THE NORTHERN PACIFIC RAILROAD

THE NORTHERN PACIFIC RAILROAD

JUBILEE WALKER SERIES BOOK 3

TIM PIPER

Book design by The Book Designers
https://bookdesigners.com/

Maps by Jon Teegarden Artwork
https://www.facebook.com/jonteegardenartwork

ISBN 979-8-9884186-6-5 (hardback)
ISBN 979-8-9884186-7-2 (paperback)
ISBN 979-8-9884186-8-9 (ebook)

Library of Congress Number: 2023917905

Published by
Sunshine Parade Publishing
1907 Sinclair Ct.
Bloomington, IL 61704
https://www.sunshineparadepublishing.com

To Lee Piper

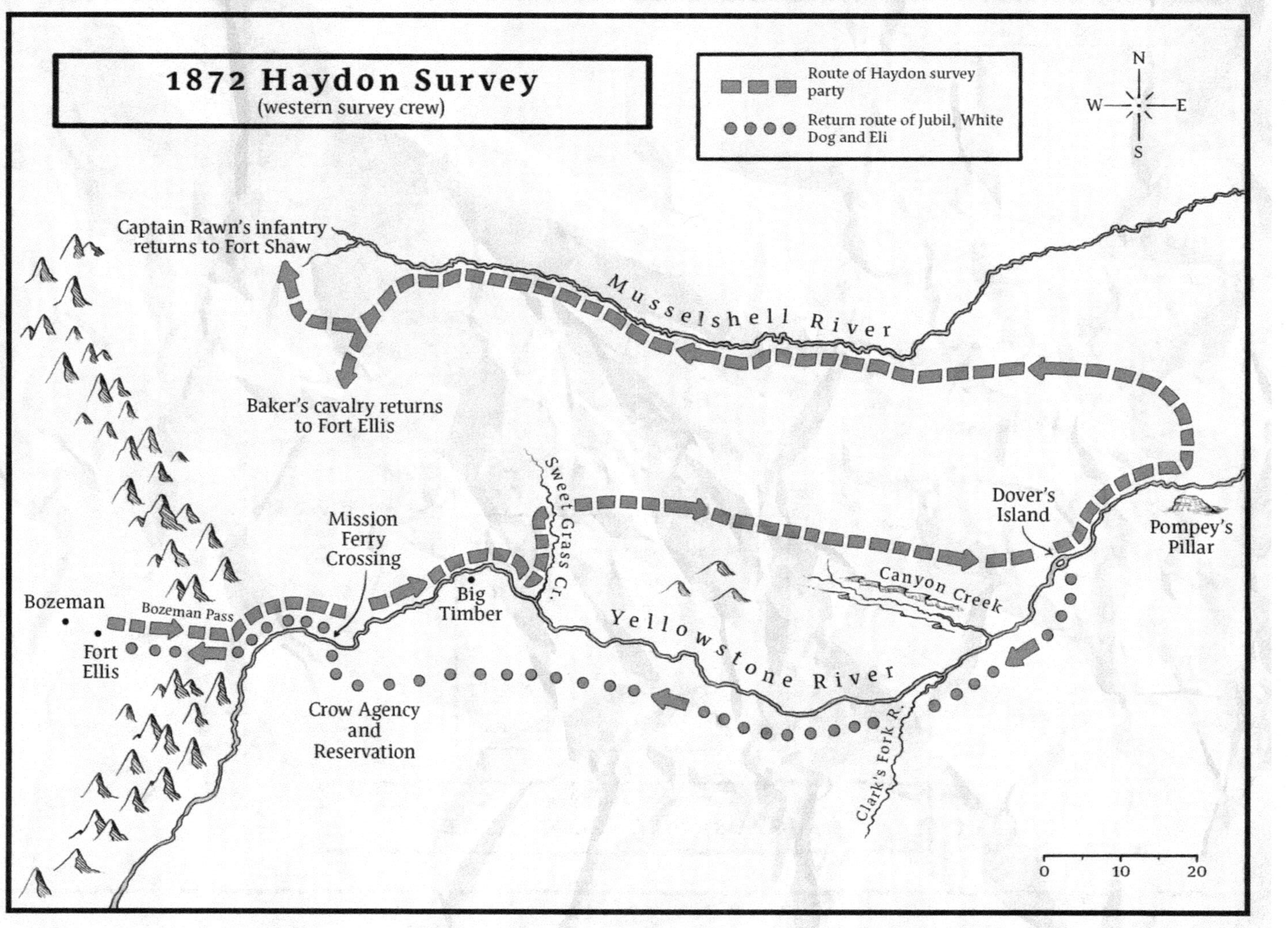

1872 Haydon Survey
(western survey crew)
Route of Haydon survey party
Return route of Jubil, White Dog and Eli
N
W E
S
Captain Rawn's infantry returns to Fort Shaw
Musselshell River
Baker's cavalry returns to Fort Ellis
Mission Ferry Crossing
Sweet Grass Cr.
Dover's Island
Pompey's Pillar
Bozeman
Bozeman Pass
Fort Ellis
Big Timber
Canyon Creek
Yellowstone River
Crow Agency and Reservation
Clark's Fork R.
0   10   20

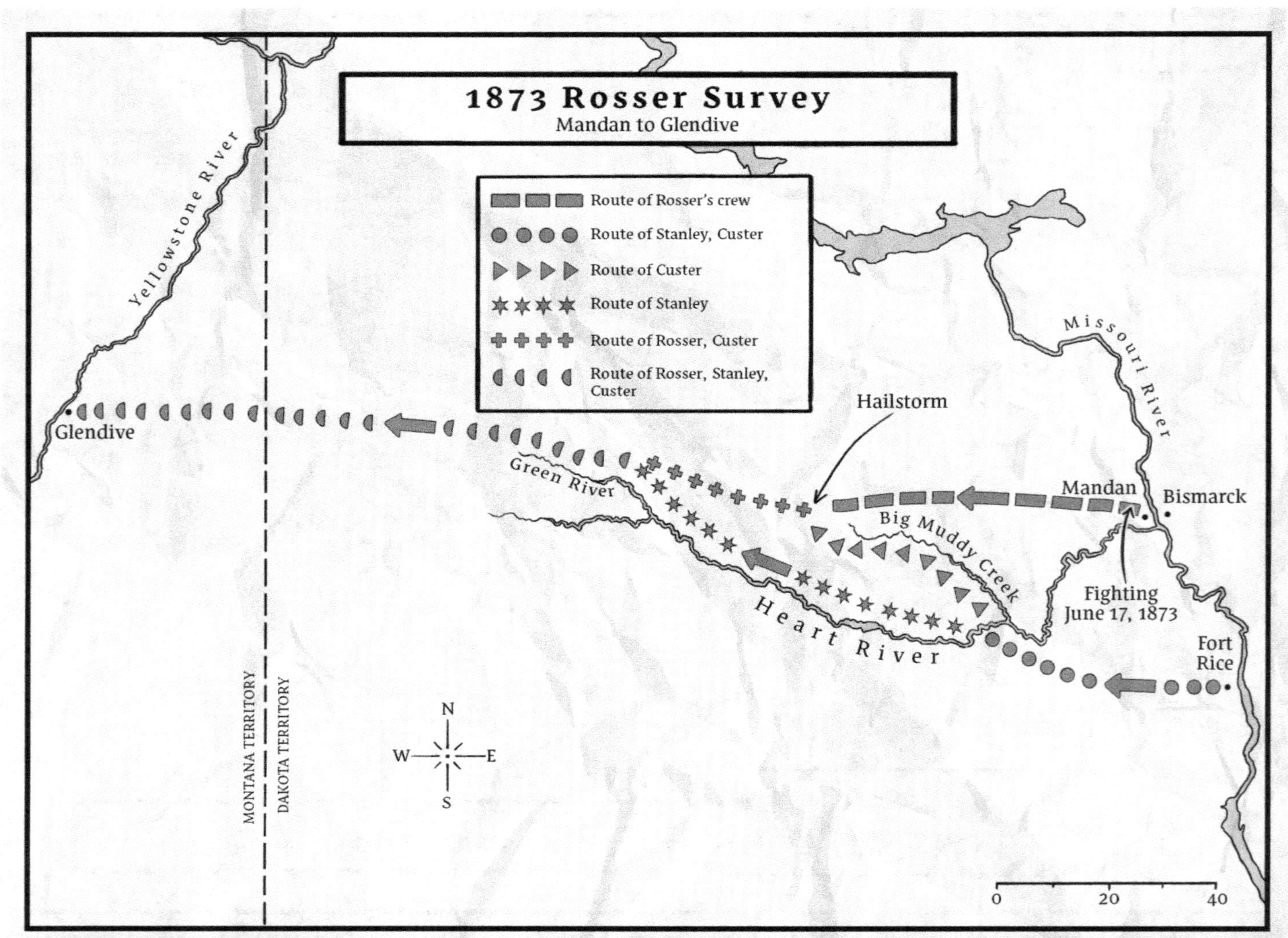

1873 Rosser Survey
Mandan to Glendive
Route of Rosser's crew
Route of Stanley, Custer
Route of Custer
Route of Stanley
Route of Rosser, Custer
Route of Rosser, Stanley, Custer
Yellowstone River
Missouri River
Hailstorm
Glendive
Green River
Mandan
Bismarck
Big Muddy Creek
Fighting June 17, 1873
Heart River
Fort Rice
MONTANA TERRITORY
DAKOTA TERRITORY
N
E
S
W
0
20
40

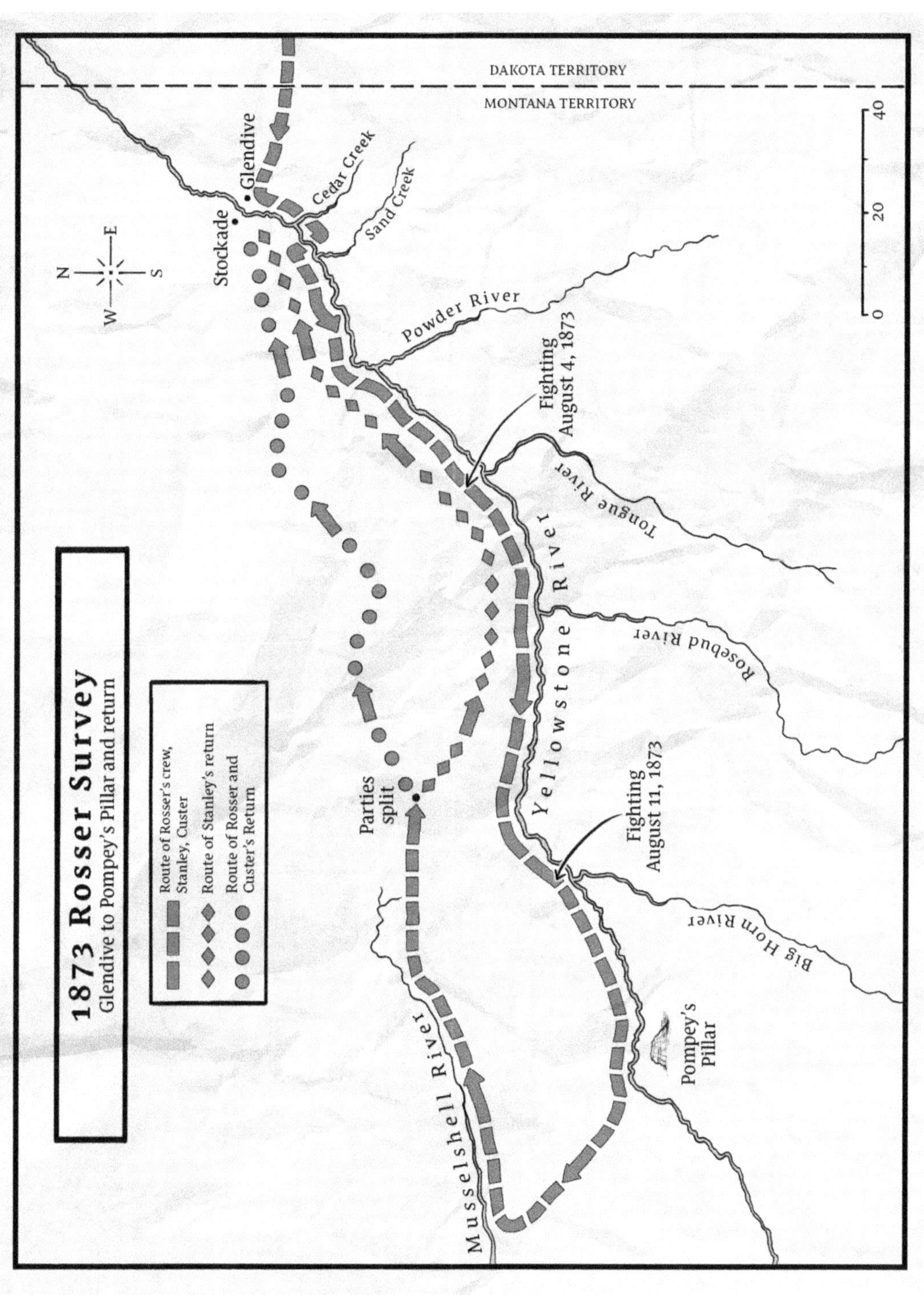

1873 Rosser Survey
Glendive to Pompey's Pillar and return

Route of Rosser's crew, Stanley, Custer
Route of Stanley's return
Route of Rosser and Custer's Return

DAKOTA TERRITORY
MONTANA TERRITORY

Glendive
Stockade
Cedar Creek
Sand Creek
Powder River
Tongue River
Rosebud River
Big Horn River
Yellowstone River
Musselshell River
Pompey's Pillar
Parties split

Fighting August 4, 1873
Fighting August 11, 1873

N
E
S
W

40
20
0

CHAPTER 1

Jubilee Walker woke in the dark of early morning in his hotel room in Poughkeepsie, New York. He lay still for a moment, until he was certain the room was real. He had half-expected to wake on his bedroll in the wilderness after an extravagant dream that Nelly Boswell had proposed marriage to him. After all, he had awakened from many fine dreams of Nelly while he was away on his expeditions.

"It was real!" he murmured as he rose from bed, grinning ear to ear.

Two years before, he and Nelly had been engaged, but when she discovered he was seriously considering the prospect of joining an expedition to the Yellowstone River that would interfere with their honeymoon trip, she called off their wedding. After some soul-searching, she had subsequently moved to Poughkeepsie to finish her education at Vassar College. She had said she still loved him, but Jubil had despaired that they would only grow further apart. He would be irresistibly drawn to another wilderness adventure, and Nelly would follow her newly discovered journalistic ambitions to cities where Jubil was not likely to want to live.

But on this visit, she had surprised him again. Nelly had proposed not only that they marry but that they live separately when their work required it. She would maintain an apartment in whichever city she was working, and Jubil would live there with her when his schedule allowed. They would be together in spirit all the time, and physically together whenever possible.

This morning they would travel to Bloomington, Illinois, their hometown, to tell Nelly's parents the news. Nelly wanted to plan the wedding in accordance with her mother's wishes, especially since she had disappointed her so much by cancelling the previous plan. Jubil was hopeful the visit would go well, but he had some concerns. Nelly's father had a long history of disagreeing with her plans, and he was not reserved about stating his position. Nelly claimed she had steeled herself to face him, and that her last birthday, her twenty-first, had emancipated her from his control. Jubil hoped her resolve held.

The sun was just rising on the cold and clear February day as Jubil knocked at Nelly's door. She was staying in the home of Maria Mitchell, who had become her mentor. Miss Mitchell was a professor of Astronomy at Vassar College and a renowned scientist. She was also a sister to Lily Warner, the wife of Jubil's business partner Abe Warner.

"Good morning, Ruthie," Jubil said to the housekeeper as he stepped into the foyer. Nelly was just coming down the stairs. She looked stylish in her skirted traveling suit, her long black hair hanging loosely. She smiled brightly, her crystal blue eyes sparkling with excitement. She was the most beautiful thing he had ever seen.

"I'll take your bag," he said. As he took the handle, she gave him a quick kiss, which was bold in front of the housekeeper, but Ruthie was a close friend.

Nelly hugged Ruthie. "I'll be back in a week. Please thank Miss Mitchell again for helping me arrange this absence from my classes."

Ruthie nodded and dabbed her eyes with a handkerchief. "We're so happy for you both," she said.

At the Poughkeepsie station, they boarded the train and found their seats. Jubil had purchased first class seating for the short trip to Philadelphia, where they would change trains for Chicago.

"This is so exciting," Nelly whispered, as she snuggled nearer to him on the comfortably padded bench seat.

"It is, isn't it?" he said smiling at her. "We've each made this trip how many times? But never together. And under such special circumstances."

"Yes—special," she said, and gave him a quick kiss. Her bold display of affection made him grin.

Once the train was underway, they went to the dining car. They had breakfast, and he watched her nibble her toast and sip her coffee, registering every second so he could recall the moment with precision for the rest of his life. After breakfast he proudly escorted her out of the busy dining car, and they returned to their seats.

"You are so beautiful," he said, leaning close to her, "and I am so proud of the person you are. I have an urge to point that out to everyone we encounter—and boast of our upcoming marriage."

She laughed and waved him off. "That's very sweet. But please don't."

"No? All right," he said with a shrug and grin. "What type of wedding are you hoping for?"

"Nothing large, or fancy," she said. "I want to hear my parents' preferences before we decide. Do you have any preferences?"

"Honestly," he said, shaking his head, "I don't. Whatever makes you happy, will make me happy." She put her head on his shoulder and reached for his hand.

"I do have one thing to ask," she said, sitting up straight again and turning to face him. "I'd like to be the one to tell my parents that the wedding is on again."

"Of course," he said, patting her hand. "I am there in a supporting role only."

"I love you," she said, and snuggled closer again.

He had expected some conversation about how her father might react to their news, but he would not spoil the mood by bringing it up. He was encouraged she did not seem worried.

The day passed quickly. Nelly worked on a paper for her journalism class, while Jubil read the newspapers and watched the snowy hills roll by.

Mid-afternoon they reached Philadelphia, and Jubil purchased two compartments in a Pullman Palace car on the westbound train to Chicago. As they waited for their train, he remembered a business matter he had not yet told Nelly about.

"While I was in Washington DC, I received an invitation to visit Jay Cooke," he said. "He lives here in Philadelphia. Before I came to visit you, I had thought I'd stop to see him on my way home."

Jubil had never met Jay Cooke, but Cooke's Northern Pacific Railroad had been involved in the lobbying effort to protect the Yellowstone Basin, which had resulted in a law that declared Yellowstone the nation's first national park. Jubil, his friend Walter Trumbull, and several other members of the 1870 Washburn Yellowstone expedition had played a major role in introducing the bill and pushing it through Congress.

"I'm sorry to have upset your business plans," Nelly teased.

"I hadn't made an appointment yet," Jubil said. "And if I had, I would have canceled it. I can visit him later. Once you're back in Poughkeepsie, I also think I'll go see the Warners. I haven't visited them since they moved to Nantucket."

In addition to being Jubil's surrogate father, Abe Warner was also his business advisor. Jubil had bought the Warners' store in Council Bluffs, Iowa, after the death of their son Luke. Though Abe no longer had a financial interest in the store, or Jubil's plans for an adventure tour business, Abe had agreed to remain available to Jubil as a consultant.

"Oh, I wish I could go see Abe and Lily with you," Nelly said, "but I can't afford more time away from classes. I've already planned to attend the National Woman Suffrage Association conference in May."

"They'll understand," Jubil said.

On the train that evening, they had a surprisingly good supper of roast chicken in a mushroom sauce with fresh baked bread. The dining car was appointed with a full bar at one end, and they enjoyed a glass of wine with their meal to celebrate. When they returned to their car, the steward had switched their compartments to sleeping rooms. He would have loved to share a room, but would not offend Nelly by making such a suggestion. They kissed good night.

In the morning they were once again in the dining car at breakfast, as the train continued on its way to Chicago.

Nelly sipped her coffee and looked pensively out the window.

"You're very quiet this morning," he said. "Everything all right?"

She looked at him and sighed. "Yes. I'm fine. I'm just uneasy about telling Mama and Papa our plans."

He was not surprised. "They'll be happy for us—don't you think?" he said. "They were before."

"Yes, I think they'll be pleased about the marriage," she agreed. "It's our living arrangements. I'm not sure they'll approve—Papa especially."

"We're not being all that unconventional," he said without conviction.

"Not in New York, perhaps. But who do you know in Bloomington that has such an arrangement?"

He had to concede her the point.

"We won't let other people's opinions stop us—will we?" He felt no concern at all over what anyone else thought of their living arrangements, but the only family members he had left were his surrogate parents, the Warners, and they were socially progressive and had always supported him unconditionally. He wondered if his own parents would have approved of his and Nelly's plans. How would he have felt if they hadn't? He did not think it would have deterred him, but then again, before his mother's death he had resigned himself to a life of farming because that was what was expected of him. He felt the seed of a worry land in his fertile imagination. But surely everything would turn out fine.

"We'll stand up for ourselves," Nelly said with a sigh of resignation. He wished he could find more reassurance in her tone.

The westbound train took them to Chicago, where they caught the morning train to Bloomington. On their way downtown in a hired carriage, they drove past the lot where Jubil and Luke had once had their own Warner and Walker store. There, they had conceived of a plan to trade on Jubil's growing reputation as an explorer, offering guided wilderness tours to adventure-minded travelers. But their store had burned down, and Luke had died in the fire. Jubil pushed away a recollection of pulling Luke's limp body across the floor of the apartment toward the window that led to the porch roof.

As though sensing his distress, Nelly put her hand on his arm.

The carriage pulled up at the Ashley House on the northwest corner of the courthouse square. Jubil would stay there during their visit.

"It's cold out here," he said to Nelly. "Would you like to come in with me while I check in?"

"I think I will," she said, stepping out of the carriage. Jubil retrieved his travel bag.

They both recognized the desk clerk in the lobby, William

Brown. He had been a childhood schoolmate of theirs and an irritation to Jubil for as long as he could remember. First, he had bullied Nelly in the schoolyard, until Jubil put a stop to that. Then he had grown up and tried to court her while Jubil was away on an expedition.

"Well, my word," Brown said as his eyes moved over them, "look who has come to Bloomington. The intrepid explorer Jubilee Walker and the sophisticated Vassar student Nelly Boswell. What brings you two back to town?"

Brown's tone was friendly, but, Jubil thought he detected a mocking edge. Jubil gave him the benefit of the doubt. "Hello, Brown. We're here to visit Nelly's parents. I need a room for the night."

"One room? For the both of you?" Brown asked, frowning slightly.

"No, Brown," Jubil said with disgust. "For me. Nelly will be staying with her parents."

"Yes, of course," Brown said. "I thought you might have gotten married since I last saw you."

"No," Jubil said curtly.

"I'm sorry about the loss of your store and your friend last year," Brown said to Jubil. Even when he seemed earnest, Jubil didn't trust his motives.

"But congratulations on the Yellowstone bill. I read about it in the *Daily Pantagraph*, and they mentioned your name."

"Thank you," Jubil said.

"Nelly, you are looking well," Brown said. "You've hardly changed a bit—by outward appearances at any rate."

"That was an awkward compliment, William," Nelly said.

"I meant no offense. I only meant you've surely grown more cultured during your time at Vassar."

"Well, I don't know about that," Nelly said guardedly.

"I've heard talk about what you were up to, but it's hard to know the truth."

"Why would anyone talk about my affairs?" Nelly asked.

"Everyone's just curious what became of you," Brown said with a shrug. "You and Jubil were planning to be married, and then the whole thing was off, and you disappeared. No one I know has heard directly from you in what—two years? People make up their own stories."

Nelly narrowed her eyes—a sure sign she was irritated. Jubil did not like Brown's comment, but he knew Nelly would not appreciate him speaking for her. But he could only hold his tongue for so long.

"Well neither have I heard from anyone here, other than my parents."

"And this is your first trip back to visit them?" Brown persisted.

"If it is any of your business, William," Nelly said firmly, "some of my family has come to visit in Poughkeepsie since I've been there."

"Some of them?" Brown asked.

"Just give me my room key, Brown," Jubil said, losing his patience but controlling his temper.

"Yes, certainly," Brown said, retrieving a key from the rack. "As I said, I meant no offense. It's good to see you both. Enjoy your visit."

Jubil took his key and addressed the porter in the lobby, who had been pretending not to listen to their conversation. "Look out for my bag until I return," Jubil ordered, and handed him a silver dollar. The porter raised his eyebrows and glanced at Brown. Jubil and Nelly stepped out of the hotel.

"Well, *that* was annoying!" Nelly said, huffing out a cloud of steam in the cold air.

"Sorry," Jubil said putting his arm around her, "I should have cut him off sooner."

"I'm fine. Let's get on with this," she said resolutely.

He reached for her hand.

"The nerve of him!" she fumed.

"Forget him," Jubil said. "He's always been annoying."

"I don't like the idea of people gossiping about me—about us."

"Even if it were true, I'd say the gossips are just jealous of you."

She turned to face him and smiled. "I love you."

"Good! Hold on to that thought and we can't go wrong!"

At the Boswell residence, Jubil paid the driver and helped Nelly step out of the carriage.

"I'm nervous," she said, slipping her hand into the crook of his arm.

"It will be fine. *You'll* be fine," Jubil assured her, patting her hand.

As they stepped onto the porch, Nelly's mother opened the front door.

"I'm so glad you're here," Nelly's mother said, as she stepped out open-armed into the cold to hug her daughter. "We were so surprised to get your telegram. I was concerned something might be wrong, but Theodore assured me you would have said so. That's true, isn't it?"

"Everything's fine, Mama," Nelly said, hugging her mother. The two looked much alike—they were about the same height and build, Nelly had inherited her mother's striking blue eyes—but her mother's hair was blond, while Nelly had inherited her father's black hair. Mr. Boswell stepped into the doorway to watch the reunion of his wife and daughter.

"Come in, come in, before the house freezes up!" he ordered congenially.

The house was warm and the aroma of something freshly baked filled the air—perhaps, he hoped, Mrs. Boswell's apple pie.

"Welcome home, Jubil," Mr. Boswell said, offering a handshake. He was a big sturdily-built man, two or three inches taller than Jubil. His carpenter's hands were callused, and his grip was firm. Even though Jubil had known him all his life, he didn't feel as close to him as he did to Abe Warner, whom he had met only a few years ago. Mr. Boswell was a kind but a no-nonsense fellow and a strict disciplinarian. In his defense, his sons entirely deserved the regulation he provided, but the whole household got much the same treatment.

"I'm sorry, Jubil," Mrs. Boswell said, coming to give him a hug. "I've ignored you completely."

"Not to worry, ma'am" he said, enjoying her attention. She reminded him of his own mother, who had died when he was seventeen. In fact, his mother and Mrs. Boswell had known each other well through church activities, and because Jubil and Nelly had always been close friends. They had even been neighbors for ten years, until Mr. Boswell gave up farming and moved his family into town. Like Jubil's mother, Mrs. Boswell was a gentle soul but was not to be trifled with. Though Mr. Boswell set the boundaries, Mrs. Boswell ruled daily operations. Ike and Eli rightly feared their mother's wrath at least as much as their father's. Jubil had seen Mrs. Boswell go from calm with them one moment to ironfisted the next, and he had come to learn that Nelly had inherited her mother's volatile temperament.

"Let's sit in the parlor," Mrs. Boswell said. "I'll go fetch us some coffee." Nelly and her mother went off to the kitchen, and Jubil followed Mr. Boswell into the parlor.

"Congratulations on the passage of the Yellowstone bill," Mr. Boswell said, sitting down in a chair near the hearth as Jubil settled onto the sofa facing the fire. "Mattie and I are very proud of you. I'm sure the Warners are too. How's business? Are the boys carrying their weight?"

Nelly's younger twin brothers, Ike and Eli, were running the Warner and Walker Outfitters store in Council Bluffs in Jubil's absence.

"Yes, sir. I'd be lost without them. I've been in Washington since mid-January, and I haven't heard of any problems at all—which I hope is good."

Mr. Boswell laughed. "Any other expeditions on the horizon?"

"No plans for the moment. I hope to finally get the adventure tourism business underway. One more delay and I'm afraid we'll lose Eli. He's as ready to bust out as I was at his age."

"Hmmph," Mr. Boswell said. "Well, I hope he's worth his salt when he does get out there. He and his brother have never known any real hardship."

Jubil nodded. Mr. Boswell had counseled him well before he set out for the West. He had even introduced him to Mr. Gulley, whose advice—*keep your wits about you, keep your gun handy, and keep hold of your valuables*—had saved Jubil's life more than once.

Mrs. Boswell and Nelly came in and served coffee and cookies.

"It is so good to see you both," Mrs. Boswell said as she and Nelly sat down.

"It's been nearly two years since you've been home!" Mr. Boswell said to Nelly, and Jubil couldn't tell whether his tone was teasing or edged with disapproval.

Nelly flinched. "I know—I'm sorry."

"He didn't mean anything by it," Mrs. Boswell said with a sideways glance at her husband. "We're just glad you're here. You've been very busy at college. We couldn't be prouder."

"Thank you, Mama," Nelly said, exhaling. Jubil wanted to reach over and hold her hand but felt that would inappropriate, at least until they announced their engagement was on again.

"What coincidence brings the two of you to Bloomington at the same time?" Mr. Boswell asked, looking quizzically from Nelly to Jubil and back again.

"Yes, we've been wondering what could bring you home, Nelly, in the middle of your term at school?" Mrs. Boswell added.

Jubil hadn't considered how confusing it would be for Nelly's parents to see them together for the first time since Nelly had ended their engagement. He waited for Nelly to speak first, the strategy they had agreed to. She was the one who had changed her mind about their marriage the first time, and she was determined to be the one to announce she had changed it again. But she said nothing, and, as the seconds ticked by, Jubil began to twitch.

Finally, Nelly reached for Jubil's hand and held it in both of hers. "Jubil and I have decided to be married."

Nelly's mother shot up out of her chair and rushed to hug Nelly, and Jubil and Mr. Boswell rose out of courtesy.

"That is excellent news!" Mrs. Boswell said, stepping back and holding Nelly's face between her hands. "We're very proud of you—both of you," she said, looking at Jubil. He smiled and gave her a little bow.

Mr. Boswell stepped forward and hugged Nelly, but it seemed to Jubil that there wasn't enough enthusiasm in it. Come to think of it, he could only think of one other time he had seen Nelly's father embrace her—the day she left for Poughkeepsie, he had given her a heartfelt hug and even shed a tear. And while Jubil had seen him tousle Ike or Eli's hair, he had never seen other displays of affection. Jubil's father had not been much for physical displays of affection either. On the other hand, Jubil's uncle Pete, his father's brother, had been free with hugs, pats on the back, and an arm around the shoulders. Jubil sometimes felt guilty for missing his uncle more than his father.

Mrs. Boswell hugged Jubil, and Mr. Boswell shook his hand and patted his shoulder.

"Have you set a date?" Mrs. Boswell asked as they returned to their seats.

Nelly looked at Jubil and reached for his hand again.

"Not yet. We'd like to set one while we're here," Nelly said. "Sometime soon after my graduation. Commencement will be on June twenty-fifth. I hope you can come."

"Oh, I hope so too," Mrs. Boswell said, looking at her husband. Mr. Boswell nodded in agreement.

"We'd like to be married here in Bloomington, of course," Nelly said. "We haven't decided on the exact details. We wanted to talk to you first. I wasn't sure if you would prefer the church or a civil ceremony, here or at Jubil's farm. We're full of ideas."

"Well, that comes as no surprise," Mr. Boswell said.

"Theodore!" Mrs. Boswell scolded. He shrugged.

"How considerate of you to ask our opinion," Mrs. Boswell said. "It will be great fun discussing the options. I wish you could stay longer than overnight."

"Me too," Nelly agreed.

"What are your plans for after the wedding?" Mr. Boswell asked.

"Jubil is going to give me a month-long tour of Colorado," Nelly said, beaming at him. "I'm even going to try roughing it a bit!"

Jubil smiled and squeezed her hand.

"And have you decided where you will live once you're married?" Mr. Boswell asked, one eyebrow raised. "Should we be looking for a house here in town, or will you be living in Council Bluffs?"

The smile faded from Nelly's face. She straightened her posture, and her grip on Jubil's hand tightened.

"I'll be looking for a position in journalism somewhere," Nelly said. "Starting employment later in the summer."

"Somewhere?" Mr. Boswell asked.

"I'm not positive where yet," Nelly said. "When I worked for the newspaper in New York last summer, Miss Mitchell gave me a letter of introduction to a magazine editor—Mr. Porter at

Scientific American. He encouraged me to contact him when I was ready for employment. I intend to do that and see what comes of it. If that fails, I'll make other plans."

"That sounds wonderful," Mrs. Boswell said. Nelly gave her a little smile.

"New York?" Mr. Boswell asked, turning his attention to Jubil. "How will that work? Are you going to move your operation to New York?"

Before Jubil could answer, Nelly interjected, "I plan to take an apartment in the same neighborhood where I lived last summer. Jubil will live with me when he can—meaning when he is not on an expedition or when he doesn't have business at the store or elsewhere that calls him away."

Jubil felt her tone was a bit more defiant than it needed to be, but he understood the tension she felt. He could no longer remain silent.

"I think it's only right for Nelly to pursue her passions as freely as I pursue my own," he said. "I'm thrilled she has decided not to let my extended absences into dangerous places prevent her from marrying me. We love each other, and we will spend as much time together as we can, and be happy for it."

Nelly squeezed his hand.

Mr. Boswell frowned. "Well, this will give folks around here something new to gossip about. *'Have you heard what the Boswell girl is up to now?'*"

"Theodore!" Mrs. Boswell said. "She is doing absolutely nothing wrong."

"That hasn't stopped people from questioning her conduct since the day she left town," he replied angrily. "Or the men at the shop from making jokes about who the boss is in my household—though I've shut that down. Which hasn't done me any good with the men I work with or Mr. Ferre."

"That problem is no one's but your own, Theodore Boswell," Mrs. Boswell said firmly.

Jubil began to feel jittery as Nelly's parents turned on each other. Nelly looked troubled.

"If you insist on working outside the home," Mr. Boswell said to Nelly, "why don't you move to Council Bluffs, and get a job with the newspaper there? Or better yet," Mr. Boswell said, turning to Jubil, "why don't *you* rebuild your store here so our boys can come back home? You can rebuild your farmhouse. And if Nelly must work, she can work at the *Pantagraph*."

"That is not how we are choosing to live our lives, Papa," Nelly said, her eyes narrowed and her lips pursed.

"Well, I don't approve!" her father said.

A deep silence came over the room, as though they had entered the eye of a hurricane.

"Nelly has opportunities," Jubil said, "well beyond those afforded by the newspapers you mention, sir. She should not be inhibited from doing whatever she is capable of." Nelly squeezed his hand again.

"Hmmph," Mr. Boswell said. "Well, I'll not have it."

"Theodore!" Mrs. Boswell said.

"I'll not condone any marriage based on such an unseemly arrangement," Mr. Boswell said, rising from his chair and looming over Nelly and Jubil. "I'll not give my permission for you to marry under such circumstances."

"I don't need your permission!" Nelly declared. She stood and faced her father. "I came for your blessing, but I don't require that either!"

"Please, Nelly," her mother said, coming to stand between them. "Try to hold your temper. We'll find some way to come to terms with this."

"No, we won't," Nelly said angrily. "You know how bullheaded he can be. We're leaving."

Jubil rose to stand beside her. It seemed like a bad idea to leave now, but he didn't know what else to do.

"Please don't leave it like this," Nelly's mother said, beginning to cry.

Jubil had seen Nelly this angry only once before—when she had called off their wedding. She was too angry to cry, which meant it was not a good time to try and reason with her.

"I'm sorry, Mama," Nelly said. "I'll write to you about the wedding plans. If we're not welcome here, maybe we'll just have it in Poughkeepsie."

"Oh, Nelly, don't say that!" Nelly's mother sobbed and clutched Nelly's arm. Nelly hugged her mother then broke away and left the room.

Jubil turned to Mr. Boswell. "With all due respect sir, I wish you'd reconsider. Nelly deserves far better treatment than this."

"I'll thank you to not lecture me in my own home," Mr. Boswell said coldly.

Jubil decided not to further upset Nelly by speaking his mind to her father. He also didn't think it would be effective if he did. This idea that women were subordinate to men was as old as Adam and Eve, but that didn't make it right. And men who used bullying to get their way, or the excuse that it was God's will, would not be argued out of their position.

Jubil followed Nelly into the foyer, where Mrs. Boswell helped Nelly into her parka.

"I'm so sorry," Mrs. Boswell said tearfully.

"I love you, Mama," Nelly said, hugging her. "I was hopeful that he might finally allow me to be my own person, but I was wrong. I'll write soon."

Mrs. Boswell hugged Jubil, and then he and Nelly stepped out of the house. Her mother stood in the open doorway watching them walk away before gently closing the door.

They only walked a few steps down the street before Nelly fell against Jubil's chest and began to sob. He held her until she calmed down.

"We'll walk back to the Ashley House," Jubil said. It was only three blocks away.

"I'm not setting foot in there," Nelly declared. "I want to leave this place. Now."

Jubil considered their situation. "If we just stay the night, Nelly, we might all have a chance to think about things and come to some agreement." As he spoke, he could see by Nelly's drawn expression that his words were falling on deaf ears. He sighed.

"All right," he said. "Let's walk up to the square. I'll fetch my bag, and we can catch a carriage to the depot. We'll take the evening train to Chicago."

He had been afraid something like this would happen. She looked at him with tears brimming in her blue eyes, and his heart broke for her.

"I'm very sorry," he said. "It shouldn't be this way. He's very wrong."

He was so disappointed in Mr. Boswell, though most men these days would agree with him about a woman's place. He was not sure how he had escaped having such a controlling attitude. Possibly because he had been raised by his mother alone most of his life and had seen that she could do everything as well as he could—and some things better. Even before his father's death, though, he had felt closer to his mother. His father would probably have agreed with Mr. Boswell, but Uncle Pete would not have. Uncle Pete believed that everyone should be free to do as they liked, as long as they respected other people in the process.

CHAPTER 2

Nelly was quiet and melancholy during the train ride back to Chicago, and Jubil found his frustration in her father's behavior growing. The last thing he wanted was for their marriage plans to be up in the air, but Nelly had no desire to discuss the events of their visit to Bloomington or to make any plans for the future until she had time to gather her thoughts and correspond with her mother. Jubil tried to soothe his uneasiness by reminding himself that Nelly's affection for him was not in doubt. He could not risk alienating her by trying to force a plan.

He turned his attention to his own affairs. He still wanted to visit the Warners, even though he dreaded telling them what had happened in Bloomington. The news would no doubt upset them. And if he really was going to Nantucket, he should send a telegram to Ike and Eli in Council Bluffs to explain his delay in returning. Then there was the invitation to visit Jay Cooke.

He turned to Nelly, and his heart sank at the sorrow in her pale face and the droop of her shoulders. He slipped his hand into hers and was rewarded by the hint of a spark in her eyes.

"We still have a day before you have to be back in Poughkeepsie," he said. "What would you think of stopping in Philadelphia overnight? We could have a nice meal, and you could rest or take in the sights while I meet with Jay Cooke, if he has time to see me."

"I would not mind that one bit," Nelly said with a weary smile. "In fact, it sounds very relaxing. What do you think Mr. Cooke wants to talk to you about?"

"I assume it has something to do with developing the area around Yellowstone," Jubil said. "I'm wondering if he has any ideas Abe Warner and I might want to factor into our plans for the summer—though I won't let *anything* upset any wedding plans you care to make." Nelly rewarded his teasing with a genuine smile.

After they checked into the hotel in Chicago, Jubil sent a telegram to Jay Cooke asking for an audience. By the next morning he had received a reply from Cooke's secretary saying Cooke would be delighted to receive him. When they arrived in Philadelphia they checked into the hotel. The next morning, before Jubil set out for Cooke's residence, he helped Nelly arrange a carriage to visit Philadelphia's historic sites, including Independence Hall, where the US Declaration of Independence and the Constitution had been debated and signed, and the Liberty Bell still hung in the tower.

Jubil stepped out of the hired carriage that had brought him to Jay Cooke's estate and gazed up—and up—at the five-story gray-yellow stone and brick walls of easily the biggest house he had ever seen—a palace for the American king of high finance. He laughed to himself as he knocked on the door. He would have to remember to keep his mouth closed and not gaping open throughout his visit.

Cooke's aide, John Carter, answered the door, and he and Jubil shared a friendly greeting. It was Carter who had extended the invitation on Cooke's behalf when he and Jubil had met at the Yellowstone exhibition Cooke had funded in Washington, DC, of photographs, paintings, maps, geological specimens, and writing generated during and after the expeditions.

Carter led Jubil around the gargantuan house, first into a drawing room that stretched at least thirty by fifty feet and was furnished with groups of chairs lit from above by gilded chandeliers. There was a grand piano in one corner, and one end of the room featured floor-to-ceiling windows that offered a view of the snowy grounds of the estate. Some distance away across the expansive lawn stood the stables and a large greenhouse. Carter pushed open a glass door, and they stepped into the conservatory, a jungle of palms and rubber plants under a glass roof. A sculptured fountain burbled away in the center of the room, and the air smelled like plowed soil after a rain. Carter led Jubil up an eight-foot-wide set of stairs to the top floor of the mansion, which held an auditorium with a stage and seating capacity for one hundred fifty people. Jubil could not imagine the cost of such luxury.

When Carter ushered him into Cooke's office, through eight-foot-high mahogany doors, Jubil was reminded of Abe Warner's office in Council Bluffs. Cooke's large desk, like Abe's, was situated in front of the windows, and the center of the room was occupied by a circle of reading chairs and side tables. Like Abe, Cooke had surrounded himself with shelves of books and collectibles. Abe had a soft spot for crafts and art objects, while Cooke seemed to prefer paintings and photographs. Jubil also guessed the two men were about the same age, early fifties, judging by the gray strands in Cooke's neatly parted brown hair and chest-length beard. He was wearing a waist-length gray wool cape fastened at the neck over his elegant black three-piece-suit. Jubil had not seen such a costume before, and while it was an odd look, he assumed it was to ward off the chill in the huge room.

Cooke greeted him with a warm smile and a handshake. He invited Jubil to sit with him in the circle of chairs.

"Congratulations on the Yellowstone bill," Cooke began. "Your contributions were material to its success."

"That may be an exaggeration," Jubil laughed, "but I appreciate the compliment."

"Nathaniel Langford was grateful to have a man of your experience in the party," Cooke said. "I'd be very interested to hear about your adventures—not only in Yellowstone, but also with Major John Wesley Powell."

Cooke seemed sincere, and at his urging, Jubil explained the loss of his mother in 1867 and his desire to follow Major Powell, an old family friend, on his expedition that year, which Powell had denied him. He had decided to impress Powell by making his way to his outfitting point in Council Bluffs, where he had met the Warners and worked briefly at their outfitting business. To further impress Powell, Jubil had ridden with a Warner and Company supply wagon train from Council Bluffs to Fort McPherson in Nebraska, escorted by General William T. Sherman.

As Jubil began to describe the 1868 expedition that Major Powell had allowed him to join, Cooke asked, "How did it feel to be among the first to summit Longs Peak?" And when Jubil went on to narrate the 1869 Grand Canyon expedition, Cooke asked, "Was it as terrifying as one would imagine to ride the Colorado through the canyon in those little boats?"

His questions put Jubil in mind of his friend Luke Warner. Luke would never have taken the risks Jubil did, but he loved to hear his stories, urging more details with a barrage of questions that made recounting his adventures more a conversation, which he enjoyed, than a monologue, which he did not. Jubil felt a pang of loss for his friend, a daily occurrence.

Cooke also had many questions about the outfitting business, but he did not mention tourism. Instead, he asked how Jubil had come to join the Yellowstone expeditions. General Sheridan had invited him on the 1870 expedition, and once the rumors of geographical wonders had been confirmed, Jubil's old acquaintance General William T. Sherman had called on him to guide the army's Yellowstone survey in 1871.

"What an exciting and accomplished life you've led," Cooke

said sincerely. "An achievement for any man, but especially impressive for one of your age."

"Thank you," Jubil said. Cooke's down-to-earth demeanor made him feel more comfortable in his company than he had expected.

"You and I have a common interest," Cooke said with a conspiratorial grin.

"Adventure tourism?" Jubil asked.

"Correct," Cooke confirmed. "I want to get people to ride the Northern Pacific Railroad. Offering to take them to Yellowstone National Park is an excellent way to do that. You want to show people the park. It seems to me our objectives are in perfect alignment."

Jubil nodded as he thought about how to phrase his response. "Yes, sir, in general I believe you're right. But my primary objective is to protect the park according to the bill's intentions. I don't think the railroad should infringe on the Yellowstone Basin, and I don't believe any accommodation should be made for tourists unless it adheres strictly to the bill's intent."

"Well said." Cooke nodded vigorously. "I do not disagree with anything you've said."

Jubil was taken aback. He had fully expected Cooke to support extracting every possible dollar from Yellowstone—pushing the railroad right to the doorstep of the most exotic features in the basin.

"You will, of course," Cooke said, "face constant battles defending the region as a park. Someone will always see money being left on the table."

"I know that for a fact," Jubil said. He described the men already operating businesses in the Yellowstone Basin—a bathhouse at Soda Mountain, and a toll bridge over the Yellowstone near the gold mines. Jubil described his encounters with a crook named Phineas Black, who was extorting these businesses for protection money. Jubil's refusal to go along with Black's schemes had led to a confrontation during which Jubil shot Black dead in self-defense and in the process was badly wounded himself.

"My heavens," Cooke said, "I assure you I am not the sort of villain who will ever attempt to murder you."

Jubil laughed. "You don't seem like a villain of any sort."

"I think my reputation is less a villain than a zealot," Cooke said with a slight smile, surprising Jubil with his self-awareness.

"I do believe enthusiastically in the potential of the Northern Pacific Railroad. And I believe a partnership would benefit both of us," Cooke said.

"How so?" Jubil asked. Of course, Cooke would have a plan, and if Jubil's instincts were correct, it would be a big one.

"I need to build the Northern Pacific Railroad, and it needs to be financially successful. But I'll never manage to complete it without the support of the public. People must clamor to have that railroad completed. And they will clamor if they know it will take them to Yellowstone National Park. Once they get there, many of them will want comfortable, safe guided tours. An adventure tour business in Yellowstone could be very successful if it were run by someone with a reputation as a wilderness explorer, someone who has the park's best interests at heart. Namely, you. You and I could create a company to provide these tours."

Cooke was not saying anything that Jubil and Luke hadn't talked about.

"But first we have to get the railroad built," Cooke said. "To do that, I need funding, and that requires bond sales. Bond sales depend on people feeling confident they're making a sound investment. Most people get that confidence from listening to what other people are saying. If people they respect are confident, most of them will feel confident too. You have a growing reputation as a respected explorer and businessman, Mr. Walker. If people heard you profess your support for the completion of the Northern Pacific Railroad and your confidence that it can be done, that would help bolster public confidence. I need your voice to support my project in the public sphere."

Major Powell routinely did public speaking tours about his expeditions, and Nathanial Langford had done the same after their Yellowstone trip in 1870. Jubil, however, had declined to participate in such events.

"I appreciate your good opinion of me," Jubil said, "but I would hate to disappoint you with my performance as a public speaker."

"After hearing your stories today, I imagine you would do better at it than you allow yourself to believe," Cooke said. "But I'm not asking you to go on a speaking tour. I want you quoted in articles that will appear in every newspaper in the country."

Jubil was relieved, but he wasn't certain how he would go about getting his name and ideas in the newspapers. He was no writer either.

"I want you to give statements to newspaper reporters in praise of the Northern Pacific Railroad and Yellowstone," Cooke said. "I will put you in contact with them, and they'll write the articles."

"And what would this new partnership look like?" Jubil asked.

"A new company—Walker and Cooke Adventure Travel. I will make an initial investment of one million dollars and retain twenty percent ownership, but I will exert no management control. However, three conditions must be met before I make my investment: First, you must join the Northern Pacific Railroad survey team this summer and simultaneously express your support for the railroad. Second, a successful survey must be completed. Third, you have to make a significant investment in my railroad venture to prove your commitment."

Jubil floundered among the details of Cooke's proposal. The amount of money he was proposing to invest was more than Jubil's wildest imaginings. He had no idea how he would even use that much capital. But the business was contingent on Cooke's three conditions, so Jubil decided to focus on those first. The first thing that came to mind was protecting his commitment to Nelly.

"When does the survey team plan to go into the field?" he asked.

"The end of July," Cooke replied.

This was troubling. That would barely allow time for the wedding and the Colorado honeymoon. They might even have to cut it a week short. Would Nelly tolerate such a change in plans? She had not taken a similar change well two years ago. But were their original plans even in effect anymore, since the argument with Mr. Boswell? He couldn't imagine she would want him to turn down such an opportunity for their future. He would discuss it with her when he returned to the hotel.

"What remains to be done on the survey?" Jubil asked.

"Last year," Cooke began, "just after you completed your Yellowstone expedition, the western survey crew arrived in Bozeman. Their goal was a point about three hundred miles down the Yellowstone, at the confluence with the Powder River, where they hoped to meet the survey crew coming from the east. If they had, that would have completed the survey from Lake Superior to Puget Sound. But winter weather forced them to turn back before they reached their goal. The eastern crew came closer, but they also were turned back. Now both routes need to be resurveyed."

"What stood in the way of their completing the survey?" Jubil asked.

"Indians…incompetence…bad luck," Cooke said with a shrug.

"Indians?" Jubil asked with raised eyebrows.

"Nothing serious…so far," Cooke said. "The surveys are going out well protected, but Sitting Bull and the Sioux are not going to sit quietly while we destroy their traditional way of life."

"How do you feel about that?" Jubil said.

"Most remorseful," Cooke said without hesitation. "It pains me that their great culture has run afoul of the crushing advance of civilization, and I am sorely pressed by being one of its instruments—but such is the world we find ourselves in. History records a litany of similar tragedies of cultures decimated by the encroachment of newcomers. However, I cannot stop the advance of civilization by not building the railroad. It will advance in spite of any reluctance on my part. I would gladly make accommodations to the tribes if any satisfactory ones were available, but from my experience, they are not. The tribes insist on clinging to a way of life that is simply unrealistic in the modern world. All I can do is be as humane as possible and play the role God gave me—which is to build the Northern Pacific Railroad."

A certain light appeared in Jay Cooke's eyes when he mentioned God's plan for him, and it became clear to Jubil how he had gained a reputation for zealotry. But Jubil found the rest of his sentiments moving. In fact, he could not have stated his own feelings about the situation, and his role in it, any more clearly. He had not expected a wildly wealthy man, a financier presumably concerned mainly with profit, to feel the same way he did about the Indians' fate.

"You mentioned incompetence," Jubil said. "Anyone's in particular?"

"Perhaps I should have said human fallibility," Cooke said. "The man in charge of the survey last year was slow in arriving, which led to a late start. He then moved too slowly because of his difficulty in managing his alcohol consumption and stayed out so long his men were trapped in a blizzard. The work he did was of no use and must be redone."

Cooke said the new team he had put together would be led by Major Eugene Baker, the commander at Fort Ellis, and one of his officers, First Lieutenant Gustavus Cheyney Doane. Major John Barlow, an Army engineer, would travel with the party to write an official report of the survey.

"You don't say," Jubil said, smiling. "They were Lieutenant Doane and Captain Barlow when I last saw them."

He had only met Major Baker briefly at Fort Ellis in 1870. But he had become friendly with Doane, who had led the military escort during the Washburn expedition, even though he and Jubil disagreed heartily about Indian policy. Jubil very much admired Doane's vivid journals that captured the strange and wondrous landscape of the Yellowstone Basin.

Barlow had been the leader of the 1871 survey conducted by the army, which Jubil was hired by General Sherman to guide. Jubil and Barlow had gotten off to a rocky start, but by the end of the survey, they had come to a mutual respect.

"You would travel with the survey as my observer," Cooke said, "and that title would give you a voice with the survey leaders," Cooke said. "You would be there to offer your experience and advice on my behalf, and you would make a report to me on your return with your recommendations."

Jubil understood his strategy. Having an observer designated by Cooke in the field might keep the survey leaders in line this year. The prospect of spending the summer on the Yellowstone survey was beginning to exert the familiar pull that the prospect of adventure always had on him. But there was still the matter of the schedule and Cooke's other terms.

"I confess there are aspects of your proposal I have some enthusiasm for," Jubil said. "But to be honest, your offer of such a huge sum of money is beyond what I can imagine a use for."

Cooke studied him in befuddlement. Jubil suddenly felt as if he had said he could see no use for an abundant supply of air to breathe.

"I'm envisioning," Cooke explained patiently, "an advertising campaign in newspapers and magazines across the country to attract people to a Yellowstone tour, and brochures available in retail outlets of every sort. Some means of making reservations and ticketing will need to be put into place, and people hired to manage it. Once we get tourists to Bozeman, they will need to get to the park. If we adhere to your restriction on rail travel into the Basin, some form of transport will be needed—thousands of people, riding in on horseback is impractical. Perhaps custom-built stagecoaches could be built. Once people are in the park, they will need to eat and sleep somewhere. The government will not likely want to operate the park, and will probably grant vendors a concession to operate. We should be one of those vendors, if not the only one. You will probably continue to escort groups of very high-paying clients on tours yourself, and ride back and forth across the country regularly. You might want your own railroad car, to give you some semblance of home. If we are wildly successful, we might even have entire trains dedicated to our tours that offer unparalleled service. These are a few investments I see as necessary to get sufficient numbers to Yellowstone to earn it the protection you desire. After we have secured success with Yellowstone, we should expand our offering of tours to other destinations. I also have ideas about the outfitting business if you'd like to hear them."

"I admit your vision far outpaces my own," Jubil said, humbled.

"I understand," Cooke said. "You are a young man and an ambitious one, or you would not have earned the respect you have and be here visiting with me today. Your dreams have been scaled to what you think is realistic. I'm offering you an opportunity to adjust your thinking regarding what is possible."

Jubil was sold on the need to complete the Northern Pacific Railroad to ensure the park's success and protection, and he had no problem with being quoted to that effect in the newspapers. The prospect of joining the western survey team with Doane and Barlow was exciting—these were the experiences he lived for. Then he remembered Cooke's other stipulation.

"What level of investment would you require from me?"

"Rather than investing cash, I propose that you invest something that will focus you on the objective, namely that you put the deeds to the real estate you own into escrow. That will allow you to continue to operate your business with no drain on your cash position or, unless I miss my guess, any entanglement with Mr. Warner's assets. If the survey is successful, you own a world-class travel business. If the survey fails, then the railroad fails, I fail, and your investment, along with my considerably larger one, are lost. The resulting bankruptcy proceeding will consume everything I own." He looked around the huge room as if imagining losing it.

This proposal stunned Jubil. He owned two pieces of real estate—his family's farm north of Bloomington and the store in Council Bluffs and the lot it sat on. Cooke was asking him to put those at risk for the possibility of owning a world-class business. The venture was starting to feel too risky, but he could not yet bring himself to decline the offer to be part of it. What would Abe think of all this?

"A point of clarification about the store," Jubil said, "I'm only risking the lot and the building, not the Warner and Walker Outfitters business?"

"Correct," Cooke said. "You are free to buy another location and build a new store."

It struck Jubil that Cooke had done a considerable amount of research and planning in advance of Jubil's visit. Cooke had not invited him here just to hear his adventure stories. He already had an elaborate plan. Jubil began to feel uneasy. Did Cooke have motives that Jubil did not fully understand?

"My family farm though..." Jubil said, thinking aloud.

"Yes, I understand the sentimental value," Cooke said sympathetically. "But ever since the tragic death of your partner and the loss of your store, have you spent much time at your farm?"

What Cooke said was true. Following Luke's death, Jubil had chosen not to rebuild the store in Bloomington. Instead, he had purchased the Council Bluffs store from Abe, when he retired. With Nelly in Poughkeepsie going to Vassar, there was very little to bring him back to Bloomington. The future he and Nelly had in mind would not change that either. Still, it tugged at his heart to think of letting the farm go.

"I appreciate the opportunity," Jubil said, "but the store and the farm are a lot for me to risk. I don't know that I'm willing to do that."

Cooke said, "Ask yourself this: Do you really believe that, with my determination to succeed, your expertise, and the support of a formidable contingent of the US Army, we will not be able to complete the last few miles of this survey, an effort that has already reached from Tacoma to Bozeman, and Duluth to Bismarck? If you believe we are likely to fail, then this will seem like a risky investment. If not, you'll feel your collateral is relatively safe and merely providing proof of your confidence."

It did seem unlikely that anything would prevent the completion of the survey and ultimately the railroad itself. The Indians could never muster enough power to defeat a full assault by the US Army. The only reason such a thing had not happened to date was that a floundering sense of morality was still at work nationally; the government was still trying to find a way, no matter how flawed, to cohabitate with Indian tribes on the continent. If patience wore out in achieving that objective, many were already prepared for the alternative—to eradicate the Indians and be done with it. What else could stop the survey—money? Surely not. Cooke either had it himself or could raise it in quantities beyond imagining. By these measures, the investment seemed nearly risk free.

"The risks do seem acceptable. But I'll have to ponder the offer and talk it over with Mr. Warner and my fiancée," Jubil said.

"I realize the scope of our agreement is significant," Cooke said, "but it is not complicated. I frankly don't see that pondering it should be necessary. And I am admittedly impatient to move on with my planning. If you are not inclined to be involved in managing a travel business as we have discussed, I intend to find someone who is. The things we discussed will happen, and someone will profit nicely by them. I intend to be in on that profit. If you are not interested, then I wish you well, and we'll part company. But I'll need your answer before you leave here today."

If Jubil did not accept Cooke's terms now, he would have no say in how the park was developed. It was the possibility of being shut out that jolted Jubil into realizing that his heart had already made its decision, even though his mind was still asking, *Are you sure? What will Nelly and Abe think?*

He recalled sitting at the campfire on the last evening before the 1870 Washburn Expedition left the Yellowstone Basin, as the men began to propose various ideas for profiting from the natural wonders they had just seen: visitor cabins near the Upper and Lower Falls; a toll booth at the base of the summit trail on Mount Washburn; a hotel in the geyser basin. Nathaniel Langford had told the men that if they were serious, they should waste no time implementing their plans, because if they did not, then Jay Cooke surely would.

The uneasiness he felt about making the decision on his own was lessened by the fact that he felt more comfortable with Jay Cooke than he had expected. He actually liked him. He was going to have to trust that Nelly and Abe would agree that the possible reward was too great to pass up. He hoped they would see it as he did— as a bold but calculated risk meant to improve the lives of his extended family.

Jubil looked Cooke in the eye. "All right, I'll do it," he said.

Cooke pointed at Jubil and smiled. "You, my friend, have just made the first of many sound decisions from which we will both profit greatly!" Cooke went to his desk and brought Jubil a sheet of paper. "I took the liberty of having my proposal drawn up in advance of our meeting."

CHAPTER 3

Jubil returned to the hotel around noon. He expected Nelly might still be out, but when he knocked on her door, she answered. Her eyes were puffy and red, and she held a handkerchief.

"Oh," he said sympathetically, "it doesn't look like you've had the best of mornings." He stepped into the room to give her a hug.

"I was too distracted by my thoughts to enjoy sightseeing," she said with disgust.

"I'm sorry," he said. "I shouldn't have gone off and left you."

"No, no," she said, "I'm fine...or I will be anyway. How did your meeting go?"

Jubil led her to take a seat on the velvet upholstered furniture in the anteroom of her hotel suite and began to tell her his news. He left the door open for propriety's sake.

Nelly's jaw dropped when he told her the amount Cooke had pledged to invest in his business if the survey were to succeed.

"My Lord, Jubil!" she said, her face lighting up. "That is marvelous! You should be proud Cooke thinks so highly of you."

"I guess I am," Jubil said. "More than anything, I was surprised by it. The deal comes with some risk though." He explained the terms of the agreement.

"Oh dear," Nelly said as she considered the news, her eyes fixed on Jubil's. "I believe in you. If you think Cooke's offer is sound, I'm with you."

"I love you even more than I did a moment ago," he said. Leaning over, he gave her a kiss. "But..." he said, working up the courage to explain the next part. "I also have to talk to you about our honeymoon schedule."

Nelly's eye's narrowed, and he hurriedly described the proposed schedule for the survey. She frowned at him for a long moment afterward. Then her shoulders sagged. "This news actually comes as something of a relief," she said.

Her response sent a chill through him. "What are you saying? How is it a relief?"

"I've been stewing all morning," she said, taking her crumpled handkerchief from her sleeve and dabbing her nose with it. "I know I said I don't require Papa's approval, but getting married without Papa there will break Mama's heart. If Papa doesn't come, Eli probably won't either. I'm not sure I can go through with it. I don't want to pull my family apart like that. I'm dedicated to my principles, but I can't do that to Mama. And I love my father too—even if he can be backward-thinking and bullheaded at times."

Jubil's pulse quickened. What did she mean she couldn't go through with it? Was she suggesting they call off the wedding entirely? He tried not to panic. "Hold on now, Nelly," he said. "Your mother said she'd help your father come to terms with our position. She'll help straighten him out."

"You don't know Papa like I do," she said. "And to be honest, I don't want to give the gossips in Bloomington more to wag their tongues over. If they're going to talk about me, I'd rather it be over my politics than my morals."

"You know you can't control what people talk about," Jubil said. "Who cares what any of them think?" He sincerely did not care, and in that moment, he felt desperate to persuade

Nelly not to care either. "They don't know anything about you or the level of determination it takes to be a strong and independent woman."

"I know," she said, her hands worrying the handkerchief that she held in her lap. "I don't want to care what they think, but I do. Maybe I would feel differently if I knew my father was on our side."

Jubil reached for Nelly's hand to reassure her, but she was looking down at her handkerchief and didn't seem to notice. He wanted to find the right words to save their marriage plans, but what came out was much plainer. "So, without your father's approval, the wedding is off?" he asked in a choked voice.

"No, Jubil!" Nelly said, turning fully toward him with concern in her eyes. "I'm sorry, I'm not being clear. I don't want to cancel our wedding plans—only delay them."

The sense of relief he felt was tinged with uneasiness.

"That will give Mama and me more time to persuade Papa to accept the situation," Nelly said, "and give me more time after graduation to secure a position somewhere and settle into an apartment before we get married."

"I can't say I'm not disappointed." He felt compelled to say it, even though he could tell it made Nelly feel worse. "Are you saying we'll set a date when I return from the survey?"

She nodded.

"I suppose that's not so bad."

"I think we could have things in better order by then—don't you? Will it be too cold to go to Colorado then?"

Jubil shrugged. "We won't be able to rough it, but we can still enjoy Denver and, if it's not too snowy, take day trips into the mountains. If it is, we'll just sit by the fire and look at them. It won't matter as long as we're together."

They shared a quick hug before Jubil retired to his room to rest before supper. Instead, he stood at the window and pondered the wildly unpredictable events of the last few days. He still had a lingering feeling that she might change her mind at any minute and decide to give up altogether on the idea of being married. He felt caught in a current of events he could not control—like running a rapid in the Grand Canyon with disaster possible at any moment. The best strategy in that situation was to go with the flow of the river but fight when it was the only way to avoid disaster. He needed to trust that Nelly and her mother could get Mr. Boswell to accept Nelly's wishes. He also needed to stand up to Nelly's father, who should have been praising his daughter for her determination, intelligence, and bravery, but instead was acting like an obstinate child in an argument that hadn't gone his way. Lecturing Mr. Boswell on his failures would not help matters, but there must be a way for Jubil to approach him that would prove effective.

When their train arrived in Poughkeepsie, Jubil escorted Nelly to the livery stand to hire a carriage to take her home. Jubil wouldn't be staying. He was on his way to visit the Warners, and then he would travel back to Council Bluffs. He wasn't sure when they would see each other again.

"I miss you already," he said.

"We'll make this work," Nelly said, reaching for his hands, "somehow."

Jubil hoped with all his heart that she was right.

The distance between Poughkeepsie and Nantucket as the crow flies was about two hundred miles, but the trip required following a labyrinthian route through four states that added another hundred miles, giving Jubil time to think about the situation with Nelly and how best to describe his agreement with Jay Cooke to Abe and Lily Warner. He expected they would be excited about the plan, but he imagined Abe would have concerns about the risk Jubil was taking with his property—some of which used to belong to Abe. He might be offended that Jubil had not consulted with him before signing the agreement, but Jubil thought he would understand that it hadn't been an option.

As the train neared Hyannis, Massachusetts, Jubil detected the smell of salt water in the air, and his worries fell away as the adventurer in him took over. He had never seen the ocean, much less traveled on it, and he was excited at the prospect of this new experience. The train pulled in just after sunset, too late for him to catch the steamship ferry to Nantucket Island, so he spent the night in an inn near the wharf.

The next morning, he and a bustle of other pedestrians boarded the *River Queen,* a large side-wheeler much like the ones he was accustomed to using at the Missouri River railroad crossing near Council Bluffs. He took a spot along the rail near the bow and breathed in the sharp tang of sea spray and musky aroma of damp wood and rope. As the ship pulled away from the dock and cut through the gentle waves of Lewis Bay, headed for open ocean, he turned his parka collar up against the bone-chilling breeze and pushed his hat tighter to his head. His oilskin rain slicker over his parka would not have been out of place in this damp wind. He made a mental note to talk with Ike about stocking gear designed for ocean travel. He shifted his footing to steady himself against the slight buck and roll of the ship, a feeling he was familiar with from his Grand Canyon trek.

In about a quarter of an hour, the steamer entered Nantucket Sound, and he got his first view of the Atlantic Ocean. He adjusted his footing again to counter the pitch of the ship as it plowed through the ocean waves. The ship was stable compared to his wild rides on the Colorado River, but rough enough to be exhilarating. At first, the Nantucket Sound seemed little different from Lake Michigan, but after about an hour an uneasy awareness had grown in him of how tiny he and this steamship were. The mainland had faded to a purplish line, and ahead of them Nantucket Island was a small hazy strip adrift on an endless horizon. Beyond it, water for thousands of miles, and his ship was just a speck of driftwood afloat on it. He had experienced a similar feeling of insignificance as he stood on the summit of Mount Washburn, staring into the expanse of the Yellowstone Basin.

In another hour Nantucket Island had grown into full view and still didn't look large—perhaps fifteen miles long. It was flat and crescent shaped, forming an open bay that led into a long narrow harbor. As he waited for the ferry to unload at an L-shaped wharf, he watched the ships at the four other docks loading and unloading people and cargo from around the world. The sight of people coming and going spurred the familiar tingle of excitement at all there was left to discover in the world. When Nelly had made her unconventional proposal for their living arrangements, she had said she might want to work in London or Paris one day, and travel the world. This visit to Nantucket was inspiring him to go along with her, should that ever happen, or maybe even to encourage it. Who knew what adventures he might find overseas?

The town of Nantucket was nestled against the port, and Jubil made his way uphill along a street of well-maintained buildings to a livery, where he hired a horse and tack. The weather was surprisingly temperate on the island, chilly but well above the freezing temperatures in Poughkeepsie and on the cold ferry crossing. Following Abe's directions, he rode uphill toward the open plateau of the island's interior and the Dutch windmill near which Abe had said their house was located.

He recognized it from Abe's description—a two-story white home with a red door and tall red-shuttered windows. The small stable and two utility sheds were also painted crisp white and bright red. The house was not grand like their

Victorian estate in Council Bluffs, but it was elegant in its own way. Abe Warner was grinning ear to ear as he opened the front door.

"You made it!" he said. He shook Jubil's hand vigorously and ushered him through the door. Jubil admitted feeling windblown and out of place. "Like a prairie dog at the beach," he said, and they laughed.

Jubil was surprised to see Abe dressed in well-worn trousers and boots and a heavy flannel shirt that lay taut over his small potbelly. When running the store in Council Bluffs, Abe and his son Luke had always been immaculately dressed in three-piece suits. Abe's hair now fell forward in a graying forelock where it had once been combed back and held in place with pomade.

"Jubilee Walker!" Lily Warner said as she appeared in the long hallway from a room at the rear of the house. Her painter's garb was more familiar to Jubil—she was wearing flat shoes and a cardigan sweater over a paint-smeared smock—but her salt-and-pepper hair had gone almost completely white in the year since he'd last seen her, just after Luke's death. He winced at the image of Luke that came to him then, as it often did, his lifeless body splayed on the ground outside the burning ruin of the store they had built together, his face smeared with ash.

But then Lily was saying, "Welcome! It's such a delight to have you here!" in her strong New England accent and enveloping him in a hug.

He felt an affection for her very much like what he had felt for his mother. Lily had welcomed him into her home in Council Bluffs and made him feel like her son even before Luke died. And she had been an important advisor to Nelly, helping her accept Jubil's desire to take dangerous expeditions. Nelly had also turned to her for advice when Jubil upended their previous wedding plans. Then Lily had made arrangements with her sister, Maria Mitchell, to host Nelly in Poughkeepsie while she finished her education at Vassar. Without Abe and Lily Warner, Jubil had no idea what would have become of him and Nelly.

They put Jubil's belongings in one of the two guest bedrooms and gave him a tour of the house, which was comfortably but simply appointed—hardwood floors and fabric upholstery rather than carpets and leather furniture, as they had at the estate in Council Bluffs. In Iowa, they had a couple, the Garcias, who took care of the house and grounds, but here they did most of the upkeep themselves.

Over a light lunch of fish and fried potatoes that they prepared together, Jubil shared his news about Nelly's proposal and the events at her parent's house. Abe and Lily were amused by Nelly's bold proposal for their living arrangements. He had expected they would be accepting of these details. And while they were distressed by Mr. Boswell's response and the subsequent delay in the wedding plans, they were not as surprised by it as Jubil had been.

"If you and Nelly are firm in your feelings, you should stand by them," Lily said.

"We are," Jubil said.

"And if your plans reflect who you are, you should follow them," Abe said.

"They do," Jubil said firmly. He meant what he said, but it was also true that the terrain of his relationship with Nelly now felt uncertain under his feet. He found it impossible to articulate these deeper feelings even to these people who were like parents to him.

After lunch, Jubil followed Lily down the hallway, toward the scent of paint and turpentine, as she returned to her studio at the back of the house while the light was still good. On the easel in the center of the room, a seascape painting was in progress of the south view through the room's many windows, across the island to the sea.

"It's beautiful, Lily," Jubil said, and Lily smiled as she took up her palette and brush.

"She's found a ready market for her artwork here," Abe said from the hallway. "A tourist shop in town sells all she places with them."

As Jubil and Abe adjourned to Abe's office, Jubil said, "Lily seems to be doing well." For a period after Luke's death the previous year, she had been debilitated by grief. "And you're looking hale and hearty. As an expert on sturdy menswear, I admire your workman's attire. I don't believe I've ever seen you so prepared for hard labor," he said jokingly.

"I've discovered a new vocation," Abe said with a smile. "I've become a home renovator and landlord. The island is still bustling, but not like it did when Lily and I were young. The population is half what it was when we moved away."

"It's such a beautiful place," Jubil said. "What happened?"

"In the old days, the whaling industry was booming, but petroleum fuel oil brought an end to that. We've found it hard to see these fine old homes standing empty. The market is so depressed I've been able to buy a few for a song—four so far. I'm enjoying polishing them up and making them rental properties. The mainland public has a growing interest in vacationing on our island, and we're helping make them comfortable."

Jubil knew this effort was out of love for their island home—they certainly didn't need the income. The Warners had holdings in several business operations in Chicago—three large tailor shops, two wholesalers of fabrics and furs, and a wholesaler of guns and camping gear. These businesses served many other accounts besides Warner and Walker Outfitters, and provided the Warners with substantial income.

"Another form of adventure tourism," Jubil said.

"You could say so, yes," Abe agreed. "I imagine some of the summer folks would be interested in following you out west one day too. We'll print up some brochures when you're ready."

"That is an excellent idea," Jubil said.

"And as long as we're talking about it, I have some news about my plans in the adventure tourism business." He explained how he had come to visit Jay Cooke in Philadelphia.

"I thought you were of the opinion the railroad would despoil the new Yellowstone National Park rather than save it," Abe said with a puzzled expression.

"I did have that concern. But it seemed polite to accept his invitation, and I was curious to meet him and express my views on protecting the park."

"Yes, that's good," Abe said. "I can see why Cooke might be interested to meet you."

"Have you met him?" Jubil asked.

"No," Abe said, furrowing his brow a bit. "I followed news of his bond sales that funded the Union during the war. He's renowned for his honesty in that effort, but I've also read that he is willfully ignorant of the distinction between political support and bribery. If the newspapers are to be believed, his Northern Pacific Railroad is beginning to seem more like a personal obsession than a business venture. But men like Cooke always have their detractors. No doubt he is a great man—with the same ruthless streak as other great men."

Jubil didn't care for the implication that the project was likely to fail, but he was not surprised that the opinion existed.

"I found him more likeable than I expected," Jubil said, unsure of why he was feeling defensive on Cooke's behalf. He explained Cooke's sincere desire to hear about his adventures and outfitting business, and more importantly how pleasantly surprised he was that Cooke agreed that the railroad should not encroach on the park and was sympathetic about its impact on the Indian tribes. Jubil offered these details with the hope that they would help explain why he had felt inclined to trust Cooke.

"You've had a unique role in the whole Yellowstone business," Abe said. "I'm surprised he didn't have some scheme for involving you in his Northern Pacific Railroad venture. Or did he?"

Abe had always been good at cutting to the chase.

"Yes, sir," Jubil said, "although I don't know that I'd call it a scheme. We would be partners in the adventure tourism business." He explained the agreement and its terms, and, as he spoke, Abe began shifting in his chair. Jubil could feel a restless irritation growing in Abe, but he did not interrupt.

When Jubil finished, Abe shook his head. He seemed to be struggling for the right words. Finally, he said, "He's using you, Jubil, taking advantage of you." He could not disguise the scorn in his voice.

"I'm sorry you see it that way," Jubil said. He was hurt by Abe's comment. The last thing he wanted to do was disappoint him. He also found himself feeling angry that Abe allowed no room for the possibility that the venture would succeed.

"Weren't you suspicious when said he had taken pains not to entangle his offer with my finances?" Abe asked. "Didn't you see a red flag waving when he wouldn't allow you time to consult with me?"

Jubil had never heard such exasperation in Abe's voice, and his comment hit home. Jubil had no good defense, since he knew that he had made the decision with his heart rather than his head. The heart did not see what it did not want to see. Cooke's friendly demeanor had set him up to yield to his insistence that Jubil sign the agreement the day of his visit or not at all. Surely Cooke could have allowed a few days for him to consult with Abe, telegraph his response, and return to sign the agreement. But Jubil had not challenged him. Cooke was relying on him to feel powerless enough that he would follow the great man's will without question. And he had. Now he was too proud to admit these things to Abe. The only recourse he could see at this point was a good offense.

"I felt capable of making my own decision," he said carefully.

"We had a full discussion of the risks involved, and I think I've weighed them with consideration. I sincerely believe that the power of the US Army and the resources and determination of the Northern Pacific Railroad will be enough to close the few hundred miles of survey still left unfinished." He cut himself off as he realized his tone had risen from explaining to orating.

Rather than stir Abe's temper, Jubil's speech seemed to trigger a kind of acceptance in him. Abe leaned back in his chair and gazed at Jubil, then sighed. "You are an optimist, Jubil," he said. "And I hope for your sake that you are right."

"I'm sorry I raised my voice," Jubil said, "but I'm passionate about it."

"Yes, I see that," Abe said. "But you've put the store and your farm at risk. I built that store and gave it to you. Your parents built that farm and gave it to you. And you've put those things at risk—things you can't replace. I fear you are in for a hard lesson. I've put a lot of faith in your judgment by naming you our heir and executor. I hope I haven't made a mistake."

Abe's comment stung badly.

"I didn't think you'd be so angry with me," Jubil said, feeling put in his place like a child. While he was honored that the Warners had decided to make him their heir, he hadn't asked for it. "I was hoping you would stand up with me at my wedding. Would you still do that?"

"Of course, I will. I'll be proud to," Abe sighed and gathered his thoughts for a moment. "I'm more disappointed than angry. I believe your love of adventure and the invincibility you feel from conquering fear has led you here. But you are not invincible, Jubil, and when you learn that, it will be painful."

Abe suggested they invite Lily in. He left it to Jubil to explain the situation and did not express his thoughts to Lily while Jubil spoke. Lily's conclusions were more generous than Abe's. She was more enthusiastic than he was about the possibility of a positive outcome on the survey, but she also found the prospect of losing the store and the farm deeply concerning. Jubil found her view to be much like his own, and he was grateful for her support.

He went to bed that night feeling chastened and diminished, but as he lay awake listening to the roar of the ocean on the shore, he decided to treat Abe's reaction as a challenge. Abe was right that Jubil had gotten himself into a tricky situation, but Jubil was more determined than ever to make the survey and his partnership with Jay Cooke succeed. He was determined to prove Abe wrong.

CHAPTER 4

After a week on Nantucket sanding and staining oak trim and replacing maple floorboards with Abe and strolling through the town with Lily, Jubil caught the ferry for the mainland and the train back to Council Bluffs. The morning he arrived was chilly, windy, and gray, and the streets were bustling as he walked from the station to Warner and Walker Outfitters, stopping at a market along the way to buy a half-dozen apples for his horses. At the store, he found Ike and Eli Boswell, and Caleb Nelson, the stock clerk, standing around the register, drinking coffee.

"Got a cup of that for a wayfaring stranger?" he said, closing the door and dumping his travel bag on the floor. He had been away for two months.

"Jubil!" the twins said in near unison. They all shook hands, and Ike poured Jubil a cup of coffee. Ike was wearing a three-piece suit, and Eli was wearing a flannel shirt, work pants, and scuffed boots. It had never been difficult to tell them apart.

"The store looks well managed," Jubil said, sipping his coffee. "Did you even miss me?"

"Of course, we did!" Ike said and then looked at him sidelong. "When did you say you were leaving again?"

Jubil feigned disgust as they all laughed. Luke had frequently joked that the store's success was due to Jubil always being away somewhere, leaving Luke to run it without interference.

The boys asked Caleb to watch the store so they could visit with Jubil, and the three of them took the surrey to the north end of town, where they all lived together in Abe and Lily's huge Victorian home, which looked smaller to Jubil after visiting Jay Cooke's home.

Jubil dropped Ike and Eli off at the front door, then drove around to the stables to put the surrey horse, Rocky, away, and see to his other horses. Mr. Garcia, the stableman and groundskeeper, was pleased to see him, and so were his other two horses—Star and Apollo.

"I sure have missed you, girl," Jubil said to Star. As he hugged the horse around the neck, she tucked her chin into his back and pulled him close. Star had been his father's horse, and he had known her for as long as he could remember. While he was growing up as an only child on the farm, she had been his constant companion. Some boys had their dogs, and he had Star. She was not just his horse; she was his friend. He pulled two apples from the pocket of his parka and fed them to her as he stroked her neck and asked her how she'd been.

The brown and white pinto stallion in the neighboring stall pawed the ground. "Yes, Apollo," Jubil said, "I've got some for you too." He had bought Apollo in Corinne, Utah, in 1870 for his first Yellowstone expedition and had found him still at the same livery when he was looking for a horse for the second expedition in 1871. He was a strong and beautiful horse who had proven his surefootedness and poise as they navigated the narrow ridges and treacherous sulfur fields of the Yellowstone Basin, which was why, at the end of the second expedition, Jubil had brought him back to Council Bluffs. But Apollo was not retired, as Star and Rocky were. "I've gotten us into another adventure, my friend," Jubil said, feeding Apollo his apples. "We're headed for Yellowstone again this summer, so rest up."

Rocky had waited patiently, as always. Rocky had been assigned to Jubil by the US Army during his first adventure after leaving home in 1867. Abe Warner had let him ride on a Warner and Company Outfitters supply wagon train bound for Fort McPherson, Nebraska, escorted by General William T. Sherman. At Fort Kearney, Sherman put Jubil on horseback in case of Indian attack. He and Rocky had survived an Indian attack together, and Rocky had carried him safely back to Council Bluffs, accompanied part of the way by Jubil's new friend, White Dog, General Sherman's Pawnee scout. When the army told Jubil to keep Rocky, he became the Warners' carriage horse. Jubil thought he felt grateful for the easy job.

Jubil told his horses good night and headed into the house. He joined Ike and Eli in Abe Warner's office in the western turret, which had a permanent aroma of Abe's cigars. Jubil loved this room with its stunning view of the Missouri River Valley and the city of Council Bluffs, with the signature rocky hills marking its eastern boundary.

Ike and Eli were lounging in the reading chairs.

"I have a lot of news," Jubil said as he sat down. "I'll start with the most important—the wedding is on again!" He knew he was exaggerating a little, since he could not cite a date. But he felt Nelly's proposal was worth celebrating. Ike shook his head and looked away, then gave Jubil the side-eye again, while Eli merely nodded.

"Well, that's not a very charitable reaction," Jubil said pointedly.

"We'll save our enthusiasm until after the ceremony," Ike said dryly. "What's the wedding date?"

"Well..." Jubil said, "it's complicated."

"Yeah, we heard," Eli said. "We got a letter from Mama about what happened. What did Nelly think Papa was going to say?"

"She thought he'd be reasonable," Jubil snapped.

Ike and Eli both shook their heads.

"Do you have a plan?" Ike asked.

"We're going to be married, but we're going to wait a little while."

"For what?" Ike asked.

"Your father to come to his senses," Jubil said.

"You'll grow old waiting for that," Eli said.

"We're not going to wait forever," Jubil said. "Only until I return from some business I have to attend to this summer."

"I knew this was coming," Ike said. "What now?"

Jubil described his visit with Jay Cooke, and the boys stared at him in silence for a long moment.

"Did I hear you correctly?" Ike asked. "He'll invest a *million* dollars?"

Jubil nodded.

"Would Eli and I be involved in this new business?" Ike asked.

"Certainly," Jubil said. "If you want to be."

Ike gazed into the distance, assumedly considering the possibilities. Eli, on the other hand, was frowning. Jubil thought he knew why.

"What happens if you lose the store?" Ike asked. "This is my only source of income, you know. What am I supposed to do if that happens?"

"We're not going to worry about that," Jubil said. "It's not going to happen. The survey will succeed."

"Hmm," Ike said. "I admire your optimism." He did not look satisfied with Jubil's answer. "And you're willing to lose your farm in this gamble?"

"I'm concerned about the possibility of course," Jubil said, growing a little irritated to be pressed on the matter again. "But like I said— the survey will succeed."

"And how does Mr. Warner feel about all this?" Ike asked.

"He understands that it was my decision to make. He

transferred the store's deed to me, you know." Jubil scolded himself silently for omitting so much of the truth. But he couldn't bring himself to describe the depth of Abe's dissatisfaction with him.

Ike nodded as he studied Jubil, while Eli regarded him with narrowed eyes and tight lips—an expression that reminded Jubil of Nelly when she was irritated.

"Looks like you've got something on your mind, Eli," Jubil said. "Spit it out."

"All right," Eli began. "It sounds like you'll be joining the Northern Pacific Railroad survey while I sit here in Council Bluffs, with my hopes of leading adventure tours dashed once again. This makes three summers in a row you've delayed the tour, Jubil, because *you* have a different adventure to go on. I'm not going to wait on you any longer to start having my own adventures. I won't abandon Ike, but as soon as he says he can manage without me, I'm gone."

Eli had been more patient than Jubil would have been himself. In fact, five years ago, when Major Powell had refused Jubil a spot on his Colorado expedition, Jubil had set out on his own for Council Bluffs. Eli deserved a chance to realize his own dreams. Jubil had anticipated Eli's dissatisfaction and had come up with a plan to placate him.

"I wouldn't blame you for striking out on your own, but why not travel with me this summer instead?" Jubil offered. "I'm going as Cooke's observer, so I have enough authority to bring you along. I'll just say you are my aide—assuming Ike is all right with it."

Eli looked surprised and pleased. They both looked to Ike.

"Can you manage?" Jubil asked Ike.

"Caleb and I can operate the store. I can hire help when we need it. Eli's our best salesman though," Ike said. "I expect he'll enjoy hearing how much sales suffer in his absence."

"Good," Jubil said. "We'll wrap the survey up this summer,

and then we'll begin to build a company that is more successful than anything we've ever imagined." Jubil wanted to believe what he was saying, and he intended to do everything in his power to make it happen. He would simply have to try harder to shrug off the uneasy feeling that had begun even before his conversation with Abe Warner.

"Have you boys ever been apart for a whole summer?" he asked the twins.

They shook their heads in unison.

"But I won't mind missing him for a while," Ike said.

They all laughed.

"When I get back," Jubil said to Ike, "you and I will have a serious talk about how we're going to manage our new business."

Ike nodded.

"Before we go," Jubil said to Eli, "I want to be sure we're clear about a few things. You've got to agree to take direction from me. Are you sure you can do that?"

"I am," Eli said with conviction.

Jubil did not detect any sign that Eli was not taking him seriously.

"Before I went out West the first time," he said, "an acquaintance of your father's gave me some advice that has saved my life more than once: keep your wits about you, keep your gun handy, and keep hold of your valuables. This is serious business, Eli."

"I understand," Eli said. "I'm ready."

The twins' eyes locked, and Jubil witnessed one of the frequent unspoken conversations that took place between them. After what seemed like a full minute, Ike shrugged, as if backing off. "All right," he said.

Jubil didn't ask what issue they had wordlessly resolved.

He was concerned about what Mr. and Mrs. Boswell would have to say about Eli going adventuring, but not enough to subject his plans to their approval. If Eli felt he needed it, he could seek it out himself.

As signs of spring began to appear in the landscape, Jubil set about making sure Eli was ready for the survey trip. Jubil had never gone hunting with any of the Boswell family—Mr. Boswell had never been one for hunting, and Jubil had always gone either with his uncle Pete or alone. Eli did not own any firearms, but claimed experience in using his father's. Jubil decided to take him out to make certain he was telling the truth, since he knew Eli was prone to exaggerating his own skills. He armed Eli with a new Colt revolver and a Winchester rifle, a lever-action repeating model like his own Henry rifle, which had been his father's. He then outfitted his charge with a new version of his own well-worn trapper's pack, including gloves, compass, field glasses, canteen, flint, tin pot, slicker, bedroll, and small tent.

He began taking Eli camping overnight in the bluffs so he could use his gear and get comfortable with his new weapons. Eli proved to be a good shot with both the pistol and the rifle and kept them clean, which Jubil was pleased to see. He told Eli to start taking long horseback rides to ready himself for days in the saddle.

He had never seen Eli so focused and motivated, even going out to camp alone in stormy weather. One pleasant evening in May, Jubil elected to accompany him into the woods for an overnight stay. There was one aspect of preparation for their trip he wanted to cover that was more mental than physical.

"You're doing well with your firearms," Jubil said.

"Thanks. They're much better guns than I've ever used," Eli said. "Much more accurate."

"We've hunted small game," Jubil said, "and you've done very well. What's the most dangerous animal you've ever encountered?"

Eli considered the question. "When we lived on the farm, Papa set me to guard the lambs from coyotes that were prowling around. A bold one tried to come right past me, snarling and crouched down like he'd jump me. I let him have it with Papa's shotgun, and shot him dead!"

The dramatic storytelling reminded him that Eli's behavior could often be boastful and cocky. Did this attitude reflect a kind of confidence that was just part of his nature, or did it reflect the insecurity of a boy bragging in the schoolyard?

"That's good," Jubil said. "You've got be prepared for coyotes, wolves, mountain lions, bears, moose, buffalo. Lots of big critters in the wilderness that can kill you."

"I'm ready for them," Eli said firmly.

"Good," Jubil said. "You know I've had to fire my weapons at Indians and even had to shoot a man in a gunfight once." Eli looked up from poking at the campfire and met Jubil's gaze. "You need to be ready to do that or you shouldn't go. I can't protect you from everything."

"I know that," Eli said defensively. "If you can do it, then I can do it. I'm ready."

Jubil nodded. He hoped they would never have to find out if Eli was right.

During the month of May, Jubil immersed himself in aspects of operating the store he had always left to Luke, and to Ike after Luke died. He had never paid much attention to managing inventory or handling relationships with suppliers in Chicago, several of which were owned in part by Abe Warner. He considered visiting them in person, to introduce himself as the Warners' heir, but he was committed to staying in Council Bluffs to keep an eye on Eli's preparations for the survey.

He and Nelly had corresponded regularly since he returned to Council Bluffs. But being busy with school and woman suffrage events, she didn't write to him as often as he would have liked. It made sense that he missed her more since they had become engaged again.

In late May, she wrote after attending the National Woman Suffrage Association conference in Washington, DC. He read it sitting at Abe's desk.

Dearest Jubil,

The conference was a three-day affair both physically and emotionally exhausting and exhilarating. I have never spent so much time in the company of those at the pinnacle of influence in the woman's rights movement. Some of them held up better in my estimation than others. I must confide that Susan B. Anthony has aspects of personality I find less than admirable. My esteem for her friend and my mentor, Mrs. Elizabeth Cady Stanton, however, has only risen. While inspirational in her fervor, bravery, and dedication, Miss Anthony is exceedingly rude at times. She publicly chastised Mrs. Stanton, her closest ally and friend, over her weight, an event that was beyond appalling for everyone else present. And in another episode, Miss Anthony was disrespectful of the whole organization. I have trouble understanding why she continues to be part of a movement to lift women up when she continues to drag women down, one by one.

A newcomer to the movement was scheduled to speak, Miss Victoria Woodhull, who I came to learn Miss Anthony holds in personal contempt. Miss Woodhull is the first woman to make her fortune on Wall Street and has formed a new political party, the Equal Rights Party, which has nominated her for the office of President. She had come to speak in search of support. Miss Anthony would not allow her the podium, quite literally standing in front of the lectern to block her access. When Miss Woodhull demanded her right to speak, Miss Anthony ordered the janitor to turn out the gas lights, bringing the meeting to an awkward end.

Mrs. Stanton has long counselled me to have patience with the progress of the movement, and I now understand better than ever the gears and workings of the machinery that sometimes move the thing forward, and other times bring it to a halt—seized up in opposition to itself. But I take heart in following Mrs. Stanton's lead, though I can hardly understand how she still loves Miss Anthony as a friend.

Nevertheless, the majority of the conference was stimulating and inspiring. I felt compelled to write a brief dispatch in support of the movement and send it to the Daily Pantagraph. I thought it might spare people in Bloomington any need to speculate on what I am doing and thinking out East. I am excited for you and my family to see it—my first byline! I hope you will approve.

As my graduation approaches, I am growing ever more anxious to see you and my family. I am excited to inform you that Mr. Porter at Scientific American in New York has offered me a position as an editorial assistant, and I have accepted. My next task is to secure my living quarters, which I hope will be in the same building I was in last summer.

Once that is in place, we will be all the closer to finally being married. I am so looking forward to that day, and love you even more for your patience in waiting out this delay.

I hope preparations for your expedition are proceeding to your satisfaction, and that Eli is meeting your expectations. You have my continued condolences that Abe does not fully approve of your agreement with Mr. Cooke, but I am confident you will prevail in proving your judgment sound.
Truly yours,
Nelly

Jubil's spirits soared when he read that Nelly had gotten the job at *Scientific American*, and he followed her description of the conference with great interest, but he couldn't help wincing when she mentioned her dispatch to the *Pantagraph*. While he understood her desire to redirect the focus of those gossiping about her, he couldn't see how the article would help the campaign to bring her father over to their side so that they could set a date for their wedding. She said she was eager for them to be married, but her words seemed at odds with her actions.

His fears were confirmed the day after he received Nelly's letter, when Ike came into Abe's office carrying a large envelope, which he dropped on the desk in front of Jubil.

"Mama bought extra copies of the *Pantagraph* with Nelly's article," Ike said and pointed to the envelope. He flopped down into one of the reading chairs. "She says that Papa is refusing to go to her graduation."

"Oh no," Jubil said. "She must not have known that when she wrote to me."

"She should have known how Papa would react," Ike said, rolling his eyes, "and the position she was putting Mama in."

"You know Nelly," Jubil said. "Staunch in her convictions." He rubbed his forehead. It was possible that Nelly had not fully considered the consequences of her actions, as Ike suggested, but it was equally likely that she had considered the consequences and had not been deterred.

He opened the envelope and removed a copy of the newspaper. Her article appeared on page two, her byline beneath the headline. She reported on conference events with no mention of dissention in the ranks, and closed with a strong assertion of the rightness of their cause and determination to prevail. An impressive effort he thought, for her first published work.

"What does Eli think of this?" Jubil asked.

"He sides with Papa," Ike said dismissively. "He thinks she's too full of herself."

Jubil's heart sank listening to Ike, knowing how proud Nelly was of her accomplishments and how much she was looking forward to sharing graduation with her family. After his conversation with Abe in Nantucket, Jubil knew all too well how it felt to have a cloud cast over one's achievement by the disapproval of a loved one.

He thought of Mrs. Boswell. She was the one dealing with the brunt of Mr. Boswell's discontent.

"Is your mother all right?" Jubil asked.

"I think so," Ike said. "She's showing some defiance of her own, which is good, but..."

"Why don't you go home for a while?" Jubil suggested. "Eli, Caleb, and I can run the store."

Ike studied Jubil while he considered the offer. "Thank you," Ike said, "that's very thoughtful. I think I will, but only for a few days before the graduation. I can't sit there for very long with nothing to do."

Jubil felt a wave of admiration for Ike very much like he had felt for Luke. Ike and Luke were similar in many ways, and Ike was growing into a fine young man and a good friend and business partner.

Eli stepped into the office. "I'm going out for a ride. Anybody want to come along?"

"Not this evening," Jubil said. "I've got to write to your sister. Ike says you don't approve of her politics."

"I didn't question her politics," Eli said. "I said she was too full of herself."

"Says the pot to the kettle," Ike said to his brother.

Jubil thought Eli's comment was harsh, but he let it pass. He had watched Nelly boss Eli around plenty of times, and Eli had never taken well to it. Eli's irritation with his dominant sister had grown into a general resentment.

"I'm going to close the store the last week of June," Jubil said, changing the subject, "so we can all attend Nelly's graduation. It's too much for Caleb to run it alone."

"You don't need to do that," Eli said. "I'm staying here."

"Why?" Jubil asked. "Don't do that. Nelly will be very disappointed."

"She'll be fine," Eli said. "She'll have plenty of people telling her how special she is. She won't even miss me."

"You're being a selfish ass, Eli," Ike said angrily.

"Let's not get all hot about it," Jubil said. Ike was normally mild mannered, but Jubil had seen Eli make him fighting mad when the boys were young. And Ike had always won. "We've still got a couple of weeks to sort it out."

But Eli didn't change his mind, and relations grew icy between the twins as the graduation approached.

The night before Ike left for Bloomington, Jubil decided to speak his mind to Eli. While Ike was painting in Mrs. Warner's studio, Jubil found Eli in his bedroom reading.

"I want to make one more appeal to you to come to Nelly's graduation," Jubil said, standing in Eli's open doorway. "This is only going happen one time, and I think you'll regret not going. I think you'll regret it for a long time to come."

Eli put down his book and looked away from Jubil.

"I'm not going," Eli said bluntly. "She'll hardly know or care if I'm there. She'll either ignore me or start ordering me around, and I'm not traveling across the whole country for that." Eli looked at Jubil. "It's always about Nelly—no matter the hardship to anyone else. She's done it to you too—cancelling your wedding and then delaying it again. Telling you where she will and won't live. I don't see why you put up with it."

Jubil's face flushed with anger as he checked an impulse to assault Eli. He clenched his fists and delivered his words carefully, "I am going to tell you something, Eli, and I'm only going to say it one time: You and I can live and work together if you hold up your end of the bargain, and part of that bargain is that you will not talk about Nelly to me in that way. She has more gumption than you and I put together. I love her, and we're going to be married, and I won't stand for you tearing her down. Is that clear?" Eli listened intently to Jubil's speech, and at the end, he nodded and said, "Yes." Jubil hadn't spoken to him this way since he and Ike had burned down the house and barn on Jubil's family farm, and he could tell that Eli took his words to heart. Jubil turned and walked away.

The next morning, Ike set out for Bloomington, and a few days later, Jubil set out by train from Council Bluffs to meet him and Mrs. Boswell in Chicago, then they made their way east together. They did not offer any report on Mr. Boswell, and he did not ask.

They arrived late in the evening in Poughkeepsie, but Nelly and the Warners were waiting at the station. As Mrs. Boswell stepped from the train, Nelly fell into her arms, sobbing.

"I'm sorry if I've ruined things with Papa," she said, "and for the hurt I've caused you. But I will not allow him to control my life."

"Don't you worry about me," her mother said. "I'm quite capable of standing up for myself. Where do you think you came by your skill for it?"

Nelly laughed and cried at the same time.

"Your father must accept the world is changing and be willing to change with it," Mrs. Boswell said, and Jubil found himself nodding. "He and his like will find it an impossible task to hold back you and your fellow Vassar graduates."

"Oh, Mattie," Lily Warner said, as she stepped up to embrace Nelly's mother, "how beautifully said."

"Well, I had time on the way here to perfect my speech," Mrs. Boswell said, laughing.

Nelly turned to Jubil, and he wrapped his arms around her. His heart ached for her, but he put on a happy face. "Congratulations on your big day," he said. "What you've done here is a great accomplishment."

"I'd have never done it if you hadn't spoiled our wedding plans!" she teased, and everyone laughed. Being the brunt of the joke was slightly embarrassing, but he had earned it.

The next morning, Jubil, the Boswells, and the Warners took a carriage from the hotel to the Vassar campus, which resembled Jubil's idea of a grand European estate. Its sprawling Main Building, made of gray stone, sat regally in the center of acres looped with walking paths and covered by trees, bushes, and flowers. The auditorium reminded Jubil of the one on the top floor of Cooke's mansion. This visit was again stirring questions in him about furthering his own education, but he still didn't have a passion to do so—and there was his answer.

Nelly met them in the lobby dressed in an elegant dark skirted suit and a crisp white blouse with her hair held back loosely by a black ribbon. Her mentor and benefactor, the stately Miss Mitchell, joined them, embracing Lily Warner, her sister, and speaking politely to each person Nelly introduced.

"Mrs. Boswell," she said, "You have a remarkable daughter. I'll miss her so. Watching her grow and find her purpose has been a delight. Her determination to accomplish difficult things and her pleasant and winning manner have her bound for great things."

"Thank you for all you have done for her," Mrs. Boswell said, smiling in spite of her glistening eyes.

Another of Nelly's mentors, Mrs. Elizabeth Cady Stanton, stopped to congratulate her and her mother, and then one of Nelly's English professors. He was pleased to meet Jubil, as Nelly had shared Lieutenant Doane's Yellowstone journal in his class. He praised Nelly's intelligence and gift for the written word.

Nelly's blue eyes sparkled, and her cheeks flushed pink with the compliments. Jubil had never seen her so happy. He thought it was a shame that Mr. Boswell was not present to see the high regard Nelly's associates had for her. Perhaps he could have understood that what he viewed as defiance was passion and dedication. It was probably just as well, however, that Eli had stayed behind. It might have been too much for him to see Nelly shine without trying to humble her.

The commencement ceremony itself was a series of speeches full of deep thoughts and lofty language that left Jubil trying to reason out parts of them while losing track of the rest of the speech. It ended with an oration by the college president, Mr. Raymond, who then bestowed the baccalaureate degree on twenty-nine members of the Class of 1872. Then everyone burst into applause, and Jubil found himself leaping to his feet and whooping along with the rest of the crowd.

Jubil did not have a chance to talk with the Warners alone that day, and they would return to Nantucket after breakfast the following morning. He was hoping that being with them would help him gauge whether Abe's position on the agreement with Jay Cooke had softened.

As they all stood in the lobby of their hotel, saying goodnight, he pulled Abe aside. He could see in the way Abe looked at him that his opinion of Jubil was not as high as it once had been. Jubil knew then that his own feelings about the agreement hadn't changed: he still felt equal measures ashamed and defiant about it.

"I'm sorry to have disappointed you," Jubil said quietly. "I hoped my decision with Jay Cooke would have had the opposite effect."

"I was already proud of you," Abe said, "and you can do no wrong in Lily's eyes. But I think this agreement shows poor judgment. I hope I'm wrong."

"Perhaps if it all ends well, you'll forgive me," Jubil said.

"Well," Abe said with a sigh, "be careful out there on the survey. We all want you back alive." He patted Jubil on the shoulder and went upstairs with Lily.

Jubil stood looking out the window of Nelly's apartment onto bustling East Eighteenth Street below, wishing he lived there with her. Following Nelly's graduation, he, Ike, and Nelly's mother had come to New York to help settle Nelly into her new home. She had lived in this same building last summer, sharing rooms with two other young women, when she worked for Mrs. Stanton and Miss Anthony's newspaper the *Revolution*. Mr. Porter, the editor at her new place of employment, *Scientific American* magazine, had helped her arrange the lease. Nelly and her mother shared the bedroom, while Ike slept on the couch. Jubil had taken a room at the St. Nicholas Hotel, a mile or so south at the corner of Broadway and Spring Streets.

Ike loved New York, and Jubil was surprised to find that he also found it more comfortable and exciting than he had during his first trip to visit Nelly after she moved to Poughkeepsie, when he had found the city intimidating. But exploring the city with Ike, he found it vibrant and filled with possibilities. When they discovered Central Park, Jubil thought he could live there quite comfortably, but of course that was not allowed.

"I wish you didn't have to leave so soon," Nelly said, appearing at his side bearing two mugs of steaming coffee. He took the coffee and kissed her forehead.

"Me too," he said. He wondered if they would ever get used to saying goodbye. The life together they had planned would be full of them.

"You'll look out for Eli, won't you?" Nelly asked.

"Of course," Jubil said, "the best I can. I wish he had come to the graduation."

"I'm more upset with Papa than Eli," Nelly said. "Eli is still a boy, and he's always gone out of his way to point out that his older sister is not his superior. But Papa is a grown man."

Jubil put his arm around her. "Maybe I can sway Eli this summer, and he can help bring your father around."

"Maybe," she said skeptically. "I just hope he survives the trip and doesn't get you killed."

"We'll be fine," he said, hoping this was true. Eli had always had a reckless streak—with Jubil's burned out farmhouse and barn as evidence—but Jubil was hopeful he would take direction.

"You'll write regularly?" she asked.

"Certainly," he said. "Which reminds me—there's something I'd like your help with, if your new job allows for it. If you come across any newspaper articles about the survey, especially if my name appears, would you clip them out and save them? I'd like to have evidence to show Cooke I did my best to promote the railroad."

"I certainly will," Nelly said. "I'll have all the time in the world to read the newspapers in the evening and keep up with your adventures."

"I hope you spend some of those evenings writing me," Jubil said, "to keep me updated on your adventures."

Nelly laughed and hugged him. When the time came, it was difficult for him to say goodbye to Nelly. So much of what he thought would be decided by now was still up in the air, hanging over him: the wedding date, the fate of the store and the farm. But the only thing he could do was get on with the railroad survey, complete it successfully, and remove the cloud of doubt he had placed over his future.

CHAPTER 5

When Jubil returned to Council Bluffs, Eli was packed and ready to go, but Jubil wanted to wait for Ike to return before they left. He had escorted his mother to Bloomington but would be along the following day.

A letter had come from Jubil's friend Walter Trumbull, who lived in Washington DC. Walter reported that the Interior Department had taken up the matter of appointing a superintendent for the new Yellowstone National Park. Walter's friend Truman Everts—who had gone missing on the Yellowstone expedition the previous year and was lucky enough to have been found weeks later—had been angling for the position, but it had been awarded to Nathaniel Pitt Langford, one of the leaders of the Washburn expedition. Jubil thought he was the right man for the job. Being acquainted with both men, he expected Langford would be more forceful in his efforts to defend the park from exploitation than Everts.

Walter worried, however, that Langford would be spread too thin, since he had simultaneously been appointed as Bank Examiner for the Territories and Pacific Coast States. Walter said that Langford was expected to be in Yellowstone this summer along with Dr. Ferdinand Hayden, who was continuing another survey of the basin he had begun last year. Captain

Barlow and Jubil had accompanied him at times while Barlow conducted the army survey.

Ike returned, reporting that not only had he been unable to sway Mr. Boswell's opinions, their discussion had turned into an argument. His father said Ike, along with Nelly, was no longer welcome in his house. His mother, out on an errand, did not witness the argument. Not wanting to upset her further, Ike had not told her. He had been planning on returning to Council Bluffs that day anyway, so she wouldn't know anything about it from him. He was unsure if his father would tell her.

Jubil had hoped that over time the situation with Mr. Boswell would improve, but it was only getting worse—the family was splintering. Jubil cared deeply about the Boswells, and his first impulse was to help, but he had to be very careful about how he went about doing it. One wrong step, and he could easily make matters worse.

The next day Jubil and Eli boarded the train. With Apollo settled into his accommodations, Jubil and Eli found their compartment in a Pullman Palace car. He would buy Eli a horse at the livery in Corrine, Utah.

As the train pulled away from Council Bluffs Jubil sat back and relaxed, enjoying his first crossing of the Union Pacific bridge across the Missouri River. It had been completed this spring, finally eliminating the need to ferry across the river.

"So, what do we do now?" Eli asked from the chair next to Jubil's in the sitting room of their compartment. "Do you want to take a stroll and explore the train?"

Jubil had ridden trains like this one many times and was content to settle in and read. He held up one of the books he had brought along to pass the time, another imaginative adventure by Jules Verne, *The Mysterious Island*.

Eli grunted with disgust, and Jubil laughed. "You go ahead," he said, unconcerned. The train was a locomotive and tender pulling six passenger cars, a dining car, a baggage car, and a stable car. There wasn't far for Eli to go or much likelihood he'd find any mischief.

The next time Jubil looked up, the train was slowing at a whistle-stop somewhere in the middle of Nebraska. Passengers stepped off to stretch their legs or visit the small restaurant next to the little depot, while the train took on water for the boiler. A short while later the train blasted its whistle and set off again, and as it did, it occurred to Jubil to wonder where Eli was. He had not seen him get off or on the train, but it was hard to imagine he would not have taken the opportunity. Jubil left the compartment to make sure Eli was still on the train.

Seating was controlled in the dining car at appointed meal times but open for socializing otherwise. He found Eli there playing cards and drinking beer with three other young men.

"Jubil!" Eli called out over the general hubbub of conversation and laughter in the crowded car. Jubil had never fancied spending his time in this way on the train. He walked down the aisle to their table.

"Howdy, fellows," Jubil said. To Eli, he said, "I just got up to stretch my legs. You winning or losing?" He was relieved to see that the pot in the center of the table was only small change.

"I'm down a few cents. These boys are sharps," Eli said, eyeing his companions dramatically.

One of the young men at the table smiled up at Jubil. "Does your associate always blame his bad luck and poor judgment on others?"

"He's normally a model citizen," Jubil said with a grin.

"See there, boys," Eli said a bit too loudly, "I've got Jubilee Walker vouching for me—top that!"

Jubil wondered how much beer Eli had consumed. He had probably been telling his business to anyone who would listen.

"I'll leave you fellows to your game. Be kind to my friend

here." To Eli, Jubil said, "Maybe tapering off on the beer would improve your luck."

"I'll take that under advisement," Eli said, hoisting his glass.

Jubil returned to his compartment, and about an hour later Eli swaggered back, and the two of them had supper together. Eli was not behaving as Jubil had as a younger man, but he was doing no harm, so Jubil declined to lecture him. The rest of the train trip followed a similar routine. Jubil did not necessarily approve of Eli's behavior, but he and Eli were different types of men, and their behavior reflected that fact. Jubil knew he would have to choose carefully when to correct Eli and when to leave him be.

At Corinne, Jubil left Eli next to the small platform by the tracks with their gear while he rode Apollo to the livery to pick out a horse for Eli and a pack horse for their gear. One horse that caught his eye was a muscular gray stallion that reminded him of his carriage horse, Rocky. He bought him and a healthy leather-brown stallion. Eli took one look at the gray stallion and claimed him as his own, naming him Max, after Jubil's Percheron draft horse who had been a favorite of the twins when they were boys. They called the friendly pack horse Buddy. Jubil coached Eli on how to properly load their gear on Buddy, a skill he had found lacking in some of his previous travel companions. First, they packed their various gear in canvas and leather panniers, then they arranged these bags so as to balance the weight on both sides of the animal, then they secured the load to the cross-braced pack saddle and to the animal with a taut diamond hitch.

"This section of the trip will hopefully be a dull ride north across the plains up to Bozeman," Jubil said. "There is the occasional band of braves roaming around showing their defiance, and highwaymen are sometimes known to prey on travelers, but I've made the ride a few times without trouble. You still need to be prepared for anything, though."

"Why not take the stagecoach to Bozeman?" Eli asked, gesturing to the sign on the booth indicating that both train and stagecoach tickets were sold there.

"The stagecoach from here to Bozeman is faster," Jubil said, "but it is also the most uncomfortable thing I've ever ridden. Even worse than one of Abe's freight wagons. I prefer horseback."

Jubil loaded his Henry rifle, removed his Colt pistol and holster from his pack, checked it over and loaded it, strapped it on, and then made sure Eli did the same. From his pack, he also removed his medicine bag, a fringed and beaded buckskin bag containing spirit tokens—two animal teeth, a claw, a little rock, a few small bones, and an arrowhead—that supposedly had the power to protect his life. Even if it did not, he was still proud to wear it. It had been given to him by General Sherman's Pawnee scout, White Dog, in return for Jubil having saved his life in a gun battle. The previous year, White Dog had returned the favor by saving Jubil's life in a gun battle with Phineas Black and his men. Jubil hoped to find White Dog somewhere along the way this trip.

As they began to ride north, Jubil began to wonder with a sick feeling in the pit of his stomach if anyone was planning a railroad spur from Corinne to Helena and Bozeman. That would be a much quicker and cheaper way to get people to the park than Cooke's Northern Pacific plan. Previously there had not been enough traffic to merit a rail spur through here, but now that Yellowstone was a park, that flow of travelers would surely increase. The idea put Jubil's own mission at risk—which was something he did not want to think about. Surely Jay Cooke knew more about building railroads than Jubil did, and Jubil was certain Cooke had considered all of these possibilities.

He turned his mind instead toward Cooke's idea of designing comfortable custom carriages to ferry wealthy travelers into and around the park. Jubil was certain that such a conveyance would be useful for many situations—replacing the uncomfortable stagecoach between Corinne and Bozeman, for one.

As they rode, Jubil and Eli chatted amiably. Eli exclaimed about the landscape as he got his first look at the mountains, and again as they came across a herd of antelope. Eli's many questions reminded Jubil of how, on his first trip West, he had switched wagons to see which of the Irish teamsters would tolerate talking with him for a while. After three days they were halfway to Bozeman, and Eli was beginning to slow down to match the pace of the journey.

"You're doing well," Jubil said as they sat by their campfire after supper. Eli was handling his share of making and breaking camp, working on the fire, and tending the animals without any prompting from Jubil. "I appreciate that. You're a good travel partner."

"I had a good model to follow," Eli said. "It was a good idea to go out camping in the bluffs this spring. This feels pretty natural. But it's a long ride. How many days before we get to Bozeman?"

"About three," Jubil said.

"I knew it would be a lot of riding," Eli said. "But knowing something in your mind and experiencing it are whole different things. My imagination was weak."

"That will happen to you a lot out here," Jubil said. "That's why you have to stay ready for anything. Even things you were expecting can still catch you by surprise."

"I'm ready! Bring it on," Eli said pulling a face and shaking his fist.

"You've got to take this seriously, Eli," Jubil said.

"I am," Eli said defensively.

"All right, all right," Jubil said. He did not want to treat Eli like a child, but he couldn't allow him to lose sight of the dangers that surrounded them out here. "We're both in for some firsts on this trip. This will be the largest expedition I've ever been on. I understand there will be about four hundred soldiers in the escort. This is also a different sort of survey than I was on last year. I'm not exactly clear what a railroad survey entails, so we'll be learning together."

Eli silently poked at the fire—still seeming to be irritated by Jubil's reprimand. With Eli no longer interested in conversation, Jubil went to bed.

The rest of the trip on to Bozeman was uneventful and the weather was cooperative. Jubil couldn't have asked for better circumstances, but in spite of Jubil's warnings, Eli seemed restless and distracted. In Bozeman, they stabled their horses at the livery and went to find rooms for themselves at the Guy House, where Jubil had spent weeks recuperating from his gunfight with Phineas Black. They settled in for the evening and went to supper in the hotel dining room. As they were seating themselves, a man Jubil recognized walked past the dining room on his way out of the hotel.

"There's Nathaniel Langford." Jubil rose and called out to him, and Langford came to their table. He was in his mid-thirties and had deep-set eyes, a chest-length beard, and a serious manner.

"What a pleasant surprise," Jubil said. "A chance meeting with the newly appointed superintendent of Yellowstone National Park."

"I hope you approve," Langford laughed.

"Wholeheartedly," Jubil said. "Can you join us for supper?"

"I'm sorry, but I'm afraid I can't," Langford said. "I'm meeting Dr. Hayden over at the Metropolitan Hotel. I have a few minutes, though."

He sat down with them, and Jubil introduced him to Eli.

"I'm pleased to make your acquaintance, Mr. Langford," Eli said. "I've heard Jubil's stories about the expedition—some of them more than once." He grinned at Jubil. "And I enjoyed your vivid account in *Scribner's Monthly*."

Jubil was surprised. He had never caught Eli reading a book or heard him mention anything he had read, let alone Langford's article.

"Thank you, Mr. Boswell," Langford said. "Welcome to Montana. Are you gentlemen opening a new outfitting store?"

Jubil explained his agreement with Cooke, and Langford sat back and stared silently at him for an uncomfortable moment.

"My word," Langford finally said, "that is a lot to take in—but excellent news."

"Thank you," Jubil said. He wondered about Langford's reserved congratulations. Had he hoped Cooke would offer him such a partnership? Perhaps not, since Langford seemed to have enough on his plate.

"Well, you and I will have a great deal of business to do together in the future," Langford said. "I'm pleased Cooke is allowing his drive for profit to be moderated by your respect for the park."

"He seems sincere about it," Jubil said. "But the first order of business is to complete the survey."

Langford furrowed his brow.

"Are you concerned?" Jubil said.

"Sorry," Langford said, "perhaps a bit. I hope this year's survey goes better than last year's—it was poorly managed. But Cooke has hired a new man, a Mr. John Haydon—no relation to Dr. Hayden. I don't know him, but hopefully he and Colonel Baker can both stay sober and get along. Haydon served in the Confederate army, and Colonel Baker is a Union man."

Jubil had only met Baker once, when he was the commander of Fort Ellis. He'd had no idea that Baker had a troubled history with alcohol.

"What about Indian problems?" Jubil asked.

"They're putting up some resistance," Langford said flatly, "but I hear the escort will take almost all the cavalry from Fort Ellis—to the dismay of the locals who feel unprotected."

Jubil had been hoping for stronger assurance that the survey was positioned well. Unsettled, he decided to change the subject before he learned about any other problems that he couldn't control.

"Are you here on park business?" Jubil asked.

"Yes," Langford said, "Dr. Hayden is continuing his survey this year—a larger team to do more collecting and sampling—and refining his maps. James Stevenson and I are going to do some reconnoitering along the Madison River to consider the feasibility of a railroad route into the park from the west. Do you remember Mr. Stevenson?"

"Yes, he took me for a ride on the lake in the *Anna*," Jubil said. Hayden's men had brought a portable boat with them the previous year to survey Yellowstone Lake. "Are you thinking a spur off the Northern Pacific from Bozeman down to the Madison, or up from the Union Pacific at Corinne?"

"Doesn't matter to me," Langford said. "I'm thinking of the park. We've got to get visitors there, or we'll get no protection for the area."

Jubil agreed with Langford about the park, but unlike Langford, it now mattered very much to Jubil that the Northern Pacific win out over the Union Pacific.

"Are you going into the Yellowstone Basin on this trip?" Eli asked Langford.

"Yes," Langford said, "Stevenson and I plan to enter from the west, along the Madison, and follow the Firehole to the Geyser Basin, where we'll meet Dr. Hayden. Then we'll come out of the Basin to the north, and follow the Yellowstone up Paradise Valley."

Eli turned his attention to Jubil. "I sure would like to see those sights."

"We don't have time for that," Jubil said. "We've got a job to do."

"Well," Eli said, "you've got a job to do. I'm just along for the ride. If Mr. Langford doesn't mind, maybe I could ride along with him instead, and meet up with you back in Bozeman?"

Jubil considered the proposition. Jubil was not sure Eli was safer with him than with Langford, but he couldn't face Nelly and the rest of the Boswells if something happened to Eli while they were separated. But then again, it might be just as bad if something happened to Eli while they were together. He could not protect him from every possibility.

"No, I think you should stay with me," Jubil said.

Eli frowned. "I would think, for our business plans, the more valuable experience for me would be seeing the park, but I'm sure you know best," Eli said, thinly covering his displeasure.

"I'm sorry to say I can't take you along this time around, son," Langford said, grinning. "You can tour the Yellowstone Basin anytime, but the railroad survey will be a once-in-a-life-time experience." Langford turned to Jubil. "Sorry to rush off, but I don't want to keep Dr. Hayden waiting. Good luck with the survey."

The next morning Jubil and Eli were on their way to Fort Ellis. The weather was warm and dry as they rode south out of Bozeman and followed the well-worn trail east to the fort, a short ride of only three miles. The fort, a collection of white-washed buildings scattered across about one hundred acres, sat on rolling open plains, surrounded by mountains on the north, east, and south. They found Colonel Baker in his office talking with another officer, Major Barlow. The men rose to greet them.

"Welcome back to Fort Ellis, Mr. Walker," Colonel Baker said, rising. He had a full short beard and wore a dusty unbut-toned frock coat and a Stetson cavalry hat. When Jubil leaned in to shake his hand, he caught the strong smell of whiskey. "I believe you are well acquainted with Major Barlow," Baker said, waving his hand dismissively as he dropped back into his chair.

"Thank you, Colonel, it's good to be back," Jubil said. "Congratulations on your promotion, Major Barlow. It's good to see you again."

"You as well, Mr. Walker," Barlow said with a slight smile. "I was pleased to learn you would be accompanying us." Jubil had learned that while Barlow had a serious demeanor, he was pleasant company. General Sherman had recruited Jubil to guide Barlow's survey through Yellowstone the previous year, but Barlow had initially thought his maps were adequate without Jubil's help. Midway through the expedition they finally learned to value one another and became friends.

Jubil turned to Eli. "This is one of my business associates, Eli Boswell—this will be his first expedition."

Eli stepped up to greet the men and shake hands. Colonel Baker rose halfway and shook hands with Eli disinterestedly.

"I understand First Lieutenant Doane will be with the escort," Jubil said.

"Yes," Major Barlow said, "you may not see him today. He's busy getting ready to move out."

"How about Mr. Haydon and the survey crew, are they here yet?" Jubil asked.

"The *colonel* you mean—or so he styles himself," Colonel Baker blurted out. Jubil realized that Baker hadn't just had a drink—he was drunk. "Pardoned Confederate army officer, you know—not a combat officer—an engineer, like Major Barlow here."

Jubil looked at Barlow but saw no sign he had taken offense—though Jubil would not have blamed him if he had.

"Yes," Major Barlow answered for Baker, ignoring his comments, "they are making their final preparations to leave.

I'll introduce you and Mr. Boswell to him, if you'd like. We can go now."

Jubil and Eli followed Barlow out of the headquarters building.

"Is Colonel Baker going to be allowed to lead the escort in his condition?" Jubil asked.

"I'm sorry to say he is," Barlow admitted. "He will have eight companies in the escort. Four cavalry companies from Fort Ellis under Captain Ball, and four infantry companies from Fort Shaw under Captain Rawn. I'm here on orders from General Hancock to deliver an official report of our leg of the survey. I've informed Baker of General Hancock's concerns, but the harder I push, the more defiant Baker becomes. His comportment is up to him, and he's aware of the possible consequences. I'll report what I see. It's all I can do."

For a moment Jubil considered sending a telegram to General Sheridan, or even General Sherman, explaining the situation and asking to have Baker relieved of duty. But that level of intervention seemed extreme, and if his request was refused, he would be in a very awkward position to continue on the survey. If Major Barlow was willing to allow Baker to lead, then Jubil would trust Barlow's decision and hope for the best.

"I understand you're here at the request of Jay Cooke," Barlow said. "I don't recall your having mentioned anything about him last year. Is your acquaintance recent?"

Jubil explained how he had come to meet Cooke and their agreement to a travel business partnership, contingent on the completion of the Northern Pacific Railroad survey.

"Speaking of which, before we meet Colonel Haydon," Jubil said, "I'd like a better understanding of the work he and his crew will be doing. How will this survey be different from what I saw you and Dr. Hayden doing last year?"

The previous year's focus had been on determining the exact locations of geographical features, platting a grid, and improving the maps of the Yellowstone region. At the same time, a science team was documenting natural resources and wildlife in each area.

"You'll find this quite different," Barlow said. "This railroad survey has no science team, and the surveyors will move along as quickly as possible. They will be marking out the straightest line possible between two given end points that has a grade along the way that will allow the expected railroad loads to be carried successfully. The overall goal is the shortest, flattest route between Bismarck and Bozeman, and our part is to locate the part of the route between Bozeman and the Powder River."

The other survey crew was heading west from Bismarck to meet them there.

"Sounds simple enough," Jubil said with a wry smile.

"It would be if the Earth were flat and dry," Barlow replied.

They found Haydon in the yard, supervising the loading of a wagon. Haydon was in his mid-forties, six inches shorter than Jubil, and had a full head of iron-gray hair. He seemed to be a quiet sort, with a serious nature. Cooke had informed him that Jubil would be joining the survey, and he seemed to have no concern about or interest in Jubil's and Eli's presence. After their brief meeting, Barlow led Jubil and Eli to their bunks in the officer's quarters, where Eli went off to begin the business of introducing himself to everyone he encountered.

"Is Colonel Haydon always that cordial," Jubil asked Barlow, "or did he just not take a shine to me?"

"He seems to have little use for anyone but the men on his crew," Barlow replied. "I'd say he views the rest of us as a necessary evil he must endure."

"Reminds me of another fellow I once worked with," Jubil said with a grin.

"Yes," Barlow laughed, "maybe he'll warm to us as time goes by. You and I seem to be here in similar roles—as observers.

So you may find everyone—including Haydon—treating you more as Jay Cooke's eyes than as yourself. I expect to be viewed as the eyes of the military command, rather than as a fellow surveyor. And yet, we have no real authority."

Jubil was surprised but pleased with Barlow's candor and acceptance.

"If there was an official report delivered last year," Jubil said, "I didn't see it."

"There wasn't," Barlow said. "Ultimately, they were forced to turn back due to winter weather. If they had moved along with more conviction, they would not have been out so late in the year. The leader of the survey, Mr. Muhlenberg, was a problem drinker, and Colonel Baker's own bad habits made things worse."

Cooke had left out some significant details during their conversation about the failed survey.

"This year, Cooke's people have replaced Muhlenberg, and they want Haydon in charge of the survey, but General Sheridan still wants Colonel Baker to lead the escort. Colonel Baker and I both report to General Hancock, who reports to Sheridan. Hancock knows Baker is a favorite of Sheridan's, but he also knows Baker may be disruptive, and thinks my presence might temper things. Not every detail will make it into my official report, but every detail will be observed and reported up the chain of command. The military wants this survey over with. If there is Indian trouble back there while we're off down the Yellowstone, the public will be outraged. If the relationship between Baker and Haydon becomes strained, any influence you can exert over Haydon to tolerate Baker and complete the mission will be greatly appreciated—for all our sakes."

"I understand," Jubil said. "So far, my prospects for influencing Haydon do not look bright."

"Oh, don't sell yourself short," Barlow said with a grin, "you can be a very charming fellow."

Jubil rolled his eyes. "Can I ask something of you?" Jubil said, encouraged by Barlow's goodwill. "My business associate, Eli Boswell—this is his first expedition. He's capable of looking out for himself, and he wouldn't want me asking you, but—if anything happens to me while we're out, would you try to watch out for him until he gets back to the fort?"

"You can rest assured I will," Barlow said.

"Thank you," Jubil said.

After Major Barlow left, Jubil lay on his bunk recalling what Cooke had said about Indians, incompetence, and bad luck. Even though his understanding of the job ahead of him was becoming clearer, he did not find that making him more comfortable—quite the opposite.

As he was about to doze off, he realized Eli had not yet returned. He was going to have to remember to keep an eye on Eli, otherwise he might as well have sent him off with Langford. Considering all that was likely to be going on, and considering Eli's congenial and energetic nature, keeping track of him would not be easy.

Just as Jubil was resigning himself to get up off his bunk to look for him, Eli returned full of enthusiasm for the adventure that lay ahead and colorful descriptions about who he had met so far. Jubil indulged him for a while, then interrupted—they needed their sleep to be ready for an early start. Eli agreed and was asleep long before Jubil, who lay there pondering all that he had gotten himself into.

CHAPTER 6

Jubil and Eli were finishing their breakfast in the officer's mess when Jubil felt a presence behind him. Eli, facing Jubil, put down his coffee cup and looked up at someone with a certain awe in his face. Then Jubil heard the low rumble of a familiar voice.

"I heard Jay Cooke sent a spy out to keep an eye on his investment."

"Lieutenant Doane," Jubil said with a smile as he rose to greet his friend with the walrus mustache with points that hung to his chin, "I'm sorry—*First Lieutenant* Doane—it's good to see you. Congratulations on your promotion."

"Thank you, good to see you too, Walker," Doane said as they shook hands.

Doane stood a good three inches above Jubil's six feet, with broad shoulders and a muscular build. When Jubil introduced Eli, who was a few inches shorter than Jubil, he looked like a child next to Doane.

"Not my first choice of available assignments," Doane shrugged. "Nothing personal, mind you. Langford is back in the Yellowstone Basin with Dr. Hayden, so that would have been a plum assignment. But my experience on the rescue party last year sealed my fate. I'm leading Company G of the Second Cavalry as part of your escort."

Jubil heard the subtle scorn in Doane's tone. He had heard it before, two years ago, when Doane informed him that he had been the first to propose an expedition through the Grand Canyon, but that the expedition had been awarded to Major Powell.

"The previous survey required rescue?" Jubil asked. Another detail Cooke had failed to mention.

"Partly just bad luck," Doane said, "though if they would have finished their job without dawdling, they might not have been caught by the weather. In any case, I may not have time to enjoy your company much this trip. I'll have my men to attend to, my commanding officer Colonel Baker to deal with, and Major Barlow keeping an eye on me."

"Well, Jay Cooke's spy rides with whomever he chooses," Jubil said with a grin.

He saw the hint of a smile beneath Doane's mustache. Having Doane along made Jubil feel a bit less concerned about Colonel Baker's drinking, even though he was not sure what Doane could do about it.

"I'd enjoy hearing more about your newfound friendship with Cooke," Doane said. He turned to Eli. "You're in good hands, Mr. Boswell," he said as he moved toward the mess line.

Jubil and Eli finished their coffee, loaded up their gear, and rode out to find Major Barlow and Colonel Haydon and his survey crew. Strung out in a procession over a mile long were about four hundred soldiers, twenty men in Haydon's survey crew, and thirty cowherds and wolfers. The survey crew's gear was stacked and strapped onto three heavy wagons, each pulled by a four-mule team, and the gear for the military escort was hauled by a small armada of sixty wagons and ambulances whose wheels creaked and moaned on the hard uneven ground. A small herd of beef cattle trailed behind the wagons, bellowing and stinking and stirring up a great cloud of reddish dirt. Tending the cattle were a few cowherds, and bringing up the rear was a heavily armed, scruffy band of characters dressed in a wild variety of skins, coats, and hats. It was like a small town on the move.

"That looks like a band of mountain men," Eli said. "Why are they here?"

"They're called 'wolfers'," Jubil said. "I've heard about them but never traveled with any. They follow along to kill and skin the wolves that are drawn to the cattle."

One of the wolfers stared at them as they rode past—he was about Eli's age, and wore a wolf's-head cap and long blond braids.

"They look like a dangerous lot," Eli said, sounding worried.

"I wouldn't play cards with them," Jubil said lightly. He was pleased to see Eli intimidated by his surroundings. He hoped that a healthy fear of the dangers around him would temper his curious nature.

Jubil spotted Major Barlow near the head of the column. He and Eli rode up beside him and matched his pace. Colonel Haydon was not with him.

Jubil settled into the saddle, relieved to finally be under-way. The trail followed the East Gallatin River over hilly country. It was near the end of July, but the weather was chilly and overcast. As they rode over the rolling plains, the aspen and willow shivered in the cool breeze, and the water in the streams looked like molten metal. Six miles from Fort Ellis they came to the Yellowstone divide, a ridge along the Gallatin Range forming the apex of two watersheds; one that sloped to the Gallatin River, the other to the Yellowstone.

"Are we going to ride right over those mountains?" Eli asked Jubil as the trail ascended.

"See that notch up there, depressed several hundred feet below the ridgeline? That's the Bozeman Pass," Jubil said, "the only tolerable wagon road across the Gallatin range."

When they reached the top of the pass, Jubil paused to show Eli where they were on the map. "There it is, Eli, Paradise

Valley," Jubil said, gazing out at the expanse before them, "down there is the Yellowstone River, and we're right here," he said, pointing out their location.

Eli sat silently in awe of the vista below him, mouth agape. All the way to the southern horizon the Yellowstone River meandered through a valley several miles wide that was bounded by snow-capped mountains. Spread across the floor of the valley were thousands of grassy acres, dotted with the habitations of pioneers.

"You follow the Yellowstone River south from here to reach the basin," Jubil said, "but we will be following it north around this big bend, where it begins to flow to the east. If you should happen to get separated from the survey, you can find your way back to the fort by just following the river back to this point—so mind what the route looks like as we make our way down Trail Creek, so you can find the pass again."

"Get separated from the survey?" Eli asked with concern. "Why would that happen?"

"It shouldn't," Jubil said, "but you have to be prepared for anything out here."

Eli looked around to get his bearings.

As they followed Trail Creek down into Paradise Valley and came into clear view of the Yellowstone, Major Barlow, Jubil, and Eli stopped and stared at the river.

"It's up considerably from last year," Jubil said staring at a river that was twice the width and depth he was familiar with.

"I was afraid of this," Barlow said, as much to himself as Jubil. "It was a very long winter, and the spring snow melt is late—it snowed in Bozeman on the first of July—and it has also been unusually rainy. The river looks to be about one hundred yards across, maybe fifteen to twenty feet deep. I'd guess it's moving at about six to eight miles an hour." Barlow sat silently looking at the river, then turned to Jubil. "We can't cross that."

"Why do we have to?" Jubil asked. "Why can't we just

survey on this side?"

"That's one of the reasons the survey failed last year," Barlow said. "The terrain on the north side of the river is far more difficult."

"What? Cooke told me they surveyed so far out that winter hit them," Jubil said.

"That's true," Barlow said. "Last year, the railroad's objective was to follow the north bank to avoid disrupting the Crow Agency and reservation along the south bank. The crew surveyed a line very close to the river along the north bank, but every night they crossed to the south bank to camp on the plains, as there was not adequate room on the north bank to make camp. The next morning, they would cross the river again and continue their survey along the north bank. They did this until they reached Clark's Fork River. Then, because of their slow pace, the weather hit them. That whole route along the north bank is too close to the river, and worthless. In fact, it's probably underwater now."

"Why didn't the survey leader recognize that in the first place?" Jubil asked.

"He said he was just following orders," Barlow said, "and trying to make the best of the situation, but it was obviously a doomed strategy. His judgment was compromised by alcohol."

Cooke had said the whole survey needed to be redone, but he had not said why. Their intended route this year would mean going right through the reservation. Another detail that Cooke had failed to mention.

"What do we do now?" Jubil asked. "How do we get across?"

Colonel Haydon had ridden up while they were talking. Now he said, "A good question. We certainly won't attempt it here. We'll continue downriver to the ferry near the Crow Agency. That's the best ford along this stretch and our best chance."

Barlow looked at Jubil and nodded. He was a chief engineer for the army and a good man, and Jubil trusted his judgment.

They fell in line with the rest of the column and continued along the river to the point where the ferry was supposed to be, but the river was no less formidable an obstacle there. The column halted, and Jubil and the survey leaders sat looking at the swollen river.

"There's normally a rudimentary ferry system here," Doane said, pointing across the river at a rickety wooden shed. Beside it, turned upside down, was a sturdy boat that looked similar to the ones Jubil had used on the Colorado River through the Grand Canyon. He could have easily crossed the river in it. Next to the shack was a trail that led toward the Crow Agency and the reservation, visible in the distance.

"It's an every-man-for-himself affair," Doane continued. "There's the skiff and a rope tow, but the river is up so high, someone at the agency has hauled the skiff up the bank to avoid it being swept away, and the rope tow is either submerged, or they've taken it down to avoid its being swept away by debris coming down the river."

"It is too late in the day to consider crossing now," Haydon said. "We'll make camp here for the night."

They had come about thirty miles from Fort Ellis.

The next morning, Jubil, Eli, and Barlow were drinking coffee as they sat by the fire in the senior officers' camp. Haydon and his men kept mostly to themselves, maintaining their own campfire and sleeping near their wagons. Lieutenant Doane was talking to one of the other officers, and after a short conversation, saluted the officer and headed in Jubil's direction.

"Good morning, gentlemen," Doane said. "Do we have a plan of action?"

"Not yet, but here comes Haydon," Barlow replied, as Colonel Haydon walked over to join them.

"Where is Colonel Baker?" Haydon asked Doane.

"He's indisposed at the moment, sir," Doane said. "Captain Ball sent me to ask your plans."

In other words, Baker was drunk. In an odd way, Jubil was relieved to see that the colonel's shortcomings would not be allowed to disturb the mission. The other officers would cover for him.

"What are our chances of making a crossing here?" Haydon asked. "Major Barlow, as an army engineer, how long would you say it would take to build a proper bridge here for us?"

"Two weeks, possibly less—if the weather cooperates," Barlow replied, looking up into the overcast sky.

"I had hoped to be well along by then," Haydon said pensively. "Can we continue along the north bank to another crossing point?"

"Moving this whole expedition along the north side of the river will be slow going," Lieutenant Doane said. "I'm not even sure it's possible. The banks are so steep along several miles of it that you can't follow the river, you have to make your way up onto a plateau that is cut with ridges and valleys. It would be better if we had an Indian scout—they know every passable route around here."

Jubil looked across the river and wondered whether White Dog was at the reservation. His friend could guide them, but he had misgivings about Haydon's plan.

"Colonel Haydon," Jubil said, "are you sure about making a departure from our planned route? If Major Barlow can build a bridge in a couple of weeks, wouldn't that be the least risky way to go?"

"I have to agree with Mr. Walker," Major Barlow said. "If we have no more rain, we can build a sound structure here in two weeks."

Haydon took a moment to consider, then shook his head. "I'm concerned you're being optimistic, and I never trust the weather to cooperate. We'll move further down river to find a suitable crossing and then double back on the south side to make our survey. In the absence of a scout, we'll find our own way."

Jubil and Barlow exchanged a glance. Jubil's instinct was to make a stronger argument for building the bridge, but he was reluctant to have a disagreement with Haydon so early in the survey. Jubil interpreted Barlow's silence to mean that he felt the same way. It appeared their roles as observers might limit them to being just that—and not influencers.

"I know someone who would help us," Jubil said, "if he's at the reservation." He was hoping to see his friend, but mainly he was concerned about Haydon's willingness to also ignore Doane's advice. Their chance for success would be better with an experienced guide.

"Tell him the army will pay his usual rate," Doane nodded.

"Your prospects are not good for crossing that river," Barlow cautioned, "if that's what you're thinking."

Jubil walked closer to the water's edge to have a better look. The river was about three hundred feet across here, and deep enough that any rocks below the surface were fully covered. The river was not a roiling rapid, and covered its power with a smooth surface that hid a strong current. Jubil and Apollo had swum the Yellowstone a few times, though never at flood stage, but it looked—and more importantly, felt—possible.

"I can do it," Jubil said.

"You can't cross that river! Look at that!" Eli exclaimed, pointing at the river as if Jubil had somehow failed to notice it.

"We'll be fine," Jubil said. "Where exactly is that rope tow? I wouldn't want to get tangled in that," Jubil said to Doane.

"If it's still in the water, it's right in here somewhere," Doane said, pointing.

"I'm going to ride back upriver before I cross," Jubil said. "That'll give me plenty of room to drift with the current. If I overshoot this point, I'll just hang on until Apollo can pull us across. I'll ride back up to let you know I've made it, then ride over to the reservation. Hopefully, they'll know White Dog's whereabouts."

"You don't have to do this," Eli said, shaking his head in disbelief.

"But I do, Eli," Jubil said seriously. "If we don't get a guide, we may not be able to complete the survey. I can't let that happen if I can prevent it. I have to try to get us a guide. Is Flynn still the Indian agent here?" Jubil asked Doane.

Jubil had once traveled with Flynn on a wagon train. He was, more recently, an associate of Phineas Black, the man Jubil had killed in a gunfight the previous year.

"Yes," Doane said. "But he has new handlers now."

Jubil nodded. "I'll try to be back by midday," he said to the group, and went to get Apollo.

"I volunteered for us to take a swim this morning," Jubil said, as Apollo pawed the ground while being saddled up. "I hope you don't mind too much."

He removed his Colt and holster and stowed them in his pack but kept his hunting knife strapped to his belt. He wore his medicine bag. If he met up with White Dog, he wanted to have it on, and if it had any power to guard his life, that might come in handy too.

He set out upriver, scouting the channel carefully for any disturbances that would indicate submerged rocks or tangles of timber—those were the most lethal. He had seen tangles of trees that trapped anything coming downriver, holding it fast until it was eventually pulled under by the force of the current. The channel looked clear, which was encouraging. He was about a quarter of a mile upriver when he decided he had come far enough.

"This looks as good a spot as any," Jubil said, reaching up to pat Apollo on the neck to calm the both of them. "That water will be chilly, but we're tough, aren't we boy? Let's get this done."

Jubil eased Apollo into the river slowly, allowing him to walk until the water reached the horse's knees. He held him still then, and allowed Apollo to become accustomed to the water pushing against him. Jubil took his medicine bag off, rolled the strap around the bag and tucked it inside his shirt so it wouldn't get swept away.

"Easy now..." Jubil said, urging Apollo a step further. Jubil's boots were wet now, and Apollo was up to his belly in the water. The horse was beginning to have trouble maintaining his balance. Jubil did not want Apollo to tip over and be swept away off balance. It was time to commit.

"All right...go, Apollo!" Jubil nudged Apollo's flanks with his heels, and the horse launched himself into the river. The strength of the current almost pushed Jubil out of the saddle. He held tight to the saddle horn and clutched Apollo with his legs. He shifted his weight into the current until they gained stability. The water was cold, but not enough to cramp his muscles, as long as he wasn't in it for too long.

Apollo kept his wits about him and pulled against the current. They were being taken downstream, but Apollo was also making good progress across. Jubil was startled as a log barreled past in front of them, missing them by only a few feet. He reminded himself to watch upriver for oncoming debris. By the time they reached the middle of the river, they had drifted about half the distance back to the survey camp.

Suddenly, something startled Apollo. He stopped swimming and reared his head. Jubil felt the horse's hindquarters begin to drift downstream. Apollo was now facing upriver headlong into the current, preventing him from swimming. At the same time, the current nearly swept Jubil backward off the horse.

He dropped the reins and held the saddle horn with both hands—his grip with his legs was more difficult to maintain facing this direction. He let go with his left hand to turn Apollo's head to the left and urge him to reorient against the current. As the horse turned his head and neck, it brought his body around again, and they began to make progress toward the opposite shore. They had drifted further downstream than Jubil had hoped to.

They were now about three quarters of the way across the river, and almost even with the survey camp, where men lined the banks watching. Jubil spotted the shack and the overturned skiff on the opposite side. They were going to overshoot that point, but they would not drift a great deal further downriver, if all went well. Apollo sensed they were nearing the opposite bank, and pulled valiantly for shore. They still had about one hundred feet to go, as they drifted downriver past the shack and skiff.

Then Jubil felt a sharp pain against the knee of his left leg as he and Apollo were jerked to a halt, pointing directly at the river bank. They were being held suspended by the current against something in the river—the ferry tow rope. Jubil pictured what must be beneath the water: there were probably posts driven into the riverbend on either shore, each supporting a block and tackle with rope looped between to allow the skiff to be hauled across the river rather than rowed. They were lucky it had not caught them at the neck instead of across Apollo's side. But the horse was not going to be able to swim forward with the pressure of the current holding him against the ropes.

Jubil felt for his hunting knife, and was relieved to find it still in the holster on his belt. Now the problem was how to cut them free. He had no trouble locating the rope—it was painfully binding his left leg to Apollo's side—but reaching it without being pushed off Apollo, dropping the knife, or cutting himself or the horse would not be easy. He had no choice but to try.

He gripped the saddle horn with his right hand and clutched Apollo with his legs, as he reached down with his left hand to locate the rope. His leg held the rope just far enough away from

Apollo's side to allow him to slide the knife in. He removed the knife from its sheath, and reached down again to find the gap. He slid the knife in and began to saw, careful not to hit Apollo's side. As he sawed at the rope, he looked upriver and his stomach dropped. About one hundred yards away and coming fast, was the root ball of a big tree headed straight downriver toward them. If he could not free them, it would slam into them like a battering ram. Jubil sawed frantically as he watched the tree approach. It was only a few feet away when the rope finally snapped and Apollo was swept sideways facing upriver, allowing the log to push past. Jubil turned Apollo's head to swim for the shore, and after drifting downriver another hundred yards or so, the horse found his footing in the shallow water and heaved up onto the shore. Jubil dismounted and comforted his horse, who was huffing and trembling.

"You are as fine a partner as a fellow could have," Jubil said, looking Apollo in the eye and rubbing his cheeks as he calmed. "But don't tell Star I said that. We don't want to hurt her feelings."

Jubil checked Apollo's side and found some rope burn near his left shoulder but no cuts. He rubbed the horse down all over to relax his muscles and warm him up, then he dumped the water out of his boots, wrung out his socks, and took off his wool shirt and cotton undershirt and rung them out the best he could. Fortunately, the sun was coming out. He checked the contents of his medicine bag to make sure all the spirit tokens were intact. They were, and apparently, they still worked. He dressed, strapped the medicine bag back on, and rode back to the ferry shack. He signaled to the men on the other shore, who cheered his success, then set off toward the Crow Agency.

As he approached, he could see the reservation spread out to the south of the stockade that enclosed the agency. There were several hundred lodges, and south of them a few acres of cultivated garden. The peaceful look of the place made Jubil uncomfortable about the Northern Pacific Railroad running right through the middle of it, and especially uncomfortable about being partly responsible for that.

The stockade was lightly built, apparently intended more for keeping food stores and horses safe from natural predators than as a military defense. He rode through the open gates. Inside was a horse corral, a few wagons, several storehouses, what Jubil guessed was a one-room school, based on the children in raggedy clothing playing outside it, and another building that he assumed was the residence of the agent. Sitting outside that building were two men, a red-haired fellow that he recognized and an Indian that he did not.

Flynn, was one of three Irishmen who had been teamsters for Abe Warner on a supply wagon train that Jubil had ridden with from Council Bluffs to Fort McPherson several years ago. Of the three—Flynn, Murphy, and O'Brien—Flynn, who was about Jubil's age, was the most pleasant company. Two years ago, Phineas Black had finagled Flynn into his position at the Crow Agency, in order to facilitate his own corrupt dealings as a government vendor to the reservation. Jubil's friend, White Dog, had killed Murphy in the same gunfight in which Jubil had killed Black. Even though Flynn took orders from Black and Murphy, Jubil did not view him as a complicit criminal. Flynn was just a victim of his own timidity. As he rode closer, Flynn stared, then slapped his thigh, laughed, and rose from his chair.

"May the saints preserve us—if it isn't Jubilee Walker! What in God's name are you doing here, Walker?"

"Good morning, Flynn," Jubil said. "Fine place you've got here."

"It's well enough," Flynn said. "Suits me, you know. Peaceful mostly. I'm just out here doing my best to help these poor buggers." Flynn gave Jubil a suspicious look. "Have you come hunting me down then? To finish off your business with

Murphy and Black? I wasn't cheating nobody, you know. I was just taking orders and doing my job."

"I know that, Flynn," Jubil said. "I'm not here to chastise you. I need your help." He explained his situation with the survey. "I thought I might find a friend of mine here. His name is Taaka Asakis, White Dog. He's Pawnee and scouts for the army sometimes."

Flynn looked at the man sitting next to him. "You know him?"

Closer up, Jubil saw that the man was not an Indian or not a full-blooded one at any rate. He had long unadorned black hair parted in the middle and a weathered, tanned face, but a white man's features.

"The soldiers call him White Man's Dog," the man said, speaking with a slight French accent.

"Yes, they do," Jubil said, "but I'm not a soldier."

"How did you come by your medicine bag?" the man asked, pointing at the pouch Jubil wore slung across his torso.

"White Dog and I were in a skirmish with some of Tall Bull's Dog Soldiers. Afterward, he gave it to me."

The man sized him up and then nodded.

"He's not here," the man said. "Off scouting to the east. Sitting Bull and the Sioux are getting itchy for a fight."

None of that information was good news.

"My name is Jubilee Walker. Who would you be, sir?" Jubil asked the man.

"My apologies gents, let me do a proper introduction," Flynn said. "Mr. Walker here is an adventurer, runs an outfitting business, and has a fierce conscience about right and wrong. And this here gentleman, Mr. Walker, is Mitch Boyer. Mitch's pa was a French-Canada trapper, and his ma was a Santee. Mitch here calls Jim Bridger a friend, and he speaks English, French, Sioux, and Crow. He knows these parts probably better than any man around."

"How do you do, Mr. Boyer?" Jubil said with a nod. "Would you consider guiding the railroad survey? I believe you'd help us out considerably. The army will pay the usual rate for a scout."

"You say Colonel Baker is in charge of the escort?" Boyer asked.

"Yes," Jubil said. He assumed Boyer knew Baker's shortcomings. "I don't know Baker well, but I do know Lieutenant Doane, one of the officers with him—and I trust him."

Boyer nodded. "All right, I'll ride with you for a while. We'll see how it goes."

"Excellent," Jubil said, pleased to be improving the survey's prospects. "Can we be on our way soon?"

"I'll fetch my horse and gear," Boyer said, reaching down to retrieve a shabby top hat as he rose from his chair. He was dressed eccentrically in a black and gold paisley vest over weathered buckskins, with beaded moccasins on his feet.

"Thank you," Jubil said to Flynn. "You were very helpful."

"Glad to be of service," Flynn said. "You know, I was not at all upset that you removed Murphy and Black from over my head."

"I found many of the townspeople in Bozeman felt the same," Jubil said.

"You know, don't you," Flynn said, "that nothing has changed, though. You run those rats off, and more just scurried in to take their place. I'm still out here accepting shoddy merchandise and filling out shady paperwork."

Jubil was not surprised to learn these details. He had not expected that the corruption in the Bureau of Indian Affairs was cleansed by the removal of one bad apple. He'd had intentions of involving himself more in efforts to make a broader change in the bureau, but his good intentions had fallen victim to the realities of his personal life—opening a new store, lobbying for the passage of the Yellowstone bill, and getting married. Now his attention was on the survey and not losing his property.

"Who are you taking orders from these days?" he asked Flynn.

"O'Brien," Flynn said. "He was supervising Black's gold mining operations, but with Murphy out of the picture, he gives me my marching orders."

Jubil and O'Brien hadn't crossed paths since Jubil had seen him on the wagon train.

"He's not the kingpin, though," Flynn said. "I don't know who is. Black was just one of the scoundrels pilfering the government's pocket—there's a whole ring of them. You'd best watch your back out here. If you start kicking at their nest again, you're going to get stung."

"I appreciate your concern," Jubil said. Perhaps when the survey was completed successfully, he would turn his focus to rooting out the next level of corruption at the Indian Agency. But for now, he had to mind his own business.

"Next time you see O'Brien, you can tell him I said hello."

"I think it would be best if I neglect to mention I saw you," Flynn said.

"Suit yourself," Jubil said.

He knew Flynn would sell him out in a moment to save his own skin, but he still found him likeable. Flynn's tales about Irish leprechauns and other magical folk helped pass many otherwise dull hours riding across the dusty plains on Abe Warner's wagon train.

Boyer returned with his horse and gear, his top hat pulled down low on his forehead. "Might as well cross back over the river while you are still wet," he said to Jubil.

Jubil bid Flynn farewell, and as he and Boyer rode toward the river, he hoped White Dog might still turn up—and that the Sioux would keep their distance.

CHAPTER 7

Jubil and Mitch Boyer made a chilly but undramatic crossing of the river. Boyer led them upriver further this time, and their downstream drift put them almost in the center of the survey camp by the time they reached the opposite bank. They emerged from the river to a cheerful greeting from the men, and Jubil and Eli made their way to Colonel Haydon's tent, where Doane, Captain Ball, and Major Barlow stood outside. Haydon stepped out of the tent to greet them, and Jubil made introductions, making a point of Boyer's credentials.

"We're fortunate to have your services, Mr. Boyer," Haydon said. "You understand our mission, and our predicament?"

"I do," Boyer said. "Your next best place to cross is downriver about thirty miles, a spot called Big Timber. There's a good ford there, if the river's not too high, which I expect it will be. Just downriver from there, Sweet Grass Creek joins the Yellowstone. We'll not be able to follow along the north bank from there for a good sixty miles or so. We'll have to go up Sweet Grass Creek to the plateau between the Yellowstone and Musselshell Rivers and make our way across it. Then follow Canyon Creek back down to the Yellowstone to Clark's Fork River, where your men crossed to the north side of the river last year. About twenty miles short of where they gave up and turned back."

"That would put us about halfway to our end goal without having surveyed an inch," Haydon said. "I suppose if we can cross the river there, we could backtrack to the Crow Agency and survey from there to the Powder River. How long do you think it will take to complete this detour?"

"Couldn't say," Boyer answered laconically. "Weather... equipment failures...livestock runaways...who knows...two weeks at least, I'd say."

"Indians?" Haydon asked.

"Not likely along this route," Boyer said.

This was the only good news Jubil heard in Boyer's assessment of the situation. It seemed to Jubil that if Major Barlow thought a bridge could be built in two weeks, they should just do that. Haydon's plan sounded like struggling around the north bank for the same length of time, or more, and still having to backtrack before the survey started. But each plan depended on things he had no real feel for, so he was willing to go along with any plan other than giving up. Whichever delay Haydon chose, it did not bode well for the success of the survey.

"What about Colonel Baker? Does he need to weigh in on the plan?" Haydon asked Captain Ball, since Baker had still not made an appearance.

"My orders are for us to follow your lead, sir," Ball said.

More good news. As long as Baker did not interfere with the survey's mission, Jubil didn't care how much the man drank. He was also pleased that Colonel Haydon seemed determined to complete his mission. Haydon was no quitter. Jubil would be sure to praise him to Jay Cooke.

"We'll set out in the morning then," Haydon said. "I'm going to survey along the northern route whether we use the results in the end or not. Muhlenberg's line last year was mostly useless, and ours may be too, but there's no reason not to stake it out along the way."

Jubil was not pleased with Haydon's decision about the

bridge, but did approve of the idea of surveying the alternate route. That seemed to Jubil to increase their odds of making a success out of this detour. As they broke camp in the morning, Jubil and Barlow talked as they made final preparations to move out.

"The role of an observer doesn't offer much in the way of specific duties," Jubil said. "It feels odd to not be the scout or the guide or the animal tender or the camp manager. Last year I helped your survey crew when I was at loose ends. I suppose Eli and I will offer our services to Haydon."

"Maybe you know something about survey work," Eli said, "but I don't."

"Not all the jobs require special skills," Barlow said to Eli, "there's always some general labor involved. Haydon is the chief of survey and his job is to select the route, as best he can, that the tracks will follow. You'll see him and Boyer out scouting ahead. Then along the route he selects, you'll see the rest of the crew define the exact line the tracks will follow. First the transitmen set up their instruments to find the line the tracks will follow and determine the angle of elevation along that route. That's a highly skilled job. They send out rodmen and chainmen to mark the next point along the line and measure the distance between the two points. Those are semi-skilled jobs.

"Along the route, the axe-men clear out any obstacles, and the picket-men drive stakes and flag them. They can always use help with general labor. Ultimately, all the measurements will be sent to the mapmakers, and they will chart them. Surveying is a good trade for a young man, Mr. Boswell. You might gain some good experience this trip if you pay attention."

Jubil appreciated Barlow's patience with Eli.

They started out along the north shore of the river the following day. Travel was not difficult that day, but on the second day, the weather grew hot, and the route, over a low ridge that extended to the river's edge, was nearly impassable for the wagons. The soldiers and axe-men attacked the rocks and soil with picks and shovels and, after several hours, leveled a path that the wagons could cross. Jubil procured two extra shovels and pitched in, and he was proud of Eli, who joined him without complaint.

That evening, as Jubil and Eli were leaving the mess tent with Lieutenant Doane, one of the wolfers walked past—a young man with blond braids wearing a wolf's-head cap. "Evenin' gents," he said, with a sneering grin.

"That one looks like trouble," Jubil said, eyeing the fellow as he passed.

"I heard he bears an uncanny resemblance to a wanted poster somebody spotted in Bozeman," Doane said.

"I remember him," Eli said. "We saw him when we set out from the fort." Jubil didn't recall having seen him.

"Might be him, I suppose, but the army doesn't arrest people on suspicion," Doane said.

Jubil nodded. Eli stared at Doane then met Jubil's gaze for a moment, and quickly looked away. He hoped this would raise Eli's sense of caution, but did not deliver a lecture. Without further discussion, they returned to their bedrolls.

The weather was too hot for their tents, so they were sleeping in the open air. Just as Jubil was dropping off to sleep, the camp was disturbed by a loud ruckus at the campfire where the wolfers had made their separate camp. Jubil rose from his bedroll, strapped on his gun belt, and, with Eli at his elbow, approached the crowd that had already gathered.

In the middle of a ring of soldiers and wolfers, two wolfers were grappling with each other as the raucous mob cheered them on. The younger of the two, with long blond braids poking out of his fur cap, got his foot behind his opponent's and tripped him then pinned him to the ground. As the young man with the braids reached for the skinning knife he carried on his hip, Jubil found the handle of his pistol. Was no one else going to put a stop to this? He pushed toward Lieutenant Doane at the front of the crowd. Just as he reached him, Doane stepped into the circle and fired his pistol into the air.

"That'll do boys! We'll not have you murdering each other!" Doane shouted, training his pistol on the wolfer with the braids.

"You're fingering the wrong man!" the young wolfer exclaimed. "I ain't done nothing." He slipped his knife back into the sheath, and stared at Doane.

A wolf's-head cap lay on the ground near Eli's feet. He picked it up and handed it to the young wolfer, who nodded at Eli as he took it, and then stormed out of the ring of spectators. As the crowd began to disperse, Doane stepped over to Jubil and Eli.

"The older one was trying to haul the kid in for bounty," Doane explained. "We'll keep an eye on all these rascals. You don't have anything to fear from them."

Jubil and Eli exchanged a glance, but Jubil did not lecture.

After two more sweltering days of difficult terrain, the column reached Big Timber, where they found Boyer's prediction accurate—the ford across the river was impassable. The river was narrower here and the bottom rockier, which sped up the flow of the channel and created whitecaps. Swimming or trying to take the wagons across it was out of the question. Boyer led the party further downriver a few miles to the mouth of Sweet Grass Creek. From there, as far downriver as Jubil could see, the Yellowstone flowed right up against a tall rocky bank. Here they would head northward, to detour around this impassable section of the river.

They moved up the Sweet Grass a few miles and made camp in an area near a stand of dead cottonwoods that provided a good supply of fuel. The tall grass lining the banks of the creek gave off a pleasant citrus aroma. Trout were abundant in the creek, and game was in good supply. Each company in the military escort had their own cook, and the senior officers had one as well. Jubil and Eli took their meal with the officers. Supper that evening was the best they had enjoyed in the week they had been on the trail. Trout cooked on a grill over a cottonwood fire gave the fish a smoky flavor that reminded Jubil of meals with his uncle Pete in the cabin on Jubil's family farm. The thought of Uncle Pete brought up the possibility of losing the farm, but Jubil set that worry aside and sat talking after supper with Doane. Meanwhile Eli wandered off to visit with whoever would indulge him. By the time Jubil was ready to turn in, Eli had not shown up at his bedroll.

Jubil found he could not sleep without knowing Eli was safe. He took a walk around camp and spotted him sitting beside a campfire with one of the wolfers. He was shocked to see it was the young man with the braids, who was in the fight a few days ago. What could Eli be thinking? He was tempted to call him away, but Eli clearly was in no immediate danger. The young wolfer appeared to be telling a tale punctuated by dramatic gestures and facial expressions. Eli listened and laughed. The wolfer looked to be near Eli's age, and it occurred to Jubil that most of the survey party and escort were older. He decided not to make a fuss. He didn't want to annoy Eli by being overprotective. Eli had not seen him, so Jubil went back to his bedroll.

When Eli returned, Jubil spoke up. "I noticed you visiting with that young wolfer who was in the fight the other day."

"Yes," Eli said, his tone defensive. "What's wrong with that? I'm nineteen—I can choose my own acquaintances."

"No need to get touchy. What's his name?" Jubil asked, intending to do some asking around about the man's character.

"He calls himself Stalker Bill," Eli said.

"Hmm," Jubil said, "the other fellow accused him of being a wanted man."

"Bill says that fellow made that up and has been picking a fight with him this whole trip," Eli said defensively. "He had to fight back to defend his honor and put that fellow in his place. We were just talking. He has some great stories."

"All right," Jubil said, "I don't want to argue about it, but—"

"I know…I need to be prepared for anything," Eli said, sounding irritable. "You're treating me like a child. I can take care of myself."

"Fine," Jubil said shaking his head in frustration. "Do what you will."

Eli lay down in his bedroll in silence.

Jubil was growing frustrated over how much discipline to exert. It did not come naturally to him, and he himself disliked being nagged at. He had to accept there was only so much he could do to protect Eli.

The next morning the column continued upstream along the banks of the Sweet Grass as they traveled north toward higher, flatter ground. They rode along the top of a ridge with the Sweet Grass flowing in a valley below. Midmorning, Boyer said they had to cross the creek for the first time. It did not look like an inviting spot to Jubil, but he was sure Boyer knew best. The ravine was so steep that the wagons had to be moved across by hand. Jubil and Eli helped the soldiers as they struggled all day, lowering the wagons by rope, pulling and pushing them across the forty-foot width of the rocky creek bed, then pulling them back up the opposite side of the ravine. Following that, the animals all had to be herded down, across, and up again, before hooking the teams up again and continuing on. Camp was made early after an exhausting day, and only four miles progress. For the next three days they made their way uphill and upstream, crossing and recrossing the creek several times—thankfully, more easily than the first crossing. Boyer said they would leave the valley of the Sweet Grass tomorrow, and emerge onto the high plains between the Yellowstone River and the Musselshell, then turn east.

After supper on the tenth day, Jubil wrote to Nelly for the first time. A courier was due to arrive soon with mail from Fort Ellis and then take mail back to the fort. In the letter, Jubil shared his concerns over Baker's drinking and dislike of Colonel Haydon, and his worry that river conditions might prevent the survey's completion before winter set in. He told her Eli was doing well, and decided not to be candid about his concerns, which would only worry her. Eli had not yet returned to his bedroll, but Jubil refused to look for him again.

He finished his letter and fell into a dreamless sleep. A few hours later, something brought him awake again. The bright moon lit the area, and a jolt of fear shot through him as he saw that Eli had still not returned to his bedroll. Where could he be at this time of night? The position of the moon told him dawn would come soon. He searched the camp, first checking the spot where he had seen Eli and Stalker Bill talking, but the fire there had gone cold, and no one was sleeping near it. A memory of Nelly asking him to look out for her brother flashed through his mind, as he gathered his wits. He searched the rest of the camp as the first light of dawn began to show on the horizon.

He headed for the corral to get Apollo, and there he encountered one of the wolfers, saddling his horse.

"Would you happen to know the whereabouts of Stalker Bill?" Jubil asked. "I think my business associate might be with him."

"Most of the boys are spread out up along the ridges, spotting for wolves while the cattle are in the valley," the wolfer said. "Can't say where he might be, any nearer than that."

"Thanks," Jubil said, his concern for Eli now elevated to worry. He had dreadful thoughts of explaining to the Boswells that some disastrous fate had befallen their son, just as he had had to explain to Abe Warner that Luke was dead.

He found Apollo in the corral and saddled him. He looked for Eli's horse, Max, but did not find him. Did this mean Eli had left camp? He put a bridle on Buddy, the pack horse. He would bring Buddy in case Eli had somehow lost his horse, as Mr. Everts had during the Washburn Yellowstone expedition. Dawn was breaking as Jubil found Doane, who was eating breakfast in the officer's dining tent. He explained his worry for Eli.

"I'm not continuing on until I find him," Jubil said, "I'm concerned he might have ridden off with one of the wolfers and gotten into trouble. I'll catch up with you."

"Give me a minute," Doane said. He went to speak with Captain Ball, who was sitting nearby, then returned.

"We'll take five men out with us to search for him today," Doane said. "But tomorrow we have to catch up to the escort."

"Thanks," Jubil said, "but I'll be staying out here until I find him."

Once Doane had assembled his men, he suggested they split into two groups and search the ridgelines on either side of the Sweet Grass valley. They would ride south for three hours then return, then ride north for three hours and return. By then, dark would be approaching. Anyone who spotted Eli was to signal with a gunshot.

Jubil and his group took the west ridge, and Doane and his men the east. The day was hot and dry. They rode south until midmorning but found no sign of Eli. The groups traded sides of the river, then turned around and rode back over the same ground again. At midday they took a break, then set out to the north to ride until midafternoon. About an hour north of the main camp Jubil heard a gunshot from one of the men near him. He turned Apollo and Buddy, stirred the horses to a gallop, and rode in that direction. He tried to keep his mind clear of a fear that he would ride up to see Eli's lifeless body sprawled on the ground. Time slowed to a crawl as he often found it did in moments of crisis, but this time it worked against him. He and Apollo flew along the ridge with seconds feeling like minutes and minutes feeling like hours. In the distance he spotted the soldier who had fired the shot and rode for him.

As Jubil got closer, he saw that the soldier was standing beside Eli, who was sitting on the ground near a burned-out campfire, drinking from the soldier's canteen. The crown of Eli's head was bloody, but Jubil felt a wave of relief spread through him to see Eli alive and alert.

"What happened?" Jubil asked as he dismounted and hitched Apollo and Buddy. He took the canteen from Eli and poured water on his bloody head, revealing a nasty bump and an inch-long gash.

"It was Stalker Bill," Eli said, wincing as Jubil cleaned the wound.

"Why were you with him again?"

"He was going to show me how to track a wolf and skin it. I thought you'd be impressed if I brought you a wolf skin. He said we'd only get one at night, so we set up camp. He went to collect more firewood, and then must have snuck up and clubbed me with a piece of it. You told me to watch my back… but I didn't listen."

"How long has he been gone?"

"Last night sometime after supper."

"He's long gone," Jubil said. He could see no point in chastising Eli further, at least not at the moment. "Where's your horse?" he said, looking around.

"He took it…he took everything—my horse, pistol and holster, rifle, my money."

Eli's shirt was torn and hanging open, and the oilcloth pouch where he had carried his cash was gone. Jubil had designed the pouch after his own money had been stolen during his first trip to Council Bluffs. Luke had made a product out of it, and they now carried them in their store.

Doane and the other men gathered around, and Jubil brought them up to date.

"You're not thinking of going after him, are you?" Doane asked Jubil.

"It's tempting, but it would be futile," Jubil said. "White Dog could track him, but I'm not that good."

"We can catch up to the escort early tomorrow, if we move out now," Doane said.

"Can you ride, Eli?" Jubil asked.

Eli slowly stood up and steadied himself, then nodded.

"You take Apollo, you'll do better riding in the saddle. I'll ride Buddy." Since Buddy was a pack horse, they had no saddle for him, but Jubil didn't mind—for a couple of days anyway.

They rode east for a few hours and found the trail of the survey party as it climbed out of the Sweet Grass valley onto the high plains between the Yellowstone and the Musselshell. They camped for the night, and Jubil did his best to clean Eli's wound. The army doctor with the escort would stitch it up, but the longer it was open to the elements the more chance it would fester. Eli endured Jubil's ministrations in a sullen silence, an unusual condition for him.

Jubil told himself he should not feel guilty for Eli's situation, but he still did. He should have insisted Eli stay away from the wolfers, instead of making suggestions and jokes about it. He knew Eli would find mischief wherever he went— he had been that way his whole life—but still Jubil preferred to encourage responsible behavior, not demand it.

His own first lessons in leadership had come from following Major Powell, whose insistence on being obeyed had resulted in rebellion and even death among his men. Jubil did not want to be that kind of leader, but he didn't want Eli getting killed either. The last thing he had promised Nelly was that he would take care of her brother. He had to do better. Jubil added a few lines to his letter to Nelly, which he had not yet mailed, telling her about Eli's misadventure and his concerns leading up to it. This had become too serious to shield her from the truth.

The landscape changed considerably as they left the Sweet Grass valley and started across the high plains. The land was dry and nearly barren of vegetation, pocked with prairie dog holes. By the end of the next day, they had caught up with the survey party and escort. They got Eli patched up and resupplied with an army issue horse and saddle, pistol, and rifle.

For the next two days it rained almost continuously. They set up their tents for the first time in several days, for what little good they did in the downpour. Jubil and Eli had their hooded oilskin slickers and knee-high oiled-leather boots, which gave them better protection than most men had, but it was still a miserable environment. The barren landscape turned into a muddy mess, and their progress slowed to a crawl. Colonel Baker went on a binge. And Jubil worried about the delay.

The courier arrived from the fort with mail, and Jubil was pleasantly surprised to receive a letter from Nelly.

Dearest Jubil,

I hope this letter finds you and Eli safe and well and moving swiftly toward the successful completion of your mission. Eli has always tended to be over-confident, so I'm hoping he measures up to expectations. It is good of you to mentor him. Please take extra caution.

My position at the magazine is proving to be all I had hoped for. I am currently serving as a proofreader of articles on a wide variety of subjects, so I am learning a great deal. Mr. Porter has been complimentary of my efforts. I have met a woman who works here and lives in my building, so we have begun to travel back and forth from the magazine offices together, which is pleasant. I love the city.

I fill my idle hours with meetings, reading, and letter writing in support of woman suffrage. The current campaign is to promote Miss Anthony's strategy of civil disobedience to test the Fifteenth Amendment to the Constitution. She thinks the wording of the amendment should have specifically included women, but feels it provides justification as written for women to vote as 'citizens,' though it needs to be clarified. If that can't be done by legislation then it should be tested in the courts. She is advocating women to test the law by attempting to vote, and if denied, sue. If arrested, resist and appeal the case to the Supreme Court.

You will not be surprised to hear that I intend to follow her lead. What may come as a surprise to you, as it has to me, is my mother's position on the matter. In her correspondence she indicates she and a small group of women intend to put the issue to the test in Bloomington. While I'm proud of her bravery and conviction, I'm concerned about Papa's reaction. I can only imagine he will be further outraged, but it is her decision to make.

I have not yet seen any newspaper coverage of your survey. I have made the acquaintance of a woman in my building who works for the Associated Press and asked for her assistance. I'm fairly confident we have not overlooked articles. If Mr. Cooke was expecting the survey to be in the news, he may be disappointed.

I love you and miss you terribly, but I do my best to not dwell on it constantly. One day all this waiting will be over, and we will be together. Please take great care on your travels to insure your safe return.
Truly yours,
Nelly

He was glad the letter he was sending told her what had happened to Eli. She would probably hope, as he did himself, that the experience had taught Eli a good lesson. The business about Mrs. Boswell was concerning. He was not sure what effect this would have on their wedding plans, but it couldn't be helpful. He was not sure what to think of the possibility of Nelly being arrested, but she was not asking his permission. He hoped if it happened, it would not affect her employment.

The courier had brought another piece of interesting mail, according to Lieutenant Doane. Colonel Baker had received a message telling him to be on the lookout for a fellow calling himself Stalker Bill. Colonel Baker was to place him under arrest and send him back to the fort. Stalker Bill was wanted in the Montana Territory—Eli was not his first victim. But this news did little to improve Eli's spirits.

Jubil had to hand it to Haydon's survey crew, they were a hearty bunch. They persisted in slogging their way through three days of rain, finding their line, taking their measurements, and staking their route. Jubil volunteered to help, but the pace was so slow that not much extra help was needed. Eli was still recovering from his head wound and was miserable on multiple fronts. His wound was sore and he was having headaches, which the pounding rain did not help. And he was cold and wet at night, but there was nothing to be done for that. To his credit, Eli did not openly complain, but Jubil could tell by his sullen silence that he was dejected.

The sun finally came out again, lifting everyone's spirits. A strong warm breeze helped to dry the muddy ground, and by midday their rate of travel was brisk. They were now about twenty miles north of the Yellowstone River and had climbed up to a high broad plain that gradually sloped down to the Yellowstone to the south and the Musselshell River to the north. If the railroad did decide to use this line, the stretch through this area would afford travelers a spectacular vista.

They were moving east to find Canyon Creek, some forty miles away. Then they would follow Canyon Creek back down to the Yellowstone, to Clark's Fork River, the end point of the previous year's survey. How long this would take was anyone's guess. Even then, if Haydon stuck to his original plan to survey south of the river, they then had to backtrack to the Crow Agency and start over, surveying from there to their end goal at the Powder River.

Dry weather allowed them to move along the plains at a good pace. Game was plentiful, firewood generally available, and Boyer always managed to find good water, though many of the streams were too alkaline to drink. The landscape was rife with prairie dogs and prairie dog holes, dangerous to humans, horses, and cattle only if they were running. Rattlesnakes, which found the terrain and the prairie dogs much to their liking, were also plentiful.

Dawn was breaking one morning as Jubil rolled up his bed-roll. The weather was warm and dry, so they were again sleeping in the open air. Eli slept on. He was using his saddle as a pillow and was cocooned in his blanket head to foot with only his face showing. Jubil hated to disturb his peaceful sleep, but soon it would be time for breakfast. As he walked over to wake him, a ray of the rising sun struck Eli like a spotlight. Jubil watched in horror as a snake slithered out from underneath his saddle into the sun and coiled itself three feet from Eli's face. The snake's greenish gray color and pale-yellow belly told him it was a Prairie Rattler—beautiful in its way, but deadly. As the sun warmed his face, Eli opened his eyes.

"Don't move, Eli," Jubil said calmly, with hands open, palms out. Eli remained perfectly still as Jubil picked up his rifle. He could not safely shoot the snake from this angle, but he might be able to sweep it away with the barrel. He moved to stand near Eli's feet and then took a step closer to the snake.

As he did, the snake cocked its head back like the hammer

of a gun, hissed, and set its rattle abuzz. Time slowed down, and Jubil saw that it was clear to fire from his position. He levered a round into the chamber of his Henry rifle, raised it to his shoulder, sighted it in, pulled the trigger, and blew the head off the snake.

Eli flinched and covered his face with his blanket.

"Good job of keeping your wits about you," Jubil said.

Eli threw off his blanket and sat up. "Are you kidding? I was scared stiff," he said dismissively.

"That usually won't work in your favor," Jubil said, "but this time it did." Jubil had found that he sometimes had the opportunity to remind himself to keep his wits about him, but sometimes he didn't—instinct took over. He was coming to see that he and Eli were made very differently, and he was concerned about that. He needed to be able to trust Eli's instincts if he was to help guide people in the wilderness.

"We need to get moving," Jubil said and went to load up Buddy.

After three days more days of travel and surveying along the ridge, they reached Canyon Creek and began to follow it down to the Yellowstone. As they descended, the terrain was cut with ravines and small creeks that made the going rough for the wagons. This section left Jubil wondering how the survey crew would find a passable route for the railroad, but in his travels, he had seen remarkable railroad trestle work over rivers and valleys, so he trusted they would find a way. He and Eli helped the axe-men work ahead with pick and shovel, leveling the way enough to make a passable wagon trail. After two days, they had carved their way back down to the lush Yellowstone River valley. The current was much closer to normal here, though the river was still high. Crossing it would not be easy, but it seemed possible.

It was now mid-August, and they were about one hundred and fifty miles from Fort Ellis and halfway to their end goal.

Haydon and his survey crew had located, marked out, and mapped a passable route from the fort to this point. If they had not had to make this detour, they should have been nearing the Powder River, and success, by now. But they still had to cross the Yellowstone and march back to the Crow Agency, which would take about a week, and then survey from there to the Powder River. It would be as though the survey had not begun until late August rather than late July. The previous year's survey had not begun until mid-September, which was too late. But they still had a chance to complete their mission this year, if all went well from here on.

They made camp a mile south of the junction of Pryor's Creek with the Yellowstone. Here the river had carved a loop, an oxbow, creating a small landmass in the river called Dover's Island, named after some long-gone trapper. Game, fish, firewood, and water were all in abundance there. Jubil was grateful for the opportunity to relax and enjoy the area. Completing the detour had given him a feeling of confidence, and he felt cautiously optimistic about their chance for success.

CHAPTER 8

Dover's Island was roughly sixty acres, a quarter-mile wide and half-mile long, with a heavy stand of cottonwoods around the oxbow perimeter. There had been no Indians along the survey route so far, just as Boyer had predicted, but here at the Yellowstone he suggested greater precautions might be in order. Colonel Baker posted a picket of about two dozen men, spread around the oxbow, and set the main encampment of the troops on the south end of the island, near the main channel of the river. The cattle, mules, and horses were herded to the north end of the island, where the river had diverted to form a channel three feet deep. Baker directed the wagons and civilians to set up camp in the center of the island. The wolfers had elected to set up their own camp a few yards upriver from the island, in the tall grass along the main channel of the Yellowstone. Jubil thought the island was the most comfortable and secure encampment they had enjoyed the whole trip. He and Eli set up their tents and enjoyed a supper of fresh antelope and trout along with rice and cornbread.

Jubil was grateful for the fact that, so far, Colonel Baker—while he had been surly, and gone on the occasional drinking binge—had not inhibited the survey or had any confrontations with Haydon. In fact, Baker had hardly dealt with Haydon directly at all, preferring to have his men relay messages.

Tonight, Baker seemed more relaxed than usual and had invited several officers to join him for social drinking and poker in the wall tent he used as his command post. Jubil and Eli sat nearby at the main campfire, listening to the survey crew tell stories of near-death experiences and humorous situations until they retired for the night.

As they were walking to their tents, they passed by Colonel Baker's tent. The lanterns inside created silhouettes of the officers on the walls, and their drunken laughter rang out into the night. Lieutenant Doane exited the poker tent, saw Jubil, gave an informal, grinning salute, and went on his way. The raucous laughter kept Jubil awake longer than he cared to be, but he finally fell into a dreamless sleep.

A gunshot woke him. He lay listening for whatever followed…silence…and then the high pitch of an Indian war cry that sent a tingle across his scalp. Gunfire erupted on the left side of the camp. Jubil pulled his boots on, grabbed his rifle and coat, threw back his tent flap, and poked his head out. Eli was doing the same thing.

"Stay there!" Jubil said. "I'll see where our defenses are forming up. Get your boots on, grab your rifle, your coat, some ammunition. Lie flat and keep watch. I'll come get you."

Jubil kept low as he exited his tent. Early dawn and a bright moon lit the scene with a soft glow. The soldiers were streaming from their tents, and the officers were shouting orders to arm and organize their men. The firing that had begun on the west side of the island had now spread to the whole perimeter. The Indians had them surrounded on all sides of the oxbow.

Captain Rawn and Lieutenant Doane came running from opposite directions to Colonel Baker's tent. Jubil ran to join them just as Captain Rawn threw open the tent flap, revealing Colonel Baker still lying on his cot, fully clothed, his back turned to the doorway, as if he were still sleeping.

"We're under attack, Colonel!" Captain Rawn shouted.

"What are your orders?"

Baker waved him away without looking at him or even turning over. "Just tell 'em to calm down…it's nothing…they're getting spooked…over nothing," he mumbled.

Captain Rawn turned to Doane with a bald look of disgust. Rawn stormed out of the tent and looked around, assessing the situation.

"First Lieutenant Doane," Captain Rawn said, "tell Captain Ball I intend to have my men pull the wagons in a line along the middle of the island. I'm going to take a company out to help defend the perimeter, and herd the livestock behind the wagons. We'll pull back from the perimeter and set our defenses on the south end of the island, behind the wagons."

"Yes sir," Doane said as Rawn moved on, shouting orders to another lieutenant.

"What can I do to help?" Jubil asked Doane.

"Just keep yourself and your young friend alive," Doane said, and he too was on his way, shouting orders to his men.

Even though the gunfire was heavy, Jubil had yet to see or hear any shots hit near him. The perimeter of the island was lined with large cottonwood trees which were providing cover for the guards and their support troops, and they stopped most of the incoming fire. As long as the Indians did not charge across the oxbow onto the island, they should be able to defend themselves. Whether the Indians would charge depended on how many of them there were, but it also depended on the disposition of their leaders. Sometimes they just wanted to make a point and earn bragging rights, but other times they wanted blood.

Jubil returned to Eli's tent and reassured him that the soldiers had everything under control. He crouched just inside the tent, looking out, and Eli lay prone beside him, as soldiers scrambled to find their units and shore up the camp's defenses. The civilian survey crew huddled near their wagons.

"Shouldn't we be helping somehow?" Eli asked.

Jubil could see the fear in Eli's eyes, and appreciated his brave front.

"Our orders are to stay put and stay out of the way."

Jubil briefly considered joining the soldiers on the front line, but he did not want to leave Eli alone. He also did not mind leaving the shooting to the soldiers. If he or Eli were threatened directly, he would fire in self-defense, but otherwise he would stay back.

The soldiers, following directions from Captain Ball and Lieutenant Doane, were positioning the wagons in an arced line across the middle of the island, creating a loose corral. While they were doing this, Captain Rawn led another group of soldiers through the midst of the livestock toward the perimeter of the island, firing as they went. As they advanced, the beef herders fell in behind them, to move the cattle behind the corral. Once the wagons and livestock were in place, Captain Rawn and his men pulled back behind the wagons. Jubil saw a dozen or more cattle and a few horses and mules lying dead on the ground, but no soldiers or Indians. Jubil was relieved to spot Apollo and know that he was safe. Eli's horse Buddy took a while longer to locate, but he was safe too.

Then Jubil heard a buzzing sound, a snap, and the tent collapsed on his head. A bullet had missed his head by inches and snapped the support pole at the front of the tent.

"Jesus!" Eli shouted, flipping the tent off his head. "Are you hit?"

"No," Jubil said, pushing the loose canvas off of his head and shoulders. "We better move. Do you have your rifle? Stay low and follow me."

The wagons closest to their position were near the western side of the island. Staying low, Jubil led Eli through the livestock between them and the wagons. Jubil spoke quietly to the agitated animals and touched their warm flanks and necks as he moved between them, jerking to a halt every so often when a steer or a horse flinched in one direction or another. It would not do to be knocked over and trampled.

They took cover behind a wagon about a hundred feet from the western perimeter. The heaviest fire was coming from this direction. From here Jubil could see upriver a short way, across the oxbow to the wolfers' camp. They had been the first to be hit by the attack. The wolfers were fighting their way backward toward the island. A dozen soldiers stepped out into the knee-deep water to give them supporting fire. For the first time since the firing began, Jubil could see Indians, ducking in and out from behind the stand of cottonwood trees along the river banks, firing and taunting.

He noticed Mitch Boyer, fighting among the ranks of the wolfers. His first instinct was to rush to Boyer's defense in some way, but he did not want to leave Eli alone. Eli's hands shook violently as he clutched his rifle and his eyes flitted back and forth. Jubil felt for him.

Jubil put a hand on Eli's shoulder. "If we sit tight, we'll be all right. The soldiers will gain their strength soon and drive them off. Focus on keeping your wits about you."

Eli had recovered enough of his composure to sneak a peek over the wagon at the wolfers' battle. About half of them had retreated across the oxbow to the relative safety of the island. Others fired from behind their cover, and moved back a bit at a time. He saw Boyer and a wolfer drop back and reach the edge of the oxbow. From there they would have to wade across the three-foot-deep channel to reach the island. Boyer backed into the water firing with pistols in both hands, the man beside him doing the same. Halfway across, Boyer's companion's head exploded in a spray of red. Jubil looked at Eli, who was staring in shock at the grisly scene. The color drained from Eli's face—then he turned and doubled over, retching. Jubil was shocked and repelled by the wolfer's grisly death, but he was propelled into action by his concern for Boyer, now standing alone. The wolfer's dramatic death seemed to breathe life into the Indians, and for the first time they surged forward toward the island.

"Stay put!" Jubil shouted at Eli. He stepped out from the cover of the wagons and waded into the oxbow, firing his rifle to provide cover for Boyer. A group of brave soldiers waded in behind him to help repel the charge and pushed past him and Boyer. The soldiers held their positions long enough to push back the charge of Indians, allowing Jubil and Boyer to fall back behind the wagons. The soldiers then dropped back across the oxbow to relative safety themselves.

Eli was huddled behind the wagon, chewing his bottom lip relentlessly. Jubil was not entirely surprised by his reaction under fire. After witnessing Eli's behavior with the rattlesnake, he had grown concerned about his ability to respond well in a crisis. In the past, when Jubil returned home from his adventures, Eli was always excited to hear stories about Indians—especially fierce ones. But the reality of such an encounter was another matter.

"It's all right," Jubil said, resting his hand on Eli's back to comfort him. "The first time I saw something like that, I was sick too. I had nightmares for a while. But I got over it."

He recalled the Indian raid that had taken place on his trek with General Sherman to Fort McPherson in 1867. He could still see Lieutenant Jenkins lying dead on the ground next to him, his head a shattered bloody mess. But Jubil had not been frozen by the sight of it. He had been sick and then continued to fight Tall Bull's Dog Soldiers with the lieutenant's dead body beside him. He had run out from behind the cover of the rocks where they were sheltering to help White Dog to safety after he was shot in the leg. He didn't know if Eli could learn to overcome his tendency to freeze.

Now, Captain Rawn led a group of soldiers to reclaim the

northern perimeter of the island. They pushed north of the line of wagons, and after a heated exchange of fire, pushed the Indians back across the oxbow. Captain Rawn then left a few guards along the perimeter, but pulled back the main force to allow the Indians to claim their dead.

As dawn broke, the firing eased, and the two sides seemed to reach a stalemate. Jubil took Eli on a walk around the camp hoping to shake off some of his anxiety. As far as Jubil knew, the wolfer was the only death in their party. The surgeon's tent was busy though, so there must have been casualties. He did not see Colonel Baker anywhere. The last time Jubil had seen him, Baker was standing outside his tent, half-dressed and ranting incoherently at both the Indians and the soldiers while everyone ignored him.

If the army was going to take the offensive, Captain Ball and Captain Rawn would have to agree on a plan. Now that things had calmed down, Jubil hoped the Indians had decided to retreat. He saw Lieutenant Doane walking along the line of wagons, talking quietly to the men. Doane noticed Jubil and came his way.

"Mostly a lot of noise," Doane said. "A few wounded, a couple of them badly. One of the wolfers is dead."

"We saw that happen," Jubil said, glancing at Eli. "What happens now? Did they leave?"

"We pushed them off the island, but they could still be in the trees on the other side of the oxbow. They may be hiding behind that bluff there too," Doane said, pointing north. About two hundred yards north of the island was a bluff about fifty feet high that ran at an angle southwest back to the Yellowstone River.

"Will the cavalry go out to chase them off?" Jubil asked.

"Maybe. Colonel Baker is useless, so that leaves Captain Ball and Captain Rawn to sort it out. They haven't had time yet to work up a plan, but I expect they will. They'll probably send someone out to scout first—try and get a look at what we're dealing with."

"I don't think that will be necessary," Eli said, pointing to the north.

All along the bluff, looking down into the island encampment were hundreds of Indians, easily as many as their own numbers.

"Where are their horses?" Jubil asked.

"Behind the bluff I expect," Doane said. "Probably a bunch more of them back there, holding the horses."

The quiet was shattered as the Indians crouched or lay prone and began to rain down gunfire on the camp. The soldiers responded. Already in a defensive position, Jubil and Eli tucked in closer to the wagon. Doane steadied his rifle on the side of the wagon and began to return fire. The fusillade continued for several minutes before settling into a pattern of occasional fire, the combatants all beginning to conserve their ammunition.

Doane lowered his rifle. He reached in his inside coat pocket and removed a small collapsible telescope. As he looked through it, the corners of his walrus moustache lifted with his grin. Jubil looked at the bluff, where a man was standing, exposed. Doane handed the telescope to Jubil. He admired the instrument and made a mental note to tell Ike they needed to stock these in the store.

"Say hello to Sitting Bull," Doane said.

Jubil looked through the glass. Even though Jubil had never seen a picture of the legendary chief, he looked much as he'd imagined. He was perhaps forty, with deeply lined and weathered features. He wore two feathers standing erect from the crown of his head, and his hair hung in two braids to his waist. He wore beaded buckskins, a bone breastplate, and a colorful sash across his chest. He stood unarmed, staring down at the camp, looking invincible. Jubil handed the telescope to Eli.

"Do you think they will attack?" Jubil asked Doane.

"Depends on what he's trying to accomplish," Doane said.

"It's real possible he wasn't looking for a fight. He might have just sent his boys out to steal our horses, and they got spotted. It might be they'll just pester us for a while, and then move on. Anyway, we're not in a good position to attack. We'd take a lot of abuse crossing that open ground between here and the bluff, then we'd have to ride or climb up it. I'd say it's best to just wait them out...but I'm not in charge."

"He's coming down," Eli said.

Sitting Bull walked about halfway down the face of the bluff, then turned and motioned for others to come. Four more Indians joined him as he continued down to the foot of the bluff, where he sat and motioned for the others to join him, two on either side. The soldiers had been holding their fire, mesmerized by the chief's theatrics, but as soon as Sitting Bull sat down, the spell broke, and the soldiers began firing again. Jubil could see bullets pinging the dirt around the Indians, but miraculously none of the shots found their mark.

"Why is he doing that?" Eli asked, handing the glass back to Doane.

"Proving he has no fear of us," Doane said. "Showing we can't harm him."

Jubil reached to his hip and touched White Dog's medicine pouch. He wondered at the power of the objects in Sitting Bull's medicine pouch, to have kept him alive this long.

Doane, watching again through the glass, looked puzzled, and then flashed the biggest smile Jubil had ever seen on him.

"Don't that beat the Dutch!" Doane said with a laugh. "He's lighting his pipe!" He shook his head and handed the telescope back to Jubil. Sure enough, Sitting Bull was pulling away at a long pipe decorated with feathers. He billowed out a puff of smoke and handed the pipe to the warrior next to him, as bullets continued to strike nearby.

"He knows how to put on a show doesn't he?" Doane said with obvious admiration.

Suddenly the level of fire from the soldiers near the center of the island increased, as the sound of an Indian war cry rang out. An Indian appeared on a pony, riding at a full gallop from east to west, straight across the open area between where Sitting Bull and his men sat and the island encampment. Jubil could hardly believe what he was seeing. Doane snatched the glass back from him.

"And that," Doane said cheerfully, "is Crazy Horse." He handed the glass back to Jubil. "Clearly demonstrating how he came by his name."

Jubil was struck by how much Doane was enjoying the morning's events. He was not the least bit afraid. He probably relished the opportunity to get the best of these brave men. Jubil hoped it would not come to that.

Eli seemed stupefied by the spectacle.

Crazy Horse had, amazingly, made it halfway across the field without being hit when another Indian rode down the side of the bluff and followed in his path.

"That's White Bull," Doane said. "Not as well known, but just as crazy."

The level of firing rose again. Crazy Horse's pony collapsed, sending its rider tumbling into the dirt. White Bull rode to Crazy Horse at a gallop. As he neared him, he reached down with his right arm. With perfect timing, Crazy Horse took a short run, locked forearms with White Bull, and swung himself up onto the rear of the horse. The two rode across the field, reached the bluff where it angled toward the river, and rode up it and out of sight—unscathed.

As if that signaled the end of the performance, Sitting Bull stood up and started walking back up the bluff, followed by his men.

"That's dime novel stuff in real life," Doane said, which is what Jubil had been thinking as well. "We won't be amused, though, if he riles those boys up so much that they get the idea our bullets can't kill them. If he tells them to do it, they'll descend on us like the hounds of hell."

Doane's tone was far too gleeful for Jubil's liking, and Eli had gone wide-eyed.

"The lieutenant is just using colorful speech," Jubil said to Eli. "We can defend ourselves, if it comes to it."

"Of course," Doane said to Eli. And then to Jubil he said, "Sorry to scare the boy. We'll know soon whether that was just a big show or they intend to attack. I should go report in with Captain Ball, just in case."

Jubil did not mind Doane's candor, but he was concerned at how frightened Eli had become.

Minutes stretched into hours as they waited to understand Sitting Bull's intentions. There had been no gunfire from either side since the chief had made his exit, and the silence was almost as unsettling as the chaos. Midmorning, Lieutenant Doane returned to where Jubil and Eli sat behind the wagons.

"Captain Ball and Mitch Boyer just returned from a scouting mission," Doane said. "The Indians are withdrawing south across the Yellowstone. They estimate about a thousand of them. Colonel Baker ordered Captain Ball to set the cavalry on them, but Ball convinced him to just let them go. By noon they should all be on the other side of the river."

Jubil breathed a sigh of relief. It had been mostly a big show. The Indians had them greatly outnumbered and had a perfect opportunity to wipe them out, but instead they had used the opportunity to display their bravery and scorn. He felt a complicated mix of emotions: respect for the Indian's values, certainly, but also remorse. If they believed white men would be swayed by their brave and honorable gesture to turn around and go home, they were certainly doomed.

In hindsight, the comfortable little island fortress had turned out to be a trap. By late in the afternoon, the party had abandoned the encampment there in favor of a new position on the open ground between the river and the bluff. Sentries were posted on the bluff to watch the surrounding area. Even if there was another attack, the open ground would allow better use of the cavalry and better prospects for escape if necessary. Colonel Baker had retired to his tent, and there would be no poker that night.

Campfires were built and supper cooked and enjoyed quietly, as the exhaustion of the long day caught up with everyone. Jubil reconnected with Major Barlow, who had taken cover behind the surveyor's wagons with Haydon and his crew on the east side of the island. They were disappointed their position had not provided a good view of the Indians' displays of bravery. After visiting with them for a while, Jubil was ready to retire early and Eli followed along. They stopped at Eli's tent, which Jubil had helped him repair.

"I've got a confession to make," Eli said, "I may not be much of an adventurer after all."

"It's all right to be scared in a gun battle, Eli," Jubil said. "Everyone is."

Eli looked at him skeptically. "I was *really* scared, Jubil," he said. "I always liked your stories, and I wanted to see the things you got to see and do the exciting things you got to do. But your gunfight with Phineas Black or the Dog Soldiers, those were just stories to me. I never really took to heart what it would be like getting shot at or shooting at anybody. I said I could do it—but I didn't really know. But I do now. I'm not cut out for this Jubil—I'm sorry."

"You don't need to apologize," Jubil said. "I know this wasn't what you were dreaming of doing. You wanted to see the wonders of nature, not be a gunfighter. Me either. But this just seems to be part of the frontier—and human nature. It's hard to take the good without occasionally getting a dose of the bad. But I don't think less of you. I can't leave this survey though, not until I've done everything I can to see it to a successful conclusion. You don't have to use your gun if you don't want to, but I need you to see this through. Can you do that?"

Eli nodded. Jubil patted him on the shoulder and ducked into his tent. He slumped onto his bedroll and felt his body sag with exhaustion, although his mind was racing. If Eli's tendency under pressure was to freeze, his chances of survival out here weren't good, and he would never be able to lead a group of tourists into the wild. Could he somehow overcome this fear and learn to keep his wits about him? Eli's outward confidence had prevented Jubil from considering that he wouldn't take to adventuring as Jubil had. Tomorrow, he hoped they would finally cross the river and get on with what they had come to do—complete the railroad survey—so that he could get Eli safely home.

CHAPTER 9

Jubil was up early the next morning, ready to move on, but no plans had been finalized the previous night, so he was forced to bide his time. After breakfast, he and Eli were having coffee with Major Barlow and Lieutenant Doane. Doane was telling stories of other displays of courage that Sitting Bull and Crazy Horse were known for. Jubil could not square Doane's admiration for these men with his willingness to kill them if so ordered, but seeing this side of him made Jubil like him more, not less. Colonel Haydon joined them as Doane was finishing a story.

"Good morning, gentlemen," Haydon said. "Lieutenant Doane, is Colonel Baker *indisposed* again this morning?"

"He's in the command tent with Captain Ball and Captain Rawn, sir," Doane said, ignoring Haydon's implication.

"Would you care to join me, Major Barlow?" Haydon asked. "I'd like to get a plan in place for moving on. I think your presence would be helpful. Mr. Walker, you're welcome to join us as well. You too, Lieutenant Doane."

"Thank you, sir," Doane said, "but I'll respectfully decline. If the other officers want me, they'll call for me."

Jubil asked Eli to wait for him at the campfire while he and Major Barlow followed Colonel Haydon to Colonel Baker's command tent. Baker was there with his captains, sober, fully dressed, standing beside a table with a map spread out on it.

Jubil waited for Colonel Haydon to reproach Baker's behavior yesterday, but to Haydon's credit, he did not.

"What is your assessment of the Indian situation now, Colonel?" Haydon asked Baker.

"Our scouts tell us they've moved on to the east," Colonel Baker said. "They were just making a show of themselves. I was trying to tell everyone yesterday that it would amount to nothing."

Tell that to the wolfer who got his head shot off, Jubil thought. The men all stood silently, each waiting for someone to dispute Baker's assessment of the situation.

"Be that as it may," Haydon said, dismissing Baker's comment. "I'm ready to cross the river, travel back to the Crow Agency, and survey along that line. The sooner the better."

"Yes," Baker said, with a nod, "well, you go right ahead… whenever you are ready."

Jubil waited along with everyone else for Baker to continue. His comment had left some doubt about his full meaning, but he remained silent. Surely, he wasn't saying what it sounded like—that Haydon could leave but Baker was going nowhere.

"And the military escort?" Haydon asked.

"We were just discussing my plan, when you came in," Baker said. Both Captain Ball and Captain Rawn looked uneasy. "Sitting Bull and his Sioux have moved east away from the river, so they'll not be a threat for a while. Your path back to the Crow Agency is unobstructed, so we'll sit tight until you make your way back here. Then we'll assess how to handle the rest of the way to the Powder River."

If Colonel Baker noticed Haydon's clenched jaw and balled fists, he gave no indication.

"Are you saying you're not sending an escort with the surveyors?" Haydon said, addressing Baker but turning to look at each of the military officers.

"No, I didn't say that," Baker replied. "We'll split the escort into two units. We'll send half the infantry, cavalry, and cattle with you. The rest will remain camped here until you return to this point. We can probably even continue with that arrangement until you reach the Powder River, but we may send more men on with you, if it seems warranted."

"Warranted!" Haydon exploded. "Of course, it's warranted! If you hadn't been drunk out of your head yesterday, you'd have seen how warranted it was. You had men killed and wounded yesterday in that fight you called 'nothing.' You surely don't expect me to send my men out into harm's way, protected by a half-hearted effort from you?"

"My officers and I feel you'll be fine," Baker said, ignoring Haydon's anger and the deep frowns on his captains' faces.

"With all due respect, Colonel," Major Barlow said—*Which is not much,* Jubil thought—"I don't think that is advisable."

"Thank you, Major," Colonel Baker said. "Be sure to note in your report that I graciously listened to your unsolicited advice but rejected it."

"I'll omit some details in my official report," Barlow said, "but you can be sure General Hancock will know everything that has happened."

Colonel Baker, his face empty of expression, stared at Major Barlow. Everyone in the tent, including Baker, was aware he would be disciplined for his behavior. The most troubling thing was that Baker did not seem to care. Jubil could not remain silent.

"Colonel Baker," Jubil said, "My understanding from Mr. Cooke was that the army escort would follow the surveyors. If Colonel Haydon says he needs your men, I believe you're obliged to follow."

"You and Mr. Cooke may believe whatever you wish, Mr. Walker," Colonel Baker said flatly. "But I'm in charge, and I'm not moving camp."

"I'll not have it!" Colonel Haydon exclaimed. "Mr. Walker, you can tell Mr. Cooke that he, and the Northern Pacific Railroad board, and all of their bondholders, can thank Colonel Baker for the failure of this attempt to finish the survey. I'm not sending my men into Indian country without a full military escort."

Haydon's declaration struck Jubil as an overreaction. He had not expected him to quit, even in the face of his disagreement with Baker.

"Colonel Haydon, we don't have to give up," Jubil said. "We can send out scouts in advance of your men. We'll still have a strong force with us, and the Indians don't seem intent on engaging us. Perhaps we can still get the job done. Are you quite sure you won't continue?"

"Well said, Mr. Walker," Colonel Baker said smugly.

"Don't get the idea that I'm agreeing with you," Jubil snapped, meeting Baker's gaze squarely. "I'm just trying to mitigate the damage you're causing."

"I take your point, Mr. Walker," Haydon said, considerately. "I don't know Mr. Cooke personally. He might be willing to risk the lives of these men to complete his railroad, but I am not. I'll not send the survey crew out without the full protection they have available."

Haydon turned to Colonel Baker. "If the survey party returns to Fort Ellis, will you follow along?"

"Certainly," Baker said.

"I'd prefer to return along the Musselshell River," Haydon said. "At least we could make a preliminary survey of it, and prevent the whole trip from being a waste."

"I see no problem with following that route back," Baker said.

Jubil thought Haydon's secondary objective was no consolation at all. The survey was being abandoned, and he seemed helpless to stop it.

"We can't give up this easily!" Jubil said. "Colonel Haydon, we have to complete this survey. There are a lot of people, and their money, counting on us."

Haydon looked at him sympathetically. "I appreciate your concern," Haydon said, "but I've made my position clear. I'll not have those men's lives on my conscience for the sake of Jay Cooke's railroad."

"I believe we're done here then," Colonel Baker said. "If you gentlemen will excuse me, my officers and I need to get busy preparing for our departure."

Major Barlow was scowling at Colonel Baker. Haydon was the first to turn and leave the tent, then Jubil and Barlow followed.

"Isn't there some way we can remove him from his command?" Jubil asked Barlow. "Some army regulation against his behavior?"

"There are such regulations, but they require a trial later that puts the mutinous officers in a defensive position. Had the captains arrested Baker yesterday, drunk in the heat of battle, their case would have been strong. Instead, they just ignored him and took command of their men to attend to the battle," Barlow explained. "Today is another day, Baker is sober, and we are under no immediate threat. They have no grounds to disobey his orders."

"I don't understand why Baker would do this," Jubil said. "He has to know he's going to be reprimanded, or worse, once we return to the fort."

"I think that is exactly why he is doing it," Barlow said. "Even though he was not arrested yesterday, he knows I will report the events to General Hancock. Baker's command is over, once we return to the fort. General Hancock may even order him arrested. Baker's lost interest in serving any further. Now he is just being spiteful. I don't think he can separate Haydon from his Confederate past."

"Do you agree it's not safe for Haydon to go out under Baker's terms?"

"I do," Barlow said. "If we had not seen that display by Sitting Bull, then possibly Baker's proposal would be reasonable. There is no guarantee that another encounter would not turn out very badly for us. They could gather forces well beyond our number. Cooke can come back next year and try again to complete his survey. In my opinion, Haydon's mistake was not taking the time to build a proper bridge over the Yellowstone at the Crow Agency. We would have gotten to the south side of the river at the outset, rather than traipse around the north bank for two weeks. It's likely things would have gone very differently. We might have entirely avoided our run-in with Sitting Bull. Now, if you'll excuse me, I'm going to go work on my report."

Jubil explained the situation to Eli.

"Does this mean the survey failed—that you've lost your farm and the store?" Eli asked.

"It would appear so," Jubil said, lost in his thoughts. "I need some time to myself right now. You go ahead and get packed up. I'll be along shortly."

Jubil walked away from camp to the bank of the Yellowstone River and climbed onto a boulder, where he sat and watched the river roll by. He was still not ready to accept that the matter was settled. There should be something he could do or say to prevent total failure. He recalled that Cooke, when asked what might stand in the way of completing the survey successfully, had replied, "Indians, incompetence, bad luck." It appeared this survey had fallen victim to all three.

Jubil touched on the idea of having lost the farm, and the emotions were too strong to face. And he could not bring himself to concentrate on the complicated logistics involved with losing the store. The pain and embarrassment of facing his loved ones, especially Abe and Lily, were too much to bear. He was too stunned to even weep. He had never experienced such a profound failure in his life.

Then a thought occurred that felt like a lifesaving hand-hold on a mountainside. Something Barlow had said: *Cooke could come back next year and try again.*

There was nothing the survey had encountered, either this year or the previous year, that could not be overcome with good management, both civilian and military. This survey was not a failure, its leaders were. Perhaps Jubil could convince Cooke to not declare this survey a failure and allow him to keep his property—for the time being. Perhaps Cooke would give him another chance. Now that he knew what could go wrong, he would gladly commit to another summer to get the job done properly. He would not think any more about failure, not until he talked to Cooke about having another chance.

Buoyed by these thoughts, Jubil rose from the boulder to return to camp. As he did, he saw an Indian on the opposite bank on horseback in a grove of cottonwoods. Jubil looked for more Indians, but the man appeared to be alone. A jolt went through him when the Indian rode out of the trees and raised his right hand in greeting—White Dog!

Jubil waved and hurriedly looked around to see if any of the army sentries had spotted White Dog yet. A private nearby was raising his rifle.

"Don't shoot!" Jubil shouted. "I know him! He's an army scout—a friend!"

The soldier obeyed but still held his rifle at the ready. Other soldiers began to mill around, to see what the commotion was about. Jubil shouted again, to make sure they were going to comply.

He turned his attention back to White Dog, who now wore his long black hair with a single braid down the right side, from which a large black feather hung. He was dressed in a beat-up army jacket, unbuttoned over a cotton shirt, and deer-skin trousers and moccasins. Jubil was elated to see him.

He watched as his friend eased his horse into the river. The land here was flatter than further west, so the river current was considerably slower. As White Dog swam his horse across the channel, Major Barlow and Eli joined Jubil at the river-bank. The soldiers from Fort Ellis all were familiar with White Dog as a scout, so once he had been identified, his presence was no longer suspect. Eli stood entranced as White Dog dismounted and he and Jubil greeted one another with a forearm grip handshake.

"Taaka Asakis," Jubil said. "It is good to see you, my friend."

"It is good the spirits protect my friend Jubilee Walker."

Jubil reached for White Dog's medicine bag and held it up in his right hand.

"The spirits were working hard yesterday," Jubil said. "Did you see Sitting Bull?"

"Yes. I watch them hunt, near Crow reservation. Make sure they not make trouble. But they see you, and make trouble here, before I can warn. It is good you live."

"Yes," Jubil said. "It is."

He turned toward Eli and Major Barlow.

"White Dog, this is Major Barlow. He is a good man. He builds things for the army—bridges, roads, forts. And this young fellow is one of my business associates, Eli Boswell."

Both Barlow and Eli stood there awkwardly, unsure whether to offer a handshake. White Dog did not, and instead nodded, so they did the same.

"Will you ride with us?" Jubil asked.

White Dog shook his head. "Army has Mitch Boyer. Does not need me."

"That may be," Jubil said, "but I'd sure enjoy your company. Maybe just ride with us for a while?"

White Dog shook his head again. "Railroad not good. Bring too much people. Scare away buffalo."

They had talked about the railroad before, and Jubil himself had been skeptical of it at that time. He wondered if he should explain that, in a very real sense, he was a railroad man now. He did not want to risk spoiling their friendship, but he did not feel right concealing that fact from his friend either. He would try to explain later, if he had the chance.

The previous year, White Dog had found him with Barlow's survey party near Yellowstone Lake. At that time, Jubil had been mired in despair. He had just lost Luke and thought Nelly was out of reach for good. White Dog had offered him the chance to ride with him, wherever the wind took them. But Jubil had decided against it.

But maybe they could ride together now, for a short time. If Haydon was ready to turn the survey around and follow the Musselshell back to Fort Ellis, then Jubil might as well head for the fort right now and get on with the business of convincing Cooke to give him another chance next summer. There was no need to slog along with the escort, wagons, and cattle to the fort. He would never have risked such a trip on his own, at least not with Eli along, but if White Dog would ride with them, they could almost certainly avoid trouble.

"What about if I were to leave the railroad men?" Jubil asked his friend. "Would you ride to Fort Ellis with me and Eli?"

White Dog considered Jubil's proposal, then nodded.

Jubil smiled at Eli's shocked expression and rubbed his palms together.

"Let's get packed up, Eli," Jubil said. "We're getting out of here."

CHAPTER 10

Colonel Baker was glad to be rid of 'Jay Cooke's man', and allowed the quartermaster to provide Jubil with a replacement pack animal and a few days rations for the trip back to the fort. Jubil planned to spend a day in Bozeman to rest up and reoutfit before setting out for Corinne. He also planned to send a telegram to Jay Cooke and hoped he might get an immediate reply.

He said his goodbyes to Major Barlow and Lieutenant Doane. In spite of the circumstances, he had enjoyed their company. Major Barlow agreed to send Jubil a copy of his report but warned that he would find it tame compared to his memories. He and Lieutenant Doane shook hands.

"I hope our paths cross again, First Lieutenant," he said, and Doane's mustache lifted in response.

Their plan was to cross to the south side of the river, then follow upriver along its wide-open banks to the Crow Agency. They would cross the river again at the Crow Agency, go over Bozeman Pass, and return to Fort Ellis. The trip was about one hundred twenty miles and, if all went well, would take them three or four days. It had taken the survey party almost three weeks to make that distance.

Eli was required to make his first river crossing on horseback. Jubil assured him all he had to do was hold on tight to the saddle horn and let the horse swim. Fortunately, Eli's horse Buddy, promoted from pack horse to mount, was an old hand at swimming rivers. Jubil and Apollo crossed, leading the new pack horse.

Jubil was in a surprisingly good frame of mind, in spite of the fact the survey had not met its objective. That was largely due to White Dog's company, but he and Eli were also both greatly relieved to be away from the antagonistic atmosphere of the survey. Jubil clung to the hope that Cooke would not want to declare the whole project a failure. He would not spend time thinking he had lost the farm and the store until he heard it from Cooke himself.

The weather remained dry and warm as they rode back to Bozeman. Firewood, clean water, and grass for the horses were always available. Jubil and Eli caught many trout, and White Dog always managed to find savory roots or sweet berries.

White Dog rode with them most of the day but from time to time would ride ahead to scout. In a sense, he was saving Jubil's life again this year, for it was only his company that allowed Jubil and Eli to leave the failed expedition. They spent most of their days in comfortable silence, but one evening White Dog asked, "Why you are with railroad men?"

"I'm helping them find a path for the railroad," Jubil said. He had intended to explain this to White Dog earlier but had allowed the days to pass without doing so. He was concerned he would alienate his friend.

"You want railroad here?"

"I regret it will disturb your people, but it will happen no matter what we think," Jubil said. He wasn't comfortable with this explanation, but it was the only one he had.

"Sitting Bull says no," White Dog said. "He will kill railroad men. Medicine may not be strong against him."

"I appreciate the warning," Jubil said. "So far, so good."

That seemed to be the end of White Dog's taste for conversation. Jubil got up to tend the fire, wondering if their friendship would end over his involvement with the railroad.

"Once we reach the fort," Jubil said to White Dog, "we're going on to Bozeman and then down to catch the train in Corinne. Would you ride with us?"

White Dog considered the question and then nodded. Jubil's spirits rose again.

They arrived at the Crow Agency, where they would camp for the night. White Dog offered Jubil the choice of setting up his tent near the lodge of White Dog's friend, Standing Horse, or inside the stockade. Jubil left the decision up to Eli, who readily preferred to spend the night with White Dog and his friends.

They set up camp beside the lodge of Standing Horse and his woman, Rains in Winter, and their two toddler children. They learned that Standing Horse was also a scout for the army. His mother was Crow, and his father was a Scottish trapper. Rains in Winter made a delicious stew of tender beef chunks with vegetables from the reservation's farm. Standing Horse spoke English well and was interested to hear Jubil retell the antics of Sitting Bull and Crazy Horse. Eli was uncharacteristically quiet the whole evening, enraptured by the whole experience. Jubil was happy to think that Eli would have at least one fond memory of this trip and a tale to tell for a lifetime.

As the three of them rode away the next morning, Jubil was struck by a feeling of regret that these people would very likely lose their land and have to move—again. If his efforts succeeded, the railroad would come right through here. Even though he believed it would happen whether he was involved in the project or not, he still could not shake this feeling of guilt.

As they rode past the stockade on their way to the mission ferry crossing, Jubil saw Flynn standing at the gates, giving directions to a man who was bringing in a wagonload of supplies. When Flynn noticed Jubil, he called out.

"Were you going to ride past without so much as a how do you do, Walker?"

Jubil guided his horse closer to Flynn. "We have a lot of miles to cover, Flynn."

"Finished with your work so soon? Heading home then, are you?"

"Yes, to both, and we need to be on our way. So, if you'll excuse us," Jubil tipped his hat and nudged Apollo.

"O'Brien paid me a visit yesterday," Flynn called out. "Your name came up."

Jubil directed Apollo to stop. "How so?"

"I may have mentioned you came calling," Flynn said. "And about the railroad survey and all. Sooner or later, he would have heard about you being in the area, and he'd have given me the devil if I hadn't told him."

"I don't care if O'Brien knows my whereabouts," Jubil said, "or my business either, for that matter."

"Well, that's very Christian of you, Mr. Walker, but O'Brien is a man who is fiercely skilled at holding a grudge. And he was one of the few people who actually liked Murphy and even appreciated Murphy's meal ticket, Phineas Black. I'm just giving you friendly notice—he knows you're in the area."

"I appreciate your good intentions," Jubil said. "Do you know where he was headed?"

"No, sorry," Flynn said. "O'Brien tells me what to do, but not what he's doing. He could be anywhere."

"I suppose I owe you thanks," Jubil said. "But at least don't put him on our trail if he shows up again."

"I didn't even see you today. I was busy with a delivery. Safe travels to you, Mr. Walker," Flynn said.

As they rode away, Jubil and White Dog exchanged a look, and Eli, riding between them, caught it.

"This O'Brien fellow is out to get you?" Eli asked Jubil.

"He's surely got better things to do than hunt for me."

White Dog shot him another look that Eli also saw.

"Don't worry," Jubil said to Eli. "We'll be on the train home before you know it."

The river had returned to its normal level since Jubil's crossing a month before. The rope tow was missing, but the skiff was beached near the river. They left it where it lay and swam the horses across, Eli managing very well this time. When they reached Bozeman Pass, they stopped to have one last look at the Yellowstone River and the beautiful valley it had carved in the landscape. It was tempting to follow the river to the Yellowstone Basin and take a few weeks to show Eli its wonders. But Jubil had business to get on with. Reluctantly he turned and rode through the pass. Fort Ellis was a ghost town, with all but two dozen men still out escorting the Haydon survey. Jubil returned Eli's army-issue rifle and sidearm, and bought the packhorse for the bargain price of fifty dollars.

White Dog had agreed to ride with them to Corinne, but he had no interest in spending time in Bozeman, so he camped south of town to wait for them. Jubil found rooms at the Guy House and took the horses to the livery stable. He asked for the best care the man could provide for Apollo and his companions—new shoes, coat and mane brushed, oats and corn, and a fresh straw bed. They had earned a rest, and they still had miles to go.

Jubil thought Eli had earned a rest as well and introduced him to Bozeman in the short time they had. He took Eli to lunch at the Feed Café on the Kirk Homestead, one of Jubil's favorite restaurants during his monthlong recovery in Bozeman the previous year. Over lunch Jubil composed his message to Cooke: *The survey is incomplete due to serious mistakes made by both Baker and Haydon, not because of Indians. Given we can find better management, I will commit to another effort to complete the survey next summer. I respectfully request you consider our agreement still in effect.*

He handed it to Eli to read.

"That's what I thought you'd say—about your intentions, I mean," Eli said. "I'll sit out next summer's survey though. Not sure what I'll do—but not that."

"At least now you know—any adventure that includes a military escort is probably not one for you," Jubil chuckled, trying to put Eli more at ease by making light of his situation. "I know you've heard it too many times before, but...we will do our guided adventure tours one of these days. You and I will lead leisurely, comfortable rides through the beautiful Rocky Mountains of sunny Colorado and through the awe-inspiring wonders of Yellowstone National Park."

"Sure," Eli said with a weak smile, "one of these days."

Jubil couldn't blame him for being doubtful.

They walked through town to the telegraph office, where Jubil sent his message and told them where to reach him with replies. Eli wanted to see the Golden Slipper, the gentlemen's club where Jubil's shootout had taken place, so they walked to the edge of town to see it, but Jubil would not go inside. Eli had also heard about Phineas Black's Metropolitan Hotel. Jubil pointed out the building, but he did not want to go in there either.

The next stop was the Bozeman Mercantile, which had also been owned by Phineas Black and which Black's business partner had reopened soon after his death. It was the only general store in town, and Jubil had a passing thought about changing that one day. Jubil wanted to buy Eli a new rifle and pistol. He hoped they would have some sentimental value to him.

As they were paying for their purchases, a man spoke up behind them.

"Hello, Walker."

Jubil turned to see O'Brien staring at him with a blank expression.

"Hello, O'Brien. You look your usual cheerful self. Mustache is different though. As I recall it was more walrus-like the last time we met. The waxed tips are a nice touch. Just like Murphy's."

"You've not changed—you still run off at the mouth. You'd do well not to mention my friend—the man your Indian murdered."

"Black and Murphy came for me first, and you know it. White Dog defended me. Just as you'd have done for Murphy, if you'd been there."

"Which I truly wish I had," O'Brien said.

Jubil shrugged.

"Who's your young friend?" O'Brien asked.

"Eli Boswell, one of my business associates."

"Hope you know how to use those weapons, laddie," O'Brien said, nodding to Eli's new guns. "It's a hard country out here."

"I can take care of myself," Eli said firmly.

Jubil was proud of his response, even if he was unsure how well he could back it up.

"I hear you're on railroad business," O'Brien said. "I hope to hear you're not staying."

"You're in luck—we're not."

"Good," O'Brien said.

Eli frowned as O'Brien walked away.

"Pay him no mind. He's full of hot air," Jubil said, hoping it was true.

Jubil got them outfitted with supplies for their trip to Corinne, and that evening he and Eli had supper at the Guy House, planning an early departure. They were just finishing supper when a boy came to their table with a telegram from Jay Cooke.

"It says—*Come to Ogontz. We will discuss. Cooke.*"

"Is that good?" Eli asked. "Where's Ogontz?"

"Philadelphia, it's his estate," Jubil answered. "Well, it's better than saying it's a bust and he's keeping my deeds. At least he's willing to hear me out," Jubil said, determined to remain optimistic.

The next morning they rode out of Bozeman on the trail to Corinne. Within the first hour, White Dog joined up with them. The warm dry weather and other favorable conditions continued, but the first couple of days, until they rode past the turnoff to Virginia City, Jubil was on high alert for an ambush. White Dog scouted both ahead and behind them, with no sign of O'Brien or anyone else. For the next three days, to Idaho Falls, they kept up the same routine out of an abundance of caution, but Jubil was much less tense. From there on, they all rode together, thinking O'Brien surely would not wait this long.

They made their final camp near the Bear River and enjoyed what Jubil expected would be their last fresh-caught trout for a while. Tomorrow they would reach Corinne and be on their way home. White Dog would see them to the outskirts of town. As they sat around the campfire enjoying their last evening together, Eli, who had usually been shy around White Dog, finally decided to address him directly.

"Next time you see your friends, Standing Horse and Rains in Winter," Eli said, "tell them I said thank you again for their hospitality. That was the high point of my trip."

White Dog nodded.

Jubil was proud of Eli for saying so and happy he had made some good memories.

"Where will you go from Corinne? Back to your family?" Eli asked.

"No," White Dog said.

"You've never had a wife?" Eli asked.

White Dog frowned and sat up straighter. "Once—killed by Sioux," White Dog said.

Jubil was stunned at his friend's revelation. Last year he and White Dog had camped near Yellowstone Lake and talked most of the night. Jubil had shared his heartache over Nelly, and yet White Dog had not mentioned the tragedy of losing his wife. But Jubil had not asked directly either. "What?" he said. "I'm very sorry to hear that."

"I'm sorry too," Eli said. "It was rude of me to ask."

White Dog sat utterly still.

It seemed only fair to Jubil then to do what White Dog had done for him when he was at a low point in this life—to offer him a chance at a different life. "Have you ever considered traveling farther east? Maybe even riding the train? There's a place for you there, with us," Jubil said.

His friend stared at him as if Jubil had lost his mind.

"I think you'd be very comfortable there—one hundred sixty acres with a log cabin. It's a big world, White Dog. I could show you some of it, if you're willing."

White Dog's gaze dropped to the fire. "Not now," he said. "Someday...maybe."

Jubil felt lightheaded at his friend's response. Such a possibility had only just occurred to him. But now that it had, he found it hard to let go. At the farm White Dog could hunt, fish, forage, and grow vegetables, and not be too close to civilization if he did not wish to be. He could live in Pete's cabin if he chose to. Jubil could build a new house or cabin for himself and Nelly, and maybe even a new store in town. Bloomington and Normal tolerated a small population of Negros, Mexicans, and Chinese, and would probably accept White Dog as Jubil's friend. With this new possibility in the air, he redoubled his determination to complete the survey successfully and hold onto his family's property.

As they were eating breakfast the next morning, Apollo, tethered nearby, raised his head and gave a little whinny. Jubil looked around but saw nothing out of the ordinary. They were camped in a little grassy valley near the Bear River, at the edge of a stand of cottonwoods lining the riverbank. To the west was a rocky hillside they had come down last night to make camp here near the river, where the grass was better for the horses. They would ride back up the hillside this morning and regain the trail to Corinne. Now something on the hillside was drawing Apollo's interest.

Jubil picked up his rifle and went to retrieve his field glasses. He scanned the hillside for predators that might be encroaching on their camp but saw nothing. He tried to calm Apollo, but the horse remained unsettled. As he raised the glasses to look again, a shot rang out. Jubil heard the buzz of the round, a sharp cry and whinny, then a thud. He turned and looked in horror at Eli's horse, Buddy, lying dead on the ground—shot in the head. That shot had been meant for Jubil.

He dropped to the ground and crawled to untie Apollo, White Dog's horse, and the pack horse and led them into the stand of cottonwoods. He saw that White Dog, crouched low, was leading Eli from the campsite into the cottonwoods as well. Jubil hitched the horses behind a brushy thicket, then crept over to join White Dog and Eli behind a double-trunked tree.

"They shot my horse!" Eli said. "Why did they shoot my horse? Is it O'Brien? You said they weren't following us!"

"Eli," Jubil said firmly, "keep your wits about you." He turned to White Dog. "Did you see where the shot came from?"

White Dog pointed to the rocky hillside and swept his finger in a short arc. Jubil scanned the hillside again, and this time he saw a man about one hundred yards away, sneaking around the edge of a boulder and running a few feet downhill to the cover of the next rock outcropping. As the man peeked around the edge of his cover, Jubil recognized O'Brien. He waved someone forward—first on his right, then on his left. Jubil pulled back from the field glasses and saw two other men, each about thirty yards from O'Brien, moving downhill to their next spot of cover.

"It's O'Brien. He's got two men with him that I can see—one there, the other there," Jubil said, pointing out the location of their attackers. "They were trying to sneak up on us, but Apollo caught wind of them. I don't think we'd have much success trying to swim the river and run for it." He met White Dog's eyes. "You want to make a stand here, or do you want to go out after them?"

"You stay," White Dog said. "I go behind them."

Jubil nodded, and White Dog ran downriver along the riverbank, darting through the cottonwoods. O'Brien and his men did not fire in that direction, so Jubil figured they had not seen him. Either that, or they were conserving their ammunition. Jubil looked around for a better defensive position.

He said to Eli, "We're going to run to that big downed cottonwood near our camp and hide behind it. Follow me and keep your head down. You ready?"

Eli clutched his rifle. His face had a worried but determined look. He nodded.

Jubil dodged from tree to tree, making his way to the cottonwood some fifty feet away. Eli followed on his right. A shot hit the ground near Jubil's feet and another hit the tree Eli was hiding behind. Jubil covered the last few feet of open ground and dove behind the massive trunk. Eli had frozen behind a tree. Jubil laid his rifle across the top of the tree trunk and aimed.

"When I fire, run for it!" he shouted. Jubil fired two rounds in O'Brien's direction, and Eli dove for safety next to Jubil. "Good man," Jubil said, pleased that Eli had been able to follow directions.

He looked through the field glasses again and found that O'Brien was now near the foot of the hill. There was a grassy fifty-yard stretch between O'Brien's position and the downed cottonwood, leaving O'Brien vulnerable if he tried to charge. Jubil had lost sight of the man on O'Brien's left among the rocks on the hillside, which was disconcerting. He could see the man on O'Brien's right behind a rocky ledge three quarters of the way down the hill, but White Dog was making his way downhill toward him from behind. White Dog caught the man off guard, clubbing him over the head with a branch, and the man went down. White Dog pounced on him, stood back up and sheathed his knife, then moved across the hillside toward O'Brien.

A shot from O'Brien hit two feet to the left of Jubil's head, taking a chunk off the top of the log. Jubil dropped down and sat with his back against the log.

"Can you keep O'Brien pinned down while I move upriver?" Jubil asked Eli. "I want to get a better angle on him and see if I can find the man on his left. Just fire a few rounds to hold him while I move, but once I'm out of sight, don't fire unless you have a clear shot. Can you do that?"

Eli chewed his bottom lip, nodded, and readied himself. Jubil started his dash upriver through the trees, and O'Brien fired at him, missing again. Eli responded with two rapid shots, and O'Brien went quiet.

Jubil dashed along the riverbank and skirted the brush where the horses were hitched. Then he took cover behind a tree and eyed the area ahead for any signs of O'Brien's hench-man. A man burst from the hillside and ran toward the trees lining the river. He ducked behind a tree and peered around it, and Jubil pulled back behind his tree, holding his rifle close and upright. The ground was too soft, and the man too far away, maybe thirty yards, for Jubil to hear his footsteps approaching. He would be forced to play cat-and-mouse, peeking out to look for his nemesis without being seen himself.

His hopes of being the cat were lost on his first peek around the tree—the man spotted him and fired, missing widely. Jubil pulled back but quickly looked around the tree trunk again and was surprised to find the man had closed half the distance between them. His foe fired again, this time hitting Jubil's tree.

Jubil stepped out and held steady in his position, aiming at the tree the man had ducked behind. After a few seconds, the man rolled out on the ground and fired at Jubil. Already aimed, Jubil returned fire. The man jerked, then lay still. Jubil held his position for a minute, then carefully made his way closer. His shot had hit the man at the top of his shoulder and gone straight down into his heart.

From behind him, Jubil heard gunfire again, and turned to run back to Eli's defense. As he ran toward Eli's position, he saw O'Brien hiding behind a rock with his back exposed, firing uphill toward White Dog. White Dog and O'Brien were now playing out their own cat-and-mouse drama. Eli could easily have hit O'Brien from behind the cottonwood trunk, but either he wasn't looking or had elected not to shoot. White Dog rose up and rushed downhill to a new position, drawing closer to O'Brien, who fired but missed. Again, White Dog switched positions, putting more pressure on O'Brien. O'Brien turned and looked across the grassy valley toward the trees. He then seemed to come to the conclusion that his chances were better rushing for the cover of the trees rather than letting White Dog get any closer. O'Brien jumped out from behind the boulder, fired a few rounds in White Dog's direction, then ran through the grass toward the safety of the cottonwoods, firing toward Eli as he ran.

Jubil shouldered his rifle and tried to aim at O'Brien as he ran, but his shot was obstructed by trees. He expected White Dog to fire, but before that could happen, he heard a shot from Eli's position and watched O'Brien drop in his tracks.

Jubil found Eli slumped against the downed cottonwood tree, staring at the ground. Jubil's eyes moved over him quickly and found no blood on him.

"Are you all right? You got him," Jubil said.

"I killed him?" Eli said, looking up at him.

"It was you or him, Eli. You had no choice."

Jubil knew his words would be little comfort, but they were all he had to offer. The truth was, he was distressed himself at having shot O'Brien's hapless associate. This was the second time Jubil had killed a man, and this time it had been much more deliberate. He had fired at Phineas Black while diving to avoid being shot himself, and he had hit Black only by chance. Today, he had stared down the barrel at his victim, pulled the trigger, and watched him die. But he believed what he had told Eli—he had had no choice. But that didn't mean it wouldn't haunt him.

By this time, White Dog had joined them.

"Where is other one?" White Dog asked Jubil.

Jubil pointed upriver.

"We'll have to make some effort to bury them," Jubil said to White Dog.

"Leave for wolves," his friend said dismissively.

Jubil frowned. "I can't do that."

Jubil used their pack horse to transport the bodies to a spot on the hillside. Without a shovel, the best they could do was pile rocks over the bodies. Jubil knew that predators would uncover them, but he had done what he could. Unfortunately, Eli's poor mount, Buddy, would be left for the wilderness to reclaim. Jubil said a few words over the makeshift graves, even though he doubted the Lord had any use for these three.

By noon they were ready to move on.

"Will you go on to Corinne with us?" Jubil asked White Dog.

White Dog shook his head. "I take horses to Flynn." White Dog had found the men's horses, hitched in the trees downriver.

"I'll write Mr. Langford and explain what happened as well," Jubil said. "If he or Flynn thinks the law needs to be involved, they can call me in."

"Do you think they will come for us?" Eli asked, without emotion. It was the first he had spoken since the battle had ended.

"No," Jubil said. "That legend of the West is true—frontier justice is swift and harsh."

Eli studied his hands for a moment, then looked up at Jubil.

"I don't think I'm cut out for the West, Jubil," Eli said. "Sorry if I'm a disappointment to you."

"You're not a disappointment, Eli" Jubil said. "You were looking for adventure, not violence. Unfortunately, out here, they often come as a pair. You did fine. You defended yourself."

Without his horse Buddy, Eli was left again with a pack horse for a mount. Without a pack horse they would have to leave their tents, cooking gear, and a few other items. He could have kept one of O'Brien's horses as a pack horse, but chose not to. He kept his trapper's pack with ammunition and other important survival items, and with those few things strapped to Apollo, they were ready to leave.

"I'll be back," Jubil said to White Dog, "to see if you're ready to ride the train with me."

"Maybe," White Dog said, smiling as they grasped forearms.

White Dog also grasped forearms with Eli, and Eli seemed proud.

Jubil watched his friend ride off to the north, leading his string of horses, and reached for his medicine bag. He thanked it for protecting his life and enriching it with White Dog's friendship. Imagining White Dog living in Uncle Pete's cabin, he realized that he had not seen the future in the farm, only the past, and he had been too quick to let it go. He would talk to Cooke not only about keeping their agreement in effect, but also the terms. He did not want to lose the farm.

Jubil and Eli arrived in Corinne late that night. Eli had grown sullen and quiet. At some point, they would have to discuss the future of the adventure tours. If he decided he was no longer interested in leading them, Jubil would need to find someone else's help. If Eli decided he was still interested, he would have to come to grips with defending himself before

Jubil could trust him to lead tourists into the wilderness. There was no need to press him about it yet.

The train ride back to Council Bluffs was a subdued affair. The gregarious and boisterous Eli who had delighted in meeting every passenger on the train was nowhere to be seen. Eli kept entirely to himself, even needing to be coaxed into going to the dining car. Jubil encouraged him to talk about his thoughts and feelings, but Eli had no interest in doing so. Jubil insisted that he should not consider himself unsuited for the West, only inexperienced. The only response Eli offered was that he wasn't 'cut out for it'.

CHAPTER 11

Jubil was relieved to be back in Council Bluffs for a few days before going on to Philadelphia to see Jay Cooke. Eli's mood improved as they approached the station at Council Bluffs. As they stepped off the train, Ike greeted them.

"Welcome back," Ike said to his brother, his beaming smile fading as he saw something in his brother that concerned him.

"Thanks," Eli said.

The brothers locked eyes for a long moment, and then Ike stepped up to Eli, and they hugged—something Jubil had never seen them do.

"I'll have to hear all about your adventures," Ike said to his brother.

Eli nodded, but kept his eyes down on the wooden platform.

"How are things with the store?" Jubil asked Ike.

"Flourishing," Ike said with a smile. "I have a stack of new clothing designs, and some other ideas to discuss."

"How about after supper?" Jubil said. "We'll adjourn to the office, like Abe always does, and talk business."

They collected their gear and Apollo and drove to the Warner residence. When Jubil and Mr. Garcia led Apollo out to the stable, Star whinnied and shook her head when Apollo walked in, and nuzzled Jubil with her nose when he approached. Star's reaction left Jubil teary-eyed. She was well cared for by Mr. Garcia, Ike rode her often, and she had Rocky the carriage horse for company. But Jubil could tell that she had missed him, and he knew he owed her more time and love than he gave her. He spent the rest of the morning grooming and caring for all three horses. Mrs. Garcia came out to the stables to greet him and plan the day's meals around his preferences—and Jubil's mouth began to water at the thought of her fried chicken and apple pie.

In the afternoon he rode Star into town and sent a telegram to Jay Cooke, asking for an audience. He also sent telegrams to Nelly, to Abe and Lily, and to the Boswells, telling them that he and Eli had arrived in Council Bluffs safely. After that, he and Star went for a long ride up into the bluffs to the east of town.

In the evening, after Mrs. Garcia's wonderful meal, Eli excused himself, saying he was tired, and went to his room. Jubil and Ike retired to Mr. Warner's office to talk business.

"I've developed a taste for Abe's whiskey, but not his cigars," Ike said, pouring himself a drink. "Would you like one—or have you sworn off completely, after witnessing its effects on Colonel Baker?"

"I think I'll join you," Jubil said with a sigh. "It might be relaxing." Ike delivered the drink and took a seat.

"Eli told you everything then?" Jubil asked. He took a tiny sip of his whiskey and winced at the burning sensation in his throat.

"Yes," Ike said, "everything."

Jubil met Ike's gaze. His and Eli's eyes were the same intense blue as Nelly's. Ike had let his blond hair grow to his shoulders and had taken to brushing it back from his forehead. He was beginning to look like a man rather than a boy. Ike and Eli had never been difficult to tell apart, but their appearance was growing even more different with time. Jubil took another tiny sip and gave up on his drink. Relaxing or not, he did not like the taste of whiskey.

"Eli wants to go back to Bloomington," Ike said. "He's going to move back in with our folks for a while. He may work in the carriage shop with Papa or maybe get a job in a store downtown. He needs to sort out what he wants to do with himself."

"That catches me by surprise," Jubil said. "I suspected he might no longer want to guide adventure tours, but I thought he would still work in the store with us...with you anyway."

"I think he's uncomfortable being around you right now," Ike said. "He's always looked up to you so much and wanted to be just like you. And now it's obvious that he is not and will never be, and he's disappointed in himself."

"I could feel him keeping his distance on the train ride home," Jubil said, as the truth of Ike's words struck home. "Is it because his fear got the best of him?"

"He says it proves he's a coward at heart," Ike nodded.

"I think he's being way too harsh on himself," Jubil said. "In the end, he was able to defend himself."

"He was in such a panic he doesn't even remember firing his gun. He didn't even know it was him that had shot that man until you told him."

Jubil remembered Eli being disoriented—but apparently far more so than Jubil had realized.

"I see," Jubil said. "I still think he's being too hard on himself. I should talk to him."

"I think you should give him a little more time," Ike said. "Just let him sort it out first."

Jubil wasn't entirely comfortable taking Ike's advice, but he decided to not risk making matters worse. Ike knew his way around Eli's feelings better than Jubil did.

"What about you?" Jubil asked, with concern. "If Eli goes home, will you go too?"

"I'm not welcome there," Ike said, "as long as Papa insists on holding onto his archaic thinking. So you're stuck with me—as long as we still have a store. Do we still have a store?"

"First, let me say I'm elated that you'll stay," Jubil said. "And, yes, we'll still have a store, no matter what. Even if Cooke declares the survey a failure and keeps my deeds, we'll relocate and start up again."

"Yes, about that," Ike said. "While you were gone, I began looking around Council Bluffs in case you came back telling me we had to move. There is currently not a single storefront or open lot available along Broadway or anywhere in the hub of the downtown that would be suitable for us. We could buy a lot on the far west end of Lower Broadway, near the railroad depot, but people will have to go out of their way to get to us. If someone opened a store in our old location that competed with us, folks might switch to them rather than drive out to our new store."

"Not if we're the only ones to carry the products they want," Jubil said. He didn't really want to spend time thinking about what they would do if the survey failed, but he didn't want to dampen Ike's enthusiasm for the business either.

"That is exactly right," Ike said, as though he was proud of Jubil's awareness. "People buy from us mostly because of the custom items you and Luke designed. We sell a lot of that, but sell almost as many standard products. We need to make even more of our merchandise special, sort of put the Warner and Walker brand on it, so to speak. Have the products so appealing that people will go out of their way to get them."

Jubil was struck by Ike's vision.

"Luke would be very proud of you," Jubil said with a smile. "What do you think about rebuilding in Bloomington instead of staying here?"

"That's not for me," Ike said. "I like the fresh start we got in Council Bluffs. Maybe we should open a store somewhere else, and I'll go there for a while—Chicago or New York or Nantucket?"

Jubil laughed. "This situation has caught you on fire, and I'm thrilled. Luke would be too. We'll start working on your product offerings idea," Jubil said. "We can do that whether we move or not."

"My sketches are in Lily's studio," Ike said.

Mrs. Warner's studio was in the turret at the east front corner of the house, mirroring Mr. Warner's office on the west front corner. Tables and shelves lined the walls, filled with painting and crafting supplies, and the room had an aroma of brush cleaner. Works in progress from when she was last there were covered with canvas cloths. Ike had taken painting lessons from her while she was there, and he had gotten her permission to use the room and its supplies however he saw fit.

Jubil sat down in one of the reading chairs arranged in a circle in the center of the room, just as the chairs were in Mr. Warner's office. Ike fetched his portfolio and handed it to Jubil, who began to flip through the sketches. The images were drawn in pencil, then filled in with watercolor paint—men's and women's coats, pants, and shirts, with materials and weights specified in margin notes for each; women's boots, fur hats, mittens, muffs. All these items were along the lines they already sold, but some were even more stylish than Luke's designs. Other merchandise was also pictured, such as camping gear and travel bags, each bearing a little badge with the letters *WW*.

"These are remarkable, Ike. Not only the ideas, which are wonderful, but the sketches are beautiful. Your artistic ability had grown by leaps and bounds. What are the little tags with the WW?"

"I'm glad you like them, thank you," Ike said, "The little tag is our 'brand'. It stands for Warner and Walker. I think we should put it on every item we sell, to identify it as being our authentic product."

"What an exceptional idea," Jubil said. "Luke would have been really excited about it. Do you know how to get these things manufactured?"

"Luke was always the one to work with our vendors in Chicago on new products," Ike said. "Since he died, I've just been ordering items that Luke had already arranged suppliers for. We need to rebuild our relationship with our suppliers and establish a plan if we want to manufacture some of these items."

"I can do that," Jubil said. "I need to establish those contacts anyway, since Abe has ownership in some of them. But you can work with them directly also, if you were hoping to."

"I was counting on you to do it for now, though I might enjoy it one day," Ike said. "Without Eli here to help run the store, I can't be running back and forth to Chicago. I can't ask Caleb to run it without help either, not on a regular basis anyway. But if it's all right with you, we could hire another clerk for the store. That would free up Caleb to handle more of the things I do, and allow me to travel—to visit our vendors and my radical sister."

"You do whatever you feel is necessary to run the store, Ike," Jubil said. "I have as much confidence in you as I had in Luke. In fact, I've been thinking about your role here. I'd like you to consider us equal partners in the store for all the decisions and profits. I'll still own it and bear any losses. If we disagree on something, we turn to Abe to decide. How would that suit you?"

Ike's jaw tightened and his eyes teared up, but he smiled.

"That would make me very proud and happy," Ike said rising to shake Jubil's hand.

Jubil felt good about having a partner again. He knew Luke would approve of this arrangement. "Do you think our partnership will further upset Eli?" Jubil asked.

"I don't," Ike said. "He feels like we already have one anyway."

Jubil nodded. It had always been clear Ike was in charge when Jubil was away.

"About your designs," Jubil said. "I won't have time on this trip to stop in Chicago to meet with our suppliers. I'm going to be in a rush to see Jay Cooke, but I'll get on it as soon as I can."

"I understand. I hope you can convince him to try the survey again next summer," Ike said. "I have one more thing to show you. It's over here." He walked over to stand next to a covered easel near the windows. Once Jubil had joined him, he pulled the cover off the painting, a landscape of Jubil's family farm—not as it looked today but as it had been when his parents were alive, when the farmhouse and barn were still standing. Star also appeared in the picture, tethered at the hitching post near Pete's cabin. Jubil's eyes brimmed with tears. He was amazed that Ike remembered the place so clearly.

"I'm going to hang it upstairs in my bedroom," Jubil said, wiping his eyes. "Ike, I have no words for how much this means to me. Lily Warner is going to be flabbergasted by your skill. Thank you."

"I'm glad you like it. I hope it helps compensate in some small way for me and Eli burning the place to the ground," Ike said with a smile.

At breakfast the next day, Eli announced that he was leaving for Bloomington on the afternoon train. He offered no explanation and did not indicate when, or if, he would return to Council Bluffs. Jubil did not press him, but exchanged a glance with Ike as they finished their meal in uncomfortable silence.

"I've got to finish packing," Eli said as he rose from his seat.

Jubil could not let him leave without speaking his mind. "I wish you would reconsider, Eli. We're going to miss having your help around here…and just miss you in general."

Eli looked at the floor, then meet Jubil's gaze. "I need to find my own way. I've got a train to catch," he said, and walked out.

Jubil looked at Ike. Ike shrugged.

CHAPTER 12

Fall colors were just beginning to appear at Ogontz and the air was chilly and crisp. The morning sun brightened the yellow and orange canopies of the hickory, sycamore, and cottonwood trees, and the red maples added their splashes of crimson. Rather than being worried about the outcome, Jubil was looking forward to hearing Cooke's verdict and getting on with whatever plans the meeting necessitated.

Cooke's attire was identical to the last time Jubil had seen him, including the short cape that he wore fastened at the neck, in spite of the heat from the blazing fireplace.

"Welcome back to Ogontz, Mr. Walker," Cooke said, walking around his desk. Jubil looked into Cooke's steely blue-gray eyes and saw the same fiery energy there as before. "Coffee?"

"Yes sir, thank you."

"Help yourself," Cooke said gesturing to a coffee service on a table. Jubil poured himself a cup, and they sat down across from each other.

"Let me be sure that I understand your proposition," Cooke said, wasting no time on small talk. "You are suggesting we keep our agreement in effect and make another survey attempt next year. Correct?"

"Yes sir."

"But our agreement stipulates that if the survey fails, you

lose your deeds," Cooke said. "In what possible sense was this survey not a failure?"

"Well—I agree, of course, that this particular *attempt* was a failure, but for reasons too easily correctable to declare the whole *effort* a failure," Jubil said. "I believe you are a fair man, Mr. Cooke. I don't want to lose my properties, and I'm willing to put my name, and my time, behind the survey effort. It wasn't Indians, or impassable geography, that stopped the survey—it was the incompetent and shameful behavior of the leaders. That should be correctable. With the right men, we can do this."

"I know the gist of what occurred," Cooke said, "but I'd like to hear your perspective."

Jubil gave Cooke a full accounting of the trip, starting with his first impression of Colonel Baker and his attitude toward Haydon, ending with Baker's refusal to move camp after the raid by Sitting Bull, followed by Haydon's subsequent decision to abandon the survey.

"Did you make any effort to persuade either to reconsider his position?" Cooke asked.

"Yes sir, to no avail. Baker was resigned to his fate. Haydon was committed to safety. They would not budge."

"I understand that Haydon pushed on another twenty miles downriver from where you separated from the survey. They surveyed to a landmark called Pompey's Pillar before turning north to the Musselshell, so that will be the new end point for any further effort. The survey and escort will be arriving soon back at Fort Ellis," Cooke said. "Colonel Baker will find himself under arrest, and Haydon will find himself looking for employment."

"Both outcomes seem appropriate to me," Jubil said, though arrest was a harsher fate than he had expected for Baker.

Cooke steepled his fingers and stared at Jubil over the top of them. "Have you read the press reports on the survey?"

"Not yet," Jubil said.

"Well, they are largely unfavorable," Cooke said. "Stories about government and railroad mismanagement don't sell newspapers, but tales about unruly Indians do. If we can't build public support for the railroad and confidence that it can be completed, our funding will dry up."

"I'm willing to do what I can," Jubil said. "I'm on my way to New York to visit my fiancée. She just graduated from Vassar and has a position with *Scientific American* magazine. She has been collecting articles for me, gathered by a friend in the Associated Press."

"Congratulations," Cooke said. "I'm surprised to hear you are a regular in New York."

"I'm nomadic," Jubil said.

"Yes," Cooke gave Jubil a sly grin. "How long will you be in New York?"

"Several weeks," Jubil said. "It depends somewhat on the outcome of our discussion."

"I see," Cooke said. "Well, I have a man in New York that I'd like for you to meet." He went to his desk and made a note, then handed it to Jubil. "His name is Samuel Wilkeson. He handles publicity for the Northern Pacific Railroad. He's the man who orchestrated the publication of the articles before the survey, announcing your support and participation. You should talk to him in person about how to make our case. It sounds like your fiancée might have some valuable connections too. She might enjoy meeting Mr. Wilkeson as well."

"We're going to continue working together?" Jubil asked. "Our agreement is still in effect?"

"Yes," Cooke said, "But we won't have a discussion like this again. If next year's survey fails, that terminates our agreement. If it fails, in all likelihood the railroad will fail."

"Yes sir, I understand," Jubil said. He was determined to find a way to make the best of his situation, though once again it was hard to say exactly what that was until the survey was completed.

"While your survey party was struggling, the eastern party was making some progress," Cooke said, "but their results have been disappointing as well. That group is being led by a veteran survey manager, Thomas Rosser, with an escort out of Fort Rice led by Colonel David Stanley. About the time your party was being entertained by Sitting Bull and Crazy Horse, Rosser and Stanley were reaching their destination at the Powder River. However, they had their own run-in with Indians—a Sioux chief named Gall and his followers put on a display of their disapproval of the railroad and their bravery. I just received word yesterday that on the return trip to Fort Rice, the column was attacked with some loss of life. Disappointingly, Rosser also reports that he is not satisfied with the line that they surveyed."

"You'll have to mount new surveys from both the west *and* the east then?" Jubil asked.

"We can't afford that, in either dollars or time," Cooke said. "I believe we should mount another survey from the east, and have it push on to the point where Haydon left off last year. I'll let you know the details once I have a confirmed plan."

"All right," Jubil nodded. "Will there be anyone going that I know? It helped considerably this year that I was already acquainted with a few people."

"None that I'm aware of," Cooke said. "You know General Sheridan though. He will be organizing the escort. You should contact him in Chicago and get his endorsement. That might make you more comfortable. He will also be the one to tell you exactly when and where to report."

"I'll get in touch with him," Jubil said. He had not warmed to General Sheridan as he had General Sherman, but he could work with him. He might talk to General Sherman as well. He could use all the backing he could get to influence the affairs to come. Being designated 'Cooke's man' on the survey had not been enough. He had been too tentative, had not pushed as hard as he could have. Next year would be his last chance.

"Before I go, I have a question," Jubil said, "Would you consider removing the deed to my farm from our agreement?"

"Why would I do that? And put what in its place?" Cooke replied.

"I thought the store might be enough," Jubil said. "I could also put up some cash I inherited from my parents."

"I'd much rather have your support than your property," Cooke said, steepling his fingers again, and studying Jubil. "But what's done is done. Our agreement stands."

This did not sit well with Jubil, but he could not find an effective line of argument. "I suppose I'm no worse off than before," he said.

"We are still doing our best to achieve the outcome we both want," Cooke said. "I get a completed survey, and you keep your property."

Jubil nodded.

"If there is nothing else," Cooke said, rising from his chair, "I'll ask Mr. Carter to show you out."

The eastern survey he would be joining next year elicited none of the enthusiasm Jubil had felt for the survey he had so recently left. None of the people involved knew him, the terrain was entirely foreign to him, and there was no chance that White Dog would join him there. The only consolation was that it was far from his entanglement with the Crow Agency Indian ring, but now that both Black and O'Brien were out of the picture, he hoped that was behind him. He still hoped to improve the treatment of the tribe, if he could find a way to do so.

His train arrived in New York in the afternoon. Jubil checked into the St. Nicholas Hotel and then walked quickly to Nelly's apartment, his anticipation building with each block. Her building was new and modern without being plush. A short walk down Eighteenth Street would take her to Bowery, where she could catch the horse-drawn streetcar down to Printer's Row and her office building. Jubil had made sure she had the very best in stylish gear to face New York's winter weather during her outdoor travels.

"Welcome home!" she said, beaming as she pulled him into the apartment.

They wrapped one another in a long embrace, punctuated with kisses. Then they prepared a light supper and settled in next to each other on the sofa in the sitting room. Jubil told Nelly the story of the survey, focusing on how Eli had managed each step of the way.

"I suppose I should be surprised," Nelly said, laconically, "but I'm actually not. You know that Eli's always been a blowhard to hide his insecurities—you saw it growing up with him. You have to admit that Ike, as mild and quiet as he is, has always been the braver of the two. Their birthday is soon—they'll be twenty years old—Can you believe it?—and they are still an odd mix of identical and opposite."

Jubil felt Nelly's summation of Eli's character was harsh, but he couldn't deny the truth in it.

"Well, the issue now is," Jubil said, "he's gone back to Bloomington to live with your folks, leaving Ike to run the store without him and me to make new plans for an assistant with the adventure tour business. If we successfully complete the railroad survey next year, Cooke's investment will turn us into a big business. I'm not sure how Eli fits in now."

"How is Ike taking all this?" Nelly asked.

"He's a wonder," Jubil said with relief. He told her about Ike's commitment to stay the course with him, his ideas for new products, his sketches and painting, and explained their new partnership agreement.

"That is wonderful!" Nelly exclaimed and gave Jubil a hug. "This will be good for both of you." Jubil nodded. He knew she would be pleased but her joyful reaction lifted his spirits.

"He took Eli's leaving better than I did," Jubil said. "His concern is more for your mother—with your father and Eli both repressing her opinions." Jubil paused, wondering if he should tell Nelly the full truth about what was going on in Bloomington. "Ike didn't want to tell you this," he said tentatively, "but he's no longer welcome at home."

"What?! Says who?"

"Your father, apparently," Jubil said. "Ike spoke out in support of your position and put himself at odds with your father."

"I guarantee you my mother does not know this," Nelly said, "or there would have been a major confrontation. She'd not allow Papa to prevent her children from coming home. Ike's just protecting Mama from the bad news." Nelly's eyes narrowed as she became more and more angry.

"Are you going to tell your mother about Ike?" Jubil asked, chagrined. "I'll admit I didn't have Ike's permission to share that information with you."

"I don't know," Nelly said, pursing her lips. "Mama still says she plans to attempt to register to vote in the upcoming presidential election. She has not told Papa, but I think she may go through with it. If she does—she knows it will cause a major scene. But if she knew about Ike, there would be a big scene anyway. I think I have to tell her."

"I'll stand by whatever you decide to do," Jubil said.

"And that fact is part of why I love you," Nelly said, taking his hand.

"About registering to vote," Jubil said. "You could be arrested?"

"It's possible."

"Aren't you worried about your job?" Jubil asked.

"Mr. Porter believes in woman suffrage," Nelly said. "He has assured me that my position is secure in the event I am held in violation of the law."

"Ah," Jubil said, relieved she had taken it into consideration. "That's good. I'll support you however I can."

"I knew you were the one for me," Nelly said with a smile.

"And to that point," Jubil said slyly, "we agreed to wait until I returned from the survey to set our wedding date. Here I am. Are you ready?"

Nelly gave him a weak smile.

"That was not the reaction I was hoping for," he said.

"I hope you won't think I'm being too selfish," she said, "but I've had some thoughts while you were away."

If she had not met him with such fervid love at the door, he would have been very worried at that moment. As it was, he fortified his ego for whatever she was about to propose.

"I'm listening," he said.

"First, my father still seems far from coming around to our way of thinking. Second, the suffrage movement is at such a crucial point right now that I can't bring myself to abandon it to get married and leave New York for our honeymoon. I feel like I wouldn't be giving my best effort to either endeavor."

"Another delay," Jubil said, still holding off judgment. "Until when?" How would they ever be able to predict when or if Mr. Boswell would ever see reason?

"Going to Colorado is important to me," Nelly said earnestly. "I want to see the places you first went adventuring, and I want to have some outdoor experiences myself. I think we should go next year, as early as the weather will allow. That will also give Papa some time to reconsider his choices."

"You want to wait until spring?" Jubil said. Delaying the wedding that long made him very uncomfortable. Too much could change in that time.

"It's not that I want to wait," Nelly said, "it's that I want it all to happen in a very specific way. I know I'm proposing things more to suit me than you, but—"

"Excuse me," Jubil interrupted, "but that's not what is

bothering me. I want you to have everything you want, but I don't want to keep putting the wedding off indefinitely. I'd like to set a date and stick to it when it arrives. Without regard to your father's opinions, or the political climate, my expeditions, the weather, or anything else. Here's my proposal—let's get married next year on the first of April and spend the month in Colorado, no matter what. How about that?"

"That sounds wonderful," Nelly agreed. "That's plenty of time to get those other things sorted out—except the weather I suppose."

"We'll go anyway," Jubil said. "If we go much later, my survey trip may get in the way. There will be snow in April, but the temperature during the day will be warm. What would you think if I asked Eli to come along to help handle our camp and animals?"

"Is that necessary?" Nelly asked, furrowing her brow.

"There will be a fair amount of work to be done," Jubil said. "It would free me up from all that and give us more time together. And it might help me reconcile with him."

"You're not concerned about how he might handle himself?" Nelly asked.

"He needs another chance," Jubil said. "I think it will help him feel better about himself."

"It's settled then," Nelly said, jokingly offering a handshake. He shook her hand as he pulled her in and kissed her. He was disappointed to have another long wait ahead of him, but these compromises seemed necessary.

"We'll have the ceremony in New York then?" Jubil asked. "Do you want a church wedding?"

Nelly considered for a moment. "Yes—in New York. I don't need a big fancy wedding, but there is nice church close by on Eighteenth Street. Let me write Mama and enlist her help in making plans."

"Whatever you decide is fine by me. Let me know how I

can help," Jubil said. "I hope you don't get tired of having me underfoot here. I'm not entirely sure what I will do with myself while you are working and otherwise busy. I don't have much of a plan for my time here. I do have one fellow I need to look up though—a publicist. Cooke wants me to get some news articles published that create a positive outlook for the railroad. He said you might enjoy meeting him as well."

"What's his name?"

"Wilkeson—Samuel Wilkeson."

"I think I know his wife—Catherine. She is Mrs. Stanton's sister. I met her at the women's conference last May. I would enjoy meeting them socially. I enjoy Catherine's company."

"Well, that turns a chore into something to look forward to," Jubil said.

"I'll support you however I can," Nelly said.

Jubil kissed her again. "I knew you were the one," he joked.

The city that had at first seemed oppressive and intimidating over the next few weeks began to feel vibrant and exciting. He had contacted Mr. Wilkeson and met him in his offices. He was an energetic and likeable fellow who was pleased to learn that his wife and Nelly were acquainted. They all met for supper at Delmonico's and had a lovely evening. Wilkeson encouraged Jubil to write out his thoughts on several topics, which he would then use to write articles to be used as source material by other journalists.

Jubil labored over his assignment and documented his honest thoughts on why the previous railroad surveys had failed; why the one planned for next year would surely succeed; why the Indian situation was truly a problem but still would not prevent the railroad's construction; why the railroad was necessary to connect people to the magnificence of nature at

Yellowstone National Park; and why it was best the railroad to Puget Sound be on American rather than Canadian soil. Nelly encouraged him and edited his efforts and Jubil considered his duty to Cooke complete with the material he turned over to Wilkeson.

In early November, Nelly presented herself at her local polling place and asked to register to vote. Jubil had gone along, but stood to the side. The poll worker politely informed her that the law did not allow her to vote; therefore she would not be allowed to register. There was a constable standing nearby, but he showed no interest in the proceedings, and the poll worker did not call for his assistance. Nelly made a brief indignant speech about the injustice and inequality that drew scowls from a few bystanders and nods from a few others. Jubil felt an expansive feeling of pride and admiration for his fiancée. When she had finished, her cheeks bright pink, she turned and took Jubil's arm and walked with him out of the building.

He felt some guilt over not being in position to vote himself. He was registered to vote in Bloomington and would miss the opportunity in this election. He was going to have to factor this into his itinerant lifestyle. He had to make sure he exercised this right that Nelly and her associates were fighting so hard to gain.

The next day, Nelly came home from work distraught.

"I got a telegram from my mother." She burst into tears. "She's coming to live with me for a while."

"Why?" Jubil asked.

"She went to register to vote and was turned away, but Papa was so angry he wouldn't speak to her. I had written her about Ike, and she told Papa if Ike and I weren't welcome at home then she didn't feel welcome either. She made up a story for her friends that I needed her help for a few weeks, and she is on her way here. I feel just terrible, Jubil! I'm the cause of all this! But I can't be any other way!"

Nelly fell into his arms, and her body trembled with her sobs.

Jubil held her close and stroked her hair until her crying subsided. "I can see how you might feel that way," he said, "but you're not at fault. Your father's hardheadedness is to blame here, nothing more. Maybe I should try to talk to him."

"I think that would only get you banished as well," Nelly said, wiping her eyes on her handkerchief.

"Maybe your father needs to feel that isolation," Jubil said. "I don't think he'll enjoy it."

Two days later while Nelly was at work, Jubil went to meet Mrs. Boswell at the train station. She was in a better mood than he had expected her to be. He retrieved her luggage and flagged down a carriage.

"Nelly's very anxious to see you," Jubil said. "She's selfishly pleased to have your company for a while—her words, not mine. I'm sorry about the circumstances, though."

"Yes, well...," Mrs. Boswell said, turning to look out the carriage window as they made their way down Park Avenue. She turned back to look Jubil in the eye. "Theodore is a good man, but he is misguided in his thinking. He is at a difficult stage in his life, and he is lashing out at us instead of reflecting on himself. He has always been the one we all depended on for everything—food, shelter, security. He has always been the master of the house. He sees that status slipping away and blames us for fostering change. I've asked him why he can't think instead of taking on a new role in the family, one in which he acknowledges the ways in which everyone contributes to the whole. I've not been able to convince him to change his views. He needs to ponder it for himself for a while."

Jubil considered Mrs. Boswell's assessment of the situation as the carriage turned on Eighteenth Street and pulled up in front of Nelly's building. He thought her view of the situation was very insightful. He wondered whether anything could change Mr. Boswell's thinking if she had been unable to. If not, that would be a sad state of affairs. He wanted to help but was unsure how, or even whether, he should. Jubil waited with Mrs. Boswell until Nelly came home from work, and then he went back to his hotel to allow them to have their reunion in private.

The next evening Nelly came home from work with distressing news about the suffrage movement. Susan B. Anthony's experience at the polls had been considerably different from Nelly's and her mother's. Miss Anthony had not only been allowed to register to vote but had cast her ballot in the presidential election without challenge. Later, a US deputy marshal had shown up at her door and arrested her for voting. She was allowed to go free on bail, but she refused to pay. She remained under arrest, but the deputy marshal declined to take her into custody. Her hearing was scheduled for late January. Nelly and her local group of activists would be closely following Miss Anthony's public speaking engagements and attending meetings to organize supporters in an effort to sway public opinion in her favor.

Nelly and her mother were going to be preoccupied with these issues, and while they interested Jubil, they were not the focus of his passion. Rather than be underfoot or alone most days, he decided to return to Council Bluffs. He missed his horses. And Ike had been more than patient with his absence and would appreciate his help in the store during the holiday season.

CHAPTER 13

The Warners' large elegant house in Council Bluffs had come to feel to Jubil like home. Mrs. Garcia, the housekeeper, doted on him like a son—which he allowed shamelessly. And when Jubil arrived in November, Mr. Garcia, the stableman and groundskeeper, told him that his horses, Apollo and Star, had become more than stablemates. They had shown interest in each other, and Jubil had allowed Mr. Garcia to give them the opportunity. Now, Star was with foal. Jubil rejoiced at the idea of such a colt. He wondered if he and Nelly would ever manage to have children—or even be married.

His first evening back, he and Ike sat in Abe's office talking about the situation in the Boswell family. "Do you think your father is capable of changing his thinking?" Jubil asked.

"I think he needs to change what it is he is thinking about," Ike said. "He's so fixed on trying to control Nelly and Mama, he's not seeing the situation clearly. He is so determined to bend everything to his will, as I suppose he's always done. He's driving away the people closest to him by clinging to his own need to be right, instead of considering the possibility that history has been wrong about women. I think he's afraid of what that might mean."

"How can we get him to see that?"

"I don't know," Ike said, with a shake of his head. "He wouldn't listen to me."

Jubil was determined to figure it out.

"I'd like your advice about something else," Jubil said. "I'm thinking of hiring Eli to do the outfitting for Nelly and me on our Colorado honeymoon. She approves. What do you think?"

Ike smiled. "I think that would be wonderful—well, it could be anyway. Yes, you should ask him. While you're at it, tell him we need him back here in the store. I miss his salesmanship and his loud stupid laugh."

"I will," Jubil said, happy that Ike was pleased with his plan and touched by Ike's fondness for his twin. "I'll visit him in Bloomington after the holidays."

"I have some news that is not so good," Ike said. "You know the lot out by the railroad depot—where we were talking about building a store if the survey fails? It's been sold, and there are no other lots out there big enough for us."

"We'll figure something out," Jubil said curtly, refusing to dwell on the possibility. "The railroad survey is not going to fail."

Ike shot him a brief questioning look, and Jubil knew what Ike was thinking. That Jubil, like Ike's father, was trying to bend everything to his will. That he needed so desperately to be right that he couldn't see the situation clearly. Was this what Ike and Eli's silent conversations felt like?

Jubil sighed loudly. "I understand your concern," he said. "I know you are trying to help, but I'm going to see that survey through successfully next summer. We'll have our store and then some."

"All right," Ike conceded.

Trade in the store over Christmas was brisk, but an air of melancholy dampened the holiday celebration. Jubil imagined the mood was much the same for the Boswells in Bloomington and New York, and the Warners on Nantucket. He remembered how beautifully Lily Warner had decorated the Council Bluffs mansion for the holidays, and he longed for Christmases past. In January he received a letter from Nelly:

Dearest Jubil,

I hope this letter finds you well. Mama and I are doing fine, but I fear the rift between her and Papa may be deeper than I first imagined. Papa has not written at all, and Mama has not set a date for returning home. In fact, she says she plans to stay until after the wedding. What she will do after the wedding, she is unsure.

I have taken the liberty of arranging our ceremony to be conducted by the Reverend J.B. Smith at the Methodist Episcopalian Church a few blocks down on Eighteenth Street. I will invite a few people from my office, friends from the women's movement, and a few of my Vassar classmates, and of course our families. You should feel free to invite guests as you see fit, though I realize your guests would have to travel much further than mine. I hope you do not mind if attendance is one-sided in my favor. Mama is so enthusiastic about helping with preparations and invitations, I can't bring myself to dampen her spirits by calling her off. I expect we will have a small but warm gathering. If you have any concerns about this plan please advise immediately.

Speaking of the women's movement, Miss Anthony's trial has once again been delayed, and our efforts to support her and the cause are in high gear. The judge ruled against dismissal of the charges and raised her bail to $1,000. She refused to pay it and said the judge should send her to jail. Her attorney then made the huge mistake of paying it himself, out of concern for her, but without her consent. This removed her strategy of being held in jail, and obtaining a writ to take her case straight to the Supreme Court. On the same day, the federal district attorney presented his charges *against her to a grand jury of twenty men, and they returned a true bill against her saying she should be brought to trial. The trial date was set for May 13.*

I suspect you will be relieved to know that I have made clear to my associates they shall have to struggle on without me while you and I honeymoon in Colorado.
Truly yours,
Nelly

He wrote back endorsing her conviction to stick to the wedding plan and commiserating with her over her parents' situation. In February he received a letter from Jay Cooke advising him to meet with General Sheridan in Chicago about the upcoming survey.

"How would you like to take a trip to Chicago with me?" Jubil asked Ike. "I'll meet with General Sheridan, and then you and I can visit with Mr. Kuppenheimer, the vendor that Luke always dealt with to create our custom products. We could show him your sketches and discuss the future."

"I would enjoy that very much," Ike said. "Caleb and the new clerk can handle the store. He'll be proud we trust him enough to do it."

In mid-February, he and Ike took the train to Chicago. The weather was cold and windy, but there was no snow to contend with. Jubil had not visited the city since the Great Fire had destroyed so much of the business district the previous October. The Tremont House, where Jubil had often stayed, was gone now, temporarily replaced by the New Tremont House at Michigan and Congress. The neighborhood looked entirely different now, something shiny that had risen out of the ashes of the disaster. Ike set out from the hotel to explore the city while Jubil set out for General Sheridan's office.

"It's good to see you, Mr. Walker," Sheridan said, stepping out from behind his desk to greet Jubil. "Have a seat."

Sheridan's manner toward Jubil felt warmer than it had in the past.

"Thank you, sir," Jubil said shaking Sheridan's hand and taking a seat. "Good to see you as well. Mr. Cooke tells me he's explained to you that I'll be traveling with the upcoming Northern Pacific Railroad survey out of Bismarck this summer?"

"Yes," Sheridan said, "I was pleased to hear it." Sheridan went on to say that Major Barlow had praised Jubil's conduct on the previous survey. Jubil considered whether to bring up the subject of Colonel Baker's performance but decided against it, since he wasn't sure what he wanted from the general. Was he going to ask Sheridan to remind his officers that it was against army policy for them to get drunk?

Instead, he asked the general to share any pertinent information about Colonel David Stanley, who would be leading the military escort, and Thomas Rosser, who would be leading the survey crew.

"They're good men. All good men," Sheridan said firmly, leaving it at that. Jubil had hoped for more but was unsure how to dig deeper. He didn't want to appear to be questioning anyone's character.

"You expect Indian trouble?" Jubil asked.

"Some harassment is likely," Sheridan admitted, "but we're sending a strong escort this year. You'll be fine."

That was not particularly encouraging but not news either. Jubil was not getting the insight he had hoped for, but he was uncomfortable trying to draw more out of Sheridan.

"Perhaps you'd be willing to send letters of recommendation for me to Colonel Stanley and Mr. Rosser?" Jubil asked. "Jay Cooke said he would. A word from you would be helpful too."

"Certainly," Sheridan said. "I'd be happy to. Rosser is coming to meet with me soon. I'll recommend you highly to him."

"Thank you."

"I have another expedition that you may be interested in," Sheridan said. "I'm ordering a reconnaissance mission up the Yellowstone River from Fort Buford, which is in northern Dakota at the confluence of the Missouri River and the Yellowstone River. We're sending out the *Key West*, a two-hundred-foot steamer, to see how far upriver the Yellowstone is navigable. It's going out in late April or May."

"That sounds exciting," Jubil said. "I've never adventured by steamboat before, but I'm going to have to pass. I've got wedding plans I can't disrupt."

"Congratulations," Sheridan said, "entirely understandable." After a pause Sheridan continued. "Is there anything else I can do for you then?"

"No, thank you for your time," Jubil said, and Sheridan showed him out. His meeting had been more congenial than he expected, but he had gotten next to no information about the men leading the survey. Perhaps he would have to go to Washington to consult with General Sherman, who was always much more forthcoming. He also wanted to talk with Sherman about the Crow Indian Agency situation, and Indian affairs in general.

His and Ike's meeting with Mr. Kuppenheimer was much more productive. Kuppenheimer was about Abe Warner's age, early fifties with a ring of neatly trimmed gray hair and a small gray mustache. He had a pleasant manner and exuded energy. He admired Jubil's attire—his best Warner and Walker Outfitters travel clothing—and offered his condolences on Luke's death.

"I've known Abe for twenty-five years, and I worked closely with Luke also. He found it very exciting to bring your wilderness experiences into the design of your products. He was very proud to be your partner. And Abe has a great deal of confidence in you."

"Thank you for your kind words," Jubil said, wondering

whether Kuppenheimer had spoken to Abe since Jubil had entered into his agreement with Cooke.

"What brings you here today?" Kuppenheimer asked.

Jubil explained the idea that he and Ike were pursuing. Ike showed him his sketches, and Kuppenheimer's interest was intense.

"You are very talented, Mr. Boswell," Kuppenheimer said. "You have no formal art training?"

"Mrs. Warner has provided some instruction," Ike answered. "She's been very patient with me."

"Your design ideas are exceptional too," Kuppenheimer added. "That can't be taught."

"Thank you, sir," Ike said. Jubil was happy for him, and proud.

Kuppenheimer described to Jubil and Ike the details of working with him to turn Ike's clothing designs into actual products, and gave them references to other suppliers for other types of products. Watching Ike with Kuppenheimer, their heads bent over one of Ike's sketches, Jubil could see that Ike was in his element. Their hour-long appointment flew by. There was a light knock on the office door, and the secretary stuck his head in.

"Mr. Ward is here, sir. Should I ask him to wait?"

"Ask him to give me just a minute," Kuppenheimer said.

"We'll be on our way," Jubil said, rising. "We don't want to disrupt your schedule."

"You might enjoy making the acquaintance of the gentleman I'm meeting with next," Kuppenheimer said. "You have much in common. He's a creative businessman, like you two, and he's driven to make his mark in the world. He started out as a traveling dry goods salesman but was inspired to give rural customers better access to general merchandise and more reasonable prices than many local retailers provided. His new mail-order company allows customers to order merchandise from an illustrated catalog which is then shipped directly to their homes. Ward would be envious of your sketches, Mr. Boswell."

"Sounds like if his business catches on, stores like ours will suffer," Ike said.

"You may be right," Kuppenheimer said, with a twinkle in his eye. "But you know the old saying: Keep your friends close and your enemies closer. Would you like to meet him?"

"I'd be pleased to," Ike said, and Jubil nodded his agreement.

Mr. Kuppenheimer stepped out of the office and returned with a portly young man just a few years older than Jubil. He had brown eyes under heavy eyelids and a full mustache.

Kuppenheimer introduced them and described Jubil and Ike's business.

"From what I understand," Jubil said with a smile, "your new business might make our store obsolete."

"Oh, very unlikely," Ward laughed good-naturedly. "Especially one with specialized merchandise like yours. I may force some merchants to offer a wider variety of goods at more reasonable prices, but if they fail to respond to the market demand, that is their own doing, not mine."

"I wish you the best of luck," Jubil said, finding himself warming to Ward's good nature.

"Thank you," Ward said. "I would enjoy hearing about your adventures." He turned to Ike. "And I'd like to hear more about your clothing line too. Perhaps we could meet for supper sometime?"

"We'd enjoy that," Jubil said as Ike nodded enthusiastically. "But it will have to wait until the next time we're in Chicago."

As they walked back to their hotel, Ike said, "Why didn't you take advantage of the opportunity to get better acquainted with Mr. Ward? His method of doing business is likely to become the future of retail sales. And he seems genuinely interested in what we're doing."

"I'm sorry to disappointment you," Jubil said, "but until

I get this survey behind me, I can't complicate my business affairs further."

"Your business affairs. I see," Ike said. "Well, as your new partner you should know I disagree with that policy, but not enough to take it to Abe. I'd be willing to bet that Luke would have made a supper date with Mr. Ward, though."

"You're probably right."

Ike's criticism stung. Part of the purpose of this trip was to show Ike how much Jubil appreciated him. He was fortunate Ike had not been more upset about being overruled. He needed to be more considerate in the future if he wanted Ike to feel they were really equal partners. He did not want to lose him.

CHAPTER 14

Ike seemed more distant after they returned from Chicago. Jubil tried to engage him in creating a budget for ordering some new products from his designs, which Ike did, but he repeatedly deferred to Jubil's opinion during the process.

Jubil spent the end of February finalizing the arrangements for the honeymoon, making train reservations, writing the hotel in Denver, and preparing a manifest of gear needed for their wilderness trip. Nelly had encouraged him to invite guests to their wedding, so he sent a letter of invitation to his friend Walter Trumbull, who he expected might be his only guest, besides the Warners. Major Powell was a family friend and had given Jubil his start in the world of adventure, but Jubil hadn't been in touch with him for three years. Still, he sent a letter to Powell and his wife Emma at their home in Normal, Illinois.

It would be wonderful to have White Dog beside him at the wedding, but that was a fantasy. Other friends he had made on his expeditions had drifted away—Lew Keplinger from the Longs Peak trip, Andy Hall from the Grand Canyon expedition—and he had no idea how to find them. He decided to send letters to Nathaniel Langford and Lieutenant Doane, though he doubted they would be able to make it. In retrospect, he was making a lot of acquaintances on his travels but very few long-lasting friends. Perhaps that was the nature of his business, to be a member of a group that dissolved after its mission was complete, or perhaps that was his own nature—to form temporary relationships and then move on. If this was true, perhaps it was a trait he had inherited from his father, because he certainly hadn't gotten it from his uncle Pete or his mother.

In early March, Nelly wrote,

Dearest Jubil,

I believe all preparations are finally in place for our wedding. Having Mama here to help organize the reception and send out invitations has been a blessing. I would have wished for her help had she not been here, but I sorely regret the circumstances that brought her in the first place.

I have not written Papa because I do not know what more to say. He expects me to renounce my sense of equality and independence and be subordinate to his wishes and to men in general. I cannot do that with my life. I knew he might prefer the world to remain unchanged, but his willingness to abandon me because I'm working to change it catches me off guard.

It was he who raised me to be intelligent, capable, hard-working, skeptical, self-sufficient, determined, and ambitious. I have tried to embody those values, but now I find that in order to have his blessing I must employ them only as a subordinate to him or other men, never as an equal. And for the sake of holding to his beliefs, he would relinquish his love for his only daughter. What words can talk a man out of that?

I do love my father, or at least I love the man that I thought my father was. If he is capable of loving me less because I insist on a life of social equality, perhaps I have never really known him. I must stop before my tears wash the ink from the page.

I love you for your understanding and strength. Hurry here soon!
Truly yours,
Nelly

Jubil found Nelly's letter very moving. He shared it with Ike.

"I'm with her," Ike said. "I don't know what more we can say that he would listen to."

Jubil was preparing to leave for New York, with a side trip to Bloomington, where he would ask Eli to handle the outfitting for the Colorado trip.

"I may not even see your father while I'm in Bloomington," Jubil said to Ike, returning the letter to its envelope and slipping it into his jacket pocket. "I'm going to try to find Eli at work instead of at home. I'll see you in New York in a few weeks. Don't lose faith in me, Ike."

Ike gave him a weak smile.

In Bloomington, Jubil went to the livery and hired the use of a horse and a small buckboard wagon, then stopped at the grocery and bought some supplies. Eli was working at Haggard and Powers Hardware Store on the courthouse square in Bloomington. This store had been the only place in town where Jubil had found a suitable pack when he was outfitting himself for his first expedition after his mother died. He had paid three dollars for a well-made trapper's pack, which he had carried on every expedition since. Jubil entered the store and found its neatly organized interior the same as he remembered it.

"Good afternoon, sir," said the store manager. Jubil did not know him.

"Good afternoon," Jubil said, "I was hoping to find—" Eli stepped out from the store's back room.

"Hello, Jubil. What a surprise," Eli said, stepping up to shake hands. "Is everything all right?"

"Yes, everything is fine," Jubil said. "I'm on my way to New York, but I wanted to stop and see you first. I'm going up to check on the farm. I was hoping you might be able to go up with me for the night."

Eli looked surprised. "Well, I work until five o'clock," Eli said.

"We're not that busy," the store manager said. "Go on, if you like."

"All right then, thank you," Eli said to the manager. "I'll just get my coat."

They stopped by the carriage shop where Mr. Boswell was working, and Eli went in to tell him he was with Jubil. Then they set out for the farm.

"Why did you come to see me?" Eli asked as they started north on Main Street.

"I have a business proposition for you," Jubil said with a smile. "But let's wait until we get settled into the cabin to get into it."

He had not been to the farm since the previous October. As they drove north through the cold, dry evening, up Main Street and past Illinois Wesleyan University, he thought of Major Powell and the Grand Canyon expedition. For a time, Jubil had thought that trip had scared the adventuring out of him. But he'd been wrong. Further north, they passed through Normal and Illinois State Normal University, the teacher's college. Many of Powell's natural science collections were housed there in a museum, collections that Jubil's uncle Pete had helped Powell gather in their early years before the war.

A strong sense of nostalgia washed over him, as if everything he was seeing was from some long-ago era, another lifetime that he missed more than he had realized.

As they pulled up to the farm, Jubil stopped next to the

foundation stones and chimney of the farmhouse and barn that had burned to the ground. He had left the stone foundations in place in case he wanted to rebuild but also as a sort of monument to his parents, who had placed every stone in that foundation, built the farmhouse and barn, and opened the land to the plow. He pictured himself and his parents in that other lifetime and fought back a wave of emotion over the possibility of losing this place.

"Did you get a chance to see the painting that Ike did of the farm?" Jubil asked. "It's very good."

Eli shook his head and looked away.

About one hundred yards west of the farmhouse stood the cabin which he had helped Pete build after Jubil's father had died in a fall from the barn roof and Pete had come to live with them. They had built it from rough-hewn timbers harvested from a grove on the farm. Beside the cabin stood a small stable Jubil had built himself after the fire, from timbers reclaimed from the charred remains of the farmhouse and barn.

The door to the cabin was firmly barred, and the shutters were still closed, which was a good sign that animals had not found their way inside. He stepped in and was pleased to find things in good order. It was small, twenty by thirty feet, but cozy, with a bed, table and two chairs, and two rockers at the hearth. Pete and Jubil had built all the furniture. A large stone fireplace had shelves on the walls on either side, and a small woodstove sat near the window on the wall facing the farmhouse. He opened the heavy oak footlocker with brass fittings, which he used to stow things while he was away. From it he removed his bedding, two heavy quilts that his mother had made, his small set of cookware, plates, and eating utensils.

In silence, Eli helped him sweep out the cabin, bring water in from the well, wash the kitchen gear and the table top, and build a fire in the fireplace and stove. Jubil roasted a chicken on a spit in the fireplace. The aroma of the sizzling bird invoked memories of how he and Pete used to enjoy such a meal together.

"Are you ready to talk about your business proposition?" Eli asked.

Jubil smiled, surprised Eli had been able to be quiet for so long. "I am," he said. "You're aware of our wedding plans?"

"Yes," Eli said, "I correspond with Ike occasionally. Papa's not going though, and if he doesn't go, then I'm not going."

Jubil studied him curiously. Was he making up his own mind about women's rights, or was he simply adopting his father's beliefs without examining them? Jubil thought about his own mother, how she expected him to be a farmer. He never would have gone against her wishes. It was only because she had died that he had left the farm behind.

"I'm disappointed to think that you might not be there," Jubil said. "We only get to do this once, and we want to share it with you. And you and I are going to be brothers."

Eli glanced over at him but then just as quickly looked away.

"Anyway, it's not the wedding I want to talk to you about—it's the honeymoon. Nelly wants to have a wilderness experience, and to do that comfortably will require a fair amount of outfitting. I'd like to hire you for the job to relieve me of the time required to attend to everything."

Eli's mouth fell open. "You would?" he said. "And Nelly agrees to have me along on her honeymoon?"

"I would, and she does," Jubil said. "I don't want to trust this trip to anyone I don't know. What do you say?"

"What about my job at the hardware store?" Eli said.

"There's always a job at Warner and Walker Outfitters waiting for you," Jubil said. "Ike says our sales are down without you. And he just misses you—and so do I."

Eli hurriedly rose to tend the fireplace and the stove.

"You'd tell me what gear we're going to need?" Eli asked with his back to Jubil. Jubil saw him swipe at his eyes.

"I've got it all written out," Jubil said. "I'll already have much of it collected in Council Bluffs." From his jacket pocket he pulled out the manifest and notes he had made. He also took out Nelly's letter. "I think this will also be a good practice run for our adventure tour business. See how well the gear we bring suits Nelly's experience level."

Eli took the manifest and notes, and as he looked them over, a slow smile spread over his face.

"I'd be happy to do it," he said.

"Excellent!" Jubil said, relieved and pleased. "We'll have a wonderful time." He looked down at the letter from Nelly. "Come to the wedding, Eli."

Eli frowned and pursed his lips. "I can't do that. Not if Papa doesn't go."

"Are you that strongly opposed to Nelly's social convictions—and mine?"

"No," Eli said. "I'm opposed to the whole family abandoning Papa. I can't leave him here alone, thinking none of us cares about him anymore."

"The rest of your family cares about him, but he's driving them away," Jubil said. "He is withholding his love and support because they will not live by his rules—rules that, when you think about them, make little sense." Jubil handed Nelly's letter to Eli. "Please read this."

Eli read the letter and then stared at the flames in the fireplace. He held out the letter to Jubil. "Keep it," Jubil said. "Show it to your father." He hoped Nelly would not mind.

In the morning they closed the cabin up. Everything Jubil had seen and touched since they had arrived had once been touched by his family and still invoked memories of them. This farm was irreplaceable. He could not lose it.

When Jubil pulled up at the Boswell house to drop Eli off, Mr. Boswell came out on the porch. "Hello, Jubil. You can come in if you'd like."

"Thank you, but I'd best be on my way. I have a train to catch."

"Suit yourself," Mr. Boswell said. "Did you and Eli come to terms?"

"He's going to handle some outfitting for me this spring. He can tell you about it."

"Hmm. You're on your way to New York then?" Mr. Boswell asked.

"Yes. I wish you'd change your mind and come," Jubil said. "It would mean the world to Nelly. It breaks her heart you don't approve of her."

"She insists on standing up for her principles," Mr. Boswell said. "I'm only doing the same."

"If I were you, I'd be asking myself whether those principles are worth doing irreparable harm to my daughter and the rest of my family." Jubil said.

Mr. Boswell turned without a word and went back inside the house.

Jubil clapped a hand on Eli's shoulder as they said goodbye. "If you don't come to the wedding, we'll meet you in Chicago on our way to Colorado," he said. "But I hope to see you in New York. Try to change your father's thinking."

Eli furrowed his brow and nodded.

***

Jubil arrived in New York a week before the wedding. Nelly was pleased to learn that Eli had agreed to help with their honeymoon trip, and she wondered aloud if he and her father would change their minds at the last minute and come to the wedding. Jubil had to confess then that he had shown her letter to Eli and even suggested he share it with their father. Maybe there was still hope. But the days ticked away, and Ike arrived and then the Warners arrived, and they heard nothing from Bloomington. The day before the ceremony, Nelly broke down in tears of sadness and frustration. Then she wiped her eyes and swore to move on.

Ike and his mother spent the day finishing the decorations for the reception tables, which were far more artful with Ike's artistic touch. They all had supper together that night, and afterward Abe began to talk at some length about the precariousness of Cooke's financial enterprise, the economy at large, and the mood on Wall Street. Many of the details he referred to were over Jubil's head, so rather than argue about them, he stood by his position that these details were irrelevant, because the survey would succeed. Lily finally intervened to insist the matter be tabled.

The morning of the wedding, as Jubil waited for Abe and Ike in the lobby of the hotel, he was more edgy than he had ever been on any wilderness adventure. He had faced life-threatening situations more calmly than he was facing his own wedding. It was a mystery to him why he was so agitated, since the events of the day would follow a preplanned schedule. The honeymoon, however, was another matter. All the knowledge he had of marital relations was unreliable hearsay. Nelly was as inexperienced as he was, but who knew what she had learned from her sophisticated friends at Vassar College. It was all he could do to keep his wits about him and focus on the moment as Ike appeared in the lobby.

"You're looking smart in your suit," Ike said, noting how rare it was to see Jubil in formal wear. "Are you ready? Do you have the ring?"

Jubil retrieved the box from his jacket pocket and showed the ring to Ike as Abe joined them. It was his mother's ruby ring, given to her by his father.

"Good morning, boys," Abe said. "All set?"

They stepped out into the beautiful spring morning and caught a carriage to the Methodist Episcopalian Church on Eighteenth Street, where the women, who had spent the night at the apartment, would meet them. The carriage deposited Jubil and the others in front of the church's beautiful stone archway. A few early guests were arriving, but no one Jubil knew. Inside, the Reverend Smith met them in the lobby.

"Good morning, Mr. Walker," the pastor said. "You and Mr. Warner will wait in my study. Once the bride has arrived and we reach our appointed time, we will begin the ceremony. Mr. Warner will stand with you and bear the ring. The bride's mother will accompany her down the aisle, followed by her son, who will accompany Miss LeVault to stand with the bride. At the conclusion of the ceremony, you and the bride will walk past the guests to the lobby. I will then invite everyone to file through the lobby to the fellowship room. Any questions?"

Jubil shook his head.

As the pipe organist began to play, Jubil and Abe made their way to the pastor's study, while Ike took up his duties as an usher. Jubil left the door of the study open so he could watch the guests arrive. There were already a dozen people seated, but none that he knew so far. The first to arrive that he recognized was Lily Warner, which meant that Nelly and her mother were also here. Lily was accompanied by her sister Maria Mitchell, Mrs. Elizabeth Cady Stanton, and one of Nelly's English professors from Vassar. Following them was Mr. Porter, Nelly's editor, and several women, some accompanied by men, some not, that Jubil assumed were Nelly's associates in the woman's rights movement or worked with her at the magazine. Samuel Wilkeson, Cooke's publicity agent, and his wife Catherine, Mrs. Stanton's sister, arrived. And following them in was Jubil's friend, Walter Trumbull. A few more people trailed in as the clock ticked toward the appointed hour, and Jubil's nervousness increased. He wiped his sweaty palms on his suit pants and thought of how his mother would scold him for that. He wished that she and his father, and Uncle Pete, and Luke Warner could be there with him.

Then the pastor appeared at the study door. It was time.

Jubil and Abe followed him out to stand in front of the altar in the center of the church. Jubil turned to face the congregation, looking for Nelly at the far end of the aisle. He had a clear view through the lobby to the front doors of the church. As the organist began to play the wedding march, the congregation rose and turned toward the doorway. Nelly appeared there, looking more beautiful than Jubil had ever seen her. Her long black hair hung loosely over her shoulders and had a small braided crown bedecked with flowers—no doubt the work of Ruthie LeVault. Her deep red satin dress, with lace at the hem and sleeves, brushed the floor. She was a vision he would never forget.

Her mother, wearing a pale pink gown, appeared beside her, and together, they began to walk down the aisle.

Ike and Ruthie LeVault followed, walking arm-in-arm. Jubil could not take his eyes off Nelly, but she had not yet looked at him. She was glancing left and right as she came toward him, acknowledging as many of the guests as she could with a smile and a nod. As she approached the altar, she finally looked at him, and the joy in her smile flooded him with happiness.

Then the front door of the church opened, and in stepped Eli Boswell. Jubil felt his jaw drop and quickly snapped his mouth shut. Nelly turned to follow his gaze, and as she did, her father stepped through the door to stand beside Eli. Nelly gasped and began to cry, and the congregation began to murmur and stir. Nelly's mother, Jubil, and Abe huddled around Nelly.

"Do you want him to be part of the ceremony, or should I ask him to take a seat?" Jubil asked Nelly, handing her his handkerchief.

"I'll talk to him myself," Nelly said, wiping her eyes. She strode away, back up the aisle.

"Nelly's father and brother have just arrived," Jubil said to the congregation. "Please give us just a minute."

Jubil and the rest of the wedding party scurried after Nelly to the lobby.

Nelly stood dry-eyed in front of her father and brother. "Hello, Papa," she said. "Eli."

"I'm very sorry we're late," Mr. Boswell said, chagrined. "Our train was delayed. We should have been here hours ago. I didn't mean to cause a scene."

"You have changed your mind about our wedding then?" she asked.

"Yes, I have. I'm here to tell you that I love you and that I am the man you thought I was. I've been a fool to hold on to my antiquated view of the world. You and your mother and your brothers mean more to me than anything in this world. I hope you will forgive me."

Nelly collapsed into his arms and wept, and as he held her, Mrs. Boswell joined their huddle. Meanwhile, Ike and Eli had their own reconciliation that began with a silent conversation and ended with an embrace. When the twins had separated, Jubil put his arm around Eli's shoulders.

"Whatever you did, thank you."

"It was Nelly's letter," Eli said. "He really took that hard."

The pastor entered the lobby and approached Jubil.

"I take it all is well?"

"Yes, everything is fine," Jubil said.

"Perhaps we can get on with the ceremony?"

Abe stepped in to help reorganize the wedding procession. Nelly would repeat her walk down the aisle, this time with both of her parents accompanying her. Ike and Eli would accompany Miss LeVault. The pastor, Jubil and Abe resumed their positions at the altar, the organist restarted the wedding march, and the ceremony began again.

Nelly's mother moved out of the apartment that evening and joined her husband in the hotel, leaving the apartment to Jubil and Nelly. Jubil had entertained some fantasies about how their wedding night would play out, but he was not prepared to find Nelly had apparently done the same. He more than gladly followed her lead and was met with a far more torrid welcome than he would have had the nerve to expect. He was learning that there were great advantages to being loved by a liberal-thinking strong-willed woman.

They spent the next two days in New York enjoying their family reunion before the Warners returned to Nantucket and Jubil and the Boswells set out for Chicago. There, Nelly's parents caught a train to Bloomington, and Jubil, Nelly, Ike, and Eli went on to Council Bluffs. There, Eli took charge of the gear Jubil had collected for the honeymoon trip and handled the transfer of it from the store to the train. The next day they were on their way west.

Jubil had booked rooms for them in Denver at Portico's Delmonico of the West on Larimar Street, which had only recently been built. It was a three-story brick-and-stone building with a wrought iron canopy and modest but well-appointed rooms. Nelly loved the cozy guest room with its tall windows facing the Rocky Mountains. To Jubil it felt intimate and warm after his recent stay at the St. Nicholas Hotel in New York.

On their first full day, Jubil and Nelly had gone out for a carriage ride to explore the city. They returned to the hotel in the afternoon to find Eli sitting by the massive fireplace in the hotel lobby, in conversation with a distinguished gentleman in a three-piece suit. Eli waved Jubil and Nelly over, and introduced them to Mr. Ritchie, the proprietor of the hotel.

"Mr. Boswell has told me of your adventures, Mr. Walker," Ritchie said. "Very impressive, I must say. I'm also quite interested in your business plans."

Jubil glanced at Eli and wondered what he had been telling

Mr. Ritchie. He hoped any exaggerations he had made were not exorbitant.

"I've been discussing your adventure tour plans with Mr. Ritchie," Eli said. "I believe if we were to make his hotel our Denver base for future tours, we might be able to make an agreement advantageous to all of us."

Jubil was impressed by Eli's suggestion, and pleased about the interest he was taking in the business. Eli's gregarious and pleasant nature was once again proving its worth. He had a friendly way of making propositions to people that drew them in. Jubil and Mr. Ritchie agreed to have further conversation about Eli's proposal.

Jubil had made arrangements to meet in Denver with an acquaintance from one of his previous expeditions. Five years ago, Jubil had been a member of Major John Wesley Powell's Colorado Exploring Expedition that summitted Longs Peak in Northern Colorado. Another member of that party was William Byers, a friend of Powell's and a newspaper publisher. Jubil took Nelly and Eli with him to visit Byers in his office at the *Rocky Mountain News*.

Byers, a hale and hearty fellow about Abe's age, was happy to recommend the most reputable local outfitters for the horses, mules, and perishable goods they would need, and Eli took careful notes. Byers was particularly smitten with Nelly, which Jubil found amusing. The newspaperman plied her with questions about Vassar, her women's movement acquaintances, and the magazine where she worked, while he and Eli stood idly by.

"You should keep a journal of your experiences out here," Byers said to her. "I'll publish them as a series in the newspaper. Perhaps you could find a publisher in New York for the whole collection?"

"That is a wonderful suggestion," Nelly said, her eyes lighting up at the idea. "Jubil once sent me the journals kept by

Lieutenant Doane on one of their Yellowstone expeditions. They were wonderfully descriptive. I'll take your advice, Mr. Byers, and I'll be in touch."

"Is Jack still operating the trading post at the Hot Springs?" Jubil asked Byers, referring to Byers's son-in-law Jack Sumner, who had also been a member of the 1868 Powell expedition and went on to join the 1869 Grand Canyon expedition as well.

"He is," Byers said. "That will be a delightful trip for you," Byers said, turning his attention once again to Nelly. "A rustic experience with a few comforts, and beauty you can find nowhere else."

While Eli finished outfitting them for their outdoor adventure, Jubil and Nelly spent a few days exploring Denver and enjoying being newlyweds. He did not see how life could get any better than this. He was living a dream, spending every day and night together. He hoped their outdoor adventure went well for her.

They set out from Denver on horseback leading a pair of mules laden with their tents and other camping supplies. Jubil was apprehensive about taking Nelly into the wilderness. There had not been Indian trouble in the area for some time, but wildlife predators were always present. Jubil and Eli were armed as usual, but Nelly wanted nothing to do with firearms. For someone who hadn't ridden a horse since she was a young girl, Nelly took to the trail remarkably well. The first night out from Denver they crossed the continental divide and set up camp on the western side of Berthoud Pass.

Their camp was in a grassy alpine meadow surrounded by aspen and birch, with a brook nearby that tumbled along with a constant soothing murmur. Nelly said it was only fitting that a place so near to heaven should begin to resemble it. She was enraptured by the beauty surrounding her, and spent the evening trying to capture it in words. Eli presented her with two heavy wool blankets for her cot, which she greatly appreciated.

The weather the next afternoon was in the seventies, but overnight it snowed four inches. Wall tents with small camp stoves, and Eli's blankets, kept them warm and dry. By noon the snow had melted.

They stayed in the area for a week. During the day they hiked and Jubil pointed out the spring wildflowers—pansies, amaryllis, snapdragons—and whatever else he recognized. Jubil and Eli shot enough hare and grouse to add nicely to their staples. Deer was in abundance, but more meat than they needed. Nelly had no interest in hunting, but tried her hand at fishing and brought in several trout. She spent her evenings recapping the day in her journals, which Jubil thought were very good. Once they were finally published, he would send copies to Lieutenant Doane.

The night before they moved on, they sat enjoying a supper of trout, fried potatoes and onions, and biscuits. Eli was becoming a very good cook.

"I doubt most of the women from Vassar College or New York City would be so comfortable in the outdoors," Jubil said proudly.

"You and Eli have made it very comfortable for me. It is so beautiful here. I can easily see now why you are so fulfilled by your outdoor experiences, though I'm grateful we've not encountered anything ferocious. The only complaint that I have is the lack of toilet facilities. I don't think I'll ever get used to that."

"I don't think anyone would fault you for that," Jubil said, and he and Eli laughed.

When they reached Middle Park and the trading post at the Hot Sulphur Springs, Jubil was disappointed to find that Jack Sumner was not there, but they would enjoy their stay anyway.

The temperature during the day was about the same as they were accustomed to, but at this lower altitude the nights were warmer.

Nelly and Eli were elated to be visiting the very trading post from which Jubil had brought her the beaded moccasins that she still owned, and the painted tomahawks he had brought Eli and Ike.

After supper the first evening they arrived, Eli surprised Jubil and Nelly with a package—something long and narrow rolled up in buckskin. He handed it to Nelly. "It's for both of you," he said, as he handed it to his sister.

"You bought us a present?" Nelly said with astonishment.

"Unwrap it," Eli said.

Nelly carefully removed the buckskin wrap to find a beautifully painted ceremonial smoking pipe, adorned with dangling feathers.

"Eli, it's beautiful!" Nelly said, beaming a smile at her brother.

"It's a peace pipe," Jubil said. He wondered whether Eli had meant to convey that symbolism, or had just purchased it as a pretty artifact.

"It is," Eli said, meeting Jubil's gaze and silently conveying his intent. "It's a wedding present to you and Jubil," Eli said. "And a way to say thank you for bringing me out here with you."

Nelly got up and hugged her brother tightly. "I will cherish this forever," she said. "It's been wonderful having your help and your company."

Jubil gave Eli a handshake and a pat on the shoulder. He could not have been more pleased at the effect this trip seemed to have had on him.

Later, as Nelly and Jubil lay down to sleep, she said, "I am having a wonderful time. I'll be wanting to do more of this with you in the future."

That was the best news Jubil could have asked for.

After about a week at the Hot Springs, they returned to Denver and spent a few more days at Portico's Delmonico of the West. Jubil and Eli came to terms with Mr. Ritchie, and signed an agreement with him to provide services for Jubil's tours. Mr. Byers met them for supper at the hotel the night before they left, and again encouraged Nelly to send him her journals.

On the train ride home, Jubil felt a new resolve to return alive and well from wherever his adventures took him. He had too much to live for now to send himself hurtling headlong down some river rapids or to hang from some mountainside.

In Council Bluffs, Eli managed the unloading of their camping gear and stayed on to help Ike with the store. Jubil was very pleased about this for everyone's sake. Eli had been indispensable on the trip, handling all the details of making and breaking camp, and tending the animals.

When Jubil and Nelly returned to New York in early May, Jubil felt rejuvenated by his new circumstances, but the possibility of losing the store and farm was like a deep shadow cast over the road up ahead.

He made contact with Mr. Wilkeson, the railroad's public relations man, and learned of another disappointment Cooke had had last year. Not only had the western survey failed, but the goal of completing the laying of track from Minneapolis to Bismarck had fallen short by about thirty miles before hard winter set in, and the crews and equipment had to be sent back to Minneapolis. This was a setback not only in terms of public confidence in the railroad project, but also the loss of expected revenue.

But the laying of track had resumed this spring and had been proceeding without incident, and the workers were expected to reach Bismarck by the time Jubil was on his way. If not, his instructions were to telegraph Rosser in Bismarck when he reached Minneapolis, and Rosser would arrange to have him brought to the end of the line. Sam Wilkeson's insights about the leaders of the survey were not much deeper than General Sheridan's, but during their conversation General Sherman's name came up. Jubil decided to pay him a visit. Sherman could most likely shed some light on the situation. He might not say what Jubil wanted to hear, but he would tell him the truth.

CHAPTER 15

With the seating of a new Congress following Grant's reelection, Washington was buzzing like a beehive. Jubil could not get a spot on General Sherman's calendar until late May.

When Sherman's assistant let Jubil into the office, Sherman rose and met him in the middle of the room. He was slight but powerfully built, with a handshake like a vice.

"Jubilee Walker," Sherman said, smiling warmly, "it's good to see you, my friend."

Jubil swelled with pride at being referred to as Sherman's friend, though they did have a history.

"It's good to see you too, General."

"So, you've gotten yourself entangled with Jay Cooke and his Northern Pacific Railroad?" Sherman asked gleefully, stroking his closely trimmed reddish-brown beard.

"I have indeed." Jubil said.

"Come in, sit down," Sherman said, "I'm curious to hear what's on your mind." For all the warmth of his manner, he pinned Jubil in place with his steely dark eyes.

"I'd like to be better prepared for the upcoming railroad survey. I joined the survey last year without knowing much about the leaders, but I knew Major Barlow was going, and I expected Lieutenant Doane would be there as well. This year, I won't know anyone. Thomas Rosser is leading the survey, and

Colonel David Stanley is leading the escort. I thought I could trust you to give me some insight into what I'm getting into."

"I appreciate your confidence," Sherman said. "Sorry you had to witness Colonel Baker's fall from grace last year. We've seen that coming for a while—I probably allow more latitude than I should in these situations sometimes. You may encounter Baker again. He's a major now, assigned to the quartermaster's office at Fort Rice, a few miles south of Bismarck. You may not see him though, if you choose to meet up with the surveyors instead of the escort—the surveyors are leaving from Mandan, across the river from Bismarck. They'll have a small escort, and be joined along the way by the full escort from Fort Rice."

"Fortunately, I'll miss Major Baker," Jubil said. "I expect to join up with the survey party. What can you tell me about Thomas Rosser?"

"He's been responsible for the eastern survey almost since its outset," Sherman said, "and overseen the construction of the railroad from Duluth to Bismarck. He's not going to quit on you, like Haydon did. As a young man, he went to West Point, but he served as a general in the Confederacy. He and Custer were friends at West Point, and then faced each other in battle during the war. Speaking of Custer—you said you didn't know anyone on the survey—you don't know him well, but you've met him. Sheridan has asked for him and his Seventh Cavalry to be assigned as part of the escort. Sheridan has authorization to select a site for a fort somewhere along the Yellowstone, to protect the railroad settlement to come. He's also itching to tame Sitting Bull."

"But Custer will report to Colonel Stanley?" Jubil asked.

"Yes," Sherman replied, looking away as he said it.

"Is there some history between those two?" Jubil asked.

"No," Sherman said, looking back at Jubil, "but Custer is notoriously impatient."

"Working with Colonel Stanley requires patience?" Jubil asked, concerned he might already know the answer.

"Colonel Stanley has been known to have a drink now and again," Sherman said.

"Why do you tolerate this in your officers?" Jubil blurted out, embarrassing himself.

"Because they've proven themselves to be good fighters. Soldiering is hard on a man."

"Yes sir, I'm sure it is. But it was Baker's drinking that triggered the failure of the survey last year. We can't allow that to happen again."

"No," Sherman agreed, "we can't."

"How about Rosser having been a Confederate general? Is that going to stir up trouble? Haydon was a colonel in the Confederacy, and Baker couldn't get over it."

"Stanley and Rosser completed this past year's survey without any trouble between them," Sherman said. "I'm not sure how the reunion between Rosser and Custer will go—but I'm guessing amiably. You'll have to drop me a line and let me know." Sherman grinned.

Jubil chuckled and shook his head.

"There's one other thing you'll find of interest," Sherman said, still grinning. "Another reason Sheridan requested Custer's reinforcements is to help protect a very special member of the survey party. It seems Fredrick Grant, President Grant's son, has a taste for adventure, and is going along."

"I don't know what to think about that," Jubil said, as he took a moment to let it register.

"I'm sure he's a pleasant fellow," Sherman said.

Jubil looked at him suspiciously. "Do you know something you're not saying?"

"No," Sherman said, grinning anew.

Jubil was not enthused about such a distraction from what was really important—which brought to mind the other subject he wanted Sherman's take on.

"What's the Indian situation?" Jubil asked.

"Far from good, I'm afraid. Colonel Stanley had a meeting with Spotted Eagle, an emissary for Sitting Bull. He refused to accept government rations, objected to the railroad being built through the heart of their territory, and said they would tear up the tracks and kill the builders. You can expect confrontations."

Jubil thought that sounded like a prize-winning understatement.

"How bad?" Jubil asked.

"Hard to say," Sherman shrugged. "We're sending a large contingent—around two thousand men—artillery also. It will look more like a combat force than an escort. Sitting Bull has pulled the Sioux tribes into a cohesive force that will require the full strength of the military to defeat."

"You once told me such a day might come," Jubil said. "Will you have no choice but to let Sheridan wipe them out?"

"Thankfully, our president has adopted a new Peace Policy intended to prevent that very eventuality," Sherman said, with a somewhat dismissive air. "It seems to me we are now expected to just tame them and then let them die quietly from neglect."

Sherman's frankness was like an arrow to Jubil's heart. He hated being party to this, but he did not know how to stop it. If Sherman couldn't—what could he possibly do? He thought about what was to come—more situations in which he would be shooting at people he actually felt sympathy for. Even letting the army do the shooting for him did not put him on higher moral ground. Peace would only come if the Sioux accepted reservation living, as the Crow had. And as Jubil had seen, the Crow were neglected, cheated, and about to be pushed out again—by advocates for the railroad.

"This brings to mind a situation I'd like your views on," Jubil said. "What can I do about the situation at the Crow Agency near Fort Ellis?" Jubil described his run-in with Phineas Black, Murphy, and O'Brien, and how he had learned that the Indian ring was still shortchanging the Crow and stealing from the government.

"To be perfectly honest with you," Sherman said, "I believe you've already embarked on the most effective course of action—shoot them."

Jubil laughed heartily.

"I'm half serious," Sherman said. "You've already made more improvement out there than anyone in Washington, DC, has. You'll waste your life walking the halls of the federal government, trying to find someone to make the kind of change you want to see. I'm sorry to be such a pessimist, but if Eli Parker, a full-blooded Seneca, couldn't put things to right at the Bureau of Indian Affairs, and got run out for trying, I'm doubtful that any of Grant's white men can do it. The only way that situation out there is going to change is if the people out there change it themselves."

Jubil wasn't sure what to make of this declaration. "Well, we're not exactly ending our conversation on a high note," he said, "but I believe I've gotten what I came for. Thank you very much for your time, and your candor. I've taken to heart everything you've said."

Sherman walked with Jubil to the door.

"I'm glad I could be of some assistance," he said. "How's White Dog?"

"He saved my hide again last summer," Jubil said. "He's one up on me now. He still insists I keep his medicine bag though. It's served me well. And you'll like this—he said he might ride the train with me someday, come visit my world."

"Wouldn't that be something," Sherman said with a smile. "I wish you the best of luck. If I know you, you'll get the job done."

Jubil caught a carriage back to the National Hotel, where he was staying. When he arrived, he went to the dining room for supper. As he was sipping a glass of water and looking over the menu, someone walked up to his table, and when Jubil glanced up, he saw that it was Major John Wesley Powell.

"It's good to see you, Jubil."

Jubil rose to shake Powell's left hand. "What a pleasant surprise, Major Powell. Can you join me?"

"I'd be delighted. Thank you. I was here to meet a gentleman on a new piece of business," Powell said, "but I found he had been forced to cancel. Fortunately, I saw you as I was leaving."

"You're looking well," Jubil said sincerely.

Powell was in his late thirties, with receding auburn hair and muttonchop whiskers that met a mustache over a bare chin. With the exception of his right arm, which was missing from the elbow down, he was hale and hearty. He was shorter in stature than Jubil by six inches, but his vigorous energy made him an imposing presence.

"Thank you, I'm managing well enough," Powell said. Jubil imagined this was an understatement. Anyone who assumed Powell's missing right arm was a liability was badly mistaken. Jubil had never known it to stop Powell from doing anything, and, in fact, Jubil had seen Powell do things he doubted a two-armed man could do. He had once seen Powell, stranded on a cliff face in the Grand Canyon, release his only handhold to grasp onto the leg of a pair of pants dangled over the edge of the cliff from above by his climbing partner.

"You actually look much better than when I last saw you," Powell said with a smile.

"Yes sir, I expect I do," Jubil laughed. Jubil had been gaunt, sunburned, and traumatized when they had finally reached the end of the Grand Canyon expedition. "That trip tamed me pretty good for a little while...but it didn't hold."

"Hard to believe that trip was three years ago," Powell said. "For a while I kept abreast of your adventures through Emma, who would see the Boswell family at church, but since we moved, I've lost track. Congratulations on your work in Yellowstone. I heard about that not only through Emma, but the Bloomington newspaper. I have a great deal of respect for both Dr. Hayden and Major Barlow's work. I'm sure you made a solid contribution to their efforts."

"Thank you," Jubil said. "Your approval means a great deal to me. I've just come off another adventure with Major Barlow. But you mentioned moving. Where are you living?"

"We sold our house in Normal last spring," Powell said. "We live here in Washington now. You must come visit if you have time."

"I'd be delighted," Jubil said. "I would love to see you more often than every three years. I don't have much connection to Bloomington anymore either. You might not be aware that Nelly Boswell and I were recently married. I sent an invitation to you and Mrs. Powell at your Normal address, but the letter must not have found you."

"My word! We do have a lot of catching up to do," Powell said. "Congratulations on your marriage. Where are you living?" Jubil explained how he had moved to Council Bluffs after Luke died, but that Nelly was living in New York.

"How is it that Nelly lives in New York—if I may ask?" Powell asked. Jubil explained how they had wound up at their unconventional living arrangement.

"Emma will be thrilled to hear this news," Powell said. "Nelly will find an ally in her. You must be very proud."

"Yes sir," Jubil said.

"What brings you to Washington?" Powell asked.

"I've been visiting with General Sherman," Jubil said, and went on to explain about his involvement with Jay Cooke and the Northern Pacific Railroad. When he explained, he gave no specifics. He did not want to have to discuss his decision to put the farm and store at risk. He just said he had made an investment that would either pay off handsomely, or he would lose it. He also explained his name might be popping up in the papers soon, as he was also committed to publicly supporting the railroad effort.

"How have you been spending your time, Major?" Jubil asked. "Why did you and Mrs. Powell decide to move to Washington?"

"The summer after the Grand Canyon expedition I decided to conduct a formal survey of the area," Powell said. "As you know, our maps were sketchy, at best, and I was well positioned for the job. Dr. Hayden had his sights set on Yellowstone, so the field for the Grand Canyon was open. I spent that year gaining congressional funding, which I've achieved, and began the survey. Last year we made another trip down the river but did not run the complete length. A formal survey, as you've no doubt learned, is a much slower affair than our dash for survival was. I expect to be at this for a few years."

"That's wonderful," Jubil said. "After my experiences in Yellowstone, surveying with Hayden and Barlow, I know exactly what you mean."

Their attempts at mapping the canyon had been ill-fated. Oramel Howland had attempted to draw maps along the way down the canyon, but he had lost them, on more than one occasion, when they traversed some rapids and their boats were swamped. He also could not forget, or entirely forgive, how Major Powell had berated Howland, and the terrible fate that had befallen Oramel and his brother after they grew tired of Powell's abuse and abandoned the trip.

"You said you were meeting someone about a new piece of business," Jubil said. "May I ask what it is?"

"I suppose," Powell said. "I do have to ask you to keep it in strict confidence and understand it is not entirely certain." Powell looked around to see if anyone was within listening range.

"Yes sir," Jubil said earnestly.

"As a part of President Grant's Peace Policy in the Bureau

of Indian Affairs, Congress recently authorized a Paiute reservation in Lincoln County, Nevada, covering almost two million acres. They would like to design a large-scale program for the Utes of Utah, the Paiutes of Utah, northern Arizona, southern Nevada, and southeastern California; the Shoshones of Idaho and Utah; and the western Shoshones of Nevada. I may soon be appointed as special Indian commissioner to undertake a full study and make recommendations."

Jubil felt a tingle in his spine at the base of his neck—he knew that feeling. He used to get it when opening the cover of a new dime novel. He'd felt it the day he learned Major Powell was leading a group of students to Colorado on an exploring expedition. He'd felt it when Abe Warner told him General Sheridan was inviting him to join the Washburn expedition to Yellowstone. He'd felt it when General Sherman had invited him to serve as Major Barlow's guide for his Yellowstone survey. He knew that involving himself somehow in what Major Powell was doing would stir his soul. Perhaps, somehow, he could do something constructive for the Indians. But he could not change directions now—there was too much at stake in his current situation.

"That is a very great responsibility," Jubil said, trying to ignore his own internal dialogue. "They are choosing the right man for the job."

Powell had always shown a true interest in the Indians, though he never hesitated to defend against aggression. He spent time bartering with them and collecting their arts and crafts, learning their languages, cultures, and traditions, and generally making friends among them, and then documenting his efforts with academic thoroughness.

"Thank you," Powell said, "remember it is not official. I was here to interview someone about possibly becoming my assistant, but he was delayed. A young man currently at Lincoln University in Pennsylvania—a Ute who speaks the languages fluently."

This detail put a damper on Jubil's thoughts of joining Powell in some capacity. Even if he was available, which he was not, Powell would probably want people with specific skills, just as he had years ago when he had refused Jubil's request to join his first expedition. He took a sip of his water as he considered whether to change the direction of the conversation.

"You are committed to your efforts with the Northern Pacific Railroad then?" Powell asked, beating him to it.

"I'm committed to completing the railroad survey this summer," Jubil said. "Beyond that, I'm only tied to the railroad as a means to get visitors to Yellowstone National Park. Seeing it protected and guiding people through it are my true goals."

"And admirable ones," Powell said.

"Thank you," Jubil said. "My only regret is the impact of the railroad on the Indians. I'm afraid it will go right through the Crow reservation, and the Sioux are going to war over it crossing their territory."

"Regrettable," Powell agreed, "but inevitable. I believe the best we can do is be the friend who brings them the bad news and helps them cope with it somehow."

This had the ring of truth, and Jubil tucked it away in his memory.

"I'm sure I'd have use for a veteran outdoorsman and out-fitter—either for my survey or my work with the Indians," Powell continued.

"I'm honored you would offer to include me," Jubil said. "My interest is surely there, but I'm a married man with business partners now. I can't drop everything and run off like I once could."

"And you are all the better and more valuable for it," Powell said with a smile. "Perhaps when your business with the railroad is finished, we can talk again. I have worked up quite an appetite. What do you say we order supper?"

After supper Powell gave him a note with his address. Jubil

promised to stop by and say hello to Mrs. Powell before his train left for New York the following afternoon.

Jubil lay awake long into the night, puzzling over how he might be of use to Powell if the railroad survey succeeded, but he saw nothing in that direction but an endless set of responsibilities and challenges that would come with running a world-class travel business. If the railroad survey failed—well, that was not an eventuality he would allow himself to dwell on.

Still, Powell's words haunted him—*be the friend that brings them the bad news and helps them cope with it.* He also thought about Sherman's advice: forget working through the government; work with the people themselves to make a difference. On the railroad surveys, he certainly was not coming to the Indians as a friend.

CHAPTER 16

In June Jubil received a telegram from Thomas Rosser saying the railroad had reached Bismarck, and Jubil made his final preparations to leave. He loaded his trapper's pack as he would for any expedition and the last thing in was his medicine bag. He didn't expect to see White Dog this trip, but he was proud to wear it and enjoyed whatever safety it provided. He would not take Apollo with him on this trip. It would not be right to take Star's mate away from her or to risk anything happening to him. He would acquire a horse when he reached his destination.

He promised Nelly that he would exercise great caution on the trip and write when he could. He intended to do as he said, but knew that caution was not always enough. Some dumb luck was always involved. But he vowed to redouble his efforts. He had too much to lose now to let carelessness take it away.

Jubil began to perk up during the Minneapolis to Bismarck leg of the trip. Not only was it exciting to be riding on the Northern Pacific Railroad, but he had always found it peaceful to watch the landscape roll by.

The scenery in Minnesota, with its lush green hills and plentiful lakes, was unlike any he had seen. He marveled at how the railroad had managed to find a way across this watery landscape. When they passed Fargo and entered the high plains of northern Dakota Territory, he could not get enough of the stunning landscape. It was an arid land, spread out flat in varied shades of brown and green and dotted with hills, valleys, small lakes, and wetlands, with occasional spires of stone, worn by wind and water. Some people might have found it desolate, but Jubil found it magnificent. The train flew straight west the whole distance across to Bismarck, unimpeded. Jubil envied the crews who surveyed this route.

The afternoon of June 16, Jubil's train pulled into Bismarck. The town did not amount to much, perhaps fifteen-hundred people, but he knew it was newly taking shape because of the railroad. Across the Missouri River was the older but smaller community of Mandan, originally an Indian settlement. It had never grown beyond a few hundred people.

As he shouldered his trapper's pack and walked toward the depot, someone called his name. He turned to see a smiling, burly, bushy-bearded fellow waving and striding his way.

"Mr. Walker?" the man said. "I'm Thomas Rosser."

Rosser was in his late thirties, a little taller than Jubil, with a stockier build. He wore an unbuttoned knee-length duster and a wide-brimmed gray Stetson hat. His handshake was firm and vigorous. He had a deep baritone voice and a slight southern drawl.

"How do you do?" Jubil said. "Thank you for meeting me."

"Happy to oblige," Rosser said, leading Jubil to a small buckboard. "Mr. Cooke has told me quite a bit about you. I'm looking forward to hearing about your adventures. I also heard from General Sheridan and General Sherman. You keep impressive company for such a young man." Rosser's tone was congenial, not fawning or sarcastic.

"Truthfully, it's all come more by chance than by design," Jubil said.

"But you wouldn't keep being invited along if you weren't useful," Rosser smiled and winked. "Toss your pack in the back, and we'll be off. Looks like you've come prepared for anything. Good man."

Jubil felt a great relief at finding Rosser so likeable and welcoming. Not only did Rosser not mind his presence, he welcomed it. It appeared their relationship would be the opposite of his with Haydon. He was relieved to not have to prove himself. He put his pack in the wagon, and unstrapped his rifle from the frame to keep it with him.

"I'd like to be useful along the way," Jubil said. "I have no surveying skills, but I'm handy at fetching and carrying. And I get along well with horses and mules."

"You'll be useful all right. Don't you worry about that," Rosser said, snapping the reins and heading the wagon west toward the Missouri River landing.

Bismarck was new, but it was off to a good start. It was considerably less ramshackle than many of the western towns Jubil had seen. It looked like a permanent town in the making, not a temporary camp. These people had risked their investments on the railroad reaching them, and they had won their bets. Jubil was feeling optimistic that his bet would pay off too.

"I appreciate your confidence," Jubil said. "Last year I didn't feel much opportunity to be useful."

"A shameful performance," Rosser said, shaking his head, "from both Haydon and Baker—in my opinion anyway." Rosser looked to Jubil.

"I agree entirely," Jubil said, happy to find they saw matters similarly.

"I understand Colonel Stanley is another officer who is fond of his whiskey," Jubil said. "But you worked with him last year, so it must be manageable?"

"Manageable...yes—just," Rosser said, obviously concerned. "Hopefully this year will go as well, or better."

Jubil did not find this assessment reassuring.

"You should know right up front," Rosser added, "I'll

not complete the survey myself this summer. There will be a Northern Pacific board meeting sometime in August, and I'll have to go back east for that. But you'll be along to represent Mr. Cooke's interests, so you'll see it through."

This came as an unpleasant surprise. "You're expecting me to be in charge of your survey team?"

"No, I have a chief of survey, Mr. Eckelson. But it won't hurt if I make it clear that your opinion has weight."

"I appreciate that," Jubil said. His relief over not having to prove himself had been short lived. These men trusted Rosser, but they would probably be skeptical of Jubil. Hopefully he wouldn't have to express any unpopular opinions. This was his last chance to complete the survey.

Rosser drove the buckboard onto the ferry, and they crossed the Missouri. On the western bank, the town of Mandan was the ramshackle affair Bismarck had avoided becoming. A large tent encampment was spread out, and behind it a few dozen wooden storefronts with every variety of roofing.

"Most of this is our escort," Rosser said, waving his hand to indicate the tents. "We're going to attempt to take the survey line straight west from here, but Fort Rice is about thirty miles south. Rather than move the whole escort north and then turn west, Colonel Stanley and Custer will move northwest at an angle to intercept us along the way—we should meet up in a week or so. To cover us in the meantime, Colonel Stanley sent us a company of three hundred men under the command of Major Townsend."

"Sheridan said to expect trouble," Jubil said.

"It's a shame," Rosser said, nodding, "but inevitable I suppose."

Jubil was glad to find Rosser shared his compassion for the Indians, but he knew that would change nothing about the upcoming conflict.

"We're here," Rosser said, drawing the buckboard to a

halt near the encampment of the survey crew. It was near to, but separate from, the larger encampment, which Jubil now recognized as the military escort. Rosser parked the buckboard near two large custom-built wagons unlike any Jubil had ever seen. They were larger and more sturdily build than a normal freight wagon and had a number of specially built compartments for carrying their surveying gear. He thought Nelly's father, who worked in a carriage shop, would be very impressed. Nearby were several large tents with the door flaps tied open. Inside Jubil could see men sitting on folding chairs and working on maps that were laid out on folding tables.

"You have a large crew," Jubil said, "impressively equipped."

"Nothing but the best for Jay Cooke and Company," Rosser grinned. "We have twenty-eight men. My assistants, transit-men, rodmen, chainmen, picket-men, axe-men, mapmakers, a hunter, and a few teamsters—all fine, industrious men. You'll enjoy their company. Oh—and we have four newspaper men. I can't recall their papers. You'll sort them out."

If Mr. Wilkeson had known that there would be journalists traveling along, he had failed to mention it. No matter, as Rosser said, he'd sort them out. As Rosser and Jubil dismounted from the wagon, two men emerged from one of the tents and approached.

"Mr. Walker, this is my principal assistant, Albert Eckelson, and my chief of party, Montgomery Meigs," Rosser said.

"Just call me Eck," said Eckelson with a smile and a handshake. He was tall and thin, late twenties, with a friendly face.

"And I'm Monty," said Meigs affably. He was near Jubil's age, a little shorter but solidly built, with an appealingly mischievous grin.

"My name is Jubilee, but call me Jubil if you'd like." This first-name familiarity was unusual, but Jubil liked the friendly tone.

"I'll be the Locating Engineer for the survey," Rosser said, his drawl becoming more exaggerated as he eased into his explanation, "meaning I'll be determining the route we follow and the line we stake out along it that the tracks will follow. You'll see me riding out frequently to scout for any adjustments to our route, and coming back to check on the progress of staking out our line along the way. You can ride with me anytime you like, or you can stay with the transit party. Eck oversees the transitmen, rodmen, and the mapmakers, and Monty oversees the chainmen, picket-men and axe-men. Monty will always have a job for you if you want it, and Eck may need a rodman sometimes."

"I'll try to be useful," Jubil said. This was a very welcome change from last year.

"Has Tex been telling you wild tales about us?" Monty asked.

"Tex?"

"General Rosser," Monty said, pulling a thumb in his direction. Rosser shrugged.

"On the contrary," Jubil replied with a smile, "he said you were all fine, industrious men." Perhaps his men called him Tex, but that felt too familiar for Jubil.

"Did he mention a pay raise?" Monty asked.

"I didn't hear that mentioned," Jubil said.

"All right," Rosser said, "enough tomfoolery—Mr. Walker will think us unprofessional. Monty will help you settle in, get some supper, and get ready to leave. We'll be on our way tomorrow. Do you prefer to ride the wagons, or on horseback?"

"Horseback, by far," Jubil said. "I did not bring a horse, but I'm prepared to buy one."

"That's not necessary," Rosser said. "Monty will help set you up with one. If there is nothing that I can do for you at the moment, I need to make sure we're ready to leave."

Jubil followed Monty for the rest of the evening. He began to meet the rest of the survey crew, and also met two of the journalists traveling along. Sam Barrows, of the *New York*

Tribune, was near his own age, shorter than Jubil, with a bushy mustache and a sunny disposition. Jubil liked him. William Phelps, of the *St. Paul Pioneer* was mid-forties, tall and thin, and very quiet. Sam Barrows told him there were two other journalists along also, one from the *Sioux City Daily Journal* and another from the *Chicago Post,* but they had gone to Fort Rice, to follow Custer and Fred Grant.

It was a pleasure to be joining a group that seemed so intelligent and good natured. At the end of the day, he retired to his tent and wrote Nelly telling her he had arrived safely, then lay on his bedroll thinking about the job ahead of them. He felt more optimistic about the survey's chance of success than he had for a while. He could not imagine how such competent men, with such a formidable military escort, could not succeed.

In the morning, Jubil saddled up his mount, Venus, chosen last night from the string of spare saddle horses. She had a chestnut brown coat similar to Star's, but she had no white markings, and her mane and tail were a rusty brown rather than flaxen. She was a beauty with a strong build, and she looked him in the eye when he talked to her, which sealed the bargain. He would not get too attached to her though. He did not need another horse, especially with a new one on the way.

On Rosser's previous surveys they had turned south at Bismarck and gone to Fort Rice, thirty miles to the south, then crossed the Heart River to the west. But this year, Rosser was determined to find a route around the Heart River.

Rosser and his scouts, whom Jubil had not yet met, headed due west of Mandan. Jubil followed along on Venus, riding beside the surveyors and their wagons. Behind them was the military escort—two-hundred-fifty infantry, fifty cavalry, two dozen supply and equipment wagons, a small herd of cattle, spare horses, and a few hunters and wolfers.

The weather was dry and warm, and Jubil felt himself

relaxing into the familiar rhythm of the saddle. He thought about Eli and wondered how he was doing. He felt a little guilty over his relief at not having him along.

On his previous expeditions, the possibility of Indian attack was always there, but they had never been given advance notice to expect it. Jubil was concerned, but he was not afraid of the prospect. He had been in enough of these situations to know that if he kept his wits about him, his chances of survival were good. They had ridden about an hour, when that assumption was tested.

Up ahead about a quarter of a mile, Rosser and the scouts were riding up a treeless hill when a few Indian riders appeared at the top. Rosser and the scouts wheeled their horses, and rode back toward the survey party. As Rosser reached them, he pulled his horse up in front of Mr. Eckelson.

"Hold up here, Eck! Keep the engineers to the rear!" Rosser shouted, then he raced past the survey wagons to the officers at the head of the escort. By this time about one hundred Indians were milling about atop the hill, firing at them from on horseback, and looking as if they might charge. Rosser and the cavalry galloped past the engineers to hold the Indians back, as the infantry slowly advanced toward the hill.

Jubil and Venus were exposed to the random incoming gunfire from the hill. There was nowhere on these flat plains to take cover until the survey teamsters could pull their wagons into a defensive line. The most helpful thing he could do at the moment was stay out of the way. A line of wagons was soon formed, and Jubil took cover behind them, along with the engineers. The infantry advanced, and the cavalry fell in close behind, waiting for a signal to charge. The Indians had fallen back over the ridge of the hill, and were now on foot, firing to hold the army at bay.

If this was just the advance party of a larger group of Indians, they might come swarming over the hill at any time.

Jubil would defend himself if he had to, but there were plenty of soldiers doing the fighting for him now.

The firing continued for an hour or so, then stopped as quickly as it had started as the Indians abandoned their position. Either they had not been an advance party, or the whole contingent had given up the idea of an attack. Once the firing died down, Rosser sent the scouts ahead and then ordered the survey to resume its advance. Remarkably, in spite of all the gunfire, no soldiers or surveyors were hit, and only two Indians had been killed. With no further trouble that day, the survey covered about ten miles and made camp. Except for it occurring so soon after leaving Mandan, Jubil had been surprisingly unrattled by the incident, but he hoped it wouldn't become a daily occurrence.

For the next week, the survey made good progress without encountering any more trouble. Rosser and the scouts rode out front, sometimes a full day ahead, to make sure the way ahead was a feasible route for the railroad. At first, Jubil rode out with them. Rosser was in high spirits, as following his hunch was proving that a straighter route around the Heart River was feasible. This would eliminate dozens of miles of expensive railroad construction. After a few days, Jubil let Venus rest and spent his days helping Eck and Monty as a laborer on the survey.

Early one afternoon, as Jubil was working as a chainman for Monty, rainclouds began to gather. The weather had been warm and dry, so rain was overdue, and would not be unwelcome if it fell in moderation. Within a few minutes, the clouds had gathered into a black mass that hung low over the plains. The sky darkened and turned a sickly green. Jubil looked up to see the bottom layer of the clouds churning in a rolling boil. The first bolts of lightning flashed. He had lived on the prairie long enough to know what a storm looked like that could spawn a tornado—it looked like this. He looked around the landscape for shelter, and saw only a stand of timber to the south growing along the banks of a small stream where a herd of antelope were watering.

The temperature dropped suddenly, lightning flashed, thunder roared, and the sky unleashed a barrage of hailstones—no rain, just little pellets of ice hurled by a forceful wind. It had been too warm for his coat, so Jubil's upper body was covered only by his shirt. At first the hail was pea-sized, and it stung as it hit, but it was tolerable. He pulled his hat down tight, and ran toward the nearby survey wagon where Venus was hitched, and his pack, coat, and hooded slicker were stashed. By the time he reached the wagon, the hailstones had begun to come down in a torrent, now the size of marbles. These pellets were large enough to be painful, and where they hit exposed flesh, they left welts or cuts. His hands stung from the pelting they were taking. The other men were either scurrying for cover or battling to keep animals under control.

Just as Jubil reached the wagon Venus was hitched to, it lurched, its team trying to agree on which way to run. Jubil unhitched her to let her run free and reached for his pack. As he grabbed the frame, the team bolted and the wagon drove off, dropping his pack to the ground in front of him. Venus ran for the trees, but Jubil was not sure he could make it that far.

The hail was now walnut size, and it began to cover the ground. The horses and mules went into a panic. The teams bolted off in all directions, with the wagons careening out of control. Men trying to shelter under the wagons scrambled to escape before they were run over, then were left exposed, wondering where to run themselves. Most ran toward the stand of trees to the south.

Jubil dropped to the ground and lay on his side, drawing up into a ball. He pulled his pack on top of him, holding it by the frame from underneath, and tried to protect his head and body as best as he could. His legs were taking a beating, but his boots helped somewhat. He had to tip the pack to cover his face as the wind blew the hail sideways. This left his back uncovered, and it was taking a pounding, but he had no choice. Without his pack, he might have been beaten to death.

How long the pounding hailstorm continued Jubil could not accurately say—it seemed interminable. When it finally stopped, he pushed his pack away and arose to a scene of devastation. The hailstones stood several inches deep over the whole area, and the wagons were strewn about in various states of disrepair. Some of the teams were still hitched to their wagons, or what was left of them, while some of the harnesses had broken and set the animals free. Nearby, a few mules lay dead on the ground, and beyond them, strewn across the landscape, at least a dozen dead antelope.

Jubil took off White Dog's medicine bag and returned it to the safety of his pack, then left the pack lying on the small patch of clear ground where he had lain. He limped toward the shelter of the trees and found Venus there among the cottonwoods. As he approached, she whinnied and shied away, and he spoke softly to her until she allowed him to put his hand on her neck and examine her for injuries. There were a few scrapes on the tender flesh of her nose, but she had no major cuts.

Dazed, the men gathered together again. Only one man was badly hurt, having taken enough blows to the head to knock him unconscious. Two soldiers were assigned to take him back to Bismarck for attention. The number of cuts, bruises, and welts was uncountable, and many felt hats had been pounded to rags. On Jubil's left side, the one that had been exposed, his hip and leg were badly bruised, and his knee had taken a pounding. He could not see all of his back but assumed it looked as bad as his leg. He felt like he had been repeatedly punched in the kidneys but was relieved to see no blood in his urine.

As the men assessed their situation, the primary problem was the state of the wagons. Without an adequate complement of wagons, the survey would not be able to continue. If they had to return to Bismarck to reoutfit themselves, chances were good it would be too late to successfully complete the survey this summer. Jubil could not believe a hailstorm could defeat the survey, and, in spite of his own injuries, he fell with a vengeance to the task of helping repair the wagons.

Jubil could not do much heavy lifting the day after the storm, but he pushed through the discomfort as the days went on to help get back underway. He helped round up the horses and mules and tend their wounds, and drag the dead ones aside for the scavengers to feast on. It saddened him to see these poor animals killed or suffering. He had never heard of such a thing happening, and hoped to never see it again. In spite of his sore knee and sore back, he helped scour the area retrieving supplies and equipment strewn about, and then helped sort and stow those items in one of the surviving wagons. It took three days, but by salvaging parts from the wreckage, they were able to put enough wagons back in service to move forward.

During this delay, Jubil was interviewed by both Sam Barrows and William Phelps. They both took an interest in his role with the survey as Cooke's observer, his experiences in Yellowstone and with Major Powell, and his opinions about the value of the Northern Pacific Railroad. Sam Barrows let Jubil read the article he had written, and Jubil felt good about what he read. He knew Nelly would see it in the *New York Tribune,* and thought Sam Erickson and Jay Cooke would be pleased. Barrows also let Jubil read the article he had written about the survey's progress so far, which focused on the Indian attack and the hailstorm. He thought Barrow's article made the Indian attack sound like more than it really amounted to, but he kept his critique to himself. His description of the hailstorm was vivid and accurate. If Mr. Phelps wrote an article after their interview, he didn't offer to let Jubil read it, and Jubil didn't ask.

On the day of the storm, Rosser had sent two scouts to find Custer and Stanley to ask for immediate help, rather than meeting them further down the line as planned. And by the time the survey was ready to move out, Lieutenant Custer and the Seventh Cavalry had arrived.

CHAPTER 17

To Jubil's amazement, he heard them before he saw them. In the distance he heard music, the familiar tune, "Garry Owen." The column came over a hill south of the surveyor's camp, with Custer in the lead and flag bearers on either side of him followed by a sixteen-piece band mounted on white horses—coronets, baritone and bass horns, flutes, clarinets, and drums. Jubil was no music critic, but he thought they sounded a bit wobbly, though for playing while mounted on moving horses he supposed they were not bad.

A row of officers followed, and behind them the ranks of cavalry, five across and one hundred rows deep. The column stopped a distance away from the surveyor's camp, and Custer rode in along with his officers. Jubil was standing beside Rosser, Eck, and Monty near their campfire, watching the show. Custer rode regally into camp and halted his horse a few yards from Rosser.

"I heard you could use some reinforcements, Tex," Custer said.

"We've got it in hand now, George," Rosser said with a smile. "But we're glad to have your company."

Custer dismounted and approached. He looked just as Jubil remembered him—tall and thin with reddish-brown curly hair hanging to his shoulders under his flat wide-brimmed hat, a narrow face and nose, and a horseshoe-shaped reddish-brown mustache. He wore a frock coat with a white shirt and a red cravat tied in a loose bow, buckskin gloves with fringed gauntlets. He was in every way a showman. He and Rosser shook hands and then exchanged a few quiet words before Rosser led Custer to meet his men. He introduced him to Eck and Monty, and then Jubil found himself shaking hands with Custer for the second time.

"Jubilee Walker," Custer said as he sized him up with piercing blue eyes. "I remember you—we met at Fort McPherson, I believe. You were chasing after Wes Powell. He sent you packing, and General Sherman's scout abandoned him to follow you home."

"I'm surprised you remember," Jubil laughed.

"I was surprised the general gave up his scout. He had really taken a shine to you, or that would not have happened. I understand you're here for Jay Cooke," Custer said.

Jubil explained his relationship to Cooke.

"We should have no problem accomplishing your mission," Custer said, "if we don't shoot ourselves in the foot."

"How so?" Rosser asked.

"Let me get my men settled. We'll talk later," Custer said.

After supper that evening, Rosser, Eck, Monty, and Jubil sat with Custer in the large wall tent that served as Rosser's mobile headquarters.

"I feel it's my duty to tell you this, Tex," Custer said, leaning in, elbows on his knees, looking at Rosser first, then at the others. "Colonel Stanley will be delayed for a while, and when we reconnect, he's likely to blame me for his delay. In my opinion, the circumstances arose from a misunderstanding." Custer paused, Jubil presumed he was waiting to see if anyone was going to argue with him.

"Colonel Stanley's column has experienced frequent Indian harassment, and a terrible muddy slog on the journey so far. While you've been hit with one bad storm, we have endured rain on most of the days we have been out. The column is moving painfully slowly, and everyone is wet, sleep deprived, miserable, and irritable. I regret to say the stress has driven Colonel Stanley into the whiskey deeper than I believe is responsible—and we've had words. He also resents General Sheridan appointing me to escort Fred Grant. He believes he could have managed that without me.

"Anyway, we were camped near Big Muddy Creek when your scouts arrived asking for help. Stanley set a 2:00 a.m. reveille, but I expected to easily catch up to him, and did not bring the cavalry forward until 5:00 a.m. Rather than having left at his appointed time, Stanley had waited for me. His column moves slowly, an hour to pass a point, so I took the cavalry ahead with the bridge building equipment to span the creek. Once we were across, we moved on to your aid, but my scouts tell me that by the time Stanley's column reached Big Muddy Creek, the bridge had washed away. They are left to find some other way across. They'll be along, hopefully, but I'm not sure how long."

"Can we help them?" Rosser asked.

"I don't see how," Custer said. "We have fewer resources at hand to come up with a solution than he does."

Custer's news raised several points of concern for Jubil—Indian harassment, drinking, disagreements—but the primary concern was the need for Stanley to rejoin the survey crew. Without Stanley's support, not only would the military escort be too light, but the survey would not have adequate supplies to complete the trip. The survey crew had only brought supplies adequate for about a month, expecting to rejoin Stanley's main column. They would have to turn back if Stanley could not cross the creek soon.

"All right then," Rosser said. "We'll move out at 5:00 a.m. so we don't waste any more supplies just sitting here. We'll survey west for another few days, but send scouts back to check on Stanley. If he can't cross in a week, we'll turn back."

Jubil thought this was a sound plan, and Eck and Monty nodded.

"I'll go get my men ready to leave," Custer said and left the tent.

"What do you make of Stanley's drinking?" Jubil asked Rosser.

"I'm sorry to say I'm not surprised," Rosser said. "I hope he can manage it."

"What about the disagreement between Custer and Stanley?" Jubil asked. "It sounds like that may get worse."

"Unfortunately," Rosser said, nodding and sighing. "Who knows what Stanley's version of events will be. George is notorious for his difficulty in dealing with any authority that interferes with his own. There is bound to be conflict—hopefully we can manage it."

"Maybe he'll listen to you," Jubil said hopefully.

"Maybe..." Rosser said, "but I'll only be along for part of the trip."

This reminder was unsettling. Jubil doubted Custer would take advice from him, but that wouldn't stop him from offering it, if necessary.

The survey crew, their original escort, and Custer's cavalry set out as planned. The first night they made camp, their scouts returned with news that Stanley was making progress at crossing the creek. They had built a bridge by floating their wagons upside down on empty kegs. It would be slow going to get the whole column across and reorganized again, but they would be along in a few days. This was some relief to Jubil, but he was still concerned about how Stanley and Custer would get along when they were together again.

The survey and cavalry continued to work their way west. The weather was hot and dry, but that was better than mud and hail. Thankfully, the Indians left them alone. This fact combined with the weather and the nightly concerts by Custer's band seemed to have improved the overall mood. It had been a week since Custer had joined them, and Stanley had still not caught up. But the scouts had reported that his column was on the move and would arrive that day. The survey had gotten off to a slow start, but the pace should pick up now, Jubil told himself. The survey line was straight and clear from here to the Yellowstone. Rosser made camp early at the confluence of the Green and Heart Rivers, about halfway between Bismarck and the Yellowstone River. They would wait there for Stanley to arrive. The area surrounding the confluence had a bounty of grass and water to refresh the livestock.

Stanley's column trudged toward camp at a weary pace, the antithesis of Custer's flamboyant entrance. Colonel Stanley rode at the head of a three-mile-long column made up of fifteen hundred infantry, dozens of mule-drawn wagons, two cannons mounted on wheeled carts, hundreds of cattle, and a pack of cowhands and wolfers. Stanley conferred with a group of his officers, and then four of them began to ride back along the column, giving orders to spread them out in the river valley and establish camp. Stanley and two of his officers rode into the surveyor's camp and dismounted at Rosser's tent, where Rosser, Custer, Eck, Monty, and Jubil were waiting to meet with him. Rosser stepped out to greet him and ushered him into the tent.

Stanley was in his late forties with dark eyes under slightly furrowed brows, and a neatly trimmed beard showing lips pursed in a thin line. Before Rosser had a chance to say anything, Stanley barked at Custer.

"Lieutenant Colonel Custer, I hold you accountable for my late arrival."

"With all due respect, sir—" Custer began.

"I'll hear no debate on the matter!" Stanley cut him off.

Custer stood down. Stanley turned away from Custer and looked at Rosser.

"We're making good progress on the survey," Rosser said cheerfully. "We've found a shortcut around the Heart River that will save miles of railroad construction and shorten our survey by weeks."

Stanley looked at Rosser as if he had said something insulting.

"So, because you were mistaken as to the route we were to follow, I'm hauling several weeks' worth of unnecessary supplies?" Stanley asked angrily.

"I would not say the supplies are unnecessary," Rosser said, tactfully ignoring the insult. "I'd say that just makes us well prepared."

"Hmph," Stanley said gruffly. Looking around he recognized Eck and Monty, but not Jubil.

"Are you Walker, then?" Stanley said, accusingly—or so it felt to Jubil.

"Yes sir, I am."

"I hear you're Jay Cooke's man, here to observe and advise," Stanley said. "Also well acquainted with General Sheridan and Sherman, I understand. Let's be clear—you are welcome to observe, but I don't need your advice. Mr. Rosser might, but I don't."

Jubil kept his composure and made no reply other than to nod shortly. Stanley turned his attention back to Rosser.

"I'm going to declare tomorrow a day of rest," Stanley announced. "The men and the livestock need it." Saying nothing more, Stanley turned and left the tent.

Jubil looked around at the others and found his was not the only astonished expression.

"I suppose Colonel Stanley has made it clear to everyone," Custer said, "that he is in charge here. Now you see what I'm faced with daily."

Jubil understood Custer's point, but he thought it was ungallant of him to voice disrespectful thoughts about his superior officer.

Stanley's day of rest would have been a tolerable delay had he not misused it so badly. The surveyors went ahead and marked out their line a few miles west, then returned to camp. That evening, Stanley hosted a whiskey-enlivened poker party in his command tent, which turned into a drunken brawl among some of his officers. Stanley had them arrested, to put an end to the melee, but they were back on duty the next morning. Custer, who was with Rosser, Jubil, Eck, and Monty, threatened to arrest Stanley himself, but Rosser convinced him otherwise. Jubil wondered with some anxiety if he or Eck would have been able to convince Custer not to mutiny on Stanley if Rosser had not been there.

The survey led out in the morning, escorted by Custer's cavalry, with Colonel Stanley's column following. The survey was headed on a line due west toward Glendive, Montana, on the Yellowstone River, with no major obstructions along the way to slow them down. The survey team hit their stride and made nineteen miles, the most they had made in a day so far.

After supper, Jubil went to his tent to relax and write to Nelly, while he listened to Custer's band. Every few days, or as events warranted, a courier was sent back to Fort Rice with mail and the journalist's dispatches, or a courier would arrive with mail from the fort. In his letter, Jubil presented a hopeful outlook but told of their difficulties so far and of his concerns, the greatest of which was that Colonel Stanley would repeat Colonel Baker's performance and upend the survey. He was not sure what he would do if that appeared imminent, but he was determined to mount a more vigorous response than he had the previous year. He told her about the journalists and alerted her to watch the *Tribune* for Barrows's articles. He hoped the interviews were enough to satisfy Sam Wilkeson and Cooke.

Jubil's hopes for another peaceful day did not survive past breakfast the next morning. He, Rosser, and his men were finishing their coffee when one of Custer's officers summoned Rosser. When Rosser returned to the table, he was steaming.

"That fool Stanley is accusing Custer of having illegally loaned an army horse to one of our survey crew. He has put him under arrest, removed him from duty, and ordered him to follow along at the end of the column for the balance of the trip."

Rosser offered to intervene on Custer's behalf, but Custer wanted to make a scene of it. As the survey and escort moved out, Custer sat off to one side at attention on his horse, watching the whole column pass him by. When it had passed, he fell in at the end.

Rosser tolerated the arrangement and put in a full day of survey work. But once camp had been established that evening, he told Jubil, Custer, and the others that he was going to talk to Stanley. When he returned to the headquarters tent where they all waited, he looked ready to explode.

"Come with me, George," Rosser commanded. "Stanley intends to offer an apology."

Custer did not get up immediately. Instead, he looked around the room and drummed his fingers on the table.

Rosser's deep resonant voice boomed out his orders, "Damn it, George, come along! I've got more important things to do than referee you and Stanley." Jubil winced, and imagined most of the surrounding camp did too.

Custer scowled at Rosser, slapped the tabletop, then stood and followed him out of the tent. Jubil looked at Eck and Monty with raised eyebrows.

"That was formidable," Jubil said admiringly. "What do you suppose he said to Stanley?"

"Nothing kindly, I expect," Monty said with a smile.

The episode raised Rosser in Jubil's regard to a new level. He doubted his own anger would have yielded the same result, but if anything like this occurred after Rosser left, Jubil was determined to emulate him as well as he could. Custer and Stanley certainly would not listen to anything less.

Stanley's apology had taken place in his command tent, with only Rosser and the second level of ranking officers present, but word of it had spread to the whole camp before they moved out the next morning. For the balance of the trip to the Yellowstone, Stanley was conspicuously absent. Whether he was drinking or just lying low, Jubil did not know. And as long as he was not threatening the success of the survey, Jubil did not care what he did.

On July 15, two days after Jubil's twenty-fourth birthday, they reached the Yellowstone River. It was the most beautiful and welcome sight he had seen on the trip so far. They were now halfway to the survey's destination of Pompey's Pillar, where the previous year's survey team had abandoned the effort and turned toward the Musselshell River. If they could just maintain the pace, and the peace, the survey would be complete. Then all he had to do was get home alive.

CHAPTER 18

General Sheridan's plan to send a steamer up the Yellowstone had succeeded. Two of them were docked at Glendive when Jubil and the survey team arrived. The army had used the ships to bring in materials and supplies for the beginnings of a fort. Sheridan had made it clear however, that nothing permanent would be built until the railroad's crossing point over the river had been fixed. Camped here were about three hundred soldiers who had come down from Fort Buford on the steamers, guarding the material that had been ferried down over the past few weeks. There was a formidable pile of building materials stored at the foot of a bluff, and their camp was between the supplies and a makeshift stockade on the river.

The Yellowstone flowed northeast here, and the survey had arrived on the south bank of the river. They had an arduous effort awaiting them, ferrying the entire column across the river, which would put the survey crew in position to move south to Pompey's Pillar, where Haydon had given up the previous year. Jubil and Rosser sat on horseback, looking across the river as Custer rode up beside them.

"Seems to me they picked a poor location to stockpile all that material," Rosser said to Custer. "They can't defend it with that bluff at their backs, looking down on them. And there's not much room to get wagons in to evacuate it. If it was up to me, I'd move it all somewhere more open, and put the stockade around it there. Plus, there's not nearly enough room on the other bank for us to move the whole column across here."

"I see your point," Custer said, as he studied the situation. "I'll go talk to Stanley."

Custer wheeled his horse around and rode off.

"Can the survey go ahead, while the army moves their materials?"

"That would not be a good idea," Rosser said, shaking his head. "We're in Sitting Bull's back yard now. We need to stay with the escort."

"How long will it take to move it all?" Jubil asked.

"A couple of weeks maybe," Rosser said with a shrug.

Jubil listened with concern—another delay.

Custer returned. "He said go ahead."

"Is that all he said?" Rosser asked.

"All that mattered," Custer said.

Rosser shook his head and frowned at Custer.

"Let's go look for a better location for our purposes," Rosser said, then started his horse toward the river.

"Mind if I ride along with you?" Jubil asked Rosser.

"Not at all," Rosser said.

The river was about two hundred feet across with a steady current, and Venus handled the challenge easily. Once across, Custer ordered the officers in charge of the supply cache to begin making preparations to move everything. Then he, Rosser, and Jubil set off upriver along the north bank, looking for a more suitable location. About ten miles south of Glendive they found a spacious flat area between Sand Creek and Cedar Creek and rode back to convey orders to start the move.

The soldiers began the process of loading the building materials onto the *Josephine* while the other steamer, the *Key West*, moved down to the stockade and waited there to ferry Stanley's column across the Yellowstone. Meanwhile, Rosser,

Jubil, and Custer crossed back over the river, with Rosser deftly carrying a bag of mail that had come for them by steamboat, and went to report to Stanley. They found him in his command tent, sitting with two other officers, a bottle of whiskey on the table. Stanley was sipping from a tin cup.

"We found a superior location upriver for the stockade and for the column to cross," Rosser explained as Stanley sat listening disinterestedly. "You can start moving down there tomorrow. The *Key West* is there to start ferrying you across."

"Or we can rest here comfortably while both steamers move the material, and then begin the ferry operation," Stanley said dismissively.

Rosser clenched his jaw and frowned.

"I thought we might go ahead and move your farriers over," Rosser said, containing his anger. "We could get a lot of animals reshod while the rest of the move is taking place."

"Yes...I was thinking of having them start their forges tomorrow," Stanley said, "but on this side of the river." He took a sip from his cup and waited for Rosser's response.

"We can decide tomorrow," Rosser said, and stalked out of Stanley's tent.

Rosser was silent until he and Jubil returned to his headquarters tent, where Eck and Monty were waiting. He tossed the mail pouch on the table, and Monty began to sort it.

"If Colonel Stanley dawdles too long, or makes matters overly difficult, I swear I'll..." Rosser stopped himself. "Well... I'll not allow it."

Monty was listening but continued sorting mail. He tossed a letter in front of Jubil. He was excited to see it was from Nelly, but he would wait until later to read it. Monty tossed a few letters in front of Rosser. Rosser flicked through them, picked one out, and opened it.

"The date for the Northern Pacific Board meeting has been set," Rosser said. "I'll need to leave in about two weeks—no later than July 29. The *Josephine* has orders to take me out whenever I'm ready. I have to be in New York by August 4."

Jubil had known it was coming, but he had hoped they would be closer to Pompey's Pillar, and the completion of the survey, before Rosser had to leave. As it was, they were only halfway, delayed by helping the army with its fort and by Colonel Stanley becoming a greater problem each week. Jubil retired to his tent to read his letter from Nelly.

Dearest Jubil,
I hope this letter finds you safe and well, and that you remain so and hurry home to me. The apartment too often has a lonely feel without you or Mama. I'm very happy she is at home again, but I had grown accustomed to her presence. She helped distract me from how much I miss you. I have been doing my best to remain busy.

Miss Anthony was finally brought to trial for having illegally voted in the last presidential election. In the end, the judge declared to the jury the evidence left them no choice but a verdict of guilty. Mrs. Stanton believes this violated Miss Anthony's right to trial by jury, but I don't know if a formal challenge will be made. The judge fined her one hundred dollars, which she refused to pay, but he released her anyway, and that was end of it. He publicly humiliated her by simply dismissing her. I believe his actions will inflame the movement—women will not allow themselves to simply be dismissed.

Thankfully, you are never guilty of such inconsiderate behavior. Another of the many reasons why I love you. I fervently hope for the successful completion of the survey and your safe return home.
Truly yours,
Nelly

Jubil agreed with what Nelly said, and wished the woman suffrage situation would show more improvement, both because it was the right thing to do, but also because of the stress he saw it putting on her. He cherished getting her letters, but always had a moment of melancholy after the sharp reminder of how much he missed her.

The next morning, Rosser convinced Stanley of the wisdom of sending the farriers across the river first. After some arguing, they also agreed to a plan for which group to position next for crossing. Early in the afternoon, once the farrier's crossing was well underway, Rosser found the next group had not been moved into position. Stanley had never given them the order.

When Rosscr returned to the headquarters tent that evening, he was angry.

"That man is sorely trying my patience," Rosser fumed. "He is intentionally making matters difficult, out of spite. If he doesn't pick up the pace tomorrow…"

Jubil and the others waited for Rosser to finish his thought, but he just sat rapping his knuckles on the tabletop.

"Would you like for me to try talking to him?" Jubil offered.

"Good of you to offer," Rosser said, looking up at Jubil. "I mean no offense, but I don't know why he would listen to you, if he won't listen to me. You're welcome to try though, but don't feel obliged."

"Your probably right," Jubil said. "I'll save my ammunition until you're gone. I'll have no choice then."

The next day was a repeat of the previous, as Rosser struggled to get Stanley's cooperation. That evening as Rosser, Jubil, Eck, and Monty had their usual evening gathering in the headquarters tent after supper, Custer came in.

"I just came to warn you to expect a slow start in the morning," Custer said to Rosser. "Part of the cargo the steamers moved today was fourteen barrels of whiskey. The sutler's wagons have been fully restocked. Stanley and his poker buddies have tapped a new keg and lit their cigars."

Rosser scowled at Custer and banged his fist on the table.

"This is too much!" Rosser fumed. "We can't have this…"

"I could order him arrested," Custer offered.

"You know you can't do that, George," Rosser said, looking at his friend with a sad smile. "You'd be tried for mutiny, and your enemies would be gleeful at the excuse to hang you."

Custer stuck his thumbs in his belt and shrugged.

"I had originally expected to reach Pompey's Pillar by now," Rosser said. "His whiskey is inexcusably slowing us down."

As long as it was available, it seemed to Jubil it was going to make matters worse, just as it had the previous year. Without it, Stanley might still be obstreperous, but at least he wouldn't also be drunk.

"Maybe we could arrange some mishap that destroys the whiskey supply," Jubil said. "It's too bad it didn't all roll off the deck of the steamer and get swept down the Yellowstone."

Rosser drummed his fingers on the tabletop, then wagged a finger at Jubil.

"That is a very devious idea," Rosser said with a grin. "Jay Cooke would be proud."

Jubil laughed.

"You'll find I'm not a very devious sort," Rosser said. "I try to go straight through whatever's in the way. So let's just go destroy it."

"Destroy the whiskey?" Monty asked with a frown. "Now?"

"Yes!" Rosser said. "Let's not rely on some plot that might fail, or further delay matters. Let's just go dump the whiskey out on the plains."

"I'm in, Tex," Custer said, smiling at his old friend.

Monty and Eck rose as well, grinning.

"Me too," Jubil said, rising from the table.

Rosser led his band of vigilantes out of the tent. It was

well past sundown, but the torches around camp provided plenty of light. All the wagons were pulled into a square on the north end of camp. The livestock were corralled inside, and a picket had been set around the perimeter. Stanley's headquarters tent and social club, was located on the south end of camp. Rosser led them to one of the surveyor wagons and opened a compartment on its side. He reached in and started handing out axes.

"These will speed up the job."

Jubil grasped the hickory handle, worn smooth by other men's hands sliding along its length thousands of times. He felt the heft of the double-edged steel head and marveled at what they were about to do. He would never have expected to feel such rowdy anticipation for what was, at its heart, an act of vandalism. Armed with their weapons of destruction, they followed Rosser down the line of wagons. The guards saluted Custer and let them pass unchallenged.

Custer pointed out the two sutler's wagons serving his cavalry and the four serving Stanley's infantry.

Jubil had never seen anything quite like the sutler's wagons. They were like miniature general stores on wheels—they carried clothing, toilet items, writing supplies, and whiskey.

Rosser and Custer each climbed into a sutler's wagon and began to hand the whiskey out. There were thirteen quarter-barrel kegs, each holding about eight gallons. Each keg stood a little over a foot tall but weighed about ninety pounds. Jubil and Monty took the kegs as they were handed out of the wagon and rolled them out onto the plains, well away from the livestock and the torches that lit the area. Two guards stood nearby, amazement dawning on their faces.

They spread out into a rough circle a few yards apart—Rosser, Custer, and Jubil each with three barrels, Eck and Monty each with two.

Once everyone was in position, Rosser called, "Don't be shy

boys!" and took a mighty swing. The blade of the axe hit the head of the oak barrel with a sound like a drum.

Jubil had to suppress laughter as he watched Rosser take his frustration out on the whiskey barrel. He then followed suit, swinging the axe lightly, just to get a feel for it, and laughing when the axe connected and his own barrel made a drum tone. He took another swing, this time with all his might, and was satisfied when the blade sank deep into the wood. Once they all were all swinging their axes, they created a crazy melody of drum tones and the sound of splintering wood.

It took a dozen or so well-positioned strikes to break through the barrel staves, but once the integrity of the barrel had been compromised, the hole was easier to expand.

"Make sure you open them up good," Rosser shouted, "and drain them out."

Jubil felt a strange mixture of emotions as he worked: he was guilty of bad behavior, certainly, but he also felt liberated because he was in good company, working toward a worthy cause. He rolled his first barrel so that it would drain and set to work on another. The pungent aroma of the whiskey began to fill the air so thickly he could literally taste it—which he did not much care for.

He had overindulged on whiskey during the Colorado River expedition through the Grand Canyon, driven to it after Major Powell had chastised him for losing control of his boat and smashing it up on the rocks, an incalculable loss. When Jubil's friend Andy Hall revealed that he had recovered a whiskey keg from the wreckage, Jubil attempted to drown his sorrows in it. He had regretted the decision later, when his aching head and pasty mouth made him even more miserable than he had been in the first place.

The men gathered again when the job was complete.

"When Stanley's poker party keg runs dry," Rosser said, grinning, "that's the end of it for this trip."

The next morning as Jubil awoke he lay worrying whether their act of vandalism might have cost him the survey. What if Colonel Stanley decided, as Baker had done last year, that he was not moving, or worse, was withdrawing? Custer would probably mutiny and who knew what that meant? But Rosser had allowed them no time to consider such possibilities, and they had all gone along with him gleefully. Jubil ate breakfast alone, quietly waiting to hear talk about last night's events, but to his surprise there was none. Later in the day, Custer reported that when Stanley was brought the news of the whiskey raid, he went into a profane tirade, but that was the end of it. There was no retaliation. Custer said he thought Stanley had realized his behavior had earned him this outcome and didn't want to have to answer for it to General Sheridan.

What did set Stanley off however, was Fred Grant. Apparently, Fred decided he had seen all of the Northern Pacific Railroad survey he had any use for and had abandoned the expedition. Stanley claimed the young Mr. Grant was being disrespectful, but Jubil thought what had really upset him was that Fred told Custer he was leaving but had not told Stanley. Jubil found himself agreeing with Stanley. He could see no good reason for Grant not taking a moment to inform Stanley. His failure to do so was then either intentional or thoughtless, but Jubil had not gotten to know Grant well enough to judge for himself which it was. But Custer liked him, so Jubil's guess was that the slight was probably intentional.

Grant had commandeered a yawl from one of the steamers, and Custer had sent a half dozen of his men along with him as an escort. That crew, along with the two journalists following him, had set off rowing down the Yellowstone for Fort Buford.

Without the whiskey to impede progress, the remaining contents of the stockade were moved, and the rest of Stanley's column was ferried across the Yellowstone. The survey and escort were now gathered along the north side of the Yellowstone, ready to move toward Pompey's Pillar. But this was the end of the line for Rosser. The *Josephine* was taking him back to Fort Buford.

Jubil was sorry to see him go. The two men sat one last time together in the survey headquarters tent the morning Rosser was to leave.

"I hope we can manage to finish the job without you," Jubil said.

"You'll do fine," Rosser said.

"You're expecting Sitting Bull to give us a friendly wave as we pass by?" Jubil asked with a grin.

"That's possible," Rosser said, matching Jubil's grin, "but not likely."

There was a more serious matter Jubil wanted to clarify before saying good-bye to Rosser. "The survey line last year was supposed to go right through the Crow reservation, on the south bank of the Yellowstone," he said, "but we couldn't get across to that side. We detoured along the high ground north of the river, and Haydon surveyed along that line, but he was planning to go back and redo the survey along the south bank—that's when Baker dug in and Haydon abandoned the survey. If we meet the line where he ended it, on the north side of the river, is our line going to be useable?"

"I understand your confusion," Rosser said. "The line on the north side that Muhlenberg surveyed in 1871 was too near the river channel to have ever been feasible—which is why he was fired and the survey had to be done over. To his credit, Haydon found a passable route to the north, along the higher ground away from the river. Even if he had completed the survey along the south bank, Cooke did not have a government agreement in place to move the reservation. He was counting on getting that done after the survey."

"So, when we connect our new line to the line we surveyed last year, we can call the survey a success?" Jubil asked.

"We'll call it that," Rosser said with a shrug. "The south bank would still be an easier route to build on, but the political cost of moving the Crow reservation will probably prevent that. Someone might call for another survey before construction starts though. Assuming it ever does."

"If it ever does? It's already finished to Bismarck," Jubil said.

"True, I should have said if construction continues," Rosser said, meeting Jubil's gaze.

"Is there some doubt?" Jubil asked.

"There is no doubt about the intent," Rosser said, "if the financing can be found. That is why I have to leave early for the board meeting. Bond sales are down, credit is getting tighter, and banks are moving onto shakier ground. Mr. Cooke's financial empire is feeling the pressure, and we are meeting to discuss strategies."

"My agreement with Mr. Cooke hinges on the successful completion of the survey," Jubil said, "not the completion of the railroad. My investment is returned if the survey succeeds."

"Then you should be fine," Rosser said, "as long as he remains financially solvent long enough to honor your agreement."

"Do you think he might not?" Jubil asked. Abe had warned that Cooke's financial empire was built on debt.

"It's not entirely dependent on what Cooke alone does or does not do," Rosser explained. "Financial networks of investors, banks, and investment houses have an interdependence that requires a certain balance to remain functional. If one part gets too far out of balance, the whole thing can fly apart."

"Is something getting out of balance?" Jubil asked, concerned he might be getting out of his depth.

"We have been living in boom times since the end of the

war," Rosser said, "particularly in the railroad business. There is such great confidence that building railroads is the key to settling this land and bringing unheralded prosperity that we have indulged excesses in building them. The most vulnerable right now are banks that have made questionable loans, betting that general prosperity will protect them from their own risky behavior."

Jubil shook his head, recognizing that he had lost the plot.

"The banks are vulnerable," Rosser explained, "because they work only on the strength of public perception and behavior. People deposit money in the bank, which the bank lends out to make a profit. Once money has been loaned and spent, but not yet repaid, the assets of the bank are less than its deposits. That is not a problem, as long as everyone does not want their deposits back at once. But if they do, the house of cards collapses. If people believe the bank has made bad loans, ones that will never be repaid, they don't want to be the last to withdraw their money from that bank before it folds. If those banks are threatened and call in a heavy load of Mr. Cooke's outstanding loans, he won't be able to service his debt."

Jubil didn't like the sound of that. A feeling of unease was hollowing out the pit of his stomach. "What are the chances of that happening?" he asked.

"I don't know," Rosser said. "It may well depend on how the rest of the survey goes—whether people believe the railroad can ever be completed and whether the people financing it can ever repay the costs of building it."

Jubil was beginning to appreciate the adage *Ignorance is bliss*. The more he learned, the more concerned he became. Rosser's openness and good nature inspired Jubil to confide in him.

"When I entered into my agreement with Cooke," Jubil said, "I was focused on the likelihood that you and your crew, backed by the force of the army, could complete the survey. I felt that risk was acceptable, and I still do. But I hadn't fully grasped the larger risk of the whole enterprise. Cooke holds the deeds to my store in Council Bluffs and my family farm in Illinois. If this whole thing goes belly up, I stand to lose them."

"Oh," Rosser said with a frown. "So that is what assures Cooke of your commitment?"

Jubil nodded.

"You might still be all right," Rosser said. "I think the odds are very good the crew will make it to Pompey's Pillar, though Sitting Bull is bound to show up along the line. If you can get back to Philadelphia quickly enough, maybe you can claim victory before anything threatens the financial system. I'm sorry to leave you, but it's time I was on my way. Best of luck to you, Mr. Walker. It has been a pleasure working with you."

Jubil walked to the dock with Rosser and watched the steamer take him down the Yellowstone to Fort Buford. Their conversation had left him shaken. If Jay Cooke's financial empire collapsed, it wouldn't matter if they completed the survey or not. Jubil's property would be lost.

CHAPTER 19

Pompey's Pillar was still one hundred ninety miles away. For the next several days, the survey and escort made their way along hard-packed treeless ground under a blazing August sun. Eck had the survey well in hand, and he had the full support of his crew, but Jubil missed riding with Rosser. He offered himself up to Eck and Monty as a general laborer and always found work with the axe-men, chainmen, or picket-men. The axe-men cleared the path for the tracks by removing brush, trees, and rocks along the line, or often helped clear or level pathways for the wagons. The chain-men extended the measuring chains from each point the transitmen staked out to the next one they set along the line. The picket-men drove the stakes at the points identified by the transitmen and tied strips of red cloth to flag the stakes. These jobs were a constructive way to pass the time, but Jubil was growing weary of the monotony.

To everyone's relief, Custer and Stanley ignored one another, and the Indians went about their business elsewhere.

After supper, he, Custer, Eck, and Monty gathered in the headquarters tent just to pass the time, as they often did. But this evening, Jubil was feeling restless. They had come about seventy miles since leaving Rosser at the stockade, and the pace of the survey was beginning to feel ponderously slow.

"If you'll be riding out tomorrow to scout for our next campsite," Jubil said to Custer, "I'd like to ride with you."

"And delay the survey by denying us our best laborer?" Monty asked with a grin.

"I was wondering when the surveying life would become too tame for our adventurous new friend," Eck said to Monty.

"I confess to being ready for a change of pace," Jubil said with a shrug.

"You know if there is trouble of any sort," Custer said, "it will find me first, and you by proximity."

"It would probably find me anyway," Jubil said.

Custer stroked his horseshoe-shaped moustache, and considered Jubil's request.

"My last ward was Fred Grant," Custer said. "He ran out on me. Will you do the same?"

"No," Jubil laughed, "I'll stick with you."

"You do that," Custer said. "Don't go wandering off where I can't see you. I do not want to explain to Jay Cooke how I lost his man."

In the morning, he retrieved White Dog's medicine bag from his pack and put it on. He did not feel right chasing after Sitting Bull without it. He cleaned and oiled his rifle, which he had not carried most of the time, and saddled up Venus. She seemed excited for a change of pace too. He rode to the south edge of camp, where Custer was organizing a company of men for the day. He stood talking with three other officers as Jubil rode up and dismounted.

"Mr. Walker, meet some of my officers," Custer said. "My brother, Captain Tom Custer, my brother-in-law, First Lieutenant James Calhoun, and Colonel Charles Varner, my chief of scouts."

Jubil shook hands with the men. He was surprised that Custer had family along on the trip but had not mentioned them when spending most of his evenings with Rosser, Jubil, and the survey crew. It appeared Custer kept his private life and military life separate.

Tom Custer was a few years younger than his older brother but bore a strong family resemblance to him. His hair and mustache were the same reddish-brown color but cut shorter, his face and nose were long and thin, very much like his brother's. It was Lieutenant Colonel Custer who seemed to have gotten all the flamboyance in the family, though.

Custer's bother-in-law was about the same age as Custer. Jubil wondered whether his wife looked like her brothers.

"I believe we're ready to go," Custer said. "Move them out, Tom."

Custer had about one hundred men in his scouting party—ninety soldiers, five officers, and a handful of Indian scouts, none of whom Jubil had met. They set off at 6:00 a.m. while the day was still cool. The survey party and Stanley's column would catch up to Custer at the end of the day. About eight miles south of their Sunday Creek campsite, the route along the Yellowstone was determined by a steep bluff that arose along the bank. The scouting party rode up a fairly steep incline of about three hundred feet with little effort, but Jubil knew the wagons would find the climb a challenge. At the top of the bluff, they found themselves riding on a ridgeline that extended several miles along the river.

As they followed a buffalo trail along the top of the ridge, one of the scouts spotted recent tracks of Indian ponies, but they saw no Indians. After about ten miles, the trail led down onto a mile-wide grassy floodplain next to the river. A large patch of cottonwood trees stood along a bend in the river. They had come about eighteen miles from their previous camp. It would be a long day for the survey and Stanley's column, but it was doable. They would camp here and wait for Stanley's column to catch up. It was late morning, and Jubil's ride for the day was already over. He would have preferred to keep moving rather than spend most of the day waiting, but that was not an option.

Custer led his company over to the stand of cottonwoods, where they unsaddled their horses and turned them out to graze. Most of the soldiers scattered out through the trees to nap or play cards, while others sat by the river or fished. A few restless souls wandered off along the river toward the big hill they had just come down. Custer was among those who chose to nap, but Jubil was not sleepy.

It would have been a good opportunity to write Nelly, but he had left his pack on the wagon and had no writing materials. Instead, he sat down and leaned against a tree in the shade of the cottonwoods and watched Venus graze among the other horses. He wondered how Star was doing with her pregnancy, how Apollo was managing without him, and how his old friend Rocky, now the carriage horse, was holding up. As noon approached, the heat of the day rose, and Jubil nodded off to sleep.

He was startled awake by someone shouting.

"Bring in your horses! Bring in your horses!"

The company bugler began to blow "Boots and Saddles."

Soldiers scrambled out of the woods to retrieve their horses. Jubil assumed that Indians had been spotted, but he had heard no gunfire. He looked across the field to pick out Venus. Her coloring was the same as many of the horses. He could have picked Apollo or Star from a herd of a thousand at a glance. He thought he spotted her and ran to check—it was her. He removed her hobbles and led her back to the woods. As he was saddling her, Custer rode up.

"The guards spotted a group of Sioux between us and that stand of trees a couple of miles upriver," Custer said. "I'm going to go have a look. I meant what I said—I'd rather you stay right with me, if you're up to it. Or you can stay here, and I'll put a guard with you."

"I'll stay with you," Jubil said. He put his jacket on and checked the pockets to confirm he had extra ammunition. He slid his rifle into the saddle scabbard, strapped on his revolver, mounted up, and followed Custer.

Custer assembled a group of twenty men, led by his brother Tom, and rode to the far end of the stand of trees. About two miles south was another stand of trees along the riverbank, and in between was an expanse of chest-high grass. In that field of grass, just out of rifle range, six Indians sat on their ponies, watching them.

Custer spread his men out in a line facing the Indians—Custer, Jubil, and Tom, in the middle—then led them forward at a trot. The Indians watched for a minute, then turned and rode away to the south, toward the other stand of trees, then stopped and turned to face them again. Custer approached them again, and they retreated again, moving closer to the trees, and stopped. Custer kept approaching, but this time they stood pat. Custer's line was now about midway between their camp and the stand of trees behind the Indians.

"I recognize the one with the full headdress—Rain-in-the-Face," Custer said to Tom. "That means Sitting Bull is either in those woods or not far away. He either wants to talk, or he's just baiting us. I'll try the former, but I expect the latter. When I ride out, take half the men on foot and sneak along in the tall grass to cover me."

"You stay with Tom," Custer said to Jubil, and turned to ride away.

Tom Custer took half the men and left the rest to hold the horses. Custer rode out at a walk, his right hand up to show he meant peace. Jubil took his rifle and followed Tom and his men through the tall grass. He had a moment of wishing he had not put himself in the front ranks of a confrontation, but now that he had he owed it to his fellows to help defend their position. About one hundred yards out, Tom signaled Jubil and the rest of his line to stop while Custer rode another fifty yards ahead. Jubil could see Custer signing a message with his hands, but he could not see the Indians. The Indians gave Custer less than a minute before they opened fire. Custer turned his horse and raced back toward Tom's line, with the Indians in pursuit. As Custer raced past them, Tom signaled the men to stay down. Tom watched the Indians approach, and when they were thirty yards out, he gave his order.

"Stand and fire!"

The men rose up out of the grass and fired. Jubil rose up along with them but his rifle misfired and the surprise slowed him for a moment. By the time he had levered a new round into the chamber he could see the startled Indians had turned and fled, so he held his fire. In spite of all the gunfire from Tom's soldiers, none of the riders were hit. As they rode for the trees, the rest of their band charged out after Custer. Jubil estimated there were at least two hundred of them. Far more than Custer's scouting party.

"Fall back," Tom ordered.

Jubil raced back to Venus. Custer was waiting there.

"We'll have to fight our way back to camp!" Custer said. "Every fourth man hold horses while the rest of you fan out in an arc—fire to hold them as we retreat."

Jubil grabbed the reins from four of the soldiers and walked the horses back toward camp as the soldiers formed their defensive line and fired. The Indians outnumbered them ten to one but did not amass a charge. Instead, they made feints toward the soldiers then fell back or rode past their line, seemingly content to harass rather than overrun them. Why this was, Jubil was not sure, but he was grateful. The Indians' fighting style allowed the soldiers to half walk, half double-time their way back to camp. In spite of all the shooting, Jubil had not seen anyone, neither soldier nor Indian, hit. He thought this was curious. Once they reached camp, the Indians fell back, firing occasionally to keep the soldiers pinned in the woods.

The stand of trees they were camped in formed a semi-circle up against the river. Along the perimeter of the trees was a raised embankment left by a previous channel of the river. To the north, about a mile away, was the big hill they had come down earlier. Colonel Stanley would be coming down that hill later, but he would not arrive for hours, though it was possible his scouts would hear the gunfire and Stanley would send reinforcements ahead. Jubil was still holding a group of horses when Custer came over.

"You all right?" Custer asked.

"I'm fine. Why haven't they just overrun us?" Jubil asked.

"Their weapons and skill with them are inferior to ours," Custer said. "Though I did notice our fire was errant on that foray. They also have limited ammunition, though we have to be cautious about that as well."

A small group of Indians, out of rifle range, rode past camp over to the base of the big hill north of them.

"What are they doing?" Jubil asked.

"They're setting a guard along the buffalo trail we followed down off the ridge," Custer said. "That will prevent us from sending a rider out to Stanley for reinforcements, and it will alert the Indians if he arrives. We're penned in." Custer noticed something. "I need you to keep those horses ready to ride."

"Yes sir," Jubil said, and Custer was off again, walking the perimeter and giving orders.

Jubil was actually relieved that Custer had assigned him a noncombat role. It took the decision about fighting out of his hands.

The battle settled into a siege. The Indians fired from a distance occasionally to keep the soldiers trapped, and the soldiers returned fire when the Indians ventured too close. It was now midafternoon, and the temperature had risen into the high nineties, with no breeze. Jubil made sure the horses he was tending were hobbled and went to retrieve his canteen. As he sipped his water, Venus gave him a look that said—how about me? The scouting party had travelled light, so they had no cooking pots for him to collect water in. He decided his hat would have to do, and headed for the river.

He walked down to the river and leaned his rifle against a large boulder before removing his hat and kneeling down to fill it. As he stood up holding his hat-full of water in both hands, he realized he would have to come back for his rifle. He stepped out from behind the boulder and saw movement to his left. Looking upriver he was startled to see a long line of Indians, sneaking along the riverbank toward camp. The one in front fired at Jubil, and he heard the buzz of the round as it missed him. Instinctively he jumped back behind the cover of the boulder and grabbed his rifle. He peeked around the edge of his cover and saw at least a dozen Indians charging up the riverbank to overwhelm him, with more behind them.

The Indians charging him were about one hundred yards away and closing fast. The safety of the trees and the cavalry was about fifty feet away with no cover in between. He had vowed at the end of the honeymoon that he would no longer put himself in life threatening situations, and yet here he was again. He wedged his wet hat onto his head and ran for the trees, holding his Henry rifle waist-high and rapid-firing as quickly as he could lever shells into the chamber. He saw one Indian spin and fall as a shot hit his shoulder. Jubil dove back into the woods where he saw Custer looking his way.

"They're trying to sneak in behind us!" Jubil shouted.

Custer ordered men to the river, and they drove the Indians back.

As the afternoon wore on, Jubil was watching the ridgeline of the big hill, hoping to see Stanley coming to the rescue, when he spotted smoke. At first it was just in a single spot, but soon it spread into a long line of gray billowing clouds. The Indians had set a line of grass on fire that was burning toward camp. At first, he was unsure what the point was, since the burning grass would pose no threat to the soldiers in the woods, but soon it became clear—they were using the smoke as cover to get closer to the soldiers. The closer the fires burned to the woods, the heavier the incoming fire was from the Indians. When soldiers caught a glimpse of any movement though the smoke, they all fired in that direction. Soon Jubil heard Custer cautioning the men.

"Guard your ammunition!" Custer said. "Wait for your shot!"

The fires continued to burn toward the woods, but the smokescreen began to thin out, as the grass closer to the river was greener, and there was less thatch to burn. As the fires failed to yield the result the Indians were hoping for, they retreated to a safer distance and resumed their pattern of occasional firing.

Another billowing cloud rose up from along the top of ridge. Jubil could not imagine how burning the grass at the top of the big hill was going to bear on the battle, when he realized the color of the cloud was tan, not gray—dust, not smoke. Jubil was not the only one to notice, as he saw Custer running along his defensive perimeter, shouting to his men and pointing in that direction.

"Stanley is coming! Prepare to mount up!"

Jubil ran to the group of horses he was tending, removed their hobbles and held their reins, waiting for their riders to claim them. Then he mounted Venus and waited for Custer's orders.

Finally, the sight he had been hoping to see appeared at the top of the ridge. The rest of Custer's Seventh Cavalry came streaming down the big hill with the bugler blowing "charge." Jubil breathed a sigh of relief and rested his rifle across his lap. The group of Indians at the bottom of the hill stirred their ponies into a gallop and rode away, alerting the rest of the band of Indians. The Indians raced south toward the farther stand of trees. Custer rode up to Jubil again.

"We're going in pursuit—you stay here. You'll be fine now," Custer said, then wheeled his horse and rode away.

That was fine with Jubil. He sat on Venus and watched the chase unfold as Custer's scouting party joined the rest of his men and went after the Indians. Stanley's infantry followed on, making their way slowly down the hill, followed by the wagons, then the cattle. It took nearly an hour for the whole column to come down the hill onto the floodplain. The grass had been depleted somewhat by the fires, but not enough to ruin the campsite. Jubil unsaddled Venus and led her down to the river to drink. In an hour or so, Custer's cavalry was back in camp, having driven the Indians away.

It had been a stressful day but not as bloody as Jubil had expected. It seemed to him a small miracle. None of the soldiers had been killed, and only two were wounded but not badly. If there had been any Indians killed, they had been removed, as no bodies were found. The only one Jubil had seen hit was the one he had wounded himself on the riverbank.

CHAPTER 20

For the next few days, the survey route along the river was unobstructed, the weather was cooler, and they saw no sign of Indians. The battle seemed to have renewed Custer's and Stanley's willingness to cooperate. Custer and his cavalry stayed with Stanley's main column rather than ride ahead, so Jubil returned to his routine of helping Eck and Monty as a chainman, picket-man, or axe-man as needed. With each day, they made good mileage toward Pompey's Pillar.

He had just begun to allow himself to believe the Indians had decided to avoid them, when they came across one of their abandoned campsites. At the junction of the Rosebud and the Yellowstone they found evidence of what Custer said was probably Sitting Bull's main camp. It was alarmingly large. The grass on the trail leading away was flattened by Indian travois in a path forty yards wide. It looked as though they had made a hasty exit. The area was littered with lodgepoles, paddles, moccasins, food, personal items, even some war paint. It had to have been a camp of several hundred. Certainly, more than had attacked them at the big hill.

If this was not unsettling enough, the next day they came across another abandoned camp and more items left in haste. This one was not quite as large as the first but still had held several hundred people who appeared to have joined the other retreating group. This meant the Indians' numbers were definitely greater than Custer's five hundred cavalry, and maybe even as many as Stanley's fifteen hundred. And there could very well be more of them out there that these people were fleeing to join. Jubil had gone to have a look at the abandoned camp and was on his way back to join Eck and Monty when Custer rode up.

"Colonel Stanley and I have decided that I should take the cavalry forward," Custer said. "It looks like Sitting Bull is retreating, and we want to keep him moving that direction. Hopefully the cavalry's presence will push him on, but we'll engage him if we must. You can either stay here with Colonel Stanley or ride ahead with me. What's your preference?"

Though staying with Stanley sounded like the safer option, there was no guarantee that would be the case. The infantry, in spite of their greater numbers, was still vulnerable to the harassing tactics of Indians on horseback, and ambush. Besides, Jubil had to admit he generally felt safer in Custer's company, especially in the face of danger. Custer seemed to live a charmed life, and being in his presence might improve Jubil's odds.

He'd had a similar feeling about his friend Lew Keplinger, with whom he had climbed Longs Peak. Lew had served in combat under General Sherman through all his major campaigns in the Civil War and never been wounded. Occasionally Lew's sense of invulnerability made him plainly reckless; nevertheless, Jubil admired and emulated it.

"My preference is to ride with you," Jubil said. "But you should know, I'll not take part in any massacre. If I'm attacked and forced to defend myself, I will, but that's where I draw the line."

"Fair enough," Custer said. "My hope is to use our presence mainly as a deterrent. I'm even taking the band along to serenade Sitting Bull. That should run him off!"

Jubil chuckled. "All right."

"Pack up and have a nap," Custer said. "We'll leave tonight and try to gain some ground on them."

Jubil was pleasantly surprised to find that Sam Barrows, the journalist for the *New York Tribune*, was also riding with Custer, and they rode together when Custer and the Seventh Cavalry left after dark.

The moonlight was adequate for the scouts to follow Sitting Bull's trail, and the route was over easy ground. The cavalry traveled considerably faster than Stanley's column, and by first light they had gone about twenty miles further up the Yellowstone. Custer ordered a three-hour break, and then they were on the move again. By afternoon, they had made another fifteen miles under a hot sun, and Custer ordered a five-hour midday break. Jubil expected another long night of riding, but late in the afternoon they came to a point where Sitting Bull's trail abruptly ended at the Yellowstone. One of the Indian scouts swam his pony across the river and came back reporting that Sitting Bull's trail continued on the other side.

It was too late in the day for Custer to try to move his whole group across the river, so he ordered his men to make camp. They were about two miles below the junction of the Bighorn River and the Yellowstone, and only about thirty miles from Pompey's Pillar—a two-day ride, at most. It felt oddly precarious to be so close to his goal, as if something might occur at any moment to dash his hopes. Last year's failed effort now seemed long ago, but the effects of its surprise ending still lingered.

In the morning, the effort to move Custer's troops across the Yellowstone did not go smoothly. The Yellowstone was about one hundred fifty yards wide here, clear of rocks and other debris, with a strong current. The Indian ponies were accustomed to the river and had no trouble crossing it, but the current was too strong for most of the cavalry horses, and they floundered or swam downstream with the current rather than across or refused to enter the river at all. Custer had his Indian scouts try to run a rope across the river, to build a raft system, but gave up after breaking the rope on three tries. The difficulty of the crossing had given Custer cause to rethink his plan.

"I'm calling off the effort to cross," Jubil heard him say to his brother. "As long as Sitting Bull stays on the south side of the river and leaves us the north side, I'll not put us to the task of chasing him."

Jubil agreed wholeheartedly with Custer's position and went to bed that evening looking forward to moving on and getting the survey completed. Sometime in the night he was awakened by what he thought was the sound of running horses, but when he lifted his head to listen, he heard nothing. He assumed it must have been a dream and went back to sleep.

At dawn, the air was cool, and a blanket of mist hung over the river. As Jubil was on his way to breakfast, he thought he saw movement on the opposite bank. He stood for a moment and watched with relief through the haze as three antelope dashed away. He joined Custer and Sam Barrows at the campfire while the cook worked on breakfast.

"Good morning, gents," Jubil said as he helped himself to a cup of coffee and returned the pot to the grill over the fire. He stood warming himself and sipping the strong brew.

"Morning, Jubil," Barrows said. "Ready for another day of adventure?"

A gunshot rang out, and a bullet struck their coffee pot with a dull clang, sending it flying. Custer sprang up and looked for the shooter as Barrows tossed his coffee aside and dove for the ground. Jubil dropped to one knee, preserving his coffee. As the guards began to return fire, Custer watched the scene for a moment.

"Hold your fire!" he ordered. "It's just a few renegades. Save your ammunition."

The guards ceased fire, and the camp activity became more organized. Soldiers scrambled for their weapons and for cover, while others, including Sam Barrows and Jubil, sat wolfing down their breakfast while they had a chance. The Indians fired occasionally, just to keep everyone on the defensive. As the sun rose and the mist lifted from the river, Jubil could see more Indians gathering on the south bank of the Yellowstone.

A small crowd was gathering around one of the guards who had a long-barreled Springfield rifle. He aimed across the river and fired, and the men around him cheered as an Indian fell from his horse.

"Pick out another one," the guard said to his companions. One of them pointed out a target, the guard fired again, and that Indian, too, dropped to the ground.

"If I were you, Private Tuttle, I'd not draw quite so much attention to myself," Custer shouted. "The Indians may not be the marksman you are, but they do get lucky."

The shooter laughed and ignored Custer's warning. He challenged his friends to choose another target. They humored him, and Private Tuttle leaned into his rifle once more and took aim. But before he could fire, a shot hit him in square in the forehead, and he flew backward in a shower of blood. The men around him scrambled for cover. Jubil watched the scene with a strange sense of detachment and acceptance. Custer had warned Tuttle what would happen, and it did. He had seen a man shot in the head before, and the experience caused him to retch and to have nightmares for days. But this time he was strangely unmoved.

"Damn fool." Custer shook his head in disgust and turned to address Jubil. "I'm sending Lieutenant Braden with a platoon to mount that ridge north of us and protect our flank, also to have a look to the east and west. He'll be away from the gunfire, for the moment at least. You and Mr. Barrows can ride with him if you'd like."

"I will, thanks," Jubil said.

Barrows considered the prospect, probably wondering where the best story would be, then agreed as well. Jubil saddled Venus, and gathered up his weapons, just in case, and slung the strap of his field glasses over his shoulder. He and Barrows rode with Lieutenant Braden and twenty soldiers across an open plain to the base of a ridge about fifty feet high some two hundred yards north of camp. Braden ordered a few men to stay at the base of the ridge to hold the horses while the rest of them scampered up for a look around.

Jubil was beside Lieutenant Braden as they crested the ridge and saw about a hundred mounted warriors fifty yards out and riding straight toward them. The warriors began firing, and beside Jubil, Lieutenant Braden jerked back and cried out in pain. Jubil saw blood gush from his thigh. Braden rolled backward down the slope as Jubil and the other soldiers dropped back below the ridgeline. The soldiers began firing on the approaching riders, who were harassing them rather than mounting a serious charge, and Jubil scooted down the slope to see if he could help Braden.

The wound was bad. The shot had entered the inside of his right leg about four inches below his crotch and hit an artery. Each of Braden's panicked heartbeats forced a stream of blood from the wound. Jubil pressed down on it as hard as he could with his left hand as he worked to remove the belt from Braden's pants to use as a tourniquet. A few years ago, White Dog had been shot in the thigh and Jubil's belt had stemmed the bleeding. But White Dog's wound was on the outside of his leg and had not hit an artery. With Braden's belt now free Jubil tried to wrap it around his leg above the wound, but the wound was so high up, there was not much room to cinch up the belt. He did the best he could, and it seemed to slow the bleeding somewhat.

Custer must have heard the shots, as Captain Tom Custer

and a full company of reinforcements rode up and over the ridge to push the warriors back and hold them at a distance. Two soldiers took Lieutenant Braden back to camp, and Jubil clambered back up to the top of the ridge to rejoin Barrows. As the Indians retreated, the soldiers formed a defensive position along the ridge to prevent the camp from being flanked. Once their position was secure, Jubil and Barrows turned to review the situation below them. Jubil raised his field glasses for a look around.

Due south of them, at their camp, Custer was holding the rest of his troops in reserve. Across the river, the number of warriors had grown to several dozen. Behind them about two hundred yards was a ridge like the one Jubil and Barrows were sitting on now. On top of that ridge, a few Indians watched the scene below. About a mile away, to the east and to the west, a steady stream of Indians was crossing to the north side of the river to surround Custer in camp.

"Look to the east and west," he said, handing the field glasses to Barrows.

Barrows scanned the field below. "That's not good."

"No," Jubil said.

"Do you think there might be more of them than of us?" Barrows asked with concern.

"More than Custer's cavalry...maybe," Jubil said, "but not more combined with Stanley's infantry."

"What do you think the odds are of him arriving soon?" Barrows asked.

"It's possible," Jubil said, "but he'd have to be moving at a quicker pace than he has been all along. My guess is that it will be this evening before he shows up."

Barrows frowned.

"But maybe earlier," Jubil added lamely.

"Do you think we can hold them that long?" Barrows said, bringing the field glasses up for another look.

"If anyone can," Jubil said, "it would be Custer." He wasn't just trying to be reassuring, he believed what he said.

As the morning wore on, Jubil and Barrows watched the battle below unfold like a chess game. Custer had five hundred soldiers, one hundred of whom were here at the ridge, guarding his flank. As the Indians continued to cross the river, Custer sent about two hundred men to the east and one hundred to the west, to push back and slow the warriors crossing there. That left one hundred with him, holding the camp. The Indians never made a decisive charge. Instead, they pushed then dropped back, then pushed again. Jubil was coming to see how this method of combat made them far less effective militarily than their numbers, weapons, and bravery would allow. If they fought more like their enemy, they would attack and overrun the camp. But he hoped they would not figure that out today.

A few Indians that had crossed the river tried to advance on Jubil's position on the ridge, but Tom Custer's men kept them at bay. With Tom's men behind them, as long as they kept their heads down, Jubil and Barrows were in a relatively safe spot. Jubil looked across the river and noticed that considerably more people had gathered along the top of the ridge on that side. He brought the field glasses up for another look. Hundreds of Indians lined the ridge, but most of them were not warriors. They were spectators, just like Jubil and Sam Barrows. Hundreds of women, children, and elderly lined the ridge watching the spectacle below. In the very center of the group, straight across from Custer, was an Indian that Jubil recognized.

"There he is," Jubil said, handing the field glasses to Barrows, and pointing across the river. "That's Sitting Bull himself."

"He looks very much as I imagined he would. What a character," Barrows said as he marveled at the notorious Sioux leader. He handed the field glasses back to Jubil. "This does not bode well for your railroad."

"I've seen Sitting Bull's antics before," Jubil said. "He puts on a big show, but he won't stop the army."

"I wasn't thinking militarily," Barrows said. "I meant more in the public relations sense. The level of resistance Sitting Bull has managed to raise has made a great number of people question whether this railroad route can ever really be safe— many are questioning the need for the railroad at all. I just meant—this won't help your story."

"No, I suppose not," Jubil said. His initial concern had simply been to see the survey completed successfully, but the definition of successful had crept outward to matters well beyond his control. It was one thing to connect the eastern and western survey lines—which they would do at Pompey's Pillar. But was the whole effort a success if the route was abandoned as unsafe? Or worse, was any of this a success if the whole project failed due to a lack of support? He would hate for this to end that way. It would confirm Abe's criticism—that he had made a rash decision without fully considering the risks.

By midafternoon, the number of warriors and cavalry forces appeared to be about equal, but there were several hundred more warriors still on the other side of the river. The day was growing hot, and the firing had subsided, as the effort focused mainly on establishing position. Jubil heard a boom in the distance—thunder?

"Did you hear that?" Jubil asked Barrows.

Barrows nodded as they both listened intently. Another boom, and this time they saw an explosion on the face of the ridge across the river. Rock and debris flew as the spectators scattered for cover.

"Stanley's coming!" Jubil said.

The troops north of camp sent up a cheer that spread to all of Custer's men. Custer pulled back the companies he had deployed to the east and west of camp but left his brother's forces in position on the ridge to the north. As Stanley's forces began to appear, marching along the river, Custer sent his band out to greet them playing "Garry Owen." The Indians began to retreat back across the river, given covering fire by warriors on the opposite bank.

As Stanley's troops began to fill the field north of Custer's camp, they fired their cannons again at the opposite bank to scatter the warriors firing across from that side. Custer organized his cavalry into ranks and began a charge to drive the Indians west of camp either back across the river or further west. Within an hour, Stanley had driven the Indians away on both sides of the river east of camp, and Custer chased the ones to the west away.

Once the whole affair was over, Captain Tom Custer brought his troops, along with Jubil and Barrows, back into camp. As Barrows questioned Custer about casualties, Jubil learned that only two soldiers were killed: Private Tuttle, the sharpshooter, and Lieutenant Braden. In spite of Jubil's efforts and the army doctor's, he had bled to death from his wound. Jubil felt badly for Braden and the loved ones who waited for him at home. Three others had lesser wounds. The estimates of Indians killed or wounded were also lighter than Jubil expected—Custer claimed to have seen only four killed, but that count seemed low to Jubil, as he had seen Tuttle shoot two. Given all the gunfire that had been exchanged, it seemed hard to believe. But Jubil was glad. Perhaps Barrows's newspaper report of the affair wouldn't be so damning.

Jubil was pleased when Stanley and Custer decided not to make camp there but to move on. He returned to help Eck and Monty with the survey for the rest of the day. They made five miles without further incident, and their good fortune continued for the next two days, for which he was most grateful.

Then on August 15, two months from when he had left

Bismarck, he spotted a large block of rock rising up along the riverbank.

"There it is, Jubil," Monty said, "Pompey's Pillar. There's something here I want to see for myself. You'll appreciate this too—come along."

Jubil followed Monty across a field toward the landmark. The base of the gray sandstone rock formation covered about one acre, and the thick column rose one-hundred-fifty feet to a flat plateau. Monty walked along the base of the pillar, looking for something on its face.

"Here it is!" Monty shouted.

Jubil joined him and saw, painstakingly carved into the rock in cursive:

W Clark

July 25, 1806

"That was made by William Clark himself, during his expedition with Captain Lewis," Monty said. "He named the rock after Sacagawea's son, Pomp, who he called Pompey."

Jubil ran his hand over the inscription. Lewis and Clark, America's most famous explorers, had stood on this very spot. They had ventured across this country before the white men and Indians had come to hate each other. Jubil picked up a loose rock from the base of the monument to add to his souvenir collection in Abe's library. He wished they had a photographer along to record the image so he could frame it.

When they rejoined Eck, he said, "We found Haydon's last set of stakes before he turned for the Musselshell. We connected up with them. The Northern Pacific survey is officially complete."

Eck offered Jubil a handshake.

"Finally," Monty said, and he also shook Jubil's hand.

"Yes," Jubil said, struck by the moment, "finally." He felt a sense of accomplishment and relief even though the trip was nowhere near over. He wished again for a photographer to document the meeting of the eastern and western surveys, but he had to admit an image of him, Eck, and Monty, standing beside a stake in the ground would not be very dramatic, or even offer real proof the survey had been completed successfully.

That was it then. There was no celebration in camp that evening, and hardly any further mention of what Jubil thought would be the high point of the expedition. The surveyors still had their Musselshell River survey work ahead of them, and the army was scouting the ideal spot for a permanent fort somewhere in the area.

Technically, the survey had been completed successfully, and the Northern Pacific Railroad finally had a route planned from Lake Superior to Puget Sound. If Jubil had had a magical conveyance to transport him to Cooke's offices, he would have appeared there immediately to collect his property deeds and be done with this whole affair.

But there was no quick resolution available for his situation. He could not just say he was finished and head home. The previous year he and Eli had left the survey early, but they had the support of White Dog. If he left right now to return on his own, he would have to ride almost two hundred miles to Glendive through country that was full of inhospitable Sioux. It was possible, but the odds of him surviving that trip were not good.

Colonel Stanley was sending a courier to Fort Benton with mail, Barrows's and Phelps's dispatches, and a report written by Custer. Jubil seriously considered traveling with him. But he thought of Nelly and the risk he would be running and decided not to let his impatience push him too far. He would have to endure the return trip before he found out whether Cooke would deem the survey a success and whether Cooke's financial world had held together long enough for Jubil to get his property back.

CHAPTER 21

The survey and escort turned north at Pompey's Pillar and moved up to the Musselshell River to complete the survey begun by Haydon the previous year. This took about two weeks to accomplish, and Jubil did his best to be useful. He was grateful there were no Indian attacks and that the weather at this higher elevation was cooler. When the survey work was finished, they turned east and started the return trip toward the stockade near Glendive.

For this stretch, Custer and Stanley split up to do more reconnaissance for the best route back. Jubil stayed with Custer, and in early September they arrived at Glendive. There he boarded the steamer *Josephine* and was on his way down the Yellowstone to Fort Buford. From there he took a steamer down the Missouri to Bismarck.

At Bismarck he sent a telegram to Cooke, telling him that he was on his way back to settle their agreement. He then took the Northern Pacific Railroad back to Minneapolis, switching trains in Des Moines to return to Council Bluffs. Though he paid first class fare and had a berth on a Palace Car, he had no clothes besides those he had worn on the survey and had not had the opportunity for a proper bath. So, he did his best to keep a respectful distance between himself and his fellow travelers.

From the day he had signed the agreement with Cooke to the day he had reached Pompey's Pillar, he had not allowed himself to think seriously about what he would do if the survey was not a success. But from the time the survey was completed on, he had found himself thinking of little else.

He passed many hours thinking of alternative ways of continuing Warner and Walker Outfitters. One was obvious—finally put his adventure tour business plan into action. But he surprised himself with some of the other ideas that emerged, and he made notes to cover with Ike. Some things he and Ike could do alone, but other ideas required Eli, and possibly even their father. But before he did anything, he would discuss all his ideas with Abe Warner.

He arrived in Council Bluffs midmorning and shouldered his trapper's pack to walk to the store. He paid close attention as he walked up Lower Broadway for possible sites to relocate Warner and Walker Outfitters. By the time he reached the store, he was convinced that Ike's assessment was correct—there was no site available between downtown and the railroad depot. If they needed to rebuild in Council Bluffs, it would have to be somewhere off the beaten path.

As he stood outside the door, he daydreamed of the days when he would open that door to find Abe and Luke tending to business—and the terrible day he had stood on this spot, knowing he had to open that door and tell Abe his son was dead. He was pulled out of this reverie by movement inside the store—it was Ike, smiling and waving him in. He stepped inside and breathed in the beloved clean smell of leather, felt the warm closeness of the full shelves, the handsome displays, the goods arranged so tidily—it looked inviting and successful.

"Welcome back, stranger," Ike said, shaking Jubil's hand and patting his shoulder. "Was your trip a success?

"Thank you. It's good to be back. I think it was a success—I'll explain later. The store looks wonderful." Jubil examined the new display of Warner and Walker branded items, available, as the sign said, only at Warner and Walker Outfitters. He picked up a pair of women's gloves, and found the tag inside bearing the letters *WW*.

"Thank you," Ike said. "All the new merchandise we order will have the tag."

"I'm going on up to the house," Jubil said. "I'm sorry that I'm not staying long. I'm going to send some telegrams, get cleaned up, then be on my way to New York with a stop in Philadelphia to see Cooke. I have some ideas about our business I'd like to discuss, but I've got to get this agreement with Cooke dealt with first."

"That's fine. Caleb's in the stockroom," Ike said. "He'll give you a ride when you're ready."

Jubil walked to the telegraph office and sent Nelly a message letting her know he was home safely and would be in New York by the end of the week. He let Abe and Lily Warner know too and added that he believed the survey had been successful. He promised to visit, once he had settled the details with Cooke. Then he telegraphed Cooke and asked for confirmation that he could see him on his way to New York.

At the house, his reunion with Mr. and Mrs. Garcia was jubilant. His horses, the pregnant Star, the proud Apollo, the steadfast Rocky, were all as happy to see him as he was to see them. The bath, clean clothes, and Mrs. Garcia's cooking made him feel civilized again.

There was a packet from Nelly waiting for him that she had sent there rather than risk missing him at Fort Buford. It was filled with clippings from newspapers covering the survey, including one from the *New York Tribune* written by Lieutenant Colonel George Armstrong Custer himself. Also in the packet were editorials questioning the wisdom and financial condition of the Northern Pacific Railroad and Jay

Cooke & Co. None of the articles praised the accomplishments of the survey, or the bright future of the railroad. It was all very disconcerting.

Equally disconcerting was the reply to his telegram from Cooke's secretary. Cooke was entertaining President Grant at Ogontz on the date Jubil requested, and would be unavailable. He considered writing back to ask if the president would like to hear an account of his son's comportment on the survey this summer but thought better of it. He supposed he could put off his departure for a day or two for the sake of Cooke's schedule, but he did not want to delay his trip to see Nelly. He would go on to New York, and see Cooke as soon as he could arrange it.

He, Ike, and Eli had supper in the kitchen with the Garcias, and they updated Jubil on matters of the store, the house, and the horses. He filled them in on the highlights of his recent adventures but made no mention of his agreement with Cooke. After supper he retired early to enjoy a night in his own bed before catching the eastbound train at dawn. As he changed trains in Chicago, he looked forward to the time he could call on Mr. Ward. He had an idea he wanted to discuss with him, but first things first.

Two days later, his train pulled into New York's Grand Central Station early in the morning. He shouldered the strap of his travel bag and stepped off the train into the milling crowd. The bustle of the city reached out and grabbed him and took him in. Surprisingly, he was coming to love it. As he walked into the main waiting area, he heard a newsboy hawking papers.

"Get your paper here! Panic on Wall Street! Read it in the *Times*. Get your paper here!"

Jubil stopped to listen again, to make sure of what he heard. Panic on Wall Street? He bought a newspaper and stared at the front page. The headline in the upper left read:

September 19, 1873 The New York Times
The Panic
Excitement in Wall Street
Suspension of Jay Cooke & Co.
What Is Thought of It Everywhere—Troubles in Other Firms

The article said that, the day before, an announcement had been made on the floor of the New York stock exchange that Jay Cooke & Co. had closed its doors. The news sent stocks into a frenzy of selling, and prices had declined frightfully. Word had spread in every direction, and investors had raced to their brokers in a panic to stem their losses. Hundreds of people had gathered on the street, many looking to sell, some trying to find loans, others just there to watch the spectacle. A member of the board of Jay Cooke & Co., Mr. Fahnestock, explained that over the past two weeks, the firm had been drawn on heavily for large cash advances to the Northern Pacific Railroad, and also for withdrawal by the firm's own depositors, and they were now forced to suspend operations. He went on to explain that they held large amounts of real and personal property but that those could not be immediately converted to cash. However, he was confident all depositors would be paid soon.

Jubil sat down on a bench and stared at nothing. Resolving their agreement would not be foremost on Cooke's mind, but nevertheless, Jubil had to try. He went to the telegraph office and sent a message to Cooke conveying his sympathy for Cooke's situation, asking how he intended to resolve their agreement, and requesting a reply at his New York address. He caught the trolley down Park Avenue to Eighteenth Street, then walked to their apartment.

He knocked, and Nelly opened the door.

"I'm so glad you are home," she said, wrapping her arms around him.

"Me too," he said, doing his best to return her hug, with the newspaper tucked under one arm and his bag slung over the other shoulder.

"Have you heard the news?" she asked, still holding him.

He kissed her check, stepped back, and held up the newspaper.

"I'm so sorry," she said.

"We can't be sure yet exactly what it means to us," he said. "I've reached out to Cooke, and hope to hear soon."

He stepped in and dropped his bag, and they kissed.

"Are you hungry?" she asked.

"I am," he said. "I'll cook if you'd like."

"We'll do it together," she said with a smile. "I hope you don't mind, but I have a meeting at work this afternoon that I really must attend."

"That's fine," he said. "I'll go see Sam Wilkeson. Find out what he knows."

Jubil carried his bag into the bedroom, then joined Nelly in the kitchen where they began putting together breakfast.

"Actually, Sam and Catherine stopped by yesterday afternoon," Nelly said, putting her apron on and starting to make hotcake batter. "They've become very good friends to me. He said that Mr. Cooke was taken completely by surprise at these events. Sam's opinion is that Mr. Cooke was unnecessarily blindsided by his board of directors."

"Hmm...I'm not sure what to make of that," Jubil said, putting the skillet on the stove to fry some bacon. "Rosser told me that Cooke's financial empire was under a lot of pressure. But he didn't give any indication that failure was imminent. He didn't mention any boardroom intrigue either, but he probably wouldn't discuss that with me."

Jubil was reaching the end of his patience with this whole situation. He wanted to feel like he was in control of his future again. "Let's not dwell on it right now. Perhaps Cooke will reply to my message soon. If not, I'll persist until I reach him.

Let's hear about you. How have you been? How is everything with you?"

Nelly answered as she stirred her batter. "My job, the apartment, New York…you. I love it all," she said with a smile. "I couldn't be happier with all that. I'm distressed by the state of affairs in the woman suffrage movement. But I'm growing accustomed to what a lengthy process this promises to be before we see any real progress. Mrs. Stanton has been telling me that all along, but I've still been impatient. I have my journals ready to send to Mr. Byers for his newspaper, and I've shown them to Mr. Porter, who suggested I add more entries and publish them as a book."

"Oh, I like the sound of that. I'm looking forward to reading them again, now that they are all polished up," Jubil said as he removed the bacon from the skillet. He took the batter from Nelly and began to fry the hotcakes, while she set the table. He had not really been hungry, but the aroma of the bacon had changed that. "I can't wait to see a book with your name on it."

She kissed him on the cheek.

With breakfast ready, Jubil put the food on the table, and Nelly poured coffee. Nelly brought him up to date on the details of her job and city living. As he listened, he had a moment of appreciation for her. It was her unconventional thinking that he had to thank for most of the good that had come to him in life. From the plan that set him off on his life of adventure—to prove himself worthy of joining Powell's expedition—to figuring out a way for them to have the best of both worlds—to marry but live apart when their careers called for it. He was fortunate to have her as a partner in life. They had finished breakfast and were washing the dishes when there was a knock at the door.

"I'll get it," Jubil said.

It was a Western Union delivery boy. Jubil took the telegram, and handed the boy a nickel. He opened it and read:

Dear Mr. Walker,

Our agreement centered around the successful completion of the survey for the Northern Pacific Railroad, which in a very real sense was accomplished, and your contributions to that effort are greatly appreciated. If the matter were as simple as that, I would return your deeds and make the investment I promised in our new business. Unfortunately, even if the survey were to be declared a success, I would be unable to meet my investment obligation for our agreement. Though you did your part to bolster public support, the violent events occurring during the surveys have turned public opinion against the railroad. Bond sales have collapsed, debts cannot be met, and my investment house has gone into bankruptcy. Given these circumstances, the survey can hardly be considered a success. I am sorry to say your investment is lost, and your property will be sold. I regret that, in spite of your best efforts, things have not turned out as we hoped. But I have the utmost respect for the dedication you showed in the effort. Call on me one day, when this situation is behind us. I would love to hear your stories.

Sincerely,

Jay Cooke

Jubil held the telegram and stared in horror at Nelly as she walked into the room. He had failed—miserably. He felt light-headed and disembodied—like he was watching himself as he stood there in stunned silence. The store was gone—and the farm. What would Ike do now? What about Eli? Would Abe remove Jubil from his will and disown him? Would his public reputation be destroyed? Would anyone ever again be interested in adventure travel with a failure?

"What is it?" she asked.

He handed her the telegram. As she read it, she covered her mouth.

"Oh, Jubil. I'm so sorry," she said.

"I didn't think he would do it," Jubil said. "I didn't think he would declare the survey a failure, then sell my property to help pay his debts. I liked him. I thought I could trust him."

"I don't know what to say," Nelly said. "He seems so congenial about it all too."

Jubil nodded "I imagine he would say it's only business—nothing personal."

"What will we do now?" Nelly asked.

He sat down and put his head in his hands. "I don't know. I can't afford to buy the store and farm back without asking Abe's help, and I'm not going to do that. What a fool I've been! Rash—that's the word Abe used. He said my desire for adventure got the better of my judgment. I guess he was right."

"Can you at least keep the store operating until someone contacts you about transferring the deeds?" Nelly asked.

"I suppose," he said, "but I need to tell Ike and Eli immediately. This is going to put them in a real fix. I want to keep working with them, but I can understand if they don't want to stay with me. I don't know if my reputation can recover from this."

CHAPTER 22

Eventually, Jubil and Nelly decided that the best thing to do would be to convene a Warner and Walker meeting on Nantucket Island. They made arrangements to meet Ike and Eli in Hyannis so that they could all travel to the Warners' together. Jubil was grateful to Nelly and his brothers-in-law for agreeing to take the trip with him. He didn't know how severely he had damaged Abe's confidence in him, and he needed their support. He would be crushed to learn that he had lost Abe's respect for good. What haunted him was that this thought should have been topmost in his mind before he signed the agreement with Cooke.

For a short time after receiving the news from Jay Cooke, Jubil had felt despondent over his losses—and he still felt a vast gaping hole where the farm had been. But he was by nature an optimist, and it wasn't long before his mind was whirring over the new set of circumstances he found himself in. While he and Nelly waited for Ike and Eli to arrive, he was experiencing an odd mix of optimism and pessimism. The seriousness of his mistakes had made him wonder if his current vision of the future was equally naïve and fraught with impending failure.

The twins arrived at the wharf, and got their first look at the ocean, but their excitement was tempered by the sober occasion.

Abe greeted them at the front door.

"Come in!" he said pleasantly, stepping back as they all filed into the house and then shaking each of their hands in turn.

Lily greeted each of them with a hug.

Jubil chided himself for feeling so awkward around them, these people who had been like parents to him.

"It's a bit early, but I have a light lunch ready if you would like," Lily said. "Or we can wait a while. We'll have supper in town this evening."

"I'd like to wait for a bit," Jubil said. "There are some business matters I'd like to discuss first, if you don't mind."

"Yes, certainly," Lily said. "I thought you might."

"Let's just gather at the dining room table," Abe said.

Once they were all seated, Jubil began the speech he had been rehearsing in his mind for the last two days.

"I feel just terrible about what's happened, and I'm sorry for the upset I've caused all of you. You were exactly right, Abe, about my agreement with Cooke—I was rash. I had a strong feeling that I could trust him. I liked him. I still feel like the survey itself succeeded. We connected the east and west survey lines, and that was all our agreement called for.

"But I hadn't considered the bigger picture. I hadn't factored in the risk from the economy, Cooke's position in it, and the impact of public opinion. If I'd consulted you, Abe, you would have schooled me on these matters and likely saved us from this outcome. I should never have signed that agreement without consulting with you. I apologize to all of you and hope to never repeat such a mistake.

"But what's done is done, and I haven't come here just to apologize. Cooke said he was offering me an opportunity to adjust my thinking regarding what is possible. In spite of my losses, I did manage to gain that from my experiences—I have some new ideas about what is possible. I think we can get the business back on track. Ike and Eli have agreed to stick with me to find a way to recover from the mistake I've made. If you'll hear me out, Abe, I've come to review some ideas about how we can continue Warner and Walker Outfitters. But if you'd rather just dissolve our partnership, I'll accept that and move on."

Everyone's eyes moved in tandem to Abe at the head of the table.

"Let's hear what you have in mind," Abe said.

"Show everyone your sketches, Ike," Jubil said.

Ike opened his portfolio of product sketches and spread them out on the table.

"Oh, my word, Ike," Lily said, "these are exquisite."

"You've gotten much better," Nelly said to Ike. "Not only the art but the products. I love that coat," she said, pointing to one of the sketches.

"Luke had already initiated the idea of custom designed merchandise," Jubil said, "but he would be the first to admit that Ike's designs are the best we've ever offered. Ike also had the idea of putting an identifying mark—*WW*—like a cattle-brand, on each product to assure authenticity and quality. People come to our store because that's the only way they can get our products."

The problem, as everyone knew, was that they no longer had a store.

"But what if we sent the products to them instead?" Jubil continued. "Ike and I met a gentleman recently who is doing just that. He produces a printed catalog of products—illustrated in a fashion similar to Ike's sketches—people order what they want and pay by mail, and he ships the goods directly to them. His name is Aaron Montgomery Ward—he calls it the Montgomery Ward Catalog."

"Have you spoken to him?" Ike asked with a broad smile.

"No," Jubil said. "I wanted to have this meeting first."

"I've heard of Ward and his catalog," Abe said. "If his method of retail is successful, you wouldn't even need a store. In fact, I imagine many stores will suffer from the competition."

"Yes," Jubil said, "but Ward said a store like ours, with unique goods, will always be viable. Plus, stores can compete on immediate access to goods, price, and friendly service."

"You've talked to Kuppenheimer then, about manufacturing?" Abe asked.

"Yes," Jubil said. "The only thing I have not done is offer a deal to Ward. I wanted to work out the financial terms with you first." Jubil looked at Nelly, who was smiling proudly at him.

"I like the idea," Abe said. "We'll work out the details later."

"This is a very good decision," Ike said. "I have a very good feeling about it." Jubil was pleased Ike was excited.

"Excellent," Jubil said, relieved to have at least preliminary approval from Abe. "I have another idea that might complement that one. What if we also made our products available to other retail stores? What if we offered them the opportunity to sell our branded merchandise? We could offer it at wholesale prices and let them set their own retail price. We send the wholesale orders straight to Mr. Kuppenheimer to fulfill just like we do the ones from Ward."

"I like the idea in general," Ike said, "but who do you expect is going to go around selling retailers on the idea of carrying our merchandise?"

"Well, this is only a suggestion," Jubil said, "but we all know who the best salesman among us has always been."

Everyone looked at Eli.

"Me?" Eli said, surprised for once to be the center of attention.

"You would be the best one for the job," Jubil said. "I was thinking you might enjoy the travel too. There's no end to the places you could go to visit retailers."

"I can picture you doing a very good job of that, Eli," Nelly said sincerely. "You'd be making new friends everywhere you went."

Eli grinned at her, and Jubil saw that there was real hope for a close relationship between them.

"Another good idea," Abe said. "We can work on those terms too."

"I'd like to have a new store too, but that will be expensive," Jubil said. "I'm going to try and finance it from income off the adventure tourism business. My agreement with Cooke has educated me as to the value of my reputation. I'm not going to be shy about the rate I ask for my tours. I think I could put ads in the *New York Times*, the Washington paper, and the Nantucket news, and charge a rate three or more times what Luke and I figured on, and still be busy all summer."

"You still want my help with that?" Eli asked.

"Absolutely," Jubil said. "If you want to do it."

"I definitely want to do it. I'm ready now," Eli said. "When we are not touring, I can visit wholesale customers."

"If you put an ad in *Scientific American* magazine," Nelly interjected, "you'd reach people all over the country—the world. You'd probably be booked well into the future."

Jubil laughed and shook his head. "You are a piece of work, Nelly Boswell."

"It's Nelly Boswell Walker," she said smartly, "but thank you."

"The higher rate will also go toward improving the comfort of the guests," Jubil said. "Our bread and butter will be Colorado tours. They'll have considerable adventure, but relatively easy access, as we did on our honeymoon trip. We can run several of them a year, and soon Eli will be able to lead his own, and we'll both take tours out."

"You don't need my approval for this idea," Abe said, "but you have it anyway. I agree about your rate—raise it. About the new store, we could discuss a loan to get you started."

Jubil swallowed hard over the lump in his throat. Abe offering a loan didn't mean all was forgiven and forgotten, but it did mean that Jubil had not destroyed his future with Abe and Lily.

"That means the world to me, Abe," Jubil said, "and I appreciate the offer very much. I'd like to try to do it under our own power if we can. I think it will keep us more motivated. But if we need support, I'm grateful to know you're there for us."

"Luke would be proud of your desire to keep things going," Abe said.

With his confidence bolstered, Jubil decided to share some of his loftier ambitions.

"I want to do Yellowstone National Park tours as well, but since the railroad won't reach there any time soon, we need another route in. I've been thinking we could bring guests up from Corinne, Utah, and go into Yellowstone from the west, along the Madison River. I'd like to explore the possibility of building custom coaches for the ride up to the park—ones that are considerably more comfortable than a stagecoach. Maybe even use them in the park, if Mr. Langford can get funding to build roads. To that point, there is a whole world of effort that could go into improving the accessibility and comfort of the park to support visitors. Cooke had planned on gaining concessions from the government to make such improvements, and I imagine it will eventually occur to someone to take up where he couldn't go. I might like to get myself involved in that effort. I know a few people in Washington now, and the park's new superintendent."

"That is very ambitious," Abe said, "and not at all impossible for you."

"We might be able to build those coaches at Papa's shop," Eli said.

"Yes," Jubil said, "that's what I was thinking too."

"I'd love to go see Yellowstone," Nelly said with a smile. "Now that I'm an experienced adventurer."

"We'll do that," Jubil said with a smile, "one of these days."

"There's one more thing too," Jubil said. "When I was in Washington visiting General Sherman, I saw Major Powell. The

Powells have sold their house in Illinois and live in Washington now. He's doing a survey of the southwest as special commissioner for the Bureau of Indian Affairs to develop policy for the tribes in that area. He's actually trying to help them. I've decided I'm not doing anything else that pits me so directly against them. I've been saying for a while now that I want to do something to improve living conditions at the Crow reservation. I'm not sure what form that will take, but I'm going to make good on my word."

"That's wonderful. I'm very proud of you," Nelly said hugging his arm.

"And I have a good feeling about persuading White Dog to ride the train east. I think he would love to stay at the farm—"

In sharing his dreams, Jubil had for a moment forgotten his reality. The room was silent, everyone's expressions pained.

Nelly reached for his hand.

"We're all very sorry for the loss of your farm," Abe said.

The sadness of a funeral hung in the air. Jubil felt his throat closing up and his eyes begin to burn. He fought to hold his emotions in check. He had rehearsed a speech about how heartbroken he was to lose the farm, and how Abe had been right that he would regret it for the rest of his life. But now there seemed no point in saying aloud what everyone already knew. And he doubted he could complete the speech without breaking down in tears. He tried to push his thoughts and feelings about the farm aside for now and focus again on his gratitude for not having alienated Abe and Lily.

"I just want to say—" Jubil said in a choked voice, but he was interrupted by a knock at the front door.

"Hold that thought, Jubil," Abe said rising from his seat. "I'll go see who it is."

Everyone sat silently while Abe went to the door. From Jubil's position at the table he could see into the living room to the front door. As Abe opened the door, he blocked Jubil's view of the visitor.

"Good day to you, sir," the visitor said. "I have come here hoping to find Jubilee Walker, or word of where I might find him."

Jubil knew that booming baritone voice with its smooth southern drawl.

"You have found him here," Abe said cheerfully. "Come in!"

Jubil hurried to the door, shaking his head in confusion, as Abe ushered in their guest.

"What a pleasant surprise to see you here," Jubil said, shaking hands with his guest. "Come in and let me introduce you to my family." He led his guest into the dining room. "Everyone, I'd like you to meet Thomas Rosser. Mr. Rosser led the Northern Pacific Railroad survey this summer." Jubil introduced each member of his family, then asked, "What brings you here?"

Jubil suspected that Rosser had been forced to do some dirty work for Cooke, or possibly for the Northern Pacific Railroad, but he had no idea what it might be.

"As you can well imagine, I've been very busy lately dealing with the aftermath of Cooke's bankruptcy," Rosser said. "I've got a piece of business in that regard that I need to conduct with you."

"We can do it now, if you'd like," Jubil said. "These folks are not only my family but my business partners. We were just wrapping up a business meeting about how to handle our own aftermath of Cooke's bankruptcy." Jubil offered Rosser a seat at the table.

"That's what I've come to talk to you about," Rosser said. "I have your deeds with me."

Can this possibly be true? Jubil's mind raced, but he couldn't form a question or a sentence. *Gather your wits*, he told himself.

"I—I thought they were to be sold—" he stammered.

"They were," Rosser said. "I convinced Cooke to sell them to me."

"What?" Jubil said. "Why would you do that?"

"When you and I parted company on the Yellowstone," Rosser said, "I was headed back to the Northern Pacific board meeting. Your story about the terms of your agreement with Cooke had stuck in my mind. I hope you won't be offended to hear this, but I was suspicious that Cooke had taken advantage of your youth and good nature."

Jubil glanced at Abe, who raised his eyebrows.

"I made a gentleman's agreement with Cooke that day, that if something other than the survey itself failed, he would allow me the right of first refusal to purchase your deeds. When I received news from Eck that the survey lines had been connected, I waited in hopes you would return in time to retrieve your deeds before they got caught up in the crash that almost surely was coming, but it happened too fast. Yesterday I managed to get time with Cooke and resolve the matter."

"So, you own the store and my farm now?" Jubil asked.

"Yes," Rosser said, "but I've come to offer you the opportunity to repurchase them."

While he was excited to know the possibility existed for him to own his property again, he doubted he would be able to afford them without a loan from Abe. Maybe he didn't need the store. But refusing to repurchase it might offend Abe. As much as he longed to keep the farm, the idea of going deeply in debt for years to repurchase it was almost more painful than just losing it. He was not sure what to do.

"At what price?" Jubil asked.

"The same price I paid for them," Rosser said. "One thousand dollars."

Jubil was in shock at the low price tag. He looked around the table, and almost everyone was smiling. Abe seemed as unsure of what was happening as Jubil felt.

"One thousand dollars—that was his price," Rosser repeated with a shrug.

"Why?" Jubil asked again.

Rosser nodded. "He agreed that the survey itself was successful, and technically satisfied the terms of your agreement. But his lawyers demanded the deeds be sold. They weren't happy with the price, but it was Cooke's decision. He said he never really wanted your property. All he wanted was your support."

Jubil studied Rosser's face for a moment then stared into space.

"He said that to me once," Jubil recalled. "After the first survey failed, I went to see if he would extend our agreement. I asked him to release the farm from our agreement, but he said no. He said he'd rather have my support than my property, but what was done was done. Why did he do this if they meant so little to him?"

"It was his way of insuring he had your full commitment," Abe said.

"I believe he's right," Rosser agreed.

Jubil tried to sort out how all this made him feel about Cooke. It was easy to be resentful of him for manipulating and bullying him into signing the agreement in the first place. And Cooke was clearly saying he did not trust Jubil to give his best effort unless he was under the pressure of losing things dear to him, which did not sit well with Jubil's pride. But Cooke had agreed to sell his property back, even if it was indirectly—so his intent, in the end, could not be called evil. Plus, if things had gone well, Cooke would likely have made his investment in their new business. And the whole thing had come about because Cooke wanted Jubil's name behind his Northern Pacific Railroad efforts enough to make him the offer, which was a huge compliment.

"I can't work out whether Cooke is a hero or a villain," Jubil said.

Rosser laughed. "You are not alone."

"What form of payment do you prefer, Mr. Rosser?" Abe asked, "to reclaim Jubil's deeds?"

"A bank draft is fine," Rosser said, "or a bank transfer. I'm in no great rush—though I would like to replace the money in my account before my wife notices it's missing." Rosser grinned.

"I'm going to repay him, Abe," Jubil said. "I've still got money sitting in the McLean County Bank in Bloomington that my parents left me. I'll feel a lot better about using that money to pay for my mistake than it coming from our partnership." He turned to Rosser. "I'll get that arranged as soon as possible."

Rosser reached inside his jacket and removed an envelope. "Your deeds," he said, handing them across the table to Jubil.

Jubil opened the envelope, saw that his deeds were actually inside it, and felt the tension of the last two years melting away. He would never again consider letting his family farm go. Quite the opposite, he felt a yearning to reestablish himself there in some new chapter. Having the store back was a great relief as well, although they would now need to rethink their plans. Jubil felt a great wave of gratitude toward Rosser.

"Thank you," Jubil said, reaching across the table to shake hands with Rosser. "You've done me a great kindness that I'll never be able to repay. But if I can ever be of service, you can count on me."

Nelly leaned over and gave Jubil a kiss on the cheek and a hug. "Congratulations! I'm so happy for you!" The joyful note that Nelly struck released a chorus of happy chatter from everyone as they all rose from the table and chimed in with their congratulations.

"I think this calls for a toast!" Abe said, going to the sideboard to pour wine.

"This doesn't have to change any of the plans you laid out, Jubil," Ike said. "In fact, it makes them all easier to achieve."

"And we'll do them all, Ike," Jubil said. He stepped up to the sideboard and picked up a glass of wine.

ACKNOWLEDGEMENTS

I would like to thank my editor, Heidi Bell, for her patient coaching and insightful comments as she helped me shape the story, and Regina McCaughey-Silvia for her meticulous proofreading. Any shortcomings in the finished product are mine alone.

My daughter Lori Kaufman served as beta reader number one, and my unflagging moral support. My friend, Rich Teegarden, provided many helpful comments on early drafts, and his talented son, Jon Teegarden, created the maps that grace the book. My deepest thanks go out to all of my friends and family who took the time to read and comment on the book.

For readers interested in a historical account of the period described in the book, I recommend: *Jay Cooke's Gamble: The Northern Pacific Railroad, The Sioux, and The Panic of 1873* by M. John Lubetkin.

ABOUT THE AUTHOR

Tim Piper retired from a career in information technology, and has been a lifelong hobbyist musician. He lives in Bloomington, Illinois. This is the third novel in the *Jubilee Walker* series. Book four in the series, *The Montana Gold Mine*, will be released later this year.